THE PIT-PROP SYNDICATE

A STORY OF CRIME

BY

FREEMAN WILLS CROFTS

PLUS

'DANGER IN SHROUDE VALLEY'

WITH AN INTRODUCTION BY
JOHN CURRAN

COLLINS
CRIME
CLUB

COLLINS CRIME CLUB

An imprint of HarperCollins*Publishers*
1 London Bridge Street
London SE1 9GF
www.harpercollins.co.uk

This Detective Story Club edition 2018

First published in Great Britain by
W. Collins Sons & Co. Ltd 1922
'Danger in Shroude Valley' first published in
The Golden Book of the Year by Blandford Press 1950

Copyright © Estate of Freeman Wills Crofts 1922, 1950
Introduction © John Curran 2018

ISBN 978-0-00-819055-2

Typeset in Bulmer MT Std by
Palimpsest Book Production Ltd, Falkirk, Stirlingshire

Printed and bound by CPI Group (UK) Ltd, Croydon CR0 4YY

THE PIT-PROP SYNDICATE

'THE DETECTIVE STORY CLUB is a clearing house for the best detective and mystery stories chosen for you by a select committee of experts. Only the most ingenious crime stories will be published under the THE DETECTIVE STORY CLUB imprint. A special distinguishing stamp appears on the wrapper and title page of every THE DETECTIVE STORY CLUB book—the Man with the Gun. Always look for the Man with the Gun when buying a Crime book.'

Wm. Collins Sons & Co. Ltd., 1929

Now the Man with the Gun is back in this series of COLLINS CRIME CLUB reprints, and with him the chance to experience the classic books that influenced the Golden Age of crime fiction.

THE DETECTIVE STORY CLUB

FURTHER TITLES IN PREPARATION

INTRODUCTION

'MR CROFTS is the master of this austere, unsensational but—to minds who enjoy stubborn but logical reasoning—enthralling type of puzzle fiction.'

This assessment of Freeman Wills Crofts' output by author and publisher Michael Sadleir in a BBC radio review of an early Crofts title was both accurate and very fair. In fact, it remained true for the rest of Croft's career; and, indeed, to this day.

To Crofts belongs the shared honour of inaugurating the Golden Age of Detective Fiction. The publication of his first novel, *The Cask*, in 1920 launched that celebrated era in the history of crime fiction. Christie's *The Mysterious Affair at Styles* is usually bracketed alongside it, although, to be strictly accurate, its 1920 publication was only in the US, with UK publication delayed until January 1921.

The Cask, in many ways, created the template for a Crofts detective story: a meticulous investigation carried out with painstaking attention to detail and focusing, for the most part, on alibis and timetables. The reader is at the detective's side throughout the book as he doggedly pursues even the slightest clue, forcing it to give up its secret. Having achieved considerable success with *The Cask*, Crofts remained faithful, to a greater or lesser degree, to this type of story for the rest of his writing career. And so it is with *The Pit-Prop Syndicate*: there is little action, and the only excitement is of the cerebral kind. But this did not prevent Crofts becoming one of the 'Big Five' of Golden Age detective fiction, alongside Agatha Christie, Dorothy L. Sayers, R. Austin Freeman and H. C. Bailey. More than half a century after its publication, the author, reviewer and crime fiction historian, Julian Symons, chose *The Pit-Prop Syndicate* for inclusion in his list of 'The Hundred Best Crime and Mystery Books', compiled for *The Sunday Times* in 1957.

Crofts followed his first novel with a more traditional country house mystery, *The Ponson Case* in 1921; his third book, *The Pit-Prop Syndicate*, appeared in 1922, and *The Groote Park Murder*, set partly in South Africa, followed the year after. In each of his first four books an official police investigator carries out the investigation: Inspector Burnley in *The Cask*; Tanner in *Ponson*; Willis in *Pit-Prop*; Vandam in *Groote Park*. This experimentation finally brought about the emergence of Crofts' signature detective, Joseph French, who made his debut in 1925 in *Inspector French's Greatest Case* and subsequently appeared in all of his remaining books. The earlier incarnations were not as immortal as Inspector French, although they differ little from the eventual series character.

In a 1932 letter to his publisher Crofts gave a description of French, notable only for its vagueness, which, as we will see, was intentional:

'. . . rather stoutish man of slightly below middle height, blue-eyed, with a pleasant, comfortable, cheery expression . . . not distinguishable in dress from any other civilian . . . suave and pleasant . . . dressed in an ordinary lounge suit.'

In clarification he goes on to explain that:

'I have tried to make French an ordinary man, carrying out his work in an ordinary way. It seemed to me that there were enough "character" detectives, such as Colonel Gethryn, Philo Vance, Poirot, etc. Thus he has no special characteristics except being thorough, painstaking, persistent and a hard worker.'

Much the same traits can be applied to Willis, and indeed to the Inspectors in Crofts' earlier books. Continuing a pattern he was to follow for the rest of his career, Crofts avoided the use of a Watson character and Inspector Willis carries out most of the *Pit-Prop* investigation on his own. Usually the Watson character accompanies the detective throughout the investigation, describing all that he (the only female Watson of note being Gladys Mitchell's Laura Menzies, sidekick to Mrs Bradley) sees and hears; the Watson's more important role is as reader-substitute, acting as the admiring audience while the Great Detective explains his deductions. Willis—and later French—has little need of such a device, as the detective himself shares his thought processes directly with the reader.

Crofts' great strength as an author was the painstaking construction of his plots rather than character delineation. In his 1937 essay 'The Writing of a Detective Novel' (included in the recent Detective Story Club reprint of *The Groote Park Murder*) he notes:

> 'If we are lucky we shall begin with a really good idea . . . it may be an idea for the opening of [the] book: some dramatic situation or happening to excite and hold the reader's attention.'

Although the premise which precipitates the mystery in *Pit-Prop* can hardly be considered either dramatic or exciting, its very ordinariness—the inexplicable circumstances of the exchange of the numbered brass-plate on a 'Landes Pit-Prop Syndicate' lorry—is sufficiently intriguing to engage the reader's curiosity. And even before we read of this minor mystery which first engages Merriman's attention, our curiosity is aroused by a paragraph of foreshadowing, early in the first chapter:

> [Merriman] did not know then that this slight action, performed almost involuntarily, was to change his whole life, and not only his, but the lives of a number of other

people of whose existence he was not then aware, was to lead to sorrow as well as happiness, to crime as well as the vindication of the law, to . . . in short, what is more to the point, had he not then looked round, this story would never have been written.

The early chapters of the novel are somewhat reminiscent of the famous Erskine Childers' 1903 spy novel *The Riddle of the Sands*. In that book two friends, while 'messing about in boats', notice something potentially sinister which demands further investigation. In the case of *Riddle* it is a matter of national and international security; in *Pit-Prop* it is of a criminal nature. But what crime exactly? That is the mystery facing Merriman and Hilliard and Willis; and Crofts manages to keep the reader equally mystified about this for most of the novel. Clearly Crofts was a fan of the sea and many of his titles reflect this: *The Sea Mystery*, *The Loss of the 'Jane Vosper'*, *Found Floating*, *Mystery in the Channel*, *Mystery on Southampton Water*. His casual use of unexplained sailing terminology in Chapter III—'flush-decked', 'a freeboard', 'binnacle'—is further indication of this.

Another personal interest merits a brief mention in the previous chapter when the 'gentle hum of traffic made a pleasant accompaniment to their conversation [Merriman and friends at their club], as the holding down of a soft pedal fills in and supports dreamy organ music'. This unusually poetic simile reflects Crofts' interest in music: he was a church organist and choir-master in his leisure time.

While Crofts' undoubted strengths lay in the intricate construction of his plots, it must be acknowledged that his emotional passages are less than compelling. Even knowing that Chapter X was written almost a century ago does not make the love scene between Merriman and Madeleine any more convincing or less embarrassing, as these excerpts demonstrate:

She covered her face with her hands. 'Oh', she cried wildly. 'Don't go on. Don't say it.' She made a despairing gesture.

'What a brute I am!' he gasped. 'Now I've made you cry. For pity's sake!'

'Madeleine,' he cried wildly, again seizing her hands, 'you don't—it couldn't be possible that you—that you *love* me?'

There can be little doubt that Crofts had read Fergus Hume's best-selling *The Mystery of a Hansom Cab*. This inexplicably popular book, published in 1886 in Australia and the following year in the UK, went on to sell over half a million copies. It is directly referenced in Chapters XIII and XIV of *Pit-Prop* after the discovery of a murdered man in the back of a London taxi, circumstances reflecting closely a similar scene in which the *Hansom* corpse was found a quarter-century earlier. And echoes of his own first novel can be detected in Chapter VII when the detective duo put a cask to investigative use. Spending many hours inside the 'confined space and inky blackness of the cask' is a severe test of the dedication of the pair to their detective adventure.

In true Golden Age fashion we have three maps/diagrams. A page of Chapter XX is devoted to the drawing of a railway line and a discussion of train times; much of that chapter is concerned with rail travel—a real Crofts trademark. Although the map adds little to our understanding of the plot and neither of the two earlier maps is vital to the solution of the mystery, true Golden Age fans are always pleased to find a diagram in a story, let alone three of them!

It has to be acknowledged that the legality of some of Willis' actions in pursuit of his investigation leaves much to be desired. Tapping phone lines, picking locks, capturing fingerprints (even when the site of one particular fingerprint is very ingenious) are questionable actions, to say the least. And that taboo element of Golden Age fiction, the secret passage, is also evident—although as the solution to the crime does not depend on its existence it does not contravene any 'rule' of fair play.

A minor mystery for modern readers concerning *The Pit-Prop Syndicate* might be the title. A 'pit prop' is a wooden beam used to support the roof of a mine, and in the days when mining was a major industry the provision of such items was an important and lucrative business. While words such as *Murder* and *Death* did not feature as frequently in the titles of crime novels at this point in the genre's development as they were shortly to do, *The Pit-Prop Syndicate* is, by any standards, a very unexciting title.

Title aside, however, Crofts' third novel offers a blend of thriller and detective story, roughly divided between Parts One and Two of the novel. Both sections show Crofts putting his engineering training to imaginative use, and are a foreshadowing of the enormously popular Inspector French novels that would soon follow.

DR JOHN CURRAN
October 2017

CONTENTS

With acknowledgments to Samuel Henry, Esq., for his kindness in advising on certain technical matters mentioned in this book.

PART I

THE AMATEURS

CHAPTER I

THE SAWMILL ON THE LESQUE

SEYMOUR MERRIMAN was tired; tired of the jolting saddle of his motor bicycle, of the cramped position of his arms, of the chug of the engine, and, most of all, of the dreary, barren country through which he was riding. Early that morning he had left Pau, and, with the exception of an hour and a half at Bayonne, where he had lunched and paid a short business call, he had been at it ever since. It was now after five o'clock, and the last post he had noticed showed him he was still twenty-six kilometres from Bordeaux, where he intended to spend the night.

'This confounded road has no end,' he thought. 'I really must stretch my legs a bit.'

A short distance in front of him a hump in the white ribbon of the road with parapet walls narrowing in at each side indicated a bridge. He cut off his engine and, allowing his machine to coast, brought it to a stand at the summit. Then dismounting, he slid it back on its bracket, stretched himself luxuriously, and looked around.

In both directions, in front of him and behind, the road stretched, straight, level, and monotonous as far as the eye could reach, as he had seen it stretch, with but few exceptions, during the whole of the day's run. But whereas farther south it had led through open country, desolate, depressing wastes of sand and sedge, here it ran through the heart of a pine forest, in its own way as melancholy. The road seemed isolated, cut off from the surrounding country, like to be squeezed out of existence by the overwhelming barrier on either flank, a screen, aromatic indeed, but dark, gloomy, and forbidding. Nor was the prospect improved by the long, unsightly gashes which the resin collectors had made on the trunks, suggesting, as they did, that the trees were stricken by some disease. To Merriman the country seemed utterly uninhabited. Indeed, since running through Labouheyre, now two hours back, he could not recall having seen a single living creature except those passing in motor cars, and of these even there were but few.

He rested his arms on the masonry coping of the old bridge and drew at his cigarette. But for the distant rumble of an approaching vehicle, the spring evening was very still. The river curved away gently towards the left, flowing black and sluggish between its flat banks, on which the pines grew down to the water's edge. It was delightful to stay quiet for a few moments, and Merriman took off his cap and let the cool air blow on his forehead, enjoying the relaxation.

He was a pleasant looking man of about eight-and-twenty, clean shaven and with gray, honest eyes, dark hair slightly inclined to curl, and a square, well-cut jaw. Business had brought him to France. Junior partner in the firm of Edwards & Merriman, Wine Merchants, Gracechurch Street, London, he annually made a tour of the exporters with whom his firm dealt. He had worked across the south of the country from Cette to Pau, and was now about to recross from Bordeaux to near Avignon, after which his round would be complete. To him this part of his business was a pleasure, and he enjoyed his annual trip almost as much as if it had been a holiday.

The vehicle which he had heard in the distance was now close by, and he turned idly to watch it pass. He did not know then that this slight action, performed almost involuntarily, was to change his whole life, and not only his, but the lives of a number of other people of whose existence he was not then aware, was to lead to sorrow as well as happiness, to crime as well as the vindication of the law, to ... in short, what is more to the point, had he not then looked round, this story would never have been written.

The vehicle in itself was in no way remarkable. It was a motor lorry of about five tons capacity, a heavy thing, travelling slowly. Merriman's attention at first focused itself on the driver. He was a man of about thirty, good-looking, with thin, clear cut features, an aquiline nose, and dark, clever-looking eyes. Dressed though he was in rough, working clothes, there was a something in his appearance, in his pose, which suggested a man of better social standing than his occupation warranted.

'Ex-officer,' thought Merriman as his gaze passed on to the lorry behind. It was painted a dirty green, and was empty except for a single heavy casting, evidently part of some large and massive machine. On the side of the deck was a brass plate bearing the words in English 'The Landes Pit-Prop Syndicate, No. 4.' Merriman was somewhat surprised to see a nameplate in his own language in so unexpected a quarter, but the matter did not really interest him and he soon dismissed it from his mind.

The machine chuffed ponderously past, and Merriman, by now rested, turned to restart his bicycle. But his troubles for the day were not over. On the ground below his tank was a stain, and even as he looked, a drop fell from the carburettor feed pipe, followed by a second and a third.

He bent down to examine, and speedily found the cause of the trouble. The feed pipe was connected to the bottom of the tank by a union, and the nut, working slack, had allowed a small but steady leak. He tightened the nut and turned to measure the petrol in the tank. A glance showed him that a mere drain only remained.

'Curse it all,' he muttered, 'that's the second time that confounded nut has left me in the soup.'

His position was a trifle awkward. He was still some twenty-five kilometres from Bordeaux, and his machine would not carry him more than perhaps two. Of course, he could stop the first car that approached, and no doubt borrow enough petrol to make the city, but all day he had noticed with surprise how few and far between the cars were, and there was no certainty that one would pass within reasonable time.

Then the sound of the receding lorry, still faintly audible, suggested an idea. It was travelling so slowly that he might overtake it before his petrol gave out. It was true it was going in the wrong direction, and if he failed he would be still farther from his goal, but when you are twenty-five kilometres from where you want to be, a few hundred yards more or less is not worth worrying about.

He wheeled his machine round and followed the lorry at full speed. But he had not more than started when he noticed his quarry turning to the right. Slowly it disappeared into the forest.

'Funny I didn't see that road,' thought Merriman as he bumped along.

He slackened speed when he reached the place where the lorry had vanished, and then he saw a narrow lane just wide enough to allow the big vehicle to pass, which curved away between the tree stems. The surface was badly cut up with wheel tracks, so much so that Merriman decided he could not ride it. He therefore dismounted, hid his bicycle among the trees, and pushed on down the lane on foot. He was convinced from his knowledge of the country that the latter must be a cul-de-sac, at the end of which he would find the lorry. This he could hear not far away, chugging slowly on in front of him.

The lane twisted incessantly, apparently to avoid the larger trees. The surface was the virgin soil of the forest only, but the ruts had been filled in roughly with broken stones.

Merriman strode on, and suddenly, as he rounded one of the bends, he got the surprise of his life.

Coming to meet him along the lane was a girl. This in itself was perhaps not remarkable, but this girl seemed so out of place amid such surroundings, or even in such a district, that Merriman was quite taken aback.

She was of medium height, slender and graceful as a lily, and looked about three-and-twenty. She was a study in brown. On her head was a brown tam, a rich, warm brown, like the brown of autumn bracken on a moor. She wore a brown jumper, brown skirt, brown stockings and little brown brogued shoes. As she came closer, Merriman saw that her eyes, friendly, honest eyes, were a shade of golden brown, and that a hint of gold also gleamed in the brown of her hair. She was pretty, not classically beautiful, but very charming and attractive looking. She walked with the free, easy movement of one accustomed to an out-of-door life.

As they drew abreast Merriman pulled off his cap.

'Pardon, mademoiselle,' he said in his somewhat halting French, 'but can you tell me if I could get some petrol close by?' and in a few words he explained his predicament.

She looked him over with a sharp, scrutinising glance. Apparently satisfied, she smiled slightly and replied:

'But certainly, monsieur. Come to the mill and my father will get you some. He is the manager.'

She spoke even more haltingly than he had, and with no semblance of a French accent—the French rather of an English school. He stared at her.

'But you're English!' he cried in surprise.

She laughed lightly.

'Of course I'm English,' she answered. 'Why shouldn't I be English? But I don't think you're very polite about it, you know.'

He apologised in some confusion. It was the unexpectedness of meeting a fellow-countryman in this out of the way wood ... It was ... He did not mean ...

'You want to say my French is not really so bad after all?' she said relentlessly, and then: 'I can tell you it's a lot better than when we came here.'

'Then you are a newcomer?'

'We're not out very long. It's rather a change from London, as you may imagine. But it's not such a bad country as it looks. At first I thought it would be dreadful, but I have grown to like it.'

She had turned with him, and they were now walking together between the tall, straight stems of the trees.

'I'm a Londoner,' said Merriman slowly. 'I wonder if we have any mutual acquaintances?'

'It's hardly likely. Since my mother died some years ago we have lived very quietly, and gone out very little.'

Merriman did not wish to appear inquisitive. He made a suitable reply and, turning the conversation to the country, told her of his day's ride. She listened eagerly, and it was borne in upon him that she was lonely, and delighted to have any one to talk to. She certainly seemed a charming girl, simple, natural and friendly, and obviously a lady.

But soon their walk came to an end. Some quarter of a mile from the wood the lane debouched into a large, D-shaped clearing. It had evidently been recently made, for the tops of many of the tree-stumps dotted thickly over the ground were still white. Round the semicircle of the forest trees were lying cut, some with their branches still intact, others stripped clear to long, straight poles. Two small gangs of men were at work, one felling, the other lopping.

Across the clearing, forming its other boundary and the straight side of the D, ran a river, apparently from its direction that which Merriman had looked down from the road bridge. It was wider here, a fine stretch of water, though still dark coloured and uninviting from the shadow of the trees. On its bank, forming a centre to the cleared semicircle, was a building, evidently the mill. It was a small place, consisting of a single long, narrow galvanised iron shed, placed parallel to the river. In front of the shed was a tiny wharf, and behind it were stacks and stacks of tree trunks, cut in short lengths and built as if for seasoning. Decauville tramways radiated from the shed, and men were running in timber in the trucks. From the mill came the hard, biting screech of a circular saw.

'A sawmill!' Merriman exclaimed rather unnecessarily.

'Yes. We cut pit-props for the English coal mines. Those are they you see stacked up. As soon as they are drier they will be shipped across. My father joined with some others in putting up the capital, and—*voilà!*' She indicated the clearing and its contents with a comprehensive sweep of her hand.

'By Jove! A jolly fine notion too, I should say. You have everything handy—trees handy, river handy—I suppose from the look of that wharf that sea-going ships can come up?'

'Shallow draughted ones only. But we have our own motor ship specially built and always running. It makes the round trip in about ten days.'

'By Jove!' Merriman said again. 'Splendid! And is that where you live?'

He pointed to a house standing on a little hillock near the edge of the clearing at the far, or down-stream side of the mill. It was a rough, but not uncomfortable looking building of galvanised iron, one storied and with a piazza in front. From a brick chimney a thin spiral of blue smoke was floating up lazily into the calm air.

The girl nodded.

'It's not palatial, but it's really wonderfully comfortable,' she explained, 'and oh, the fires! I've never seen such glorious wood fires as we have. Cuttings, you know. We have more blocks than we know what to do with.'

'I can imagine. I wish we had 'em in London.'

They were walking not too rapidly across the clearing towards the mill. At the back of the shed were a number of doors, and opposite one of them, heading into the opening, stood the motor lorry. The engine was still running, but the driver had disappeared, apparently into the building. As the two came up, Merriman once more ran his eye idly over the vehicle. And then he felt a sudden mild surprise, as one feels when some unexpected though quite trivial incident takes place. He had felt sure that this lorry standing at the mill door was that which had passed him on the bridge, and which he had followed down the lane. But now he saw that it wasn't. He had noted, idly but quite distinctly, that the original machine was No. 4. This one had a precisely similar plate, but it bore the legend 'The Landes Pit-Prop Syndicate, No. 3.'

Though the matter was of no importance, Merriman was a

little intrigued, and he looked more closely at the vehicle. As he did so his surprise grew and his trifling interest became mystification. The lorry *was* the same. At least there on the top was the casting, just as he had seen it. It was inconceivable that two similar lorries should have two identical castings, arranged in the same way, and at the same time and place. And yet, perhaps it *was* just possible.

But as he looked he noticed a detail which settled the matter. The casting was steadied by some rough billets of wood. One of these billets was split, and a splinter of curious shape had partially entered a bolt hole. He recalled now, though it had slipped from his memory, that he had noticed that queer shaped splinter as the lorry passed him on the bridge. It was therefore unquestionably and beyond a shadow of doubt the same machine.

Involuntarily he stopped and stood staring at the number plate, wondering if his recollection of that seen at the bridge could be at fault. He thought not. In fact, he was certain. He recalled the shape of the 4, which had an unusually small hollow in the middle. There was no shadow of doubt of this either. He remained motionless for a few seconds, puzzling over the problem and was just about to remark on it when the girl broke in hurriedly.

'Father will be in the office,' she said, and her voice was sharpened as from anxiety. 'Won't you come and see him about the petrol?'

He looked at her curiously. The smile had gone from her lips, and her face was pale. She was frowning, and in her eyes there showed unmistakable fear. She was not looking at him, and his gaze followed the direction of hers.

The driver had come out of the shed, the same dark, aquiline featured man as had passed him on the bridge. He had stopped and was staring at Merriman with an intense regard in which doubt and suspicion rapidly changed to hostility. For the moment neither man moved, and then once again the girl's voice broke in.

'Oh, there is father,' she cried, with barely disguised relief in her tones. 'Come, won't you, and speak to him.'

The interruption broke the spell. The driver averted his eyes and stooped over his engine; Merriman turned towards the girl, and the little incident was over.

It was evident to Merriman that he had in some way put his foot in it, how he could not imagine, unless there was really something in the matter of the number plate. But it was equally clear to him that his companion wished to ignore the affair, and he therefore expelled it from his mind for the moment, and, once again following the direction of her gaze, moved towards a man who was approaching from the far end of the shed.

He was tall and slender like his daughter, and walked with lithe, slightly feline movements. His face was oval, clear skinned, and with a pallid complexion made still paler by his dark hair and eyes and a tiny moustache, almost black and with waxed and pointed ends. He was good-looking as to features, but the face was weak and the expression a trifle shifty.

His daughter greeted him, still with some perturbation in her manner.

'We were just looking for you, daddy,' she called a little breathlessly. 'This gentleman is cycling to Bordeaux and has run out of petrol. He asked me if there was any to be had hereabouts, so I told him you could give him some.'

The newcomer honoured Merriman with a rapid though searching and suspicious glance, but he replied politely, and in a cultured voice:

'Quite right, my dear.' He turned to Merriman and spoke in French. 'I shall be very pleased to supply you, monsieur. How much do you want?'

'Thanks awfully, sir,' Merriman answered in his own language. 'I'm English. It's very good of you, I'm sure, and I'm sorry to be giving so much trouble. A litre should run me to Bordeaux, or say a little more in case of accidents.'

'I'll give you two litres. It's no trouble at all.' He turned and spoke in rapid French to the driver.

'*Oui*, monsieur,' the man replied, and then, stepping up to his chief, he said something in a low voice. The other started slightly, for a moment looked concerned, then instantly recovering himself, advanced to Merriman.

'Henri, here, will send a man with a two litre can to where you left your machine,' he said, then continued with a suave smile:

'And so, sir, you're English? It is not often that we have the pleasure of meeting a fellow-countryman in these wilds.'

'I suppose not, sir, but I can assure you your pleasure and surprise is as nothing to mine. You are not only a fellow-countryman but a friend in need as well.'

'My dear sir, I know what it is to run out of spirit. And I suppose there is no place in the whole of France where you might go farther without finding any than this very district. You are on pleasure bent, I presume?'

Merriman shook his head.

'Unfortunately, no,' he replied. 'I'm travelling for my firm, Edwards & Merriman, Wine Merchants of London. I'm Merriman, Seymour Merriman, and I'm going round the exporters with whom we deal.'

'A pleasant way to do it, Mr Merriman. My name is Coburn, You see, I am trying to change the face of the country here?'

'Yes, Miss'—Merriman hesitated for a moment and looked at the girl—'Miss Coburn told me what you were doing. A splendid notion, I think.'

'Yes, I think we're going to make it pay very well. I suppose you're not making a long stay?'

'Two days in Bordeaux, sir, then I'm off east to Avignon.'

'Do you know, I rather envy you. One gets tired of these tree trunks and the noise of the saws. Ah, there is your petrol.' A workman had appeared with a red can of Shell. 'Well, Mr Merriman, a pleasant journey to you. You will excuse my not going farther with you, but I am really supposed to be busy.' He turned to his daughter with a smile. 'You, Madeleine, can see Mr Merriman to the road?'

He shook hands, declined Merriman's request to be allowed to pay for the petrol and, cutting short the other's thanks with a wave of his arm, turned back to the shed.

The two young people strolled slowly back across the clearing, the girl evidently disposed to make the most of the unwonted companionship, and Merriman no less ready to prolong so delightful an interview. But in spite of the pleasure of their conversation, he could not banish from his mind the little incident which had taken place, and he determined to ask a discreet question or two about it.

'I say,' he said, during a pause in their talk, 'I'm afraid I upset your lorry man somehow. Did you notice the way he looked at me?'

The girl's manner, which up to this had been easy and careless, changed suddenly, becoming constrained and a trifle self-conscious. But she answered readily enough.

'Yes, I saw it. But you must not mind Henri. He was badly shell-shocked, you know, and he has never been the same since.'

'Oh, I'm sorry,' Merriman apologised, wondering if the man could be a relative. 'Both my brothers were hit the same way. They were pretty bad, but they're coming all right. It's generally a question of time, I think.'

'I hope so,' Miss Coburn rejoined, and quietly but decisively changed the subject.

They began to compare notes about London, and Merriman was sorry when, having filled his tank and pushed his bicycle to the road, he could no longer with decency find an excuse for remaining in her company. He bade her a regretful farewell, and some half-hour later was mounting the steps of his hotel in Bordeaux.

That evening, and many times later, his mind reverted to the incident of the lorry. At the time she made it, Miss Coburn's statement about the shell-shock had seemed entirely to account for the action of Henri, the driver. But now Merriman was not so sure. The more he thought over the affair, the more certain he felt that he had not made a mistake about the number plate, and the more likely it appeared that the driver had guessed what he, Merriman, had noticed, and resented it. It seemed to him that there was here some secret which the man was afraid might become known, and Merriman could not but admit to himself that all Miss Coburn's actions were consistent with the hypothesis that she also shared that secret and that fear.

And yet the idea was grotesque that there could be anything serious in the altering of the number plate of a motor lorry, assuming that he was not mistaken. Even if the thing had been done, it was a trivial matter and, so far as he could see, the motives for it, as well as its consequences, must be trivial. It was intriguing, but no one could imagine it to be important. As Merriman cycled eastward through France his interest in the affair gradually waned, and when, a fortnight later, he reached England, he had ceased to give it a serious thought.

But the image of Miss Coburn did not so quickly vanish from his imagination, and many times he regretted he had not taken an opportunity of returning to the mill to renew the acquaintanceship so unexpectedly begun.

CHAPTER II

ABOUT ten o'clock on a fine evening towards the end of June, some six weeks after the incident described in the last chapter, Merriman formed one of a group of young men seated round the open window of the smoking room in the Rovers' Club in Cranbourne Street. They had dined together, and were enjoying a slack hour and a little desultory conversation before moving on, some to catch trains to the suburbs, some to their chambers in town, and others to round off the evening with some livelier form of amusement. The Rovers had premises on the fourth floor of a large building near the Hippodrome. Its membership consisted principally of business and professional men, but there was also a sprinkling of members of Parliament, political secretaries and minor government officials, who, though its position was not ideal, were attracted to it because of the moderation of its subscription and the excellence of its cuisine.

The evening was calm, and the sounds from the street below seemed to float up lazily to the little group in the open window, as the smoke of their pipes and cigars floated up lazily towards the ceiling above. The gentle hum of the traffic made a pleasant accompaniment to their conversation, as the holding down of a soft pedal fills in and supports dreamy organ music. But for the six young men in the bow window the room was untenanted, save for a waiter who had just brought some fresh drinks, and who was now clearing away empty glasses from an adjoining table.

The talk had turned on foreign travel, and more than one member had related experiences which he had undergone while abroad. Merriman was tired and had been rather silent, but it was suddenly borne in on him that it was his duty, as one of the hosts of the evening, to contribute somewhat more fully towards the conversation. He determined to relate his little adventure at the saw-mill of the Pit-Prop Syndicate. He therefore lit a fresh cigar, settled himself more comfortably in his chair, and began to speak.

'Any of you fellows know the country just south of Bordeaux?' he asked, and, as no one responded, he went on: 'I know it a bit, for I have to go through it every year on my trip round the wine exporters. This year a rather queer thing happened when I was about half an hour's run from Bordeaux; absolutely a trivial thing and of no importance, you understand, but it puzzled me. Maybe some of you could throw some light on it?'

'Proceed, my dear sir, with your trivial narrative,' invited Jelfs, a man sitting at one end of the group. 'We shall give it the weighty consideration which it doubtless deserves.'

Jelfs was a stockbroker and the professional wit of the party. He was a good soul, but boring. Merriman took no notice of the interruption.

'It was between five and six in the evening,' he went on, and he told in some detail of his day's run, culminating in his visit to the sawmill and his discovery of the alteration in the number of the lorry. He gave the facts exactly as they had occurred, with the single exception that he made no mention of his meeting with Madeleine Coburn.

'And what happened?' asked Drake, another of the men, when he had finished.

'Nothing more happened,' Merriman returned. 'The manager came and gave me some petrol, and I cleared out. The point is, why should that number plate have been changed?'

Jelfs fixed his eyes on the speaker, and gave the little sidelong nod which indicated to the others that another joke was about to be perpetrated.

'You say,' he asked impressively, 'that the lorry was at first 4 and then 3. Are you sure you haven't made a mistake of 4?'

'How do you mean?'

'I mean that it's a common enough phenomenon for a No. 4 lorry to change, after lunch, let us say, into No. 44. Are you sure it wasn't 44?'

Merriman joined in the laugh against him.

'It wasn't forty-anything, you old blighter,' he said good-humouredly. 'It was 4 on the road, and 3 at the mill, and I'm as sure of it as that you're an amiable imbecile.'

'Inconclusive,' murmured Jelfs, 'entirely inconclusive. But,' he persisted, 'you must not hold back material evidence. You haven't told us yet what you had at lunch.'

'Oh, stow it, Jelfs,' said Hilliard, a thin-faced, eager looking young man who had not yet spoken. 'Have you no theory yourself, Merriman?'

'None. I was completely puzzled. I would have mentioned it before only it seemed to be making a mountain out of nothing.'

'I think Jelf's question should be answered, you know,' Drake said critically, and after some more good-natured chaff the subject dropped.

Shortly after one of the men had to leave to catch his train, and the party broke up. As they left the building Merriman found Hilliard at his elbow.

'Are you walking?' the latter queried. 'If so I'll come along.'

Claud Hilliard was the son of a clergyman in the Midlands, a keen, not to say brilliant student who had passed through both school and college with distinction, and was already at the age of eight-and-twenty making a name for himself on the headquarters staff of the Customs Department. His thin, eager face, with its hooked nose, pale blue eyes and light, rather untidy looking hair, formed a true index of his nimble, somewhat speculative mind. What he did, he did with his might. He was keenly interested in whatever he took up, showing a tendency, indeed, to ride his hobbies to death. He had a particular penchant for puzzles of all kinds, and many a knotty problem brought to him as a last court of appeal received a surprisingly rapid and complete solution. His detractors, while admitting his ingenuity and the almost uncanny rapidity with which he seized on the essential facts of a case, said he was lacking in staying power, but if this were so, he had not as yet shown signs of it.

He and Merriman had first met on business, when Hilliard was sent to the wine merchants on some matter of Customs. The acquaintanceship thus formed had ripened into a mild friendship, though the two had not seen a great deal of each other.

They passed up Coventry Street and across the Circus into Piccadilly. Hilliard had a flat in a side street off Knightsbridge, while Merriman lived farther west in Kensington. At the door of his flat Hilliard stopped.

'Come in for a last drink, won't you?' he invited. 'It's ages since you've been here.'

Merriman agreed, and soon the two friends were seated at another open window in the small, but comfortable sitting-room of the flat.

They chatted for some time, and then Hilliard turned the conversation to the story Merriman had told in the club.

'You know,' he said, knocking the ash carefully off his cigar, 'I was rather interested in that tale of yours. It's quite an intriguing little mystery. I suppose it's not possible that you could have made a mistake about those numbers?'

Merriman laughed.

'I'm not exactly infallible, and I have, once or twice in my life, made mistakes. But I don't think I made one this time. You see, the only question is the number at the bridge. The number at the mill is certain. My attention was drawn to it, and I looked at it too often for there to be the slightest doubt. It was No. 3 as certainly as that I'm alive. But the number at the bridge is different. There was nothing to draw my attention to it, and I only glanced at it casually. I would say that I was mistaken about it only for one thing. It was a black figure on a polished brass ground, and I particularly remarked that the black lines were very wide, leaving an unusually small brass triangle in the centre. If I noticed that, it must have been a 4.'

Hilliard nodded.

'Pretty conclusive, I should say.' He paused for a few moments, then moved a little irresolutely. 'Don't think me impertinent, old man,' he went on with a sidelong glance, 'but I imagined from your manner you were holding something back. Is there more in the story than you told?'

It was now Merriman's turn to hesitate. Although Madeleine Coburn had been in his thoughts more or less continuously since he returned to town, he had never mentioned her name, and he was not sure that he wanted to now.

'Sorry I spoke, old man,' Hilliard went on. 'Don't mind answering.'

Merriman came to a decision.

'Not at all,' he answered slowly. 'I'm a fool to make any mystery of it. I'll tell you. There is a girl there, the manager's daughter. I met her in the lane when I was following the lorry, and asked her about petrol. She was frightfully decent; came back with me and told her father what I wanted, and all that. But, Hilliard, here's the point. She *knew*! There's something, and she knows it too. She got quite scared when that driver fixed me with his eyes, and tried to get me away, and she was quite unmistakably relieved when the incident passed. Then later her father suggested she should see me to the road, and on the way I mentioned the thing—said I was afraid I had upset the driver somehow—and she got embarrassed at once, told me the man was shell-shocked, implying that he was queer, and switched off on to another subject so pointedly I had to let it go at that.'

Hilliard's eyes glistened.

'Quite a good little mystery,' he said, 'I suppose the man couldn't have been a relation, or even her fiancé?'

'That occurred to me, and it is possible. But I don't think

so. I believe she wanted to try to account for his manner, so as to prevent me smelling a rat.'

'And did she not account for it?'

'Perhaps she did, but again I don't think so. I have a pretty good knowledge of shell-shock, as you know, and it didn't look like it to me. I don't suggest she wasn't speaking the truth. I mean that this particular action didn't seem to be so caused.'

There was silence for a moment and then Merriman continued:

'There was another thing which might bear in the same direction, or again it may only be my imagination—I'm not sure of it. I told you the manager appeared just in the middle of the little scene, but I forgot to tell you that the driver went up to him and said something in a low tone, and the manager started and looked at me and seemed annoyed. But it was very slight and only for a second; I would have noticed nothing only for what went before. He was quite polite and friendly immediately after, and I may have been mistaken and imagined the whole thing.'

'But it works in,' Hilliard commented. 'If the driver saw what you were looking at and your expression, he would naturally guess what you had noticed, and he would warn his boss that you had tumbled to it. The manager would look surprised and annoyed for a moment, then he would see he must divert your suspicion, and talk to you as if nothing had happened.'

'Quite. That's just what I thought. But again, I may have been mistaken.'

They continued discussing the matter for some time longer, and then the conversation turned into other channels. Finally the clocks chiming midnight aroused Merriman, and he got up and said he must be going.

Three days later he had a note from Hilliard.

'Come in tonight about ten if you are doing nothing,' it read. 'I have a scheme on, and I hope you'll join in with me. Tell you when I see you.'

It happened that Merriman was not engaged that evening, and shortly after ten the two men were occupying the same arm-chairs at the same open window, their glasses within easy reach and their cigars well under way.

'And what is your great idea?' Merriman asked when they had conversed for a few moments. 'If it's as good as your cigars, I'm on.'

Hilliard moved nervously, as if he found a difficulty in replying. Merriman could see that he was excited, and his own interest quickened.

'It's about that tale of yours,' Hilliard said at length. 'I've been thinking it over.'

He paused, as if in doubt. Merriman felt like Alice when she had heard the mock-turtle's story, but he waited in silence, and presently Hilliard went on.

'You told it with a certain amount of hesitation,' he said. 'You suggested you might be mistaken in thinking there was anything in it. Now I'm going to make a suggestion with even more hesitation, for it's ten times wilder than yours, and there is simply nothing to back it up. But here goes all the same.'

His indecision had passed now, and he went on fluently and with a certain excitement.

'Here you have a trade with something fishy about it. Perhaps you think that's putting it too strongly; if so, let us say there is something peculiar about it; something, at all events, to call one's attention to it, as being in some way out of the common. And when we do think about it, what's the first thing we discover?'

Hilliard looked inquiringly at his friend. The latter sat listening carefully, but did not speak, and Hilliard answered his own question.

'Why, that it's an export trade from France to England—an export trade only, mind you. As far as you learnt, these people's boat runs the pit-props to England, but carries nothing back. Isn't that so?'

'They didn't mention return cargoes,' Merriman answered, 'but that doesn't mean there aren't any. I did not go into the thing exhaustively.'

'But what could there be? What possible thing could be shipped in bulk from this country to the middle of a wood near Bordeaux? Something, mind you, that you, there at the very place, didn't see. Can you think of anything?'

'Not at the moment. But I don't see what that has to do with it.'

'Quite possibly nothing, and yet it's an interesting point.'

'Don't see it.'

'Well, look here. I've been making inquiries, and I find most of our pit-props come from Norway and the Baltic. But the ships that bring them don't go back empty. They carry coal. Now do you see?'

It was becoming evident that Hilliard was talking of something quite definite, and Merriman's interest increased still further.

'I dare say I'm a frightful ass,' he said, 'but I'm blessed if I know what you're driving at.'

'Costs,' Hilliard returned. 'Look at it from the point of view of costs. Timber in Norway is as plentiful and as cheap to cut as in the Landes, indeed, possibly cheaper, for there is water there available for power. But your freight will be much less if you can get a return cargo. Therefore *a priori*, it should be cheaper to bring props from Norway than from France. Do you follow me so far?'

Merriman nodded.

'If it costs the same amount to cut the props at each place,' Hilliard resumed, 'and the Norwegian freight is lower, the Norwegian props must be cheaper in England. How then do your friends make it pay?'

'Methods more up to date perhaps. Things looked efficient, and that manager seemed pretty wideawake.'

Hilliard shook his head.

'Perhaps, but I doubt it. I don't think you have much to teach the Norwegians about the export of timber. Mind you, it may be all right, but it seems to me a question if the Bordeaux people have a paying trade.'

Merriman was puzzled.

'But it must pay or they wouldn't go on with it. Mr Coburn said it was paying well enough.'

Hilliard bent forward eagerly.

'Of course he would say so,' he cried. 'Don't you see that his saying so is in itself suspicious? Why should he want to tell you that if there was nothing to make you doubt it?'

'There is nothing to make me doubt it. See here, Hilliard, I don't for the life of me know what you're getting at. For the Lord's sake, explain yourself.'

'Ah,' Hilliard returned with a smile, 'you see you weren't brought up in the Customs. Do you know, Merriman, that the thing of all others we're keenest on is an import trade that doesn't pay?' He paused a moment then added slowly: 'Because if a trade which doesn't pay is continued, there must be something else to make it pay. Just think, Merriman. What would make a trade from France to this country pay?'

Merriman gasped.

'By Jove! Hilliard. You mean smuggling?'

Hilliard laughed delightedly.

'Of course I mean smuggling, what else?'

He waited for the idea to sink in to his companion's brain, then he went on:

'And now another thing. Bordeaux, as no one knows better than yourself, is just the centre of the brandy district. You see what I'm getting at? My department would naturally be interested in a mysterious trade from the Bordeaux district. You accidentally find one. See? Now what do you think of it?'

'I don't think much of it,' Merriman answered sharply, while a wave of unreasoning anger passed over him. The suggestion annoyed him unaccountably. The vision of Madeleine Coburn's clear, honest eyes, returned forcibly to his recollection. 'I'm afraid you're out of it this time. If you had seen Miss Coburn you would have known she is not the sort of girl to lend herself to anything of that kind.'

Hilliard eyed his friend narrowly and with some surprise, but he only said:

'You think not? Well, perhaps you are right. You've seen her and I haven't. But those two points are at least interesting—the changing of the numbers and the absence of a return trade.'

'I don't believe there's anything in it.'

'Probably you're right, but the idea interests me. I was going to make a proposal, but I expect now you won't agree to it.'

Merriman's momentary annoyance was subsiding.

'Let's hear it anyway, old man,' he said in conciliatory tones.

'You get your holidays shortly, don't you?'

'Monday week. My partner is away now, but he'll be back on Wednesday. I go next.'

'I thought so. I'm going on mine next week—taking the motor launch, you know. I had made plans for the Riviera—to go by the Seine, and from there by canal to the Rhone and out at Marseilles. Higginson was coming with me, but as you know he's crocked up and won't be out of bed for a month. My proposal is that you come in his place, and that instead of crossing France in the orthodox way by the Seine, we try to work through from Bordeaux by the Garonne. I don't know if we can do it, but it would be rather fun trying. But any way the point would be that we should pay a call at your sawmill on the way, and see if we can learn anything more about the lorry numbers. What do you say?'

'Sounds jolly fascinating.' Merriman had quite recovered his good humour. 'But I'm not a yachtsman. I know nothing about the business.'

'Pooh! What do you want to know? We're not sailing, and motoring through these rivers and canals is great sport. And then we can go on to Monte and any of those places you like.

I've done it before and had no end of a good time. What do you say? Are you on?'

'It's jolly decent of you, I'm sure, Hilliard. If you think you can put up with a hopeless landlubber, I'm certainly on.'

Merriman was surprised to find how much he was thrilled by the proposal. He enjoyed boating, though only very mildly, and it was certainly not the prospect of endless journeyings along the canals and rivers of France that attracted him. Still less was it the sea, of which he hated the motion. Nor was it the question of the lorry lumbers. He was puzzled and interested in the affair, and he would like to know the solution, but his curiosity was not desperately keen, and he did not feel like taking a great deal of trouble to satisfy it. At all events he was not going to do any spying, if that was what Hilliard wanted, for he did not for a moment accept that smuggling theory. But when they were in the neighbourhood he supposed it would be permissible to call and see the Coburns. Miss Coburn had seemed lonely. It would be decent to try to cheer her up. They might invite her on board, and have tea and perhaps a run up the river. He seemed to visualise the launch moving easily between the tree-clad banks, Hilliard attending to his engine and steering, he and the brown-eyed girl in the taffrail, or the cockpit, or the well, or whatever you sat in on a motor boat. He pictured a gloriously sunny afternoon, warm and delightful, with just enough air made by the movement to prevent it's being too hot. It would . . .

Hilliard's voice broke in on his thoughts, and he realised his friend had been speaking for some time.

'She's over engined, if anything,' he was saying, 'but that's all to the good for emergencies. I got fifteen knots out of her once, but she averages about twelve. And good in a sea-way, too. For her size, as dry a boat as ever I was in.'

'What size is she?' asked Merriman.

'Thirty feet, eight feet beam, draws two feet ten. She'll go down any of the French canals. Two four-cylinder engines, either of which will run her. Engines and wheel amidships, cabin aft, decked over. Oh, she's a beauty. You'll like her, I can tell you.'

'But do you mean to tell me you would cross the Bay of Biscay in a boat that size?'

'The Bay's maligned. I've been across it six times and it was only rough once. Of course, I'd keep near the coast and run for shelter if it came on to blow. You need not worry. She's as safe as a house.'

'I'm not worrying about her going to the bottom,' Merriman answered. 'It's much worse than that. The fact is,' he went on in a burst of confidence, 'I can't stand the motion. I'm ill all the time. Couldn't I join you later?'

Hilliard nodded.

'I had that in my mind, but I didn't like to suggest it. As a matter of fact it would suit me better. You see, I go on my holidays a week earlier than you. I don't want to hang about all that time waiting for you. I'll get a man and take the boat over to Bordeaux, send the man home, and you can come overland and join me there. How would that suit you?'

'A1, Hilliard. Nothing could be better.'

They continued discussing details for the best part of an hour, and when Merriman left for home it had been arranged that he should follow Hilliard by the night train from Charing Cross on the following Monday week.

CHAPTER III

THE START OF THE CRUISE

DUSK was already falling when the 9.00 p.m. Continental boat-train pulled out of Charing Cross, with Seymour Merriman in the corner of a first-class compartment. It had been a glorious day of clear atmosphere and brilliant sunshine, and there was every prospect of a spell of good weather. Now, as the train rumbled over the bridge at the end of the station, sky and river presented a gorgeous colour scheme of crimson and pink and gold, shading off through violet and gray to nearly black. Through the latticing of the girders the great buildings on the northern bank showed up for a moment against the light beyond, dark and sombre masses with nicked and serrated tops, then, the river crossed, nearer buildings intervened to cut off the view, and the train plunged into the maze and wilderness of South London.

The little pleasurable excitement which Merriman had experienced when first the trip had been suggested had not waned as the novelty of the idea passed. Not since he was a boy at school had he looked forward so keenly to holidays. The launch, for one thing, would be a new experience. He had never been on any kind of cruise. The nearest approach had been a couple of days' yachting on the Norfolk Broads, but he had found that monotonous and boring, and had been glad when it was over. But this, he expected, would be different. He delighted in poking about abroad, not in the great cosmopolitan hotels, which after all are very much the same all the world over, but where he came in contact with actual foreign life. And how better could a country be seen than by slowly motoring through its waterways? Merriman was well pleased with the prospect.

And then there would be Hilliard. Merriman had always enjoyed his company, and he felt he would be an ideal companion on the tour. It was true Hilliard had got a bee in his bonnet about this lorry affair. Merriman was mildly interested in the thing, but he would never have dreamt of going back to the sawmill to investigate. But Hilliard seemed quite excited about it. His attitude, no doubt, might be partly explained by his love of puzzles and mysteries. Perhaps also he half believed in his absurd suggestion about the smuggling, or at least felt that if it *were* true there was the chance of his making some *coup* which would also make his name. How a man's occupation colours his mind! thought Merriman. Here was Hilliard, and because he was in the Customs his ideas ran to Customs operations, and when he came across anything he did not understand he at once suggested smuggling. If he had been a soldier he would have guessed gunrunning, and if a politician, a means of bringing anarchist literature into the country. Well, he had not seen Madeleine Coburn! He would soon drop so absurd a notion when he had met her. The idea of her being party to such a thing was too ridiculous even to be annoying.

However, Hilliard insisted on going to the mill, and he, Merriman, could then pay that call on the Coburns. It would not be polite to be in the neighbourhood and not do so. And it would be impossible to call without asking Miss Coburn to come on the river. As the train rumbled on through the rapidly darkening country Merriman began once again to picture the details of that excursion. No doubt they could have tea on board . . . He mustn't forget to buy some decent cakes in Bordeaux . . . Perhaps she would help him to get it ready while Hilliard steered and pottered over his old engines . . . He could just imagine her bending over a tea tray, her graceful figure, the little brown tendrils of her hair at the edge of her tam-o'-shanter, her brown eyes perhaps flashing up to meet his own . . .

Dover came unexpectedly soon and Merriman had to postpone the further consideration of his plans until he had gone on board the boat and settled down in a corner of the smoke room. There, however, he fell asleep, not awaking until aroused by the bustle of the arrival in Calais.

He reached Paris just before six and drove to the Gare Quai d'Orsay, where he had time for a bath and breakfast before catching the 7.50 a.m. express for Bordeaux. Again it was a perfect day, and as the hours passed and they ran steadily southward through the pleasing but monotonous central plain of France, the heat grew more and more oppressive. Poictiers was hot, Angoulême an oven, and Merriman was not sorry when at a quarter to five they came in sight of the Garonne at the outskirts of Bordeaux and a few moments later pulled up in the Bastide Station.

Hilliard was waiting at the platform barrier.

'Hallo, old man,' he cried. 'Jolly to see you. Give me one of your handbags. I've got a taxi outside.'

Merriman handed over the smallest of the two small suit-cases he carried, having, in deference to Hilliard's warnings, left behind most of the things he wanted to bring. They found the taxi and drove out at once across the great stone bridge leading from the Bastide Station and suburb on the east bank to the main city on the west. In front of them lay the huge concave sweep of quays fronting the Garonne, here a river of over a quarter of a mile in width, with behind the massed build-ings of the town, out of which here and there rose church spires and, farther down-stream, the three imposing columns of the Place des Quinconces.

'Some river, this,' Merriman said, looking up and down the great sweep of water.

'Rather. I have the *Swallow* 'longside a private wharf farther up-stream. Rather tumbled down old shanty, but it's easier than mooring in the stream and rowing out. We'll go and leave your things aboard, and then we can come up town again and get some dinner.'

'Right-o,' Merriman agreed.

Having crossed the bridge they turned to the left, up-stream, and ran along the quays towards the south. After passing the railway bridge the taxi swung down towards the water's edge, stopping at a somewhat decrepit enclosure over the gate of which was the legend 'Andre Leblanc, Location de Canots'. Hilliard jumped out, paid the taxi man, and, followed by Merriman, entered the enclosure.

It was a small place, with a wooden quay along the river frontage and a shed at the opposite side. Between the two lay a number of boats. Trade appeared to be bad, for there was no life about the place and everything was dirty and decaying.

'There she is,' Hilliard cried, with a ring of pride in his voice. 'Isn't she a beauty?'

The *Swallow* was tied up alongside the wharf, her bow up-stream, and lay tugging at her mooring ropes in the swift run of the ebb tide. Merriman's first glance at her was one of disappointment. He had pictured a graceful craft of well-polished wood, with white deck planks, shining brass work and cushioned seats. Instead he saw a square-built, clumsy looking boat, painted, where the paint was not worn off, a sickly greenish white, and giving a general impression of dirt and want of attention. She was flush-decked, and sat high in the water, with a freeboard of nearly five feet. A little forward of amidships was a small deck cabin containing a brass wheel and binnacle. Aft of the cabin, in the middle of the open space of the deck, was a skylight, the top of which formed two short seats placed back to back. Forward rose a stumpy mast carrying a lantern cage near the top, and still farther forward, almost in the bows, lay an unexpectedly massive anchor, housed in grids, with behind it a small hand winch for pulling in the chain.

'We had a bit of a blow coming round the Coubre into the river,' Hilliard went on enthusiastically, 'and I tell you she didn't ship a pint. The cabin bone dry, and green water coming over her all the time.'

Merriman could believe it. Though his temporary home was

not beautiful, he could see that she was strong; in fact, she was massive. But he thanked his stars he had not assisted in the test. He shuddered at the very idea, thinking gratefully that to reach Bordeaux the Paris-Orleans Railway was good enough for him.

But, realising it was expected of him, he began praising the boat, until the unsuspecting Hilliard believed him as enthusiastic as himself.

'Yes, she's all of that,' he agreed. 'Come aboard and see the cabin.'

They descended a flight of steps let into the front of the wharf, wet, slippery, ooze-covered steps left bare by the receding tide, and, stepping over the side entered the tiny deck-house.

'This is chart-house, shelter, and companion-way all in one,' Hilliard explained. 'All the engine controls come up here, and I can reach them with my left hand while steering with my right.' He demonstrated as he spoke, and Merriman could not but agree that the arrangements were wonderfully compact and efficient.

'Come below now,' went on the proud owner, disappearing down a steep flight of steps against one wall of the house.

The hull was divided into three compartments; amidships the engine room with its twin engines, forward a store containing among other things a collapsible boat, and aft a cabin with lockers on each side, a folding table between them, and a marble-topped cupboard on which was a Primus stove.

The woodwork was painted the same greenish white as the outside, but it was soiled and dingy, and the whole place looked dirty and untidy. There was a smell of various oils, paraffin predominating.

'You take the port locker,' Hilliard explained. 'You see, the top of it lifts and you can stow your things in it. When there are only two of us we sleep on the lockers. You'll find a sheet and blankets inside. There's a board underneath that turns up to keep you in if she's rolling; not that we shall want it until we get to the Mediterranean. I'm afraid,' he went on, answering Merriman's unspoken thought, 'the place is not very tidy. I hadn't time to do much squaring—I'll tell you about that later. I suppose'—reluctantly—'we had better turn to and clean up a bit before we go to bed. But'—brightening up again—'not now. Let's go up town and get some dinner as soon as you are ready.'

He fussed about, explaining with the loving and painstaking minuteness of the designer as well as the owner, the various contraptions the boat contained, and when he had finished, Merriman felt that, could he but remember his instructions, there were few situations with which he could not cope or by which he could be taken unawares.

A few minutes later the two friends climbed once more up the slippery steps, and, strolling slowly up the town, entered one of the large restaurants in the Place de la Comedie.

Since Merriman's arrival Hilliard had talked vivaciously, and his thin, hawk-like face had seemed even more eager than the wine merchant had ever before seen it. At first the latter had put it down to the natural interest of his own arrival, the showing of the boat to a newcomer, and the start of the cruise generally, but as dinner progressed he began to feel there must be some more tangible cause for the excitement his friend was so obviously feeling. It was not Merriman's habit to beat about the bush.

'What is it?' he asked during a pause in the conversation.

'What is what?' returned Hilliard, looking uncomprehendingly at his friend.

'Wrong with you. Here you are, jumping about as if you were on pins and needles and gabbling at the rate of a thousand words a minute. What's all the excitement about?'

'I'm not excited,' Hilliard returned seriously, 'but I admit being a little interested by what has happened since we parted that night in London. I haven't told you yet. I was waiting until we had finished dinner and could settle down. Let's go and sit in the Jardin and you shall hear.'

Leaving the restaurant, they strolled to the Place des Quinconces, crossed it, and entered the Jardin Public. The band was not playing and, though there were a number of people about, the place was by no means crowded, and they were able to find under a large tree set back a little from one of the walks, two vacant chairs. Here they sat down, enjoying the soft evening air, warm, but no longer too warm, and watching the promenading Bordelais.

'Yes,' Hilliard resumed as he lit a cigar, 'I have had quite an interesting time. You shall hear. I got hold of Maxwell of the telephones, who is a yachtsman, and who was going to Spain on holidays. Well, the boat was laid up at Southampton, and we got down about midday on Monday week. We spent that day overhauling her and getting in stores, and on Tuesday we ran down Channel, putting into Dartmouth for the night and to fill up with petrol. Next day was our big day—across to Brest, something like 170 miles, mostly open sea, and with Ushant at the end of it—a beastly place, generally foggy and always with bad currents. We intended to wait in the Dart for good weather, and we wired the Meteorological Office for forecasts. It happened that on Tuesday night there was a first-rate forecast, so on Wednesday we decided to risk it. We slipped out past the old castle at Dartmouth at 5 a.m., had a topping run, and were in Brest at seven that evening. There we filled up again, and next day, Thursday, we made St Nazaire, at the mouth of the Loire. We had intended to make a long day of it on Friday and come right here, but as I told you it came on to blow a bit off the Coubre, and we could only make the mouth of the river. We put in to a little place called Le Verdon, just inside the Pointe de Grave—that's the end of that fork of land on the southern side of the Gironde Estuary. On Saturday we got here about midday, hunted round, found that old wharf and moored. Maxwell went on the same evening to Spain.'

Hilliard paused, while Merriman congratulated him on his journey.

'Yes, we hadn't bad luck,' he resumed. 'But that really wasn't what I wanted to tell you about. I had brought a fishing rod and outfit, and on Sunday I took a car and drove out along the Bayonne Road until I came to your bridge over that river—the Lesque I find it is. I told the chap to come back for me at six, and I walked down the river and did a bit of prospecting. The works were shut, and by keeping the mill building between me and the manager's house, I got close up and had a look round unobserved—at least, I think I was unobserved. Well, I must say the whole business looked genuine. There's no question those tree cuttings are pit-props, and I couldn't see a single thing in the slightest degree suspicious.'

'I told you there could be nothing really wrong,' Merriman interjected.

'I know you did, but wait a minute. I got back to the forest again in the shelter of the mill building, and I walked around through the trees and chose a place for what I wanted to do next morning. I had decided to spend the day watching the lorries going to and from the works, and I naturally wished to remain unobserved myself. The wood, as you know, is very open. The trees are thick, but there is very little undergrowth, and it's nearly impossible to get decent cover. But at last I found a little hollow with a mound between it and the lane and road— just a mere irregularity in the surface like what a tommy would make when he began to dig himself in. I thought I could lie there unobserved, and see what went on with my glass. I have a very good prism monocular—twenty-five diameter magnification, with a splendid definition. From my hollow I could just see through the trees vehicles passing along the main road, but I had a fairly good view of the lane for at least half its length. The view, of course, was broken by the stems, but still I should be able to tell if any games were tried on. I made some innocent looking markings so as to find the place again, and then went back to the river and so to the bridge and my taxi.'

Hilliard paused and drew at his cigar. Merriman did not

speak. He was leaning forward, his face showing the interest he felt.

'Next morning, that was yesterday, I took another taxi and returned to the bridge, again dressed as a fisherman. I had brought some lunch, and I told the man to return for me at seven in the evening. Then I found my hollow, lay down and got out my glass. I was settled there a little before nine o'clock.

'It was very quiet in the wood. I could hear faintly the noise of the saws at the mill and a few birds were singing, otherwise it was perfectly still. Nothing happened for about half an hour, then the first lorry came. I heard it for some time before I saw it. It passed very slowly along the road from Bordeaux, then turned into the lane and went along it at almost a walking pace. With my glass I could see it distinctly and it had a label plate same as you described, and was No. 6. It was empty. The driver was a young man, clean shaven and fairhaired.

'A few minutes later a second empty lorry appeared coming from Bordeaux. It was No. 4, and the driver was, I am sure, the man you saw. He was like your description of him at all events. This lorry also passed along the lane towards the works.

'There was a pause then for an hour or more. About half-past ten the No. 4 lorry with your friend appeared coming along the lane outward bound. It was heavily loaded with firewood and I followed it along, going very slowly and bumping over the inequalities of the lane. When it got to a point about a hundred yards from the road, at, I afterwards found, an S curve which cut off the view in both directions, it stopped and the driver got down. I need not tell you that I watched him carefully and, Merriman, what do you think I saw him do?'

'Change the number plate?' suggested Merriman with a smile.

'Change the number plate!' repeated Hilliard. 'As I'm alive, that's exactly what he did. First on one side and then on the other. He changed the 4 to a 1. He took the 1 plates out of his pocket and put the 4 plates back instead, and the whole thing just took a couple of seconds, as if the plates slipped in and out of a holder. Then he hopped up into his place again and started off. What do you think of that?'

'Goodness only knows,' Merriman returned slowly. 'An extraordinary business.'

'Isn't it? Well, that lorry went on out of sight. I waited there until after six, and four more passed. About eleven o'clock No. 6 with the clean shaven driver passed out, loaded, so far as I could see, with firewood. That was the one that passed in empty at nine. Then there was a pause until half-past two, when your friend returned with his lorry. It was empty this time, and it was still No. 1. But I'm blessed, Merriman, if he didn't stop at the same place and change the number back to 4!'

'Lord!' said Merriman tersely, now almost as much interested as his friend.

'It only took a couple of seconds, and then the machine lumbered on towards the mill. I was pretty excited, I can tell you, but I decided to sit tight and await developments. The next thing was the return of No. 6 lorry and the clean shaven driver. You remember it had started out loaded at about eleven. It came back empty shortly after the other, say about quarter to three. It didn't stop and there was no change made with its number. Then there was another pause. At half-past three your friend came out again with another load. This time he was driving No 1, and I waited to see him stop and change it. But he didn't do either. Sailed away with the number remaining 1. Queer, isn't it?'

Merriman nodded and Hilliard resumed.

'I stayed where I was, still watching, but I saw no more lorries. But I saw Miss Coburn pass about ten minutes later— at least I presume it was Miss Coburn. She was dressed in brown, and was walking smartly along the lane towards the road. In about an hour she passed back. Then about five minutes past five some workmen went by—evidently the day ends at five. I waited until the coast was clear, then went down to the lane and had a look round where the lorry had stopped, and saw it was a double bend and therefore the most hidden point. I walked back through the wood to the bridge, picked up my taxi and got back here about half-past seven.'

There was silence for some minutes after Hilliard ceased speaking, then Merriman asked:

'How long did you say those lorries were away unloading?'

'About four hours.'

'That would have given them time to unload in Bordeaux?'

'Yes; an hour and a half in, the same out, and an hour in the city. Yes, that part of it is evidently right enough.'

Again silence reigned, and again Merriman broke it with a question.

'You have no theory yourself?'

'Absolutely none.'

'Do you think that driver mightn't have some private game of his own on—be somehow doing the syndicate?'

'What about your own argument?' answered Hilliard. 'Is it likely Miss Coburn would join the driver in anything shady? Remember, your impression was that she knew.'

Merriman nodded.

'That's right,' he agreed, continuing slowly: 'Supposing for a moment it was smuggling. How would that help you to explain this affair?'

'It wouldn't. I can get no light anywhere.'

The two men smoked silently, each busy with his thoughts. A certain aspect of the matter which had always lain subconsciously in Merriman's mind was gradually taking concrete form. It had not assumed much importance when the two friends were first discussing their trip, but now that they were actually at grips with the affair it was becoming more obtrusive, and Merriman felt it must be faced. He therefore spoke again.

'You know, old man, there's one thing I'm not quite clear about. This affair that you've discovered is extraordinarily interesting and all that, but I'm hanged if I can see what business of ours it is.'

Hilliard nodded swiftly.

'I know,' he answered quickly. 'The same thing has been bothering me. I felt really mean yesterday when that girl came by, as if I were spying on her, you know. I wouldn't care to do it again. But I want to go on to this place and see into the thing farther, and so do you.'

'I don't know that I do specially.'

'We both do,' Hilliard reiterated firmly, 'and we're both justified. See here. Take my case first. I'm in the Customs Department, and it is part of my job to investigate suspicious import trades. Am I not justified in trying to find out if smuggling is going on? Of course I am. Besides, Merriman, I can't pretend not to know that if I brought such a thing to light I should be a made man. Mind you, we're not out to do these people any harm, only to make sure they're not harming us. Isn't that sound?'

'That may be all right for you, but I can't see that the affair is any business of mine.'

'I think it is.' Hilliard spoke very quietly. 'I think it's your business and mine—the business of any decent man. There's a chance that Miss Coburn may be in danger. We should make sure.'

Merriman sat up sharply.

'In Heaven's name, what do you men, Hilliard?' he cried fiercely. 'What possible danger could she be in?'

'Well, suppose there is something wrong—only suppose, I say,' as the other shook his head impatiently. 'If there is, it'll be on a big scale, and therefore the men who run it won't be over squeamish. Again, if there's anything, Miss Coburn knows about it. Oh, yes, she does,' he repeated as Merriman would have dissented, 'there is your own evidence. But if she knows about some large, shady undertaking, she undoubtedly may be in both difficulty and danger. At all events, as long as the chance exists it's up to us to make sure.'

Merriman rose to his feet and began to pace up and down,

his head bent and a frown on his face. Hilliard took no notice of him and presently he came back and sat down again.

'You may be right,' he said. 'I'll go with you to find that out, and that only. But I'll not do any spying.'

Hilliard was satisfied with his diplomacy. 'I quite see your point,' he said smoothly, 'and I confess I think you are right. We'll go and take a look round, and if we find things are all right we'll come away again, and there's no harm done. That agreed?'

Merriman nodded.

'What's the programme then?' he asked.

'I think tomorrow we should take the boat round to the Lesque. It's a good long run and we mustn't be late getting away. Would five be too early for you?'

'Five? No, I don't mind if we start now.'

'The tide begins to ebb at four. By five we shall get the best of its run. We should be out of the river by nine, and in the Lesque by four in the afternoon. Though that mill is only seventeen miles from here as the crow flies, it's a frightful long way round by sea, most of 130 miles, I should say.' Hilliard looked at his watch. 'Eleven o'clock. Well, what about going back to the *Swallow* and turning in?'

They left the Jardin, and, sauntering slowly through the well-lighted streets, reached the launch and went on board.

CHAPTER IV

A COMMERCIAL PROPOSITION

MERRIMAN was aroused next morning by the feeling rather than the sound of stealthy movements going on not far away. He had not speedily slept after turning in. The novelty of his position, as well as the cramped and somewhat knobby bed made by the locker, and the smell of oils, had made him restless. But most of all the conversation he had had with Hilliard had banished sleep, and he had lain thinking over the adventure to which they had committed themselves, and listening to the little murmurings and gurglings of the water running past the piles and lapping on the woodwork beside his head. The launch kept slightly on the move, swinging a little backwards and forwards in the current as it alternately tightened and slackened its mooring ropes, and occasionally quivering gently as it touched the wharf. Three separate times Merriman had heard the hour chimed by the city clocks, and then at last a delightful drowsiness had crept over him, and consciousness had gradually slipped away. But immediately this shuffling had begun, and with a feeling of injury he roused himself to learn the cause. Opening his eyes he found the cabin was full of light from the dancing reflections of sunlit waves on the ceiling, and that Hilliard, dressing on the opposite locker, was the author of the sounds which had disturbed him.

'Good!' cried the latter cheerily. 'You're awake? Quarter to five and a fine day.'

'Couldn't be,' Merriman returned, stretching himself luxuriously. 'I heard it strike two not ten seconds ago.'

Hilliard laughed.

'Well, it's time we were under way anyhow,' he declared. 'Tide's running out this hour. We'll get a fine lift down to the sea.'

Merriman got up and peeped out of the porthole above his locker.

'I suppose you tub over the side?' he inquired. 'Lord, what sunlight!'

'Rather. But I vote we wait an hour or so until we're clear of the town. I fancy the water will be more inviting lower down. We could stop and have a swim, and then we should be ready for breakfast.'

'Right-o. You get way on her, or whatever you do, and I shall have a shot at clearing up some of the mess you keep here.'

Hilliard left the cabin, and presently a racketing noise and vibration announced that the engines had been started. This presently subsided into a not unpleasing hum, after which a hail came from forward.

'Lend a hand to cast off, like a stout fellow.'

Merriman hurriedly completed his dressing and went on deck, stopping in spite of himself to look around before attending to the ropes. The sun was low down over the opposite bank, and transformed the whole river down to the railway bridge into a sheet of blinding light. Only the southern end of the great structure was visible stretching out of the radiance, as well as the houses on the western bank, but these showed out with incredible sharpness in high lights and dark shadows. From where they were lying they could not see the great curve of the quays, and the town in spite of the brilliancy of the atmosphere looked drab and unattractive.

'Going to be hot,' Hilliard remarked. 'The bow first, if you don't mind.'

He started the screw, and kept the launch alongside the wharf while Merriman cast off first the bow and then the stern ropes. Then, steering out towards the middle of the river, he swung round and they began to slip rapidly down-stream with the current.

After passing beneath the huge mass of the railway bridge they got a better view of the city, its rather unimposing buildings clustering on the great curve of the river to the left, and with the fine stone bridge over which they had driven on the previous evening stretching across from bank to bank in front of them. Slipping through one of its seventeen arches, they passed the long lines of quays with their attendant shipping, until gradually the houses got thinner and they reached the country beyond.

About a dozen miles below the town Hilliard shut off the engines, and when the launch had come to rest on the swift current they had a glorious dip—in turn. Then the odour of hot ham mingled in the cabin with those of paraffin and burnt petrol, and they had an even more glorious breakfast. Finally the engines were restarted, and they pressed steadily down the ever-widening estuary.

About nine they got their first glimpse of the sea horizon, and, shortly after, a slight heave gave Merriman a foretaste of what he must soon expect. The sea was like a mill pond, but as they came out from behind the Pointe de Grave they began to feel the effect of the long, slow ocean swell. As soon as he dared Hilliard turned southwards along the coast. This brought the swells abeam, but so large were they in relation to the launch that she hardly rolled, but was raised and lowered bodily on an almost even keel. Though Merriman was not actually ill, he was acutely unhappy and experienced a thrill of thanksgiving when, about five o'clock, they swung round east and entered the estuary of the Lesque.

'Must go slowly here,' Hilliard explained, as the banks began to draw together. 'There's no sailing chart of this river, and we shall have to feel our way up.'

For some two miles they passed through a belt of sand-dunes, great yellow hillocks shaded with dark green where grasses had seized a precarious foothold. Behind these the country grew flatter, and small, blighted looking shrubs began to appear, all leaning eastwards in witness to the devastating winds which blew in from the sea. Farther on these gave place to stunted trees, and by the time they had gone ten or twelve miles they were in the pine forest. Presently they passed under a girder bridge, carrying the railway from Bordeaux to Bayonne and the south.

'We can't be far from the mill now,' said Hilliard a little later. 'I reckoned it must be about three miles above the railway.'

They were creeping up very slowly against the current. The engines, running easily, were making only a subdued murmur inaudible at any considerable distance. The stream here was narrow, not more than about a hundred yards across, and the tall, straight stemmed pines grew down to the water's edge on either side. Already, though it was only seven o'clock, it was growing dusk in the narrow channel, and Hilliard was beginning to consider the question of moorings for the night.

'We'll go round that next bend,' he decided, 'and look for a place to anchor.'

Some five minutes later they steered close in against a rapidly shelving bit of bank, and silently lowered the anchor some twenty feet from the margin.

'Jove! I'm glad to have that anchor down,' Hilliard remarked, stretching himself. 'Here's eight o'clock, and we've been at it since five this morning. Let's have supper and a pipe, and then we'll discuss our plans.'

'And what are your plans?' Merriman asked, when an hour later they were lying on their lockers, Hilliard with his pipe and Merriman with a cigar.

'Tomorrow I thought of going up in the collapsible boat until I came to the works, then landing on the other bank and watching what goes on at the mill. I thought of taking my glass and keeping cover myself. After what you said last night you probably won't care to come, and I was going to suggest that if you cared to fish you would find everything you wanted in that forward locker. In the evening we could meet here and I would tell you if I saw anything interesting.'

Merriman took his cigar from his lips and sat up on the locker.

'Look here, old man,' he said, 'I'm sorry I was a bit ratty last night. I don't know what came over me. I've been thinking of what you said, and I agree that your view is the right one. I've decided that if you'll have me, I'm in this thing until we're both satisfied there's nothing going to hurt either Miss Coburn or our own country.'

Hilliard sprang to his feet and held out his hand.

'Cheers!' he cried. 'I'm jolly glad you feel that way. That's all I want to do too. But I can't pretend my motives are altogether disinterested. Just think of the kudos for us both if there *should* be something.'

'I shouldn't build too much on it.'

'I'm not, but there is always the possibility.'

Next morning the two friends got out the collapsible boat, locked up the launch, and paddling gently up the river until the galvanised gable of the Coburn's house came in sight through the trees, went ashore on the opposite bank. The boat they took to pieces and hid under a fallen trunk, then, screened by the trees, they continued their way on foot.

It was still not much after seven, another exquisitely clear morning giving promise of more heat. The wood was silent though there was a faint stir of life all around them, the hum of invisible insects, the distant singing of birds as well as the murmur of the flowing water. Their footsteps fell soft on the carpet of scant grass and decaying pine needles. There seemed a hush over everything, as if they were wandering amid the pillars of some vast cathedral with, instead of incense, the aromatic smell of the pines in their nostrils. They walked on, repressing the desire to step on tiptoe, until through the trees they could see across the river the galvanised iron of the shed.

A little bit higher up-stream the clearing of the trees had allowed some stunted shrubs to cluster on the river bank. These appearing to offer good cover, the two men crawled forward and took up a position in their shelter.

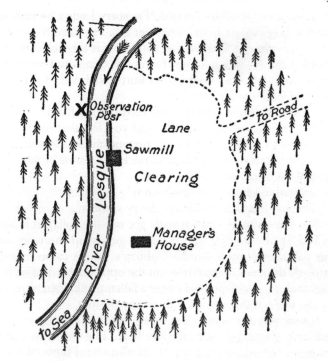

The bank they were on was at that point slightly higher than that on the opposite side, giving them an excellent view of the wharf and mill as well as of the clearing generally. The ground, as has already been stated, was in the shape of a D, the river bounding the straight side. About half-way up this straight side was the mill, and about half-way between it and the top were the shrubs behind which the watchers were seated. At the opposite side of the mill from the shrubs, at the bottom of the D pillar, the Coburn's house stood on a little knoll.

'Jolly good observation post, this,' Hilliard remarked as he stretched himself at ease and laid his glass on the ground beside him. 'They'll not do much that we shall miss from here.'

'There doesn't seem to be much to miss at present,' Merriman answered, looking idly over the deserted space.

About a quarter to eight a man appeared where the lane from the road debouched into the clearing. He walked towards the shed, disappearing presently behind it. Almost immediately blue smoke began issuing from the metal chimney in the shed roof. It was evident he had come before the others to get up steam.

In about half an hour those others arrived, about fifteen men in all, a rough-looking lot in labourers' kit. They also vanished behind the shed, but most of them reappeared almost immediately, laden with tools, and, separating into groups, moved off to the edge of the clearing. Soon work was in full swing. Trees were being cut down by one gang, the branches lopped off fallen trunks by another, while a third was loading up and running the stripped stems along a Decauville railway to the shed. Almost incessantly the thin screech of the saws rose penetratingly above the sounds of hacking and chopping and the calls of men.

'There doesn't seem to be much wrong there,' Merriman said when they had surveyed the scene for nearly an hour.

'No,' Hilliard agreed, 'and there didn't seem to be much wrong when I inspected the place on Sunday. But there can't be anything *obviously* wrong. If there is anything, in the nature of things it won't be easy to find.'

About nine o'clock Mr Coburn, dressed in gray flannel, emerged from his house and crossed the grass to the mill. He remained there for a few minutes, then they saw him walking to the workers at the forest edge. He spent some moments with each gang, afterwards returning to his house.

For nearly an hour things went on as before, and then Mr Coburn reappeared at his hall door, this time accompanied by his daughter. Both were dressed extraordinarily well for such a backwater of civilisation, he with a gray Homburg hat and gloves, she as before in brown, but in a well-cut coat and skirt and a smart toque and motoring veil. Both were carrying dust coats. Mr Coburn drew the door to, and they walked towards the mill and were lost to sight behind it. Some minutes passed, and between the screaming of the saws the sound of a motor engine became audible. After a further delay a Ford car came out from behind the shed and moved slowly over the uneven sward towards the lane. In the car were Mr and Miss Coburn and a chauffeur.

Hilliard had been following every motion through his glass, and he now thrust the instrument into his companion's hand, crying softly:

'Look, Merriman. Is that the lorry driver you saw?' Merriman focused the glass on the chauffeur and recognised him instantly. It was the same dark, aquiline featured man who had stared at him so resentfully on the occasion of his first visit to the mill, some two months earlier.

'By Jove, what an extraordinary stroke of luck!' Hilliard went on eagerly. 'All three of them that know you out of the way! We can go down to the place now and ask for Mr Coburn, and maybe we shall have a chance to see inside of that shed. Let's go at once, before they come back.'

They crawled away from their point of vantage into the wood, and retracing their steps to the boat, put it together and carried it to the river. Then rowing up-stream, they reached the end of the wharf, where a flight of wooden steps came down into the stream. Here they went ashore, after making the painter fast to the woodwork.

The front of the wharf, they had seen from the boat, was roughly though strongly made. At the actual edge, there was a row of almost vertical piles, pine trees driven unsquared. Behind these was a second row, inclined inwards. The feet of both rows seemed to be pretty much in the same line, but the tops of the raking row were about six feet behind the others, the arrangement, seen from the side, being like a *V* of which one leg is vertical. These tops were connected by beams, supporting a timber floor. Behind the raking piles rough tree stems had been laid on the top of each other horizontally to hold back the earth filled behind them. The front was about a hundred feet long, and was set some thirty feet out in the river.

Parallel to the front and about fifty feet behind it was the wall of the shed. It was pierced by four doors, all of which were closed, but out of each of which ran a line of narrow gauge railway. These lines were continued to the front of the wharf and there connected up by turn-tables to a cross line, evidently with the idea that a continuous service of loaded trucks could be sent out of one door, discharged, and returned as empties through another. Stacks of pit-props stood ready for loading between the lines.

'Seems a sound arrangement,' Hilliard commented as they made their inspection.

'Quite. Anything I noticed before struck me as being efficient.'

When they had seen all that the wharf appeared to offer, they walked round the end of the shed. At the back were a number of doors, and through these also narrow gauge lines were laid which connected with those radiating to the edge of the clearing. Everywhere between the lines were stacks of pit-props as well as of blocks and cuttings. Three or four of the doors were open, and in front of one of them, talking to some one in the building, stood a man.

Presently he turned and saw them. Immediately they advanced and Hilliard accosted him.

'Good-morning. We are looking for Mr Coburn. Is he about?'

'No, monsieur,' the man answered civilly, 'he has gone into Bordeaux. He won't be back until the afternoon.'

'That's unfortunate for us,' Hilliard returned conversationally. 'My friend and I were passing up the river on our launch, and we had hoped to have seen him. However, we shall get hold of him later. This is a fine works you have got here.'

The man smiled. He seemed a superior type to the others and was evidently a foreman.

'Not so bad, monsieur. We have four saws, but only two are running today.' He pointed to the door behind him as he spoke, and the two friends passed in as if to have an idle look round.

The interior was fitted up like that of any other sawmill, but the same element of design and efficiency seemed apparent here as elsewhere. The foreman explained the process. The lopped trunks from the wood came in by one of two roads through a large door in the centre of the building. Outside each road was a saw, its axle running parallel to the roads. The logs were caught in grabs, slung on to the table of the saws and, moving automatically all the time, were cut into lengths of from seven to ten feet. The pieces passed for props were dumped on to a conveyor which ran them out of the shed to be stacked for seasoning and export. The rejected pieces by means of another conveyor moved to the third and fourth saws, where they were cut into blocks for firewood, being finally delivered into two large bins ready for loading onto the lorries.

The friends exhibited sufficient non-technical interest to manage to spend a good deal of time over their survey, drawing out the foreman in conversation and seeing as much as they could. At one end of the shed was the boiler house and engine room, at the other the office, with between it and the mill proper a spacious garage in which, so they were told, the six lorries belonging to the syndicate were housed. Three machines were there, two lying up empty, the third, with engine running and loaded with blocks, being ready to start. They would have liked to examine the number plate, but in the presence of the foreman it was hardly possible. Finally they walked across the clearing to where felling and lopping was in progress, and inspected the operations. When they left shortly after with a promise to return to meet Mr Coburn, there was not much about the place that they had missed.

'That business is just as right as rain,' Merriman declared when they were once more in the boat. 'And that foreman's all right too. I'd stake my life he wasn't hiding anything. He's not clever enough for one thing.'

'So I think too,' Hilliard admitted. 'And yet, what about the game with the number plates? What's the idea of that?'

'I don't know. But all the same I'll take my oath there's nothing wrong about the timber trade. It's no go, Hilliard. Let's drop chasing wild geese and get along with our trip.'

'I feel very like it,' the other replied as he sucked moodily at his pipe. 'We'll watch for another day or so, and if we see nothing suspicious we can clear out.'

But that very evening an incident occurred which, though trifling, revived all their suspicions and threw them once again into a sea of doubt.

Believing that the Coburns would by that time have returned, they left the launch about five o'clock to call. Reaching the edge of the clearing almost directly behind the house, they passed round the latter and rang.

The door was opened by Miss Coburn herself. It happened that the sun was shining directly in her eyes, and she could not therefore see her visitors' features.

'You are the gentlemen who wished to see Mr Coburn, I presume?' she said before Merriman could speak. 'He is at the works. You will find him in his office.'

Merriman stepped forward, his cap off.

'Don't you remember me, Miss Coburn,' he said earnestly. 'I had the pleasure of meeting you in May, when you were so kind as to give me petrol to get me to Bordeaux.'

Miss Coburn looked at him more carefully, and her manner, which had up to then been polite, but coolly self-contained, suddenly changed. Her face grew dead white and she put her hand sharply to her side, as though to check the rapid beating of her heart. For a moment she seemed unable to speak, then, recovering herself with a visible effort, she answered in a voice that trembled in spite of herself:

'Mr Merriman, isn't it? Of course I remember. Won't you come in. My father will be back directly.'

She was rapidly regaining self-control, and by the time

Merriman had presented Hilliard her manner had become almost normal. She led the way to a comfortably furnished sitting-room looking out over the river.

'Hilliard and I are on a motor launch tour across France,' Merriman went on. 'He worked from England down the coast to Bordeaux, where I joined him, and we hope eventually to cross the country to the Mediterranean and do the Riviera from the sea.'

'How perfectly delightful,' Miss Coburn replied. 'I envy you.'

'Yes, it's very jolly doing these rivers and canals,' Hilliard interposed. 'I have spent two or three holidays that way now, and it has always been worth while.'

As they chatted on in the pleasant room the girl seemed completely to have recovered her composure, and yet Merriman could not but realise a constraint in her manner, and a look of anxiety in her clear brown eyes. That something was disturbing her there could be no doubt, and that something appeared to be not unconnected with himself. But, he reasoned, there was nothing connected with himself that could cause her anxiety, unless it really was that matter of the number plates. He became conscious of an almost overwhelming desire to share her trouble whatever it might be, to let her understand that so far from willingly causing a shadow to fall across her path there were few things he would not do to give her pleasure; indeed, he began to long to take her in his arms, to comfort her . . .

Presently a step in the hall announced Mr Coburn's return.

'In here, daddy,' his daughter called and the steps approached the door.

Whether by accident or design it happened that Miss Coburn was seated directly opposite the door, while her two visitors were placed where they were screened by the door itself from the view of any one entering. Hilliard, his eyes on the girl's face as her father came in, intercepted a glance of what seemed to be warning. His gaze swung round to the newcomer, and here again he noticed a start of surprise and anxiety as Mr Coburn recognised his visitor. But in this case it was so quickly over that had he not been watching intently he would have missed it. However, slight though it was, it undoubtedly seemed to confirm the other indications which pointed to the existence of some secret in the life of these two, a secret shared apparently by the good-looking driver and connected in some way with the lorry number plates.

Mr Coburn was very polite, suave and polished as an accomplished man of the world. But his manner was not really friendly, in fact, Hilliard seemed to sense a veiled hostility. A few deft questions put him in possession of the travellers' ostensible plans, which he discussed with some interest.

'But,' he said to Hilliard, 'I am afraid you are in error in coming up this River Lesque. The canal you want to get from here is the Midi, it enters the Mediterranean not far from Narbonne. But the connection from this side is from the Garonne. You should have gone up-stream to Langon, nearly forty miles above Bordeaux.'

'We had hoped to go from still farther south,' Hilliard answered. 'We have penetrated a good many of the rivers, or rather I have, and we came up here to see the sand-dunes and forests of the Landes, which are new to me. A very desolate country, is it not?'

Mr Coburn agreed, continuing courteously:

'I am glad at all events that your researches have brought you into our neighbourhood. We do not come across many visitors here, and it is pleasant occasionally to speak one's own language to some one outside one's household. If you will put up with pot-luck I am sure we should both be glad—' he looked at his daughter '—if you would wait and take some dinner with us now. Tomorrow you could explore the woods, which are really worth seeing though monotonous, and if you are at all interested I should like to show you our little works. But I warn you the affair is my hobby, as well as my business for the time being, and I am apt to assume others have as great an interest in it as myself. You must not let me bore you.'

Hilliard, suspicious and critically observant, wondered if he had not interrupted a second rapid look between father and daughter. He could not be sure, but at all events the girl hastened to second her father's invitation.

'I hope you will wait for dinner,' she said. 'As he says, we see so few people, and particularly so few English, that it would be doing us a kindness. I'm afraid that's not very complimentary—' she laughed brightly—'but it's at least true.'

They stayed, and enjoyed themselves. Mr Coburn proved himself an entertaining host, and his conversation, though satirical, was worth listening to. He and Hilliard talked, while Merriman, who was something of a musician, tried over songs with Miss Coburn. Had it not been for an uneasy feeling that they were to some extent playing the part of spies, the evening would have been a delight to the visitors.

Before they left for the launch it was arranged that they should stay over the following day, lunch with the Coburns, and go for a tramp through the forest in the afternoon. They took their leave with cordial expressions of good will.

'I say, Merriman,' Hilliard said eagerly as they strolled back through the wood, 'did you notice how your sudden appearance upset them both? There can be no further doubt about it, there's something. What it may be I don't know, but there *is* something.'

'There's nothing wrong at all events,' Merriman asserted doggedly.

'Not wrong in the sense you mean, no,' Hilliard agreed quickly, 'but wrong for all that. Now that I have met Miss Coburn I can see that your estimate of her was correct. But any one with half an eye could see also that she is frightened and upset about something. There's something wrong, and she wants a helping hand,'

'Damn you, Hilliard, how you talk,' Merriman growled with

a sudden wave of unreasoning rage. 'There's nothing wrong and no need for our meddling. Let us clear out and go on with our trip.'

Hilliard smiled under cover of darkness.

'And miss our lunch and excursion with the Coburns tomorrow?' he asked maliciously.

'You know well enough what I mean,' Merriman answered irritably. 'Let's drop this childish tomfoolery about plots and mysteries and try to get reasonably sane again. Here,' he went on fiercely as the other demurred, 'I'll tell you what I'll do if you like. I'll have no more suspicions or spying, but I'll ask—her—if there is anything wrong: say I thought there was from her manner and ask her the direct question. Will that please you?'

'And get well snubbed for your pains?' Hilliard returned. 'You've tried that once already. Why did you not persist in your inquiries about the number plate when she told you about that driver's shell-shock?'

Merriman was silent for a few moments, then burst out:

'Well, hang it all, man, what do you suggest?'

During the evening an idea had occurred to Hilliard and he returned to it now.

'I'll tell you,' he answered slowly, and instinctively he lowered his voice. 'I'll tell you what we must do. We must see their steamer loaded. I've been thinking it over. We must see what, if anything, goes on board that boat beside pit-props.'

Merriman only grunted in reply, but Hilliard, realising his condition, was satisfied.

And Merriman, lying awake that night on the port locker of the *Swallow*, began himself to realise his condition, and to understand that his whole future life and happiness lay between the dainty hands of Madeleine Coburn.

CHAPTER V

THE VISIT OF THE 'GIRONDIN'

NEXT morning found both the friends moody and engrossed with their own thoughts.

Merriman was lost in contemplation of the new factor which had come into his life. It was not the first time he had fancied himself in love. Like most men of his age he had had affairs of varying seriousness, which in due time had run their course and died a natural death. But this, he felt, was different. At last he believed he had met the one woman, and the idea thrilled him with awe and exultation, and filled his mind to the exclusion of all else.

Hilliard's preoccupation was different. He was considering in detail his idea that if a close enough watch could be kept on the loading of the syndicate's ship it would at least settle the smuggling question. He did not think that any article could be shipped in sufficient bulk to make the trade pay, unnoticed by a skilfully concealed observer. Even if the commodity were a liquid—brandy, for example—sent aboard through a flexible pipe, the thing would be seen.

But two unexpected difficulties had arisen since last night. Firstly, they had made friends with the Coburns. Excursions with them were in contemplation, and one had actually been arranged for that very day. While in the neighbourhood they had been asked virtually to make the manager's house their headquarters, and it was evidently expected that the two parties should see a good deal of each other. Under these circumstances how were the friends to get away to watch the loading of the boat?

And then it occurred to Hilliard that here, perhaps, was

evidence of design; that this very difficulty had been deliberately caused by Mr Coburn with the object of keeping himself and Merriman under observation and rendering them harmless. This, he recognised, was guesswork, but still it might be the truth.

He racked his brains to find some way of meeting the difficulty, and at last, after considering many plans, he thought he saw his way. They would as soon as possible take leave of their hosts and return to Bordeaux, ostensibly to resume their trip east. From there they would come out to the clearing by road, and from the observation post they had already used keep a close eye on the arrival of the ship and subsequent developments. At night they might even be able to hide on the wharf itself. In any case they could hardly fail to see if anything other than pit-props was loaded.

So far, so good, but there was a second and more formidable difficulty. Would Merriman consent to this plan and agree to help? Hilliard was doubtful. That his friend had so obviously fallen in love with this Madeleine Coburn was an unexpected and unfortunate complication. He could, of course, play on the string that the girl was in danger and wanted help, but he had already used that with disappointing results. However, he could see nothing for it but to do his best to talk Merriman round.

Accordingly, when they were smoking their after breakfast pipes, he broached the subject. But as he had feared, his friend would have none of it.

'I tell you I won't do anything of the kind,' he said angrily. 'Here we come, two strangers, poking our noses into what does not concern us, and we are met with kindness and hospitality and invited to join a family party. Good Lord, Hilliard, I can't believe that it is really you that suggest it! You surely don't mean that you believe that the Coburns are smuggling brandy?'

'Of course not, you old fire-eater,' Hilliard answered good-humouredly, 'but I do believe, and so must you, that there is something queer going on. We want to be sure there is nothing sinister behind it. Surely, old man, you will help me in that?'

'If I thought there was anything wrong you know I'd help you,' Merriman returned, somewhat mollified by the other's attitude. 'But I don't. It is quite absurd to suggest the Coburns are engaged in anything illegal, and if you grant that your whole case falls to the ground.'

Hilliard saw that for the moment at all events he could get no more. He therefore dropped the subject and they conversed on other topics until it was time to go ashore.

Lunch with their new acquaintances passed pleasantly, and after it the two friends went with Mr Coburn to see over the works. Hilliard thought it better to explain that they had seen something of them on the previous day, but notwithstanding this assurance Mr Coburn insisted on their going over the whole place again. He showed them everything in detail, and when the inspection was complete both men felt more than ever convinced that the business was genuine, and that nothing was being carried on other than the ostensible trade. Mr Coburn, also, gave them his views on the enterprise, and these seemed so eminently reasonable and natural that Hilliard's suspicions once more became dulled, and he began to wonder if their host's peculiar manner could not have been due to some cause other than that he had imagined.

'There is not so much money in the pit-props as I had hoped,' Mr Coburn explained. 'When we started here the Baltic trade, which was, of course, the big trade before the war, had not revived. Now we find the Baltic competition growing keener, and our margin of profit is dwindling. We are handicapped also by having only a one way traffic. Most of the Baltic firms exporting pit-props have an import trade in coal as well. This gives them double freights and pulls down their overhead costs. But it wouldn't pay us to follow their example. If we ran coal it could only be to Bordeaux, and that would take up more of our boat's time than it would be worth.'

Hilliard nodded and Mr Coburn went on:

'On the other hand, we are doing better in what I may call "sideshows". We're getting quite a good price for our firewood, and selling more and more of it. Three large firms in Bordeaux have put in wood-burning fireboxes and use nothing else, and two others are thinking of following suit. Then I am considering two developments; in fact, I have decided on the first. We are going to put in an air compressor in our engine-room, and use pneumatic tools in the forest for felling and lopping. I estimate that will save us six men. Then I think there would be a market for pine paving blocks for streets. I haven't gone into this yet, but I'm doing so.'

'That sounds very promising,' Hilliard answered. 'I don't know much about it, but I believe soft wood blocks are considered better than hard.'

'They wear more evenly, I understand. I'm trying to persuade the Paris authorities to try a piece of it, and if that does well it might develop into a big thing. Indeed, I can imagine our giving up the pit-props altogether in the future.'

After a time Miss Coburn joined them, and, the Ford car being brought out, the party set off on their excursion. They visited a part of the wood where the trees were larger than near the sawmill, and had a pleasant though uneventful afternoon. The evening they spent as before at the Coburn's house.

Next day the friends invited their hosts to join them in a trip up the river. Hilliard tactfully interested the manager in the various 'gadgets' he had fitted up in the launch, and Merriman's dream of making tea with Miss Coburn materialised. The more he saw of the gentle, brown-eyed girl, the more he found his heart going out to her, and the more it was borne in on him that life without her was becoming a prospect more terrible than he could bring himself to contemplate.

They went up-stream on the flood tide for some twenty miles, until the forest thinned away and they came on vineyards. There they went ashore, and it was not until the shades of evening were beginning to fall that they arrived back at the clearing.

As they swung round the bend in sight of the wharf Mr Coburn made an exclamation.

'Hallo!' he cried. 'There's the *Girondin*. She has made a good run. We weren't expecting her for another three or four hours.'

At the wharf lay a vessel of about 300 tons burden, with bluff, rounded bows sitting high up out of the water, a long, straight waist, and a bridge and cluster of deck-houses at the stern.

'Our motor ship,' Mr Coburn explained with evident pride. 'We had her specially designed for carrying the pit-props, and also for this river. She only draws eight feet. You must come on board and have a look over her.'

This was of all things what Hilliard most desired. He recognised that if he was allowed to inspect her really thoroughly, it would finally dispel any lingering suspicion he might still harbour that the syndicate was engaged in smuggling operations. The two points on which that suspicion had been founded—the absence of return cargoes and the locality of the French end of the enterprise—were not, he now saw, really suspicious at all. Mr Coburn's remarks met the first of these points, and showed that he was perfectly alive to the handicap of a one way traffic. The matter had not been material when the industry was started, but now, owing to the recovery of the Baltic trade after the war, it was becoming important, and the manager evidently realised that it might easily grow sufficiently to kill the pit-prop trade altogether. And the locality question was even simpler. The syndicate had chosen the pine forests of the Landes for their operations because they wanted timber close to the sea. On the top of these considerations came the lack of secrecy about the ship. It could only mean that there really was nothing aboard to conceal.

On reaching the wharf all four crossed the gangway to the deck of the *Girondin*. At close quarters she seemed quite a big boat. In the bows was a small forecastle, containing quarters for the crew of five men as well as the oil tanks and certain stores. Then amidships was a long expanse of holds, while aft were the officers' cabins and tiny mess room, galley, navigating bridge, and last, but not least, the engine-room with its set of Diesel engines. She seemed throughout a well-appointed boat, no money having apparently been spared to make her efficient and comfortable.

'She carries between six and seven thousand props every trip,' Mr Coburn told them, 'that is, without any deck cargo. I dare say in summer we could put ten thousand on her if we tried, but she is rather shallow in the draught for it, and we don't care to run any risks. Hallo, captain! Back again?' he broke off, as a man in a blue pilot cloth coat and peaked cap emerged from below.

The newcomer was powerfully built and would have been tall, but for rather rounded shoulders and a stoop. He was clean shaven, with a heavy jaw and thin lips which were compressed into a narrow line. His expression was vindictive as well as somewhat crafty, and he looked a man who would not be turned from his purpose by nice points of morality or conscience.

Though Hilliard instinctively noted these details, they did not particularly excite his interest. But his interest was nevertheless keenly aroused. For he saw the man, as his gaze fell on himself and Merriman, give a sudden start, and then flash a quick, questioning glance at Mr Coburn. The action was momentary, but it was enough to bring back with a rush all Hilliard's suspicions. Surely, he thought, there must be *something* if the sight of a stranger upsets all these people in this way.

But he had not time to ponder the problem. The captain instantly recovered himself, pulled off his cap to Miss Coburn and shook hands all round, Mr Coburn introducing the visitors.

'Good trip, captain?' the manager went on. 'You're ahead of schedule.'

'Not so bad,' the newcomer admitted in a voice and manner singularly cultivated for a man in his position. 'We had a good wind behind us most of the way.'

They chatted for a few moments, then started on their tour of inspection. Though Hilliard was once again keenly on the alert, the examination, so far as he could see, left nothing to be desired. They visited every part of the vessel, from the forecastle storerooms to the tunnel of the screw shaft, and from the chart-house to the bottom of the hold, and every question either of the friends asked was replied to fully and without hesitation.

That evening, like the preceding, they passed with the Coburns. The captain and the engineer—a short, thick-set man named Bulla—strolled up with them and remained for dinner, but left shortly afterwards on the plea of matters to attend to on board. The friends stayed on, playing bridge, and it was late when they said good-night and set out to walk back to the launch.

During the intervals of play Hilliard's mind had been busy with the mystery which he believed existed in connection with the syndicate, and he had decided that to try to satisfy his curiosity he would go down to the wharf that night and see if any interesting operations went on under cover of darkness. The idea of a midnight loading of contraband no longer appealed to his imagination, but vaguely he wished to make sure that no secret activities were in progress.

He was at least certain that none had taken place up to the present—that Mr Coburn was personally concerned in, at all events. From the moment they had first sighted the ship until they had left the manager's house at the conclusion of the game of bridge, not five minutes ago, he had been in Mr Coburn's company. Next day it was understood they were to meet again, so that if the manager wished to carry out any secret operations they could only be done during the night.

Accordingly when they reached the launch he turned to Merriman.

'You go ahead, old man. I'm going to have a look round before turning in. Don't wait up for me. Put out the light when you've done with it and leave the companion unlatched so that I can follow you in.'

Merriman grunted disapprovingly, but offered no further objection. He clambered on board the launch and disappeared below, while Hilliard, remaining in the collapsible boat, began to row silently up-stream towards the wharf.

The night was dark and still, but warm. The moon had not risen, and the sky was overcast, blotting out even the small light of the stars. There was a faint whisper of air currents among the trees, and the subdued murmur of the moving mass of water was punctuated by tiny splashes and gurgles as little eddies formed round the stem of the boat or wavelets broke against the banks. Hilliard's eyes had by this time become accustomed to the gloom, and he could dimly distinguish the serrated line of the trees against the sky on either side of him, and later, the banks of the clearing, with the faint, ghostly radiance from the surface of the water.

He pulled on with swift, silent strokes, and presently the dark mass of the *Girondin* loomed in sight, with behind it the wharf and the shed. The ship, being longer than the wharf, projected for several feet above and below the latter. Hilliard turned his boat in-shore with the object of passing between the hull and the bank and so reaching the landing steps. But as he rounded the vessel's stern he saw that her starboard side was lighted up, and he ceased rowing, sitting motionless and silently holding water, till the boat began to drift back into the obscurity down-stream. The wharf was above the level of his head, and he could only see, appearing over its edge, the tops of the piles of pit-props. These, as well as the end of the ship's navigating bridge and the gangway, were illuminated by, he imagined, a lamp on the side of one of the deck-houses. But everything was very still, and the place seemed deserted.

Hilliard's intention had been to land on the wharf and, crouching behind the props, await events. But now he doubted if he could reach his hiding place without coming within the radius of the lamp and so exposing himself to the view of any one who might be on the watch on board. He recollected that the port or river side of the ship was in darkness, and he thought it might therefore be better if he could get directly aboard there from the boat.

Having removed his shoes he rowed gently round the stern and examined the side for a possible way up. The ship being light forward was heavily down in the stern, and he found the lower deck was not more than six or seven feet above water level. It occurred to him that if he could get hold of the mooring rope pawls he might be able to climb aboard. But this after a number of trials he found impossible, as in the absence of some one at the oars to steady the boat, the latter always drifted away from the hull before he could grasp what he wanted.

He decided he must risk passing through the lighted area, and, having for the third time rowed round the stern, he brought the boat up as close to the hull as possible until he reached the wharf. Then passing in between the two rows of piles and feeling his way in the dark, he made the painter fast to a diagonal, so that the boat would lie hidden should any one examine the steps with a light. The hull lay touching the vertical piles, and Hilliard, edging along a waling to the front of the wharf, felt with his foot through the darkness for the stern belting. The tide was low and he found this was not more than a foot above the timber on which he stood. He could now see the deck light, an electric bulb on the side of the captain's cabin, and it showed him the top of the taffrail some little distance above the level of his eyes. Taking his courage in both hands and stepping upon the belting, he succeeded in grasping the taffrail. In a moment he was over it and on the deck, and in another moment he had slipped round the deck-house and out of the light of the lamp. There he stopped, listening for an alarm, but the silence remained unbroken, and he believed he had been unobserved.

He recalled the construction of the ship. The lower deck, on which he was standing, ran across the stern and formed a narrow passage some forty feet long at each side of the central cabin. This cabin contained the galley and mess-room as well as the first officer's quarters. Bulla's state-room, Hilliard remembered, was down below beside the engine-room.

From the lower deck two ladders led to the bridge deck, at the forward end of which was situated the captain's state-room. Aft of this building most of the remaining bridge deck was taken up by two lifeboats, canvas covered and housed in chogs. On the top of the captain's cabin was the bridge and chart-house, reached by two ladders which passed up at either side of the cabin.

Hilliard, reconnoitring, crept round to the port side of the ship. The lower deck was in complete darkness, and he passed the range of cabins and silently ascended the steps to the deck above. Here also it was dark, but a faint light shone from the window of the captain's cabin. Stealthily Hilliard tiptoed to the porthole. The glass was hooked back, but a curtain hung across the opening. Fortunately, it was not drawn quite tight to one side, and he found that by leaning up against the bridge ladder he could see into the interior. A glance showed him that the room was empty.

As he paused irresolutely, wondering what he should do next, he heard a door open. There was a step on the deck below, and the door slammed sharply. Some one was coming to the ladder at the top of which he stood.

Like a shadow Hilliard slipped aft and, as he heard the unknown ascending the steps, he looked round for cover. The starboard boat and a narrow strip of deck were lighted up, but the port boat was in shadow. He could distinguish it merely as a dark blot on the sky. Recognising that he must be hidden should the port deck light be turned on, he reached the boat, felt his way round the stern, and, crouching down, crept as far underneath it as he could. There he remained motionless.

The newcomer began slowly to pace the deck, and the aroma of a good cigar floated in the still air. Up and down he walked with leisurely, unhurried footsteps. He kept to the dark side of the ship, and Hilliard, though he caught glimpses of the red point of the cigar each time the other reached the stern, could not tell who he was.

Presently other footsteps announced the approach of a second individual, and in a moment Hilliard heard the captain's voice.

'Where are you, Bulla?'

'Here,' came in the engineer's voice from the first-comer.

The captain approached and the two men fell to pacing up and down, talking in low tones. Hilliard could catch the words when the speakers were near the stern, but lost them when they went forward to the break of the poop.

'Confound that man Coburn,' he heard Captain Beamish mutter. 'What on earth is keeping him all this time?'

'The young visitors, doubtless,' rumbled Bulla with a fat chuckle; 'our friends of the evening.'

'Yes, confound them too,' growled Beamish, who seemed to be in an unenviable frame of mind. 'Damned nuisance their coming round. I should like to know what they are after.'

'Nothing particular, I should fancy. Probably out doing some kind of holiday.'

They passed round the deck-house and Hilliard could not hear the reply. When they returned Captain Beamish was speaking.

'—thinks it would about double our profits,' Hilliard heard him say. 'He suggests a second depot on the other side, say at Swansea. That would look all right on account of the South Wales coalfields.'

'But we're getting all we can out of the old hooker as it is,' Bulla objected. 'I don't see how she could do another trip.'

'Archer suggests a second boat.'

'Oh.' The engineer paused, then went on: 'But that's no new suggestion. That was proposed before ever the thing was started.'

'I know, but the circumstances have changed. Now we should—'

Again they passed out of earshot, and Hilliard took the opportunity to stretch his somewhat cramped limbs. He was considerably interested by what he had heard. The phrase Captain Beamish had used in reference to the proposed depot at Swansea—'it would look all right on account of the coal-fields'—was suggestive. Surely that was meaningless unless there was some secret activity—unless the pit-prop trade was only a blind to cover some more lucrative and probably more sinister undertaking? At first sight it seemed so, but he had not time to think it out then. The men were returning.

Bulla was speaking this time, and Hilliard soon found he was telling a somewhat improper story. As the two men disappeared round the deck-house he heard their hoarse laughter ring out. Then the captain cried: 'That you, Coburn?' the murmur of voices grew louder and more confused and immediately sank. A door opened, then closed, and once more silence reigned.

To Hilliard it seemed that here was a chance which he must not miss. Coming out from his hiding place, he crept stealthily along the deck in the hope that he might find out where the men had gone, and learn something from their conversation.

The captain's cabin was the probable meeting place, and Hilliard slipped silently back to the window through which he had glanced before. As he approached he heard a murmur of voices, and he cautiously leaned back against the bridge ladder and peeped in round the partly open curtain.

Three of the four seats the room contained were now occupied.

The captain, engineer and Mr Coburn sat round the central table, which bore a bottle of whisky, a soda syphon and glasses, as well as a box of cigars. The men seemed preoccupied and a little anxious. The captain was speaking.

'And have you found out anything about them?' he asked Mr Coburn.

'Only what I have been able to pick up from their own conversation,' the manager answered. 'I wrote Morton asking him to make inquiries about them, but of course there hasn't been time yet for a reply. From their own showing one of them is Seymour Merriman, junior partner of Edwards & Merriman, Gracechurch Street, Wine Merchants. That's the dark, square-faced one—the one who was here before. The other is a man called Hilliard. He is a clever fellow, and holds a good position in the Customs Department. He has had this launch for some years, and apparently has done the same kind of trip through the Continental rivers on previous holidays. But I could not find out whether Merriman had ever accompanied him before.'

'But you don't think they smell a rat?'

Mr Coburn hesitated.

'I don't think so,' he said slowly, 'but I'm not at all sure. Merriman, we believe, noticed the number plate that day. I told you, you remember. Henri is sure that he did, and Madeleine thinks so too. It's just a little queer his coming back. But I'll swear they've seen nothing suspicious this time.'

'You can't yourself account for his coming back?'

Again Mr Coburn hesitated.

'Not with any certainty,' he said at last, then with a grimace he continued: 'But I'm a little afraid that it's perhaps Madeleine.'

Bulla, the engineer, made a sudden gesture.

'*I* thought so,' he exclaimed. 'Even in the little I saw of them this evening I thought there was something in the wind. I guess that accounts for the whole thing. What do you say, skipper?'

The big man nodded.

'I should think so,' he admitted with a look of relief. 'I think it's a mare's nest, Coburn. I don't believe we need worry.'

'I'm not so sure,' Coburn answered slowly. 'I don't think we need worry about Merriman, but I'm hanged if I know what to think about Hilliard. He's pretty observant, and there's not much about this place that he hasn't seen at one time or another.'

'All the better for us, isn't it?' Bulla queried.

'So far as it goes, yes,' the manager agreed, 'and I've stuffed him with yarns about costs and about giving up the props and going in for paving blocks and so on which I think he swallowed. But why should he want to know what we are doing? What possible interest can the place have for him—unless he suspects?'

'They haven't done anything suspicious themselves?'

'Not that I have seen.'

'Never caught them trying to pump any of the men?'

'Never.'

Captain Beamish moved impatiently.

'I don't think we need worry,' he repeated with a trace of aggression in his manner. 'Let's get on to business. Have you heard from Archer?'

Mr Coburn drew a paper from his pocket, while Hilliard instinctively bent forward, believing he was at last about to learn something which would throw a light on these mysterious happenings. But alas for him! Just as the manager began to speak he heard steps on the gangway which passed on board and a man began to climb the starboard ladder to the upper deck.

Hilliard's first thought was to return to his hiding place under the boat, but he could not bring himself to go so far away from the centre of interest, and before he had consciously thought out the situation he found himself creeping silently up the ladder to the bridge. There he believed he would be safe from observation while remaining within earshot of the cabin, and if any one followed him up the ladder he could creep round on the roof of the cabin to the back of the chart-house, out of sight.

The newcomer tapped at the captain's door and after a shout of 'Come in,' opened it. There was a moment's silence, then Coburn's voice said:

'We were just talking of you, Henri. The skipper wants to know—' and the door closed.

Hilliard was not long in slipping back to his former position at the porthole.

'By Jove!' Bulla was saying. 'And to think that two years ago I was working a little coaster at twenty quid a month! And you, Coburn; two years ago you weren't much better fixed, if as well, eh?'

Coburn ignored the question.

'It's good, but it's not good enough,' he declared. 'This thing can't run for ever. If we go on too long somebody will tumble to it. What we want is to try to get our piles made and close it down before anything happens. We ought to have that other ship running. We could double our income with another ship and another depot. And Swansea seems to me the place.'

'Bulla and I were just talking of that before you came aboard,' the captain answered. 'You know we have considered that again and again, and we have always come to the conclusion that we are pushing the thing strongly enough.'

'Our organisation has improved since then. We can do more now with less risk. It ought to be reconsidered. Will you go into the thing, skipper?'

'Certainly. I'll bring it before our next meeting. But I won't promise to vote for it. In our business it's not difficult to kill the goose, etcetera.'

The talk drifted to other matters, while Hilliard, thrilled to the marrow, remained crouching motionless beneath the port-hole, concentrating all his attention on the conversation in the hope of catching some word or phrase which might throw further light on the mysterious enterprise under discussion.

While the affair itself was being spoken of he had almost ceased to be aware of his surroundings, so eagerly had he listened to what was being said, but now that the talk had turned to more ordinary subjects he began more or less subconsciously to take stock of his own position.

He realised in the first place that he was in very real danger. A quick movement either of the men in the cabin or of some member of the crew might lead to his discovery, and he had the uncomfortable feeling that he might pay the forfeit for his curiosity with his life. He could imagine the manner in which the 'accident' would be staged. Doubtless his body, showing all the appearance of death from drowning, would be found in the river with alongside it the upturned boat as evidence of the cause of the disaster.

And if he should die, his secret would die with him. Should he not then be content with what he had learned and clear out while he could, so as to ensure his knowledge being preserved? He felt that he ought, and yet the desire to remain in the hope of doing still better was overpowering.

But as he hesitated the power of choice was taken away. The men in the cabin were making a move. Coburn finished his whisky, and he and Henri rose to their feet.

'Well,' the former said, 'there's one o'clock. We must be off.'

The others stood up also, and at the same moment Hilliard crept once more up the ladder to the bridge and crouched down in the shadow of the chart-house. Hardly was he there when the men came out of the cabin to the deck beneath the bridge, then with a brief exchange of 'Good-nights', Coburn and the lorry driver passed down the ladder, crossed the gangway and disappeared behind a stack of pit-props on the wharf. Bulla with a grunted 'Night' descended the port steps, and Hilliard heard the door leading below open and shut; the starboard deck lamp snapped off, and finally the captain's door shut and a key turned in the lock. Some fifteen minutes later the faint light from the porthole vanished and all was dark and silent.

But for more than an hour Hilliard remained crouching motionless on the bridge, fearing lest some sound that he might make in his descent should betray him if the captain should still be awake. Then, a faint light from the rising moon appearing towards the east, he crept from his perch, and crossing the gangway, reached the wharf and presently his boat.

Ten minutes later he was on board the launch.

CHAPTER VI

A CHANGE OF VENUE

STILL making as little noise as possible, Hilliard descended to the cabin and turned in. Merriman was asleep, and the quiet movements of the other did not awake him.

But Hilliard was in no frame of mind for repose. He was too much thrilled by the adventure through which he had passed, and the discovery which he had made. He therefore put away the idea of sleep, and instead gave himself up to consideration of the situation.

He began by trying to marshall the facts he had already learnt. In the first place, there was the great outstanding point that his suspicions were well founded, that some secret and mysterious business was being carried on by this syndicate. Not only, therefore, was he justified in all he had done up to the present, but it was clear he could not leave the matter where it stood. Either he must continue his investigations further, or he must report to headquarters what he had overheard.

Next, it seemed likely that the syndicate consisted of at least six persons; Captain Beamish (probably from his personality the leader,) Bulla, Coburn, Henri, and the two men to whom reference had been made, Archer, who had suggested forming the depot at Swansea, and Morton, who had been asked to make inquiries as to himself and Merriman. Madeleine Coburn's name had also been mentioned, and Hilliard wondered whether she could be a member. Like his companion he could not believe that she would be willingly involved, but on the other hand Coburn had stated that she had reported her suspicion that Merriman had noticed the changed number plate. Hilliard could come to no conclusion about her, but it remained clear that there were certainly four members, and probably six or more.

But if so, it followed that the operations must be on a fairly large scale. Educated men did not take up a risky and presumably illegal enterprise unless the prize was worth having. It was unlikely that £1000 a year would compensate any one of them for the risk. But that would mean a profit of from £4000 to £6000 a year. Hilliard realised that he was here on shaky ground, though the balance of probability was in his favour.

It also seemed certain that the whole pit-prop business was a sham, a mere blind to cover those other operations from which the money came. But when Hilliard came to ask himself what those operations were, he found himself up against a more difficult proposition.

His original brandy smuggling idea recurred to him with renewed force, and as he pondered it he saw that there really was something to be said for it. Three distinct considerations were consistent with the theory.

There was first of all the size of the fraud. A theft of £4000 to £6000 or more a year implied as victim a large corporation. The sum would be too big a proportion of the income of a moderate sized firm for the matter to remain undiscovered, and, other things being equal, the larger the corporation the more difficult to locate the leakage.

But what larger corporation was there than a nation, and what so easy to defraud as a government? And how could a government be more easily defrauded than by smuggling? Here again Hilliard recognised he was only theorising; still the point had a certain weight.

The second consideration was also inconclusive. It was that all the people who, he had so far learnt, were involved, were engaged in transport operations. The ostensible trade also, the blind under which the thing was worked, was a transport trade. If brandy smuggling were in progress something of precisely this kind would have to be devised. In fact anything more suitable than the pit-prop business would be hard to discover.

The third point he had thought of before. If brandy were to be smuggled, no better locality could have been found for the venture than this country round about Bordeaux. As one of the staple products of the district, brandy could be obtained here, possibly more easily than anywhere else.

The converse argument was equally inconclusive. What hypothesis other than that of brandy smuggling could meet the facts? Hilliard could not think of any, but he recognised that his failure did not prove that none existed.

On the other hand, in spite of these considerations he had to admit that he had seen nothing which in the slightest degree supported the theory, nor had he heard anything which could not equally well have referred to something else.

But whatever their objective, he felt sure that the members of the syndicate were desperate men. They were evidently too far committed to hesitate over fresh crime to keep their secret. If he wished to pursue his investigations, it was up to him to do so without arousing their suspicions.

As he pondered over the problem of how this was to be done he became more and more conscious of its difficulty. Such an inquiry to a trained detective could not be easy, but to him, an amateur at the game, it seemed wellnigh impossible. And particularly he found himself handicapped by the intimate terms with the Coburns on which he and Merriman found themselves. For instance, that very morning an excursion had been arranged to an old château near Bordeaux. How could he refuse to go? And if he went how could he watch the loading of the *Girondin*?

He had suspected before that the Coburn's hospitality was due to something other than friendliness, and now he was sure of it. No longer had he any doubt that the object was to get him out of the way, to create that very obstacle to investigation which it had created. And here again Miss Coburn had undoubtedly lent herself to the plot.

He was not long in coming to the conclusion that the sooner he and Merriman took leave of the Coburns the better. Besides this question of handicap, he was afraid with so astute a man as Coburn he would sooner or later give himself away.

The thought led to another. Would it not be wise to keep Merriman in ignorance of what he had learned, at least for the present? Merriman was an open, straightforward chap, transparently honest in all his dealings. Could he dissemble sufficiently to hide his knowledge from his hosts? In particular could he deceive Madeleine? Hilliard doubted it. He felt that under the special circumstances his friend's discretion could not be relied on. At all events Merriman's appearance of ignorance would be more convincing if it were genuine.

On the whole, Hilliard decided, it would be better not to tell him. Let them once get away from the neighbourhood, and he could share his discoveries and they could together decide what was to be done. But first, to get away.

Accordingly next morning he broached the subject. He had expected his friend would strenuously oppose any plan involving separation from Madeleine Coburn, but to his relief Merriman immediately agreed with him.

'I've been thinking we ought to clear out too,' he declared ungrammatically. 'It's not good enough to be accepting continuous hospitality which you can't return.'

Hilliard assented carelessly, remarked that if they started the following morning they could reach the Riviera by the following Friday, and let it go at that. He did not refer again to the subject until they reached the Coburn's door, when he asked quickly: 'By the way, will you tell them we're leaving tomorrow or shall I?'

'I will,' said Merriman, to his relief.

The *Girondin* was loading props as they set out in the Ford car, and the work was still in progress on their return in the late afternoon. Mr Coburn had excused himself from joining the party on the ground of business, but Captain Beamish had

taken his place, and had proved himself a surprisingly entertaining companion. At the old château they had a pleasant al
fresco lunch, after which Captain Beamish took a number of
photographs of the party with his pocket Kodak.

Merriman's announcement of his and Hilliard's impending
departure had been met with a chorus of regrets, but though
these sounded hearty enough, Hilliard noticed that no definite
invitation to stay longer was given.

The friends dined with the Coburns for the last time that
evening. Mr Coburn was a little late for the meal, saying he had
waited on the wharf to see the loading completed, that all the
cargo was now aboard, and that the *Girondin* would drop down
to sea on the flood tide in the early morning.

'We shall have her company so far,' Hilliard remarked. 'We
must start early too, so as to make Bordeaux before dark.'

When the time came to say good-bye, Mr Coburn and his
daughter went down to the launch with their departing visitors.
Hilliard was careful to monopolise the manager's attention, so
as to give Merriman his innings with the girl. His friend did
not tell him what passed between them, but the parting was
evidently affecting, as Merriman retired to his locker practically
in silence.

Five o'clock next morning saw the friends astir, and their
first sight on reaching the deck was the *Girondin* coming down-
stream. They exchanged hand waves with Captain Beamish on
the bridge, then, swinging their own craft, followed in the wake
of the other. A couple of hours later they were at sea.

Once again they were lucky in their weather. A sun of molten
glory poured down from the clearest of blue skies, burnishing
a track of intolerable brilliance across the water. Hardly a ripple
appeared on the smooth surface, though they rose and fell
gently to the flat ocean swell. They were running up the coast
about four miles out, and except for the *Girondin*, now almost
hull down to the north-west, they had the sea to themselves. It
was hot enough to make the breeze caused by the launch's

progress pleasantly cool, and both men lay smoking on the deck, lazily watching the water and enjoying the easy motion. Hilliard had made the wheel fast, and reached up every now and then to give it a slight turn.

'Jolly, I call this,' he exclaimed as he lay down again after one of these interruptions. 'Jolly sun, jolly sea, jolly everything, isn't it?'

'Rather. Evan a landlubber like me can appreciate it. But you don't often have it like this, I bet.'

'Oh, I don't know,' Hilliard answered absently, and then, swinging round and facing his friend he went on:

'I say, Merriman, I've something to tell you that will interest you, but I'm afraid it won't please you.'

Merriman laughed contentedly.

'You arouse my curiosity anyway,' he declared. 'Get on and let's hear it.'

Hilliard answered quietly, but he felt excitement arising in him as he thought of the disclosure he was about to make.

'First of all,' he began, speaking more and more earnestly as he proceeded. 'I have to make you an apology. I quite deliberately deceived you up at the clearing, or rather I withheld from you knowledge that I ought to have shared. I had a reason for it, but I don't know if you'll agree that it was sufficient.'

'Tell me.'

'You remember the night before last when I rowed up to the wharf after we had left the Coburn's? You thought my suspicions were absurd, or worse. Well, they weren't. I made a discovery.'

Merriman sat up eagerly, and listened intently as the other recounted his adventure aboard the *Girondin*. Hilliard kept nothing back; even the reference to Madeleine he repeated as nearly word for word as possible, finally giving a bowdlerised version of his reasons for keeping his discoveries to himself while they remained in the neighbourhood.

Merriman received the news with a dismay approaching

positive horror. He had but one thought—Madeleine. How did the situation affect her? Was she in trouble? In danger? Was she so entangled that she could not get out? Never for a moment did it enter his head that she could be willingly involved.

'My God! Hilliard,' he cried hoarsely, 'whatever does it all mean? Surely it can't be criminal? They'—he hesitated slightly, and Hilliard read in a different pronoun—'they never would join in such a thing.'

Hilliard took the bull by the horns.

'That *Miss* Coburn would take part in anything shady I don't for a moment believe,' he declared, 'but I'm afraid I wouldn't be so sure of her father.'

Merriman shook his head and groaned.

'I know you're right,' he admitted to the other's amazement. 'I saw—I didn't mean to tell you, but now I may as well. That first evening, when we went up to call, you probably don't remember, but after he had learned who we were he turned round to pull up a chair. He looked at you; I saw his face in a mirror. Hilliard, it was the face of a—I was going to say, a devil—with hate and fear. But the look passed instantly. When he turned round he was smiling. It was so quick I half thought I was mistaken. But I know I wasn't.'

'I saw fear on his face when he recognised you that same evening,' Hilliard replied. 'We needn't blink it, Merriman. Whether willingly or unwillingly, Mr Coburn's in the thing. That's as certain as that we're here.'

'But what is it? Have you any theory?'

'No, not really. There was that one of brandy smuggling that I mentioned before. I suggest it because I can suggest nothing else, but I admit I saw no evidence of it.'

Merriman was silent for several minutes as the boat slid over the smooth water. Then with a change of manner he turned once more to his friend.

'I suppose we couldn't leave it alone? Is it our business after all?'

'If we don't act we become accessories, and besides we leave that girl to fight her own battles.'

Merriman clenched his fists and once more silence reigned. Presently he spoke again.

'You had something in your mind?'

'I think we must do one of two things. Either continue our investigations until we learn what is going on, or else clear out and tell the police what we have learnt.'

Merriman made a gesture of dissent.

'Not that, not that,' he cried. 'Anything rather than the police.'

Hilliard gazed vacantly on the long line of the coast.

'Look here, old man,' he said, 'wouldn't it be better if we discussed this thing quite directly? Don't think I mean to be impertinent—God knows I don't—but am I not right in thinking you want to save Miss Coburn all annoyance, and her father also, for her sake.'

'We needn't talk about it again,' Merriman said in a hard voice, looking intently at the stem of the mast, 'but if it's necessary to make things clear, I want to marry her if she'll have me.'

'I thought so, old man, and I can only say,—The best of luck! As you say, then, we musn't call in the police, and as we can't leave the thing, we must go on with our own inquiry. I would suggest that if we find out their scheme is something illegal, we see Mr Coburn and give him the chance to get out before we lodge our information.'

'I suppose that is the only way,' Merriman said doubtfully. After a pause Hilliard went on.

'I'm not very clear, but I'm inclined to think we can do no more good here at present. I think we should try the other end.'

'The other end?'

'Yes, the unloading of the ship and the disposal of the pit-props. You see, the first thing we're up against is that these people are anything but fools, and the second is that they already suspect us and will keep a watch on us. A hundred to one they make inquiries and see that we really do go through that Canal du Midi to the Riviera. We can't hang about Bordeaux without their knowing it.'

'That's true.'

'Of course,' Hilliard went on, 'we can see now we made a frightful mess of things by calling on the Coburns or letting Mr Coburn know we were about, but at the time it seemed the wisest thing.'

'It was the only thing,' Merriman asserted positively. 'We didn't know then there was anything wrong, and besides, how could we have hidden the launch?'

'Well, it's done anyway. We needn't worry about it now, except that it seems to me that for the same reason the launch has served its purpose. We can't use it here because the people at the clearing know it, and we can't use it at the unloading end for all on board the *Girondin* would recognise it directly they saw it.'

Merriman nodded without speaking and Hilliard continued:

'I think therefore that we should leave the launch at Bordeaux tonight and go back to London overland. I shall write Mr Coburn saying we have found Poste Restante letters recalling us. You can enclose a note to Miss Coburn if you like. When we get to town we can apply at the Enquiry Office at Lloyd's to find out where the *Girondin* calls in England. Then let us go there and make inquiries. The launch can be worked back to England some other time. How does that strike you?'

'Seems all right. But I should leave the launch at Bordeaux. We may have to come back, and it would furnish us with an excuse for our presence if we were seen.'

Hilliard gave a little sigh of relief. Merriman's reply took a weight off his mind, not because of the value of the suggestion—though in its way it was quite useful—but because of its indication of Merriman's frame of mind. He had feared that because of Miss Coburn's connection with the affair he would lose his friend's help, even that they might quarrel. And now he saw these fears were groundless. Thankfully he recognised that they would co-operate as they had originally intended.

'Jolly good notion, that,' he answered cordially.

'I confess,' Merriman went on slowly, 'that I should have liked to stay in the neighbourhood and see if we couldn't find out something more about the lorry numbers. It may be a trivial point, but it's the only direct and definite thing we know of. All the rest are hints or suspicions or probabilities. But here we have a bit of mystery, tangible, in our hands, as it were. Why were those number plates changed? It seems to me a good point of attack.'

'I thought of that too and I agree with every word you say,' Hilliard replied eagerly, 'but there is the question of our being suspects. I believe we shall be watched out of the place, and I feel sure our only chance of learning anything is to satisfy them of our *bona fides*.'

Merriman agreed, and they continued discussing the matter in detail, at last deciding to adopt Hilliard's suggestion and set to work on the English end of the mysterious traffic.

About two that afternoon they swung round the Pointe de Grave into the estuary of the Gironde. The tide, which was then flowing, turned when they were some two-thirds of the way up, and it was well on to seven o'clock when they made fast to the same decaying wharf from which they had set out. Hilliard saw the owner, and arranged with him to let the launch lie at one of his moorings until she should be required. Then the friends went up town, got some dinner, wrote their letters, and took the night train for Paris. Next evening they were in London.

'I say,' Hilliard remarked when later on that same evening they sat in his rooms discussing their plans, 'I believe we can find out about the *Girondin* now. My neighbour on the next landing above is a shipping man. He might have a copy of Lloyd's Register. I shall go and ask him.'

In a few moments he returned with a bulky volume. 'One of the wonders of the world, this, I always think,' he said as he began to turn over the pages. 'It gives, or is supposed to give, information about everything over a hundred tons that floats anywhere over the entire globe. It'll give the *Girondin* anyway.' He ran his finger down the columns. 'Ah! what's this? Motor ship *Girondin*, 350 tons, built and so on. "The Landes Pit-Prop Syndicate, Ferriby, Hull." Hull, my son. There we are.'

'Hull? I know Hull,' Merriman remarked laconically. 'Rotten place.'

'We shall find it a jolly interesting place before we're through, it seems to me,' his friend replied. 'Let's hope so anyway.'

'What's the plan, then? I'm on provided I have a good sleep at home tonight first.'

'Same here,' Hilliard agreed as he filled his pipe. 'I suppose Hull by an early train tomorrow is the scheme.'

Merriman borrowed his friend's pouch and refilled his pipe in his turn.

'You think so?' he said slowly. 'Well, I'm not so sure. Seems to me we can very easily dish ourselves if we're not careful.'

'How so?'

'We agreed these folk were wideawake and suspicious of us. Very well. Directly our visit to them is over, we change our plans and leave Bordeaux. Will it not strike them that our interest in the trip was only on their account?'

'I don't see it. We gave a good reason for leaving.'

'Quite; that's what I'm coming to. We told them you were recalled to your office. But what about that man Morton, that was to spy on us before? What's to prevent them asking him if you really have returned?'

Hilliard sat up sharply.

'By Jove!' he cried. 'I never thought of that.'

'And there's another thing,' Merriman went on. 'We turn up at Hull, find the syndicate's depot and hang about. The fellow in charge there sees us. Well, that's all right *if* he hasn't had a letter from France describing us and enclosing a copy of that group that Captain Beamish took at the château.'

Hilliard whistled.

'Lord! It's not going to be so simple as it looks, is it?'

'It isn't. And what's more, we can't afford to make any mistakes. It's too dangerous.'

Hilliard got up and began to pace the room.

'I don't care,' he declared savagely. 'I'm going through with it now no matter what happens.'

'Oh, so am I, for the matter of that. All I say is we shall have to show a bit more intelligence this time.'

For an hour more they discussed the matter, and at last decided on a plan. On the following morning Hilliard was to go to his office, see his chief and ask for an extension of leave, then hang about and interview as many of his colleagues as possible, telling them he had been recalled, but was not now required. His chief was not very approachable, and Hilliard felt sure the subject would not be broached to him. In the evening they would go down to Hull.

This programme they would have carried out, but for an unforeseen event. While Hilliard was visiting his office Merriman took the opportunity to call at his, and there he learned that Edwards, his partner, had been taken ill the morning before. It appeared there was nothing seriously wrong, and Edwards expected to be back at work in three or four days, but until his return Merriman was required, and he had reluctantly to telephone the news to Hilliard. But no part of their combined holiday was lost. Hilliard by a stroke of unexpected good fortune was able to spend the same time at work, and postpone the remainder of his leave until Merriman was free. Thus it came to pass that it was not until six days later than they had intended that the two friends packed their bags for Hull.

They left King's Cross by the 5.40 p.m. train, reaching their destination a little before eleven. There they took rooms at the George, a quiet hotel in Baker Street, close to the Paragon Station.

CHAPTER VII

THE FERRIBY DEPOT

The two friends, eager and excited by their adventure, were early astir next morning, and before breakfast Hilliard went out and bought the best map of the city and district he could find.

'Why, Ferriby's not in the town at all,' he exclaimed after he had studied it for some moments. 'It's up the river—must be seven or eight miles up by the look of it. The North Eastern runs through it and there's a station. We'd better go out there and prospect.'

Merriman agreeing, they called for a time-table, found there was a train at 10.35, and going down to Paragon Station, got on board.

After clearing the suburbs the line came down close to the river, and the two friends kept a good look out for the depot. About four and a half miles out they stopped at a station called Hessle, then a couple of miles farther their perseverance was rewarded and they saw a small pier and shed, the latter bearing in large letters on its roof the name of the syndicate. Another mile and a half brought them to Ferriby, where they alighted.

'Now what about walking back to Hessle,' Hilliard suggested, 'and seeing what we can see?'

They followed the station approach road inland until they reached the main thoroughfare, along which they turned eastwards in the direction of Hull. In a few minutes they came in sight of the depot, half a mile off across the fields. A lane led towards it, and this they followed until it reached the railway. There it turned in the direction of Hull and ran parallel to the line for a short distance, doubling back, as they learned afterwards, until it reached the main road half-way to Hessle. The railway tracks were on a low bank, and the men could just see across them to the syndicate's headquarters.

The view was not very good, but so far as they could make out, the depot was a replica of that in the Landes clearing. A timber wharf jutted out into the stream, apparently of the same size and construction as that on the River Lesque. Behind it was the same kind of galvanised iron shed, but this one, besides having windows in the gables, seemed the smaller of the two. Its back was only about a hundred feet from the railway, and the space between was taken up by a yard surrounded by a high galvanised iron fence, above which appeared the tops of many stacks of pit-props. Into the yard ran a siding from the railway. From a door in the fence a path led across the line to a wicket in the hedge of the lane, beside which stood a 'Beware of the Train' notice. There was no sign of activity about the place, and the gates through which the siding entered the enclosure were shut.

Hilliard stopped and stood looking over.

'How the mischief are we to get near that place without being seen?' he questioned. 'It's like a German pill-box. There's no cover anywhere about.'

It was true. The country immediately surrounding the depot was singularly bare. It was flat except for the low bank, four or five feet high, on which lay the railway tracks. There were clumps of trees farther inland, but none along the shore, and the nearest building, a large block like a factory with beside it a cottage, was at least three hundred yards away in the Hull direction.

'Seems an element of design in that, eh, Hilliard?' Merriman remarked as they turned to continue their walk. 'Considering the populous country we're in, you could hardly find a more isolated place.'

Hilliard nodded as they turned away.

'I've just been thinking that. They could carry on any tricks they liked there and no one would be a bit the wiser.'

They moved on towards the factory-like building. It was on the inland side of the railway, and the lane swung away from the line and passed what was evidently its frontage. A siding ran into its rear, and there were connections across the main lines and a signal cabin in the distance. A few yards on the nearer side stood the cottage, which they now saw was empty and dilapidated.

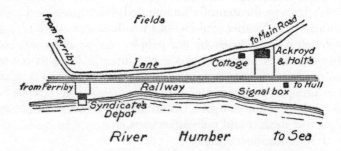

'I say, Hilliard, look there!' cried Merriman suddenly.

They had passed along the lane until the façade of the building had come into view and they were able to read its signboard: 'Ackroyd & Holt, Licensed Rectifiers.'

'I thought it looked like a distillery,' continued Merriman in considerable excitement. 'By Jove! Hilliard, that's a find and no mistake! Pretty suggestive that, isn't it?'

Hilliard was not so enthusiastic.

'I'm not so sure,' he said slowly. 'You mean that it supports my brandy smuggling theory? Just how?'

'Well, what do you think yourself? We suspect brandy smuggling, and here we find at the import end of the concern the nearest building in an isolated region is a distillery—a rectifying house, mind you! Isn't that a matter of design too? How better could they dispose of their stuff than by dumping it on to rectifiers.'

'You distinguish between distillers and rectifiers?'

'Certainly; there's less check on rectifiers. Am I not right in saying that while the regulations for the measurement of spirit actually produced from the stills are so thorough as to make fraud almost impossible, rectifiers, because they don't themselves produce spirit, but merely refine what other firms have produced, are not so strictly looked after? Rectifiers would surely find smuggled stuff easier to dispose of than distillers.'

Hilliard shook his head.

'Perhaps so, theoretically,' he admitted, 'but in practice there's nothing in it. Neither could work a fraud like that, for both are watched far too closely by our people. I'm afraid I don't see that this place being here helps us. Surely it's reasonable to suppose that the same cause brought Messrs Ackroyd & Holt that attracted the syndicate? Just that it's a good site. Where in the district could you get a better? Cheap ground and plenty of it, and steamer and rail connections.'

'It's a coincidence anyway.'

'I don't see it. In any case unless we can prove that the ship brings brandy the question doesn't arise.'

Merriman shrugged his shoulders good-humouredly.

'That's a blow,' he remarked. 'And I was so sure I had got hold of something good! But it just leads us back to the question that somehow or other we must inspect that depot, and if we find nothing we must watch the *Girondin* unloading. If we can only get near enough it would be *impossible* for them to discharge anything in bulk without our seeing it.'

Hilliard murmured an agreement, and the two men strolled on in silence, the thoughts of each busy with the problem Merriman had set. Both were realising that detective work was a very much more difficult business than they had imagined. Had not each had a strong motive for continuing the investigation, it is possible they might have grown faint-hearted. But Hilliard had before him the vision of the kudos which would accrue to him if he could unmask a far-reaching conspiracy, while to Merriman the freeing of Madeleine Coburn from the toils in which she seemed to have been enmeshed had become of more importance than anything else in the world.

The two friends had already left the distillery half a mile behind, when Hilliard stopped and looked at his watch.

'Ten minutes to twelve,' he announced. 'As we have nothing to do let's go back and watch that place. Something may happen during the afternoon, and if not we'll look out for the workmen leaving and see if we can't pick up something from them.'

They retraced their steps past the distillery and depot, then creeping into a little wood, sat down on a bank within sight of the enclosure and waited.

The day was hot and somewhat enervating, and both enjoyed the relaxation in the cool shade. They sat for the most part in silence, smoking steadily, and turning over in their minds the problems with which they were faced. Before them the country sloped gently down to the railway bank, along the top of which the polished edges of the rails gleamed in the midday sun. Beyond was the wide expanse of the river, with a dazzling track of shimmering gold stretching across it and hiding the low-lying farther shore with its brilliancy. A few small boats moved slowly near the shore, while farther out an occasional larger steamer came into view going up the fairway to Goole. Every now and then trains roared past, the steam hardly visible in the dry air.

The afternoon dragged slowly but not unpleasantly away, until about five o'clock they observed the first sign of activity about the syndicate's depot which had taken place since their arrival. The door in the galvanised fence opened and five figures emerged and slowly crossed the railway. They paused for a moment after reaching the lane, then separated, four going eastwards towards the distillery, the fifth coming north towards the point at which the watchers were concealed. The latter thereupon moved out from their hiding place on to the road.

The fifth figure resolved itself into that of a middle-aged man of the labouring class, slow, heavy, and obese. In his rather bovine countenance hardly any spark of intelligence shone. He did not appear to have seen the others as he approached, but evinced neither surprise nor interest when Hilliard accosted him.

'Any place about here you can get a drink?'

The man slowly jerked his head to the left.

'Oop in village,' he answered. 'Raven bar.'

'Come along and show us the way and have a drink with us,' Hilliard invited.

The man grasped this and his eyes gleamed.

'Ay,' he replied succinctly.

As they walked Hilliard attempted light conversation, but without eliciting much response from their new acquaintance, and it was not until he had consumed his third bottle of beer that his tongue became somewhat looser.

'Any chance of a job where you're working?' Hilliard went on. 'My pal and I would be glad to pick up something.'

The man shook his head, apparently noticing nothing incongruous in the question.

'Don't think it.'

'No harm in asking the boss anyway. Where might we find him?'

'Down at works likely. He be there most times.'

'I'd rather go to his house. Can you tell me where he lives?'

'Ay. Down at works.'

'But he doesn't sleep at the works surely?'

'Ay. Sleeps in tin hut.'

The friends exchanged glances. Their problem was even more difficult than they had supposed. A secret inspection seemed more and more unattainable. Hilliard continued the laborious conversation.

'We thought there might be some stevedoring to do. You've a steamer in now and then, haven't you?'

The man admitted it, and after a deal of wearisome questioning they learned that the *Girondin* called about every ten days, remaining for about forty-eight hours, and that she was due in three or four days.

Finding they could get no further information out of him, they left their bovine acquaintance with a fresh supply of beer, and returning to the station, took the first train back to Hull.

As they sat smoking that evening after dinner they once more attacked the problem which was baffling them.

'It seems to me,' Hilliard asserted, 'that we should concentrate on the smuggling idea first, not because I quite believe in it, but because it's the only one we have. And that brings us again to the same point—the unloading of the *Girondin*.'

Merriman not replying, he continued:

'Any attempt involves a preliminary visit to see how the land lies. Now we can't approach that place in the day time; if we try to slip round secretly we shall be spotted from those windows or from the wharf; on the other hand, if we invent some tale and go openly, we give ourselves away if they have our descriptions or photographs. Therefore we must go at night.'

'Well?'

'Obviously we can only approach the place by land or water. If we go by land we have either to shin up on the pier from the shore, which we're not certain we can do, or else risk making a noise climbing over the galvanised iron fence. Besides we might leave footmarks or other traces. But if we go by water we can muffle our oars and drop down absolutely silently to the wharf. There are bound to be steps, and it would be easy to get up without making any noise.'

Merriman's emphatic nod expressed his approval.

'Good,' he cried warmly. 'What about getting a boat tomorrow and having a try that night?'

'I think we should. There's another thing about it too. If there should be an alarm we could get away by the river far more easily than across the country. It's a blessing there's no moon.'

Next day the object of their search was changed. They wanted a small, handy skiff on hire. It did not turn out an easy quest, but by the late afternoon they succeeded in obtaining the desired article. They purchased also close-fitting caps and rubber-soled shoes, together with some food for the night, a couple of electric torches, and a yard of black cloth. Then, shortly before dusk began to fall, they took their places and pulled out on the great stream.

It was a pleasant evening, a fitting close to a glorious day. The air was soft and balmy, and a faint haze hung over the water, smoothing and blurring the sharp outlines of the buildings of the town and turning the opposite bank into a gray smudge. Not a breath was stirring, and the water lay like plate glass, unbroken by the faintest ripple. The spirit of adventure was high in the two men as they pulled down the great avenue of burnished gold stretching westwards towards the sinking sun.

The tide was flowing, and but slight effort was needed to keep them moving up-stream. As darkness grew they came nearer inshore, until in the fading light they recognised the railway station at Hessle. There they ceased rowing, drifting slowly onwards until the last faint haze of light had disappeared from the sky.

They had carefully muffled their oars, and now they turned north and began sculling gently inshore. Several lights had come out, and presently they recognised the railway signals and cabin at the distillery sidings.

'Two or three hundred yards more,' said Hilliard in low tones.

They were now close to the beach, and they allowed themselves to drift on until the dark mass of the wharf loomed up ahead. Then Hilliard dipped his oars and brought the boat silently alongside.

As they had imagined from their distant view of it, the wharf was identically similar in construction to that on the River Lesque. Here also were the two lines of piles like the letter V, one, in front, vertical, the other raking to support the earthwork behind. Here in the same relative position were the steps, and to these Hilliard made fast the painter with a slip hitch that could be quickly released. Then with the utmost caution both men stepped ashore, and slowly mounting the steps, peeped out over the deck of the wharf.

As far as they could make out in the gloom, the arrangement here also was similar to that in France. Lines of narrow gauge tramway, running parallel from the hut towards the water, were connected along the front of the wharf by a cross road and turn-tables. Between the lines were stacks of pit-props, and Decauville trucks stood here and there. But these details they saw afterwards. What first attracted their attention was that lights shone in the third and fourth windows from the left hand end of the shed. The manager evidently was still about.

'We'll go back to the boat and wait,' Hilliard whispered, and they crept down the steps.

At intervals of half an hour one or other climbed up and had a look at the windows. On the first two occasions the light was unchanged, on the third it had moved to the first and second windows, and on the fourth it had gone, apparently indicating that the manager had moved from his sitting-room to his bedroom and retired.

'We had better wait at least an hour more,' Hilliard whispered again.

Time passed slowly in the darkness under the wharf, and in a silence broken only by the gentle lapping of the water among the piles. The boat lay almost steady, except when a movement of one of its occupants made it heel slightly over and started a series of tiny ripples. It was not cold, and had the men not been so full of their adventure they could have slept. At intervals Hilliard consulted his luminous-dialled watch, but it was not until the hands pointed to the half-hour after one that they made a move. Then once more they softly ascended to the wharf above.

The sides of the structure were protected by railings which

ran back to the gables of the tin house, the latter stretching entirely across the base of the pier. Over the space thus enclosed the two friends passed, but it speedily became apparent that here nothing of interest was to be found. Beyond the stacks of props and wagons there was literally nothing except a rusty steam winch, a large water butt into which was led the down-spout from the roof, a tank raised on a stand and fitted with a flexible pipe, evidently for supplying crude oil for the ship's engines, and a number of empty barrels in which the oil had been delivered. With their torch carefully screened by the black cloth the friends examined these objects, particularly the oil tank which, forming as it did a bridge between ship and shore, naturally came in for its share of suspicion. But they were soon satisfied that neither it nor any of the other objects were connected with their quest, and retreating to the edge of the wharf, they held a whispered consultation.

Hilliard was for attempting to open one of the doors in the shed at the end away from the manager's room, but Merriman, obsessed with the idea of seeing the unloading of the *Girondin*, urged that the contents of the shed were secondary, and that their efforts should be confined to discovering a hiding place from which the necessary observations could be made.

'If there was any way of getting inside one of those stacks of props,' he said, 'we could keep a perfect watch. I could get in now, for example; you relieve me tomorrow night; I relieve you the next night, and so on. Nothing could be unloaded that we wouldn't see. But,' he added regretfully, 'I doubt even if we could get inside that we should be hidden. Besides, they might take a notion to load the props up.'

'Afraid that's hardly the scheme,' Hilliard answered, then went on excitedly: 'But there's that barrel! Perhaps we could get into that.'

'The barrel! That's the ticket.' Merriman was excited in his turn. 'That is, if it has a lid.'

They retraced their steps. With the tank they did not trouble;

it was a galvanised iron box with the lid riveted on, and moreover was full of oil; but the barrel looked feasible.

It was an exceptionally large cask or butt, with a lid which projected over its upper rim and which entirely protected the interior from view. It was placed in the corner beside the right hand gable of the shed, that is, the opposite end to the manager's rooms, and the wooden downspout from the roof passed in through a slot cut in the edge of the lid. A more ideal position for an observation post could hardly have been selected.

'Try to lift the lid,' whispered Hilliard.

They found it was merely laid on the rim; cleats nailed on below preventing it from slipping off. They raised it easily and Hilliard flashed in a beam from his electric torch. The cask was empty, evidently a result of the long drought.

'That'll do,' Merriman breathed. 'That's all we want to see. Come away.'

They lowered the cover and stood for a moment. Hilliard still wanted to try the doors of the shed, but Merriman would not hear of it.

'Come away,' he whispered again. 'We've done well. Why spoil it?'

They returned to the boat and there argued it out. Merriman's proposal was to try to find out when the *Girondin* was expected, then come the night before, bore a few eyeholes in the cask, and let one of them, properly supplied with provisions, get inside and assume watch. The other one would row away, rest and sleep during the day, and return on the following night, when they would exchange roles, and so on until the *Girondin* left. In this way, he asserted, they must infallibly discover the truth, at least about the smuggling.

'Do you think we could stand twenty-four hours in that barrel?' Hilliard questioned.

'Of course we could stand it. We've got to. Come on, Hilliard, it's the only way.'

It did not require much persuasion to get Hilliard to fall in with the proposal, and they untied their painter and pulled silently away from the wharf. The tide had turned, and soon they relaxed their efforts and let the boat drift gently downstream. The first faint light appeared in the eastern sky as they floated past Hessle, and for an hour afterwards they lay in the bottom of the boat, smoking peacefully and entranced by the gorgeous pageant of the coming day.

Not wishing to reach Hull too early, they rowed inshore, and landing in a little bay, lay down in the lush grass and slept for three or four hours. Then re-embarking, they pulled and drifted on until, between seven and eight o'clock, they reached the wharf at which they had hired their boat. An hour later they were back at their hotel, recuperating from the fatigues of the night with the help of cold baths and a substantial breakfast.

CHAPTER VIII

THE UNLOADING OF THE 'GIRONDIN'

AFTER breakfast Hilliard disappeared. He went out ostensibly to post a letter, but it was not until nearly three o'clock that he turned up again.

'Sorry, old man,' he greeted Merriman, 'but when I was going to the post office this morning an idea struck me, and it took me longer to follow up than I anticipated. I'll tell you. I suppose you realise that life in that barrel won't be very happy for the victim?'

'It'll be damnable,' Merriman agreed succinctly, 'but we needn't worry about that; we're in for it.'

'Oh, quite,' Hilliard returned. 'But just for that reason we don't want more of it than is necessary. We could easily bury ourselves twenty-four hours too soon.'

'Meaning?'

'Meaning that we mustn't go back to the wharf until the night before the *Girondin* arrives.'

'Don't see how we can be sure of that.'

'Nor did I till I posted my letter. Then I got my idea. It seemed worth following up, so I went round the shipping offices until I found a file of Lloyd's List. As you know it's a daily paper which gives the arrivals and departures of all ships at the world's ports. My notion was that if we could make a list of the *Girondin's* Ferriby arrivals and departures, say, during the last three months, and if we found she ran her trip regularly, we could forecast when she would be next due. Follow me?'

'Rather.'

'I had no trouble getting out my list, but I found it a bit disappointing. The trip took either ten, eleven, or twelve days, and for a long time I couldn't discover any rule. But at last I found it was Sunday. If you omit each Sunday the *Girondin* is in port, the round trip always takes the even ten days. I had the Lesque arrival and departure for that one trip when we were there, so I was able to make out the complete cycle. She takes two days in the Lesque to load, three to run to Hull, two at Ferriby to discharge, and three to return to France. Working from that and her last call here, she should be due back early on Friday morning.'

'Good!' Merriman exclaimed. 'Jolly good! And today is Thursday. We've just time to get ready.'

They went out and bought a one-inch auger and a three-sixteenths bradawl, a thick footstool and a satchel. This latter they packed with a loaf, some cheese, a packet of figs, a few bottles of soda water and a flask of whisky. These, with their caps, rubber shoes, electric torches and the black cloth, they carried to their boat, then returning to the hotel, they spent the time resting there until eleven o'clock. Solemnly they drew lots for the first watch, recognising that the matter was by no means a joke, as, if unloading were carried on by night, relief might be impossible during the ship's stay. But Merriman, to whom the fates were propitious, had no fear of his ability to hold out even for this period.

By eleven-thirty they were again sculling up the river. The weather was as perfect as that of the night before, except that on this occasion a faint westerly breeze had covered the surface of the water with myriads of tiny wavelets, which lapped and gurgled round the stem of their boat as they drove it gently through them. They did not hurry, and it was after one before they moored to the depot steps.

All was dark and silent above, as, carrying their purchases, they mounted to the wharf and crept stealthily to the barrel. Carefully they raised the lid, and Merriman, standing on the footstool, with some difficulty squeezed himself inside. Hilliard then lifted the footstool on to the rim and lowered the lid on to it, afterwards passing in through the opening thus left the satchel of food and the one-inch auger.

A means of observation now remained to be made. Two holes, they thought, should afford all the view necessary, one looking towards the front of the wharf, and the other, at right angles, along the side of the shed. Slowly, from the inside, Merriman began to bore. He made a sound like the nibbling of a mouse, but worked at irregular speeds so as not to suggest human agency to any one who might be awake and listening. Hilliard, with his hand on the outside of the barrel, stopped the work when he felt the point of the auger coming through, and himself completed the hole from the outside with his bradawl. This gave an aperture imperceptible on the rough exterior, but large within, and enabled the watcher to see through a much wider angle than he could otherwise have done. Hilliard then once more raised the lid, allowing Merriman to lift the footstool within, where it was destined to act as a seat for the observer.

All was now complete, and with a whispered exchange of good wishes, Hilliard withdrew, having satisfied himself by a careful look round that no traces had been left. Regaining the boat, he loosed the painter and pulled gently away into the night.

Left to himself in the confined space and inky blackness of the cask, Merriman proceeded to take stock of his position. He was anxious if possible to sleep, not only to pass some of the time, which at the best would inevitably be terribly long, but also that he might be the more wakeful when his attention should be required. But his unusual surroundings stimulated his imagination, and he could not rest.

He was surprised that the air was so good. Fortunately, the hole through the lid which received the down spout was of large dimensions, so that even though he might not have plenty of air, he would be in no danger of asphyxiation.

The night was very still. Listening intently, he could not hear the slightest sound. The silence and utter darkness indeed soon became overpowering, and he took his watch from his pocket that he might have the companionship of its ticking and see the glimmering hands and ring of figures.

He gave himself up for the thousandth time to the consideration of the main problem. What were the syndicate people doing? Was Mr Coburn liable to prosecution, to penal servitude? Was it possible that by some twist of the legal mind, some misleading circumstantial evidence, Miss Coburn—Madeleine—could be incriminated? Oh, if he but knew what was wrong, that he might be able to help! If he could but get her out of it, and for her sake Mr Coburn! If they were once safe he could pass on his knowledge to the police and be quit of the whole business. But always there was this enveloping cloak of ignorance baffling him at every turn. He did not know what was wrong, and any step he attempted might just precipitate the calamity he most desired to avoid.

Suppose he went and asked her? This idea had occurred to him many times before, and he had always rejected it as impracticable. But suppose he did? The danger was that she might be alarmed or displeased, that she might refuse to admit there was anything wrong and forbid him to refer to the matter again or even send him away altogether. And he felt he was not strong enough to risk that. No, he must know where he stood first. He must understand his position, so as not to bungle the thing. Hilliard was right. They must find out what the syndicate was doing. There was no other way.

So the hours dragged slowly away, but at last after interminable ages had gone by, Merriman noticed two faint spots of light showing at his eyeholes. Seating himself on his footstool, he bent forward and put his eye first to one and then to the other.

It was still the cold, dead light of early dawn before the sun had come to awaken colour and sharpen detail, but the main outlines of objects were already clear. As Merriman peered out he saw with relief that no mistake had been made as to his outlooks. From one hole or the other he could see the entire area of the wharf.

It was about five a.m., and he congratulated himself that what he hoped was the most irksome part of his vigil was over. Soon the place would awaken to life, and the time would then pass more quickly in observation of what took place.

But the three hours that elapsed before anything happened seemed even longer than those before dawn. Then, just as his watch showed eight o'clock, he heard a key grind in a lock, a door opened, and a man stepped out of the shed on the wharf.

He was a young fellow, slight in build, with an extremely alert and intelligent face, but a rather unpleasant expression. The sallowness of his complexion was emphasised by his almost jet black hair and dark eyes. He was dressed in a loose gray Norfolk jacket and knickerbockers, but wore no hat. He moved forward three or four feet and stood staring down-stream towards Hull.

'I see her, Tom,' he called out suddenly to some one in the shed behind. 'She's just coming round the point.'

There was another step and a second man appeared. He was older and looked like a foreman. His face was a contrast to that of the other. In it the expression was good—kindly, reliable, honest—but ability was not marked. He looked a decent, plodding, stupid man. He also stared eastward.

'Ay,' he said slowly. 'She's early.'

'Two hours,' the first agreed. 'Didn't expect her till between ten and eleven.'

The other murmured something about 'getting things ready,' and disappeared back into the shed. Presently came the sounds of doors being opened, and some more empty Decauville trucks were pushed out on to the wharf. At intervals both men reappeared and looked down-stream, evidently watching the approach of the ship.

Some half an hour passed, and then an increase of movement seemed to announce her arrival. The manager walked once more down the wharf, followed by the foreman and four other men—apparently the whole staff—among whom was the bovine-looking fellow whom the friends had tried to pump on their first visit to the locality. Then came a long delay during which Merriman could catch the sound of a ship's telegraph and the churning of the screw, and at last the bow of the *Girondin* appeared, slowly coming in. Ropes were flung, caught, slipped over bollards, drawn taut, made fast—and she was berthed.

Captain Beamish was on the bridge, and as soon as he could, the manager jumped aboard and ran up the steps and joined him there, In a few seconds both men disappeared into the captain's cabin.

The foreman and his men followed on board and began in a leisurely way to get the hatches open, but for at least an hour no real activity was displayed. Then work began in earnest. The clearing of the hatches was completed, the ship's winches were started, and the unloading of the props began.

This was simply a reversal of the procedure they had observed at the clearing. The props were swung out in bundles by the *Girondin's* crew, lowered on to the Decauville trucks, and pushed by the depot men back through the shed, the empty trucks being returned on another road, and brought by means of the turn-tables to the starting point. The young manager watched the operations and took a tally of the props.

Merriman kept a close eye on the proceedings, and felt certain he was witnessing everything that was taking place. Every truck-load of props passed within ten feet of his hiding place, and he was satisfied that if anything other than props were put ashore he would infalliby see it. But the close watching was a considerable strain, and he soon began to grow tired. He had some bread and fruit and a whisky and soda, and though he would have given a good deal for a smoke, he felt greatly refreshed.

The work kept on without intermission until one o'clock, when the men knocked off for dinner. At two they began again, and worked steadily all through the afternoon until past seven. During all that time only two incidents, both trifling, occurred to relieve the monotony of the proceedings. Early in the forenoon Bulla appeared, and under his instructions the end of the flexible hose from the crude oil tank was carried aboard and connected by a union to a pipe on the lower deck. A wheel valve at the tank was turned, and Merriman could see the hose move and stiffen as the oil began to flow through it. An hour later the valve was turned off, the hose relaxed, the union was uncoupled and the hose, dripping black oil, was carried back and left in its former place on the wharf. The second incident was that about three o'clock Captain Beamish and Bulla left the ship together and went out through the shed.

Merriman was now horribly tired, and his head ached intolerably from the strain and the air of the barrel, which had by this time become very impure. But he reflected that now when the men had left was the opportunity of the conspirators. The time for which he had waited was approaching, and he nerved himself to resist the drowsiness which was stealing over him and which threatened the success of his vigil.

But hour after hour slowly dragged past and nothing happened. Except for the occasional movement of one of the crew on the ship, the whole place seemed deserted. It was not till well after ten, when dusk had fallen, that he suddenly heard voices.

At first he could not distinguish the words, but the tone was Bulla's, and from the sounds it was clear the engineer and some others were approaching. Then Beamish spoke.

'You'd better keep your eyes open anyway,' he said. 'Morton says they only stayed at work about a week. They're off somewhere now. Morton couldn't discover where, but he's trying to trace them.'

'I'm not afraid of them,' returned the manager's voice. 'Even if they found this place, which of course they might, they couldn't find out anything else. We've got too good a site.'

'Well, don't make the mistake of underestimating their brains,' counselled Beamish, as the three men moved slowly down the wharf. Merriman, considerably thrilled, watched them go on board and disappear into the captain's cabin.

So it was clear, then, that he and Hilliard were seriously suspected by the syndicate and were being traced by their spy! What luck would the spy have? And if he succeeded in his endeavour, what would be their fortune? Merriman was no coward, but he shivered slightly as he went over in his mind the steps of their present quest, and realised how far they had failed to cover their traces, how at stage after stage they had given themselves away to any one who cared to make a few inquiries. What fools, he thought, they were not to have disguised themselves! Simple disguises would have been quite enough. No doubt they would not have deceived personal friends, but they would have made all the difference to a stranger endeavouring to trace them from descriptions and those confounded photographs. Then they should not have travelled together to Hull, still less have gone to the same hotel. It was true they had had the sense to register under false names, but that would be but a slight hindrance to a skilful investigator. But their crowning folly, in Merriman's view, was the hiring of the boat and the starting off at night from the docks and arriving back there in the morning. What they should have done, he now thought bitterly, was to have taken a boat at Grimsby or some other distant town and kept it continuously, letting no one know when they set out on or returned from their excursions.

But there was no use in crying over spilt milk. Merriman repeated to himself the adage, though he did not find it at all comforting. Then his thoughts passed on to the immediate present, and he wondered whether he should not try to get out of the barrel and emulate Hilliard's exploit in boarding the

Girondin and listening to the conversation in the captain's cabin. But he soon decided he must keep to the arranged plan, and make sure nothing was put ashore from the ship under cover of darkness.

Once again ensued a period of waiting, during which the time dragged terribly heavily. Everything without was perfectly still until at about half-past eleven the door of the captain's cabin opened and its three occupants came out into the night. The starboard deck light was on and by its light Merriman could see the manager take his leave, cross the gangway, pass up the wharf and enter the shed. Bulla went down towards his cabin door and Beamish, snapping off the deck light, returned to his. In about fifteen minutes his light also went out and complete darkness and silence reigned.

Some two hours later Merriman, who had kept awake and on guard only by the most determined effort, heard a gentle tap on the barrel and a faint 'Hist!' The lid was slowly raised, and to his intense relief he was able to stand upright and greet Hilliard crouching without.

'Any news?' queried the latter in the faintest of whispers.

'Absolutely none. Not a single thing came out of that boat but props. I had a splendid view all the time. Except this, Hilliard'—Merriman's whisper became more intense—'They suspect us and are trying to trace us.'

'Let them try,' breathed Hilliard. 'Here, take this in.'

He handed over a satchel of fresh food and took out the old one. Then Merriman climbed out, held up the lid until Hilliard had taken his place, wished his friend good luck, and passing like a shadow along the wharf, noiselessly descended the steps and reached the boat. A few seconds later he had drifted out of sight of the depot, and was pulling with long, easy strokes down-stream.

The air and freedom felt incredibly good after his long confinement, and it was a delight to stretch his muscles at the oars. So hard did he row that it was barely three when he reached the boat slip in Hull. There he tied up the skiff and walked to the hotel. Before four he was sound asleep in his room.

That evening about seven as he strolled along the water front waiting until it should be time to take out his boat, he was delighted to observe the *Girondin* pass out to sea. He had dreaded having to take another twenty-four hours' trick in the cask, which would have been necessary had the ship not left that evening. Now all that was needed was a little care to get Hilliard out, and the immediate job would be done.

He took out the boat about eleven and duly reached the wharf. All was in darkness, and he crept to the barrel and softly raised the lid.

Hilliard was exhausted from the long strain, but with his friend's help he succeeded in clambering out, having first examined the floor of the barrel to see that nothing had been overlooked, as well as plugging the two holes with corks. They regained the boat in silence, and it was not until they were some distance from the wharf that either spoke.

'My God! Merriman,' Hilliard said at last, 'but that was an awful experience! You left the air in that cursed barrel bad, and it got steadily worse until I thought I should have died or had to lift the lid and give the show away. It was just everything I could do to keep going till the ship left.'

'But did you see anything?' Merriman demanded eagerly.

'See anything? Not a blessed thing! We are barking up the wrong tree, Merriman. I'll stake my life nothing came out of that boat but props. No; what those people are up to I don't know, but there's one thing a dead cert, and that is that they're not smuggling.'

They rowed on in silence, Hilliard almost sick with weariness and disappointment, Merriman lost in thought over their problem. It was still early when they reached their hotel, and they followed Merriman's plan of the morning before and went straight to bed.

Next day they spent in the hotel lounge, gloomily smoking and at intervals discussing the affair. They had admitted themselves outwitted—up to the present at all events. And neither could suggest any further step. There seemed to be no line of investigation left which might bear better fruit. They agreed that the brandy smuggling theory must be abandoned, and they had nothing to take its place.

'We're fairly up against it as far as I can see,' Hilliard admitted despondently. 'It's a nasty knock having to give up the only theory we were able to think of, but it's a hanged sight worse not knowing how we are going to carry on the inquiry.'

'That is true,' Merriman returned, Madeleine Coburn's face rising before his imagination, 'but we can't give it up for all that. We must go on until we find something.'

'That's all very well. What are we to go on doing?'

Silence reigned for several minutes and then Hilliard spoke again.

'I'm afraid it means Scotland Yard after all.'

Merriman sat up quickly.

'Not that, not that!' he protested, as he had protested in similar terms on a previous occasion when the same suggestion had been made. 'We must keep away from the police at all costs.' He spoke earnestly.

'I know your views,' Hilliard answered, 'and agree with them. But if neither of us can suggest an alternative, what else remains?'

This was what Merriman had feared and he determined to play the one poor trump in his hand.

'The number plates,' he suggested. 'As I said before, that is the only point at which we have actually come up against this mystery. Why not let us start in on it? If we knew why those plates were changed, the chances are we should know enough to clear up the whole affair.'

Hilliard, who was suffering from the reaction of his night of stress, took a depressed view and did not welcome the suggestion. He seemed to have lost heart in the inquiry, and again urged dropping it and passing on their knowledge to Scotland Yard. But this course Merriman strenuously opposed, pressing his view that the key to the mystery was to be found in the changing of the lorry numbers. Finally they decided to leave the question over until the following day, and to banish the affair from their minds for that evening by a visit to a music hall.

CHAPTER IX

THE SECOND CARGO

MERRIMAN was awakened in the early hours of the following morning by a push on the shoulder and, opening his eyes, he was amazed to see Hilliard, dressed only in his pyjamas, leaning over him. On his friend's face was an expression of excitement and delight which made him a totally different man from the gloomy pessimist of the previous day.

'Merriman, old man,' he cried, though in repressed tones—it was only a little after five. 'I'm frightfully sorry to stir you up, but I just couldn't help it. I say, you and I are a nice pair of idiots!'

Merriman grunted.

'I don't know what you're talking about,' he murmured sleepily.

'Talking about?' Hilliard returned eagerly. 'Why, this affair, of course! I see it now, but what I don't see is how we missed it before. The idea struck me like a flash. Just while you'd wink I saw the whole thing!'

Merriman, now thoroughly aroused, moved with some annoyance.

'For Heaven's sake, explain yourself,' he demanded. 'What whole thing?'

'How they do it. We thought it was brandy smuggling, but we couldn't see how it was done. Well, I see now. It's brandy smuggling right enough, and we'll get them this time. We'll get them, Merriman, we'll get them yet.'

Hilliard was bubbling over with excitement. He could not remain still, but began to pace up and down the room. His emotion was infectious, and Merriman began to feel his heart beat quicker as he listened. Hilliard went on:

'We *thought* there might be brandy, in fact we couldn't suggest anything else. But we didn't *see* any brandy; we saw pit-props. Isn't that right?'

'Well?' Merriman returned impatiently. 'Get on. What next?'

'That's all,' Hilliard declared with a delighted laugh. 'That's the whole thing. Don't you see it now?'

Merriman felt his anger rising.

'Confound it all, Hilliard,' he protested. 'If you haven't anything better to do than coming round wakening—'

'Oh, don't get on your hind legs,' Hilliard interrupted with another ecstatic chuckle. 'What I say is right enough. Look here, it's perfectly simple. We thought brandy would be unloaded! And what's more, we both sat in that cursed barrel and watched it being done! But all we saw coming ashore was pit-props, Merriman, *pit-props*! Now don't you see?'

Merriman suddenly gasped.

'Lord!' he cried breathlessly. 'It was *in* the props?'

'Of course it was in the props!' Hilliard repeated triumphantly. 'Hollow props; a few hollow ones full of brandy to unload in their shed, many genuine ones to sell! What do you think of that, Merriman? Got them at last, eh?'

Merriman lay still as he tried to realise what this idea involved. Hilliard, moving jerkily about the room as if he were a puppet controlled by wires, went on speaking.

'I thought it out in bed before I came along. All they'd have to do would be to cut the props in half and bore them out, attaching a screwed ring to one half and a screwed socket to the other so that they'd screw together like an ordinary gas thimble. See?'

Merriman nodded.

'Then they'd get some steel things like limelight gas cylinders to fit inside. They'd be designed of such a thickness that their weight would be right; that their weight plus the brandy would be equal to the weight of the wood bored out.'

He paused and looked at Merriman. The latter nodded again.

'The rest would be as easy as tumbling off a log. At night Coburn and company would screw off the hollow ends, fill the cylinders with brandy, screw on the ends again, and there you have your props—harmless, innocent props—ready for loading up on the *Girondin*. Of course, they'd have them marked. Then when they're being unloaded that manager would get the marked ones put aside—they could somehow be defective, too long or too short or too thin or too anything you like—he would find some reason for separating them out—and then at night he would open the things and pour out the brandy, screw them up again and—there you are!'

Hilliard paused dramatically, like a conjurer who has just drawn a rabbit from a lady's vanity bag.

'That would explain that Ferriby manager sleeping in the shed,' Merriman put in.

'So it would. I hadn't thought of that.'

'And,' Merriman went on, 'there'd be enough genuine props carried on each trip to justify the trade.'

'Of course. A very few faked ones would do all they wanted— say two or three per cent. My goodness, Merriman, it's a clever scheme; they deserve to win. But they're not going to.' Again he laughed delightedly.

Merriman was thinking deeply. He had recovered his composure, and had begun to weigh the idea critically.

'They mightn't empty the brandy themselves at all,' he said slowly. 'What's to prevent them running the faked props to the firm who plants the brandy?'

'That's true,' Hilliard returned. 'That's another idea. My eyes, what possibilities the notion has!'

They talked on for some moments, then Hilliard, whose first excitement was beginning to wane, went back to his room for some clothes. In a few minutes he returned full of another side of the idea.

'Let's just work out,' he suggested, 'how much you could put into a prop. Take a prop say nine inches in diameter and nine feet long. Now you can't weaken it enough to risk its breaking if it accidentally falls. Suppose you bored a six inch hole down its centre. That would leave the sides one and a half inches thick, which should be ample. What do you think?'

'Take it at that anyway,' answered Merriman.

'Very well. Now how long would it be? If we bore too deep a hole we may split the prop. What about two feet six inches into each end? Say a five foot tube?'

'Take it at that,' Merriman repeated.

'How much brandy could you put into a six inch tube, five feet long?' He calculated aloud, Merriman checking each step. 'That works out at a cubic foot of brandy, six and a quarter gallons, fifty pints or four hundred glasses—four hundred glasses per prop.'

He paused, looked at his friend, and resumed:

'A glass of brandy in France costs you sixpence; in England it costs you half a crown. Therefore if you can smuggle the stuff over you make a profit of two shillings a glass. Four hundred glasses at two shillings. There's a profit of £40 a prop, Merriman!'

Merriman whistled. He was growing more and more impressed. The longer he considered the idea, the more likely it seemed. He listened eagerly as Hilliard, once again excitedly pacing the room, resumed his calculations.

'Now you have a cargo of about seven thousand props. Suppose you assume one per cent of them are faked, that would be seventy. We don't know how many they have, of course, but one out of every hundred is surely a conservative figure. Seventy props means £2800 profit per trip. *And* they have a trip every ten days—say thirty trips a year to be on the safe side—£84,000 a year profit! My eyes, Merriman, it would be worth running some risks for £84,000 a year!'

'Risks?' cried Merriman, now as much excited as his friend. 'They'd risk hell for it! I bet, Hilliard, you've got it at last. £84,000 a year! But look here'—his voice changed—'you have to divide it among the members.'

'That's true, you have,' Hilliard admitted, 'but even so—how many are there? Beamish, Bulla, Coburn, Henri, the manager here, and the two men they spoke of, Morton and Archer—that makes seven. That would give them £12,000 a year each. It's still jolly well worth while.'

'Worth while? I should just say so.' Merriman lay silently pondering the idea. Presently he spoke again.

'Of course those figures of yours are only guesswork.'

'They're only guesswork,' Hilliard agreed with a trace of impatience in his manner, 'because we don't know the size of the tubes and the number of the props, but it's not guesswork that they can make a fortune out of smuggling in that way. We see now that the thing can be done, and *how* it can be done. That's something gained anyway.'

Merriman nodded and sat up in bed.

'Hand me my pipe and baccy out of that coat pocket like a good man,' he asked, continuing slowly:

'It'll be some job, I fancy, proving it. We shall have to see first if the props are emptied at that depot, and if not we shall have to find out where they're sent, and investigate. I seem to see a pretty long programme opening out. Have you any plans?'

'Not a plan,' Hilliard declared cheerfully. 'No time to make 'em yet. But we shall find a way somehow.'

They went on discussing the matter in more detail. At first the testing of Hilliard's new theory appeared a simple matter, but the more they thought over it the more difficult it seemed to become. For one thing there would be the investigations at the depot. Whatever unloading of the brandy was carried on there would probably be done inside the shed and at night. It would therefore be necessary to find some hiding place within the building from which the investigations could be made. This alone was an undertaking bristling with difficulties. In the first place, all the doors of the shed were locked and none of them opened without noise. How were they without keys to open the doors in the dark, silently and without leaving traces?

Observations might be required during the entire ten day cycle, and that would mean that at some time each night one of these doors would have to be opened and shut to allow the watcher to be relieved. And if the emptying of the props were done at night how were they to ensure that this operation should not coincide with the visit of the relief? And this was all pre-supposing that a suitable hiding place could be found inside the building in such a position that from it the operations in question could be overlooked.

Here no doubt were pretty serious obstacles, but even were they all successfully overcome it did not follow that they should have solved the problem. The faked props might be loaded up and forwarded to some other depot, and, if so, this other depot might be by no means easy to find. Further, if it were found, nocturnal observation of what went on within would then become necessary.

It seemed to the friends that all they had done up to the present would be the merest child's play in comparison to what was now required. During the whole of that day and the next they brooded over the problem, but without avail. The more they thought about it the more hopeless it seemed. Even Hilliard's cheery optimism was not proof against the wave of depression which swept over them.

Curiously enough it was to Merriman, the plodding rather than the brilliant, that light first came. They were seated in the otherwise empty hotel lounge when he suddenly stopped smoking, sat motionless for nearly a minute, and then turned eagerly to his companion.

'I say, Hilliard,' he exclaimed. 'I wonder if there mightn't be another way out after all—a scheme for making them separate the faked and the genuine props? Do you know Leatham—Charlie Leatham of Ellerby, somewhere between Selby and Houghton? No? Well, he owns a group of mines in that district. He's as decent a soul as ever breathed, and is just rolling in money. Now, how would it do if we were to go to Charlie and tell him the whole thing, and ask him to approach these people to see if they would sell him a cargo of props—an entire cargo. I should explain that he has a private wharf for lighters on one of those rivers up beyond Goole, but the approach is too shallow for a sea-going boat. Now, why shouldn't he tell these people about his wharf, saying he had heard the *Girondin* was shallow in the draught, and might get up? He would then say he would take an entire cargo on condition that he could have it at his own place and so save rail carriage from Ferriby. That would put the syndicate in a hole. They couldn't let any of the faked props out of their possession, and if they agreed to Leatham's proposal they'd have to separate out the faked props from the genuine, and keep the faked aboard. On their way back from Leatham's they would have to call at Ferriby to put these faked ones ashore, and if we are not utter fools we should surely be able to get hold of them then. What do you think, Hilliard?'

Hilliard smote his thigh.

'Bravo!' he cried with enthusiasm. 'I think it's just splendid. But is there any chance your friend would take a cargo? It's rather a large order, you know. What would it run into? Four or five thousand pounds?'

'Why shouldn't he? He has to buy props anyway, and these are good props and they would be as cheap as any he could get elsewhere. Taking them at his own wharf would be good business. Besides, 7000 props is not a big thing for a group of mines. There are a tremendous lot used.'

'That's true.'

'But the syndicate may not agree,' Merriman went on. 'And yet I think they will. It would look suspicious for them to refuse so good an offer.'

Hilliard nodded. Then a further idea seemed to strike him and he sat up suddenly.

'But, Merriman, old man,' he exclaimed, 'you've forgotten one thing. If they sent a cargo of that kind they'd send only genuine props. They wouldn't risk the others.'

But Merriman was not cast down.

'I dare say you're right,' he admitted, 'but we can easily prevent that. Suppose Leatham arranges for a cargo for some indefinite date ahead, then on the day after the *Girondin* leaves France he goes to Ferriby and says some other consignment has failed him, and could they let him have the next cargo? That would meet the case, wouldn't it.'

'By Jove, Merriman, but you're developing the detective instinct and no mistake! I think the scheme's worth trying anyway. How can you get in touch with your friend?'

'I'll phone him now that we shall be over tomorrow to see him.'

Leatham was just leaving his office when Merriman's call reached him.

'Delighted to see you and meet your friend,' he answered. 'But couldn't you both come over now and stay the night? You would be a perfect godsend to me, for Hilda's in London and I have the house to myself.'

Merriman thanked him, and later on the two friends took the 6.35 train to Ellerby. Leatham's car was waiting for them at the station, and in a few minutes they had reached the mine-owner's house.

Charles Leatham was a man of about five-and-thirty, tall, broad, and of muscular build. He had a strong, clean shaven face, a kindly though direct manner, and there was about him a suggestion of decision and efficiency which inspired the confidence of those with whom he came in contact.

'This is very jolly,' he greeted them. 'How are you, old man? Glad to meet you, Hilliard. This is better than the lonely evening I was expecting.'

They went in to dinner presently, but it was not until the meal was over and they were stretched in basket chairs on the terrace in the cool evening air that Merriman reverted to the subject which had brought them together.

'I'm afraid,' he began, 'it's only now when I am right up

against it that I realise what appalling cheek we show in coming to you like this, and when you hear what we have had in our minds, I'm afraid you will think so too. As a matter of fact we've accidentally got hold of information that a criminal organisation of some kind is in operation. For various reasons our hands are tied about going to the police, so we're trying to play the detectives ourselves, and now we're up against a difficulty we don't see our way through. We thought if we could interest you sufficiently to induce you to join us, we might devise a scheme.'

Amazement had been growing on Leatham's face while Merriman was speaking.

'Sounds like the *New Arabian Nights*!' he exclaimed. 'You're not by any chance pulling my leg?'

Merriman reassured him.

'The thing's really a bit serious,' he continued. 'If what we suspect is going on, the parties concerned won't be squeamish about the means they adopt to keep their secret. I imagine they'd have a short way with meddlers.'

Leatham's expression of astonishment did not decrease, but 'By Jove!' was all he said.

'For that reason we can only tell you about it in confidence.'

Merriman paused and glanced questioningly at the other, who nodded without replying.

'It began when I was cycling from Bayonne to Bordeaux,' Merriman went on, and he told his host about his visit to the clearing, his voyage of discovery with Hilliard and what they had learned in France, their trip to Hull, the Ferriby depot and their adventures thereat, ending up by explaining their hollow pit-prop idea and the difficulty with which they found themselves faced.

Leatham heard the story with an interest which could hardly fail to gratify its narrator. When it was finished he expressed his feelings by giving vent to a long and complicated oath. Then he asked how they thought he could help. Merriman explained.

The mineowner rather gasped at first, then he laughed and slapped his thigh.

'By the Lord Harry!' he cried, 'I'll do it! As a matter of fact I want the props, but I'd do it anyway to see you through. If there's anything at all in what you suspect it'll make the sensation of the year.'

He thought for a moment then went on:

'I shall go down to that depot at Ferriby tomorrow, have a look at the props, and broach the idea of taking a cargo. It'll be interesting to have a chat with that manager fellow, and you may bet I'll keep my eyes open. You two had better lie low here, and in the evening we'll have another talk and settle what's to be done.'

The next day the friends 'lay low', and evening saw them once more on the terrace with their host. It seemed that he had motored to Ferriby about mid-day. The manager had been polite and even friendly, had seemed pleased at the visit of so influential a customer, and had shown him over the entire concern without the slightest hesitation. He had appeared delighted at the prospect of disposing of a whole cargo of props, and had raised no objection to the *Girondin* unloading at Leatham's wharf. The price was moderate, but not exceptionally so.

'I must admit,' Leatham concluded, 'that everything appeared very sound and businesslike. I had a look everywhere in that shed and enclosure, and I saw nothing even remotely suspicious. The manager's manner, too, was normal, and it seems to me that either he's a jolly good actor or you two chaps are on a wild goose chase.'

'We may be about the hollow props,' Merriman returned, 'and we may be about the brandy smuggling. But there's no mistake at all about something being wrong. That's certain from what Hilliard overheard.'

Leatham nodded.

'I know all that,' he said, 'and when we've carried out this present scheme we shall know something more. Now let's see. When does that blessed boat next leave France?'

'Thursday morning, we reckon,' Hilliard told him.

'Then on Friday afternoon I shall call up those people and pitch my yarn about my consignment of props having gone astray, and ask if they can send their boat direct here. How's that?'

'Nothing could be better.'

'Then I think for the present you two had better clear out. Our connection should not be known. And don't go near London either. That chap Morton has lost you once, but he'll not do it a second time. Go and tramp the Peak District, or something of that kind. Then you'll be wanted back in Hull on Saturday.'

'What's that for?' both men exclaimed in a breath.

'That blessed barrel of yours. You say the *Girondin* will leave France on Thursday night. That means she will be in the Humber on Sunday night or Monday morning. Now you reckoned she would unload here and put the faked props ashore and load up oil at Ferriby on her way out. But she mightn't. She might go into Ferriby first. It would be the likely thing to do, in fact, for then she'd get here with nothing suspicious aboard and could unload everything. So I guess you'll have to watch in your barrel on Sunday, and that means getting into it on Saturday night.'

The two friends swore and Leatham laughed.

'Good heavens,' Hilliard cried, 'it means about four more nights of the damned thing. From Saturday night to Sunday night for the arrival; maybe until Monday night if she lies over to discharge the faked props on Monday. Then another two nights or maybe three to cover her departure. I tell you, it's a tall order.'

'But think of the prize.' Leatham smiled maliciously. 'As a matter of fact I don't see any other way.'

'There is no other way,' Merriman declared with decision. 'We may just set our teeth and go through with it.'

After further discussion it was arranged that the friends would leave early next day for Harrogate. There Leatham would wire them on Friday the result of his negotiations about the *Girondin*. They could then return to Hull and get out their boat on Saturday should that be necessary. When about midnight they turned in, Leatham was quite as keen about the affair as his guests, and quite as anxious that their joint experiment should be crowned with success.

The two friends spent a couple of lazy days amusing themselves in Harrogate, until towards evening on the Friday Merriman was called to the telephone.

'That'll be Leatham,' he exclaimed. 'Come on, Hilliard, and hear what he has to say.'

It was the mineowner speaking from his office.

'I've just rung up our friends,' he told them, 'and that business is all right. There was some delay about it at first, for Benson—that's the manager—was afraid he hadn't enough stock of props for current orders. But on looking up his records he found he could manage, so he is letting the ship come on.'

'Jolly good, Leatham.'

'The *Girondin* is expected about seven tomorrow evening. Benson then asked about a pilot. It seems their captain is a certified pilot of the Humber up to Ferriby, but he could not take the boat farther. I told him I'd lend him the man who acted for me, and what I've arranged is this. I shall send Angus Menzies, the master of one of my river tugs, to the wharf at Ferriby about six on Saturday evening. When the *Girondin* comes up he can go aboard and work her on here. Menzies is a good man, and I shall drop him a hint that I've bought the whole cargo, and to keep his eyes open that nothing is put ashore that I don't get. That'll be a still further check.'

The friends expressed their satisfaction at this arrangement, and it was decided that as soon as the investigation was over all three should meet and compare results at Leatham's house.

Next evening saw the two inquirers back at their hotel in

Hull. They had instructed the owner of their hired boat to keep it in readiness for them, and about eleven o'clock, armed with the footstool and the satchel of food, they once more got on board and pulled out on to the great stream. Merriman not wishing to spend longer in the barrel than was absolutely necessary, they went ashore near Hessle and had a couple of hours' sleep, and it was well past four when they reached the depot. The adventure was somewhat more risky than on the previous occasion, owing to the presence of a tiny arc of moon. But they carried out their plans without mishap, Merriman taking his place in the cask, and Hilliard returning to Hull with the boat.

If possible, the slow passage of the heavily weighted hours until the following evening was even more irksome to the watcher than on the first occasion. Merriman felt he would die of weariness and boredom long before anything happened, and it was only the thought that he was doing it for Madeleine Coburn that kept him from utter collapse.

At intervals during the morning, Benson, the manager, or one of the other men came out for a moment or two on the wharf, but no regular work went on there. During the interminable hours of the afternoon no one appeared at all, the whole place remaining silent and deserted, and it was not until nearly six that the sound of footsteps fell on Merriman's weary ears. He heard a gruff voice saying: 'Ah'm no so sairtain o' it mesel',' which seemed to accord with the name of Leatham's skipper, and then came Benson's voice raised in agreement.

The two men passed out of the shed and moved to the edge of the wharf, pursuing a desultory discussion, the drift of which Merriman could not catch. The greater part of an hour passed, when first Benson and then Menzies began to stare eastwards down the river. It seemed evident to Merriman that the *Girondin* was in sight, and he began to hope that something more interesting would happen. But the time dragged wearily for another half-hour, until he heard the bell of the engine-room telegraph and the wash of the screw. A moment later the ship appeared,

drew alongside, and was berthed, all precisely as had happened
before.

As soon as the gangway was lowered, Benson sprang aboard,
and running up the ladder to the bridge, eagerly addressed
Captain Beamish. Merriman could not hear what was said, but
he could see the captain shaking his head and making little
gestures of disapproval. He watched him go to the engine-room
tube and speak down it. It was evidently a call to Bulla, for
almost immediately the engineer appeared and ascended to the
bridge, where all three joined in a brief discussion. Finally
Benson came to the side of the ship and shouted something to
Menzies, who at once went on board and joined the group on
the bridge. Merriman saw Benson introduce him to the others,
and then apparently explain something to him. Menzies nodded
as if satisfied and the conversation became general.

Merriman was considerably thrilled by this new development. He imagined that Benson while, for the benefit of
Menzies, ostensibly endeavouring to make the arrangements
agreed on, had in reality preceded the pilot on board in order
to warn the captain of the proposal, and arrange with him some
excuse for keeping the ship where she was for the night. Bulla
had been sent for to acquaint him with the situation, and it was
not until all three were agreed as to their story that Menzies
was invited to join the conclave. To Merriman it certainly looked
as if the men were going to fall into the trap which he and his
friends had prepared, and he congratulated himself on having
adhered to his programme and hidden himself in the barrel,
instead of leaving the watching to be done by Menzies, as he
had been so sorely tempted to do. For it was clear to him that
if any secret work was to be done, Menzies would be got out
of the way until it was over. Merriman was now keenly on the
alert, and he watched every movement on the ship or wharf
with the sharpness of a lynx. Bulla presently went below, leaving
the other three chatting on the bridge, then a move was made
and, the engineer reappearing, all four entered the cabin.

Apparently they were having a meal, for in about an hour's time they emerged, and bringing canvas chairs to the boat deck, sat down and began to smoke—all except Bulla, who once again disappeared below. In a few moments he emerged with one of the crew, and began to superintend the coupling of the oil hose. The friends had realised the ship would have to put in for oil, but they had expected that an hour's halt would have sufficed to fill up. But from the delay in starting and the leisurely way the operation was being conducted, it looked as if she was not proceeding that night.

In about an hour the oiling was completed, and Bulla followed his friends to the captain's cabin, where the latter had retired when dusk began to fall. An hour later they came out, said 'Good-night,' and separated, Benson coming ashore, Bulla and Menzies entering cabins on the main deck, and Captain Beamish snapping off the deck light and re-entering his own room.

'Now or never,' thought Merriman, as silence and darkness settled down over the wharf.

But apparently it was to be never. Once again the hours crept slowly by and not a sign of activity became apparent. Nothing moved on either ship or wharf, until about two in the morning he saw dimly in the faint moonlight the figure of Hilliard coming to relieve him.

The exchange was rapidly effected, and Hilliard took up his watch, while his friend pulled back into Hull, and following his own precedent, went to the hotel and to bed.

The following day Merriman took an early train to Goole, returning immediately. This brought him past the depot, and he saw that the *Girondin* had left.

That night he again rowed to the wharf and relieved Hilliard. They had agreed that in spite of the extreme irksomeness of a second night in the cask it was essential to continue their watch, lest the *Girondin* should make another call on her way to sea and then discharge the faked props.

The remainder of the night and the next day passed like a hideous dream. There being nothing to watch for in the first part of his vigil, Merriman tried to sleep, but without much success. The hours dragged by with an incredible deliberation, and during the next day there was but slight movement on the wharf to occupy his attention. And then just before dark he had the further annoyance of learning that his long-drawn-out misery had been unnecessary. He saw out in the river the *Girondin* passing rapidly seawards.

Their plan then had failed. He was too weary to think consec-utively about it, but that much at least was clear. When Hilliard arrived some five hours later, he had fallen into a state of partial coma, and his friend had considerable trouble in rousing him to make the effort necessary to leave his hiding place with the requisite care and silence.

The next evening the two friends left Hull by a late train, and reaching Leatham's house after dusk had fallen, were soon seated in his smoking-room with whiskies and sodas at their elbows and Corona Coronas in their mouths. All three were somewhat gloomy, and their disappointment and chagrin were very real. Leatham was the first to put their thoughts into words.

'Well,' he said, drawing at his cigar, 'I suppose we needn't say one thing and think another. I take it our precious plan has failed?'

'That's about the size of it,' Hilliard admitted grimly.

'Your man saw nothing?' Merriman inquired.

'He saw you,' the mineowner returned. 'He's a very depend-able chap, and I thought it would be wise to give him a hint that we suspected something serious, so he kept a good watch. It seems when the ship came alongside at Ferriby, Benson told the captain not to make fast as he had to go farther up the river. But the captain said he thought they had better fill up with oil first, and he sent to consult the engineer, and it was agreed that when they were in they might as well fill up as it would save a call on the outward journey. Besides, no one concerned was on for going up in the dark—there are sandbanks, you know, and the navigation's bad. They gave Menzies a starboard deck cabin—that was on the wharf side—and he sat watching the wharf through his porthole for the entire night. There wasn't a thing unloaded, and there wasn't a movement on the wharf until you two changed your watch. He saw that, and it fairly thrilled him. After that not another thing happened until the cook brought him some coffee and they got away.'

'Pretty thorough,' Hilliard commented. 'It's at least a blessing to be sure beyond a doubt nothing was unloaded.'

'We're certain enough of that,' Leatham went on, 'and we're certain of something else too. I arranged to drop down on the wharf when the discharging was about finished, and I had a chat with the captain; superior chap, that. I told him I was interested in his ship, for it was the largest I have ever seen up at my wharf, and that I had been thinking of getting one something the same built. I asked him if he would let me see over her, and he was most civil and took me over the entire boat. There was no part of her we didn't examine, and I'm prepared to swear there were no props left on board. So we may take it that whatever else they're up to, they're not carrying brandy in faked pit-props. Nor, so far as I can see, in anything else either.'

The three men smoked in silence for some time and then Hilliard spoke.

'I suppose, Leatham, you can't think of any other theory, or suggest anything else that we should do.'

'I can't suggest what you should do,' returned Leatham, rising to his feet and beginning to pace the room, 'but I know what I should do in your place. I'd go down to Scotland Yard, tell them what I know, and then wash my hands of the whole affair.'

Hilliard sighed.

'I'm afraid we shall have no option,' he said slowly, 'but I needn't say we should much rather learn something more definite first.'

'I dare say, but you haven't been able to. Either these fellows are a deal too clever for you, or else you are on the wrong track altogether. And that's what *I* think. I don't believe there's any smuggling going on there at all. It's some other game they're on to. I don't know what it is, but I don't believe it's anything so crude as smuggling.'

Again silence fell on the little group, and then Merriman, who had for some time been lost in thought, made a sudden movement.

'Lord!' he exclaimed, 'but we have been fools over this thing! There's another point we've all missed which alone proves it couldn't have been faked props. Here, Hilliard, this was your theory, though I don't mean to saddle you with more imbecility than myself. But anyway, according to your theory, what happened to the props after they were unloaded?'

Hilliard stared at this outburst.

'After they were unloaded?' he repeated. 'Why, returned of course for the next cargo.'

'But that's just it,' cried Merriman. 'That's just what wasn't done. We've seen that boat unload twice, and on neither occasion were any props loaded to go back.'

'That's a point, certainly; yes,' Leatham interposed. 'I suppose they would have to be used again and again? Each trip's props couldn't be destroyed after arrival, and new ones made for the next cargo?'

Hilliard shook his head reluctantly.

'No,' he declared. 'Impossible. Those things would cost a lot of money. You see, no cheap scheme, say of shipping bottles into hollowed props, would do. The props would have to be thoroughly well made, so that they wouldn't break and give the show away if accidentally dropped. They wouldn't pay unless they were used several times over. I'm afraid Merrimans point is sound, and we may give up the idea.'

Further discussion only strengthened this opinion, and the three men had to admit themselves at a total loss as to their next move. The only suggestion in the field was that of Leatham, to inform Scotland Yard, and this was at last approved by Hilliard as a counsel of despair.

'There's nothing else for it that I can see,' he observed gloomily. 'We've done our best on our own and failed, and we may let some one else have a shot now. My leave's nearly up anyway.'

Merriman said nothing at the time, but next day, when they had taken leave of their host and were in the train for King's Cross, he reopened the subject.

'I needn't say, Hilliard,' he began, 'I'm most anxious that the police should not be brought in, and you know the reason why. If she gets into any difficulty about the affair, you understand my life's at an end for any good it'll do me. Let's wait a while and think over the thing further, and perhaps we'll see daylight before long.'

Hilliard made a gesture of impatience.

'If you can suggest any single thing that we should do that we haven't done, I'm ready to do it. But if you can't, I don't see that we'd be justified in keeping all that knowledge to ourselves for an indefinite time while we waited for an inspiration. Is not that reasonable?'

'It's perfectly reasonable,' Merriman admitted, 'and I don't suggest we should wait indefinitely. What I propose is that we wait for a month. Give me another month, Hilliard, and I'll be satisfied. I have an idea that something might be learned from tracing that lorry number business, and if you have to go back to work I'll slip over by myself to Bordeaux and see what I can do. And if I fail I'll see her, and try to get her to marry me in spite of the trouble. Wait a month, Hilliard, and by that time I shall know where I stand.'

Hilliard was extremely unwilling to agree to this proposal. Though he realised that he could not hand over to his superiors a complete case against the syndicate, he also saw that considerable kudos was still possible if he supplied information which would enable their detectives to establish one. And every day he delayed increased the chance of some one else finding the key to the riddle, and thus robbing him of his reward. Merriman realised the position, and he therefore fully appreciated the sacrifice Hilliard was risking when after a long discussion that young man gave his consent.

Two days later Hilliard was back at his office, while Merriman, after an argument with his partner not far removed from a complete break, was on his way once more to the south of France.

CHAPTER X

MERRIMAN BECOMES DESPERATE

THE failure of the attempt to learn the secret of the Pit-Prop Syndicate affected Merriman more than he could have believed possible. His interest in the affair was not that of Hilliard. Neither the intellectual joy of solving a difficult problem for its own sake, nor the kudos which such a solution might bring, made much appeal to him. His concern was simply the happiness of the girl he loved, and though, to do him justice, he did not think overmuch of himself, he recognised that any barrier raised between them was the end for him of all that made life endurable.

As he lay back with closed eyes in the corner seat of a first-class compartment in the boat train from Calais, he went over for the thousandth time the details of the problem as it affected himself. Had Mr Coburn rendered himself liable to arrest or even to penal servitude, and did his daughter know it? The anxious, troubled look which Merriman had on different occasions surprised on the girl's expressive face made him fear both these possibilities. But if they were true did it stop there? Was her disquietude due merely to knowledge of her father's danger, or was she herself in peril also? Merriman wondered could she have such knowledge and not be in peril herself. In the eyes of the law would it not be guilty knowledge? Could she not be convicted as an accessory?

If it were so he must act at once if he were to save her. But how? He writhed under the terrible feeling of impotence produced by his ignorance of the syndicate's real business. If he were to help Madeleine he *must* know what the conspirators were doing.

128

And he had failed to learn. He had failed, and Hilliard had failed, and neither they nor Leatham had been able to suggest any method by which the truth might be ascertained.

There was, of course, the changing of the number plates. A trained detective would no doubt be able to make something of that. But Merriman felt that without even the assistance of Hilliard, he had neither the desire nor the ability to tackle it.

He pondered the question, as he had pondered it for weeks, and the more he thought, the more he felt himself driven to the direct course—to see Madeleine, put the problem to her, ask her to marry him and come out of it all. But there were terrible objections to this plan, not the least of which was that if he made a blunder it might be irrevocable. She might not hear him at all. She might be displeased by his suggestion that she and her father were in danger from such a cause. She might decide not to leave her father for the very reason that he was in danger. And all these possibilities were, of course, in addition to the much more probable one that she would simply refuse him because she did not care about him.

Merriman did not see his way clearly, and he was troubled. Once he had made up his mind he was not easily turned from his purpose, but he was slow in making it up. In this case, where so much depended on his decision, he found his doubt actually painful.

Mechanically he alighted at the Gare du Nord, crossed Paris, and took his place in the southern express at the Quai d'Orsay. Here he continued wrestling with his problem, and it was not until he was near his destination that he arrived at a decision. He would not bother about further investigations. He would go out and see Madeleine, tell her everything, and put his fate into her hands.

He alighted at the Bastide Station in Bordeaux, and driving across to the city, put up at the Gironde Hotel. There he slept the night, and next day after lunch he took a taxi to the clearing. Leaving the vehicle on the main road, he continued on foot down the lane and past the depot until he reached the manager's house.

The door was opened by Miss Coburn in person. On seeing her visitor she stood for a moment quite motionless, while a look of dismay appeared in her eyes and a hot flush rose on her face and then faded, leaving it white and drawn.

'Oh!' she gasped faintly. 'It's you!' She still stood holding the door, as if overcome by some benumbing emotion.

Merriman had pulled off his hat.

'It is I, Miss Coburn,' he answered gently. 'I have come over from London to see you. May I not come in?'

She stepped back.

'Come in, of course,' she said, making an obvious effort to infuse cordiality into her tone. 'Come in here.'

He fumbled with his coat in the hall, and by the time he followed her into the drawing-room she had recovered her composure.

She began rather breathlessly to talk commonplaces. At first he answered in the same strain, but directly he made a serious attempt to turn the conversation to the subject of his call she adroitly interrupted him.

'You'll have some tea?' she said presently, getting up and moving towards the door.

'Er—no—no, thanks, Miss Coburn, not any. I wanted really—'

'But *I* want some tea,' she persisted smiling. 'Come, you may help me to get it ready, but you must have some to keep me company.'

He had perforce to obey, and during the tea making she effectually prevented any serious discussion. But when the meal was over and they had once more settled down in the drawing-room he would no longer be denied.

'Forgive me,' he entreated, 'forgive me for bothering you, but it's so desperately important to me. And we may be interrupted. *Do* hear what I've got to say.'

Without waiting for permission he plunged into his subject.

Speaking hoarsely, stammering, contradicting himself, boggling over the words, he yet made himself clear. He loved her; had loved her from that first day they had met; he loved her more than anything else in the world; he—

She covered her face with her hands.

'Oh!' she cried wildly. 'Don't go on! Don't say it!' She made a despairing gesture. 'I can't listen. I tried to stop you.'

Merriman felt as if a cold weight was slowly descending upon his heart.

'But I will speak,' he cried hoarsely. 'It's my life that's at stake. Don't tell me you can't listen. Madeleine! I love you. I want you to marry me. Say you'll marry me. Madeleine! Say it!'

He dropped on his knees before her and seized her hands in his own.

'My darling,' he whispered fiercely, 'I love you enough for us both. Say you'll marry me. Say—'

She wrenched her hands from him. 'Oh!' she cried as if heartbroken, and burst into an uncontrollable flood of tears.

Merriman was maddened beyond endurance by the sight.

'What a brute I am!' he gasped. 'Now I've made you cry. For pity's sake! Do stop it! Nothing matters about anything else if only you stop!'

He was almost beside himself with misery as he pleaded with her. But soon he pulled himself together and began to speak more rationally.

'At least tell me the reason,' he besought. 'I know I've no right to ask, but it matters so much. Have pity and tell me, is it some one else?'

She shook her head faintly between her sobs.

'Thank goodness for that anyway. Tell me once again. Is it that you don't like me?'

Again she shook her head.

'You *do* like me!' he exclaimed breathlessly. 'You do, Madeleine. Say it! Say that you do!'

She made a resolute effort for self-control.

'You know I do, but—' she began in a tremulous whisper.

In a paroxysm of overwhelming excitement he interrupted her. 'Madeleine,' he cried wildly, again seizing her hands, 'you don't—It couldn't be possible that you—that you *love* me?'

This time she did not withdraw her hands. Slowly she raised her eyes to his, and in them he read his answer. In a moment she was in his arms and he was crushing her to his heart.

For a breathless space she lay, a happy little smile on her lips, and then the moment passed. 'Oh!' she cried, struggling to release herself, 'what have I done? Let me go! I shouldn't have—'

'Darling,' he breathed triumphantly. 'I'll never let you go as long as I live! You love me! What else matters?'

'No, no,' she cried again, her tears once more flowing. 'I was wrong. I shouldn't have allowed you. It can never be.'

He laughed savagely.

'Never be?' he repeated. 'Why, dear one, it *is*. I'd like to know the person or thing that could stop it now!'

'It can never be,' she repeated in a voice of despair. 'You don't understand. There are obstacles.'

She argued. He scoffed first, then he pleaded. He demanded to be told the nature of the barrier, then he besought, but all to no purpose. She would say no more than that it could never be.

And then suddenly the question of the syndicate flashed into his mind, and he sat, almost gasping with wonder as he realised that he had entirely forgotten it! He had forgotten this mysterious business which had occupied his thoughts to the exclusion of almost all else for the past two months! It seemed to him incredible. Yet so it was.

There surged over him a feeling of relief, so that once more he all but laughed. He turned to Madeleine.

'I know,' he cried triumphantly, 'the obstacle. And it's just nothing at all. It's this syndicate business that your father has got mixed up in. Now tell me! Isn't that it?'

The effect of his words on the girl was instantaneous. She started and then sat quite still, while the colour slowly drained from her face, leaving it bleached and deathlike. A look of fear and horror grew in her eyes, and her fingers clasped until the knuckles showed white.

'Oh!' she stammered brokenly, 'what do you mean by that?'

Merriman tried once more to take her hand.

'Dear one,' he said caressingly, 'don't let what I said distress you. We know the syndicate is carrying on something that—well, perhaps wouldn't bear too close investigation. But that has nothing to do with us. It won't affect our relations.'

The girl seemed transfixed with horror.

'*We* know?' she repeated dully. 'Who are we?'

'Why, Hilliard; Hilliard and I. We found out quite by accident that there was something secret going on. We were both interested; Hilliard has a mania for puzzles, and besides he thought he might get some kudos if the business was—illegal and he could bring it to light, while I knew that because of Mr Coburn's connection with it the matter might affect you.'

'Yes?' She seemed hardly able to frame the syllable between her dry lips.

Merriman was profoundly unhappy. He felt it was out of the question for him to tell her anything but the exact truth. Whether she would consider he had acted improperly in spying on the syndicate he did not know, but even at the risk of destroying his own chance of happiness he could not deceive her.

'Dear one,' he said in a low tone, 'don't think any worse of me than you can help, and I will tell you everything. You remember that first day that I was here, when you met me in the lane and we walked to the mill?'

She nodded.

'You may recall that a lorry had just arrived, and that I stopped and stared at it? Well, I had noticed that the number plate had been changed.'

'Ah,' she exclaimed, 'I was afraid you had.'

'Yes, I saw it, though it conveyed nothing to me. But I was interested, and one night in London, just to make conversation in the club, I mentioned what I had seen. Hilliard was present, and he joined me on the way home and insisted on talking over the affair. As I said, he has a mania for puzzles, and the mystery appealed to him. He was going on that motor boat tour across France, and he suggested that I should join him and that we should call here on our way, so as to see if we could find the solution. Neither of us thought then, you understand, that there was anything wrong; he was merely interested. I didn't care about the mystery, but I confess I leaped at the idea of coming back in order to meet you again, and on the understanding that there was to be nothing in the nature of spying, I agreed to his proposal.'

Merriman paused, but the girl, whose eyes were fixed intently on his face, made no remark and he continued:

'While we were here, Hilliard, who is very observant and clever, saw one or two little things which excited his suspicion, and without telling me, he slipped on board the *Girondin* and overheard a conversation between Mr Coburn, Captain Beamish, Mr Bulla, and Henri. He learned at once that something serious and illegal was in progress, but he did not learn what it was.'

'Then there *was* spying,' she declared accusingly.

'There was,' he admitted. 'I can only say that under the circumstances he thought himself justified.'

'Go on,' she ordered shortly.

'We returned then to England, and were kept at our offices for about a week. But Hilliard felt that we could not drop the matter, as we should then become accomplices. Besides, he was interested. He proposed we should try to find out more about it. This time I agreed, but I would ask you, Madeleine, to believe me when I tell you my motive, and to judge me by it. He spoke of reporting what he had learned to the police, and if I hadn't agreed to help him he would have done so. I wanted at all costs to avoid that, because if there was going to be any trouble I wanted Mr Coburn to be out of it first. Believe me or not, that was my only reason for agreeing.'

'I do believe you,' she said, 'but finish what you have to tell me.'

'We learned from Lloyd's List that the *Girondin* put into Hull. We went there and at Ferriby, seven miles up-stream, we found the depot where she discharged the props. You don't know it?'

She shook her head.

'It's quite like this place; just a wharf and shed, with an enclosure between the river and the railway. We made all the inquiries and investigations we could think of, but we learned absolutely nothing. But that, unfortunately, is the worst of it. Hilliard is disgusted with our failure and appears determined to tell the police.'

'Oh!' cried the girl with an impatient gesture. 'Why can't he let it alone? It's not his business.'

Merriman shrugged his shoulders.

'That's what he said at all events. I had the greatest difficulty in getting him to promise even to delay. But he has promised, and we have a month to make our plans. I came straight over to tell you, and to ask you to marry me at once and come away with me to England.'

'Oh, no, no, no!' she cried, putting up her hand as if to shield herself from the idea. 'Besides, what about my father?'

'I've thought about him too,' Merriman returned. 'We will tell him the whole thing, and he will be able to get out before the crash comes.'

For some moments she sat in silence, then she asked had Hilliard any idea of what was being done.

'He suggested brandy smuggling, but it was only a theory. There was nothing whatever to support it.'

'Brandy smuggling? Oh, if it only were!'

Merriman stared in amazement.

'It wouldn't be so bad as what I had feared,' the girl added, answering his look.

'And that was—? Do trust me, Madeleine.'

'I do trust you, and I will tell you all I know; it isn't much. I was afraid they were printing and circulating false money.'

Merriman was genuinely surprised.

'False money?' he repeated blankly.

'Yes; English Treasury notes. I thought they were perhaps printing them over here, and sending some to England with each trip of the *Girondin*. It was a remark I accidentally over-heard that made me think so. But, like you, it was only a guess. I had no proof.'

'Tell me,' Merriman begged.

'It was last winter, when the evenings closed in early. I had had a headache and I had gone to rest for a few minutes in the next room, the dining-room, which was in darkness. The door between it and this room was almost, but not quite closed. I must have fallen asleep, for I suddenly became conscious of voices in here, though I had heard no one enter. I was going to call out when a phrase arrested my attention. I did not mean to listen, but involuntarily I stayed quiet for a moment. You understand?'

'Of course. It was the natural thing to do.'

'Captain Beamish was speaking. He was just finishing a sentence and I only caught the last few words. "So that's a profit of six thousand, eight hundred and fifty pounds," he said; "fifty pounds loss on the props, and six thousand eight hundred netted over the other. Not bad for one trip?"'

'Lord!' Merriman exclaimed in amazement. 'No wonder you stopped!'

'I couldn't understand what was meant, and while I sat undecided what to do I heard my father say, "No trouble planting the stuff?" Captain Beamish answered, "Archer said not, but then Archer is—Archer. He's planting it in small lots—

ten here, twenty there, fifty in t'other place; I don't think he put out more than fifty at any one time. And he says he's only learning his way round, and that he'll be able to form better connections to get rid of it." Then Mr Bulla spoke, and this was what upset me so much and made me think. "Mr Archer is a wonderful man," he said with that horrible fat chuckle of his, "he would plant stuff on Old Nick himself with the whole of the C.I.D. looking on." I was bewildered and rather horrified, and I did not wait to hear any more. I crept away noiselessly, as I didn't want to be found as it were listening. Even then I did not understand that anything was wrong, but it happened that the very next day I was walking through the forest near the lane, and I noticed Henri changing the numbers on the lorry. He didn't see me, and he had such a stealthy, surreptitious air, that I couldn't but see it was not a joke. Putting two and two together I felt something serious was going on, and that night I asked my father what it was.'

'Well done!' Merriman exclaimed admiringly.

'But it was no use. He made little of it at first, but when I pressed him he said that against his will he had been forced into an enterprise which he hated and which he was trying to get out of. He said I must be patient and we should get away from it as quickly as possible. But since then,' she added despondently, 'though I have returned to the subject time after time he has always put me off, saying that we must wait a little longer.'

'And then you thought of the false notes?'

'Yes, but I had no reason to do so except that I couldn't think of anything else that would fit the words I had overheard. Planting stuff by tens or twenties or fifties seemed to—'

There was a sudden noise in the hall and Madeleine broke off to listen.

'Father,' she whispered breathlessly. 'Don't say anything.'

Merriman had just time to nod when the door opened and Mr Coburn appeared on the threshold. For a moment he stood looking at his daughter's visitor, while the emotions of doubt, surprise and annoyance seemed to pass successively through his mind. Then he advanced with outstretched hand and a somewhat satirical smile on his lips.

'Ah, it is the good Merriman,' he exclaimed. 'Welcome once more to our humble abode. And where is brother Hilliard? You don't mean to say you have come without him?'

His tone jarred on Merriman, but he answered courteously:

'I left him in London. I had business bringing me to this neighbourhood, and when I reached Bordeaux I took the opportunity to run out to see you and Miss Coburn.'

The manager replied suitably, and the conversation became general. As soon as he could with civility, Merriman rose to go. Mr Coburn cried out in protest, but the other insisted.

Mr Coburn had become more cordial, and the two men strolled together across the clearing. Merriman had had no opportunity of further private conversation with Madeleine, but he pressed her hand and smiled at her encouragingly on saying good-bye.

As the taxi bore him swiftly back towards Bordeaux, his mind was occupied with the girl to the exclusion of all else. It was not so much that he thought definitely about her, as that she seemed to fill all his consciousness. He felt numb, and his whole being ached for her as with a dull physical pain. But it was a pain that was mingled with exultation, for if she had refused him, she had at least admitted that she loved him. Incredible thought! He smiled ecstatically, then, the sense of loss returning, once more gazed gloomily ahead into vacancy.

As the evening wore on his thoughts turned towards what she had said about the syndicate. Her forged note theory had come to him as a complete surprise, and he wondered whether she really had hit on the true solution of the mystery. The conversation she had overheard undoubtedly pointed in that direction. 'Planting stuff' was, he believed, the technical phrase for passing forged notes, and the reference to 'tens', 'twenties', and 'fifties', tended in the same direction. Also 'forming connections to get rid of it' seemed to suggest the finding of agents who would take a number of notes at a time, to be passed on by ones and twos, no doubt for a consideration.

But there was the obvious difficulty that the theory did not account for the operations as a whole. The elaborate mechanism of the pit-prop industry was not needed to provide a means of carrying forged notes from France to England. They could be secreted about the person of a traveller crossing by any of the ordinary routes. Hundreds of notes could be sewn into the lining of an overcoat, thousands carried in the double bottom of a suitcase. Of course, so frequent a traveller would require a plausible reason for his journeys, but that would present no difficulty to men like those composing the syndicate. In any case, by crossing in rotation by the dozen or so well-patronised routes between England and the Continent, the continuity of the travelling could be largely hidden. Moreover, thought Merriman, why print the notes in France at all? Why not produce them in England and so save the need for importation?

On the whole there seemed but slight support for the theory and several strong arguments against it, and he felt that Madeleine must be mistaken, just as he and Hilliard had been mistaken.

Oh! how sick of the whole business he was! He no longer cared what the syndicate was doing. He never wanted to hear of it again. He wanted Madeleine, and he wanted nothing else. His thoughts swung back to her as he had seen her that afternoon; her trim figure, her daintiness, her brown eyes clouded with trouble, her little shell-like ears escaping from the tendrils of her hair, her tears . . . He broke out once more into a cold sweat as he thought of those tears.

Presently he began wondering what his own next step should be, and he soon decided he must see her again, and with as little delay as possible.

The next afternoon, therefore, he once more presented

himself at the house in the clearing. This time the door was opened by an elderly servant, who handed him a note and informed him that Mr and Miss Coburn had left home for some days.

Bitterly disappointed he turned away, and in the solitude of the lane he opened the note. It read:

'Friday.

'DEAR MR MERRIMAN,—I feel it is quite impossible that we should part without a word more than could be said at our interrupted interview this afternoon, so with deep sorrow I am writing to say to you, dear Mr Merriman, "Good-bye." I have enjoyed our short friendship, and all my life I shall be proud that you spoke as you did, but, my dear, it is just because I think so much of you that I could not bring your life under the terrible cloud that hangs over mine. Though it hurts me to say it, I have no option but to ask you to accept the answer I gave you as final, and to forget that we met.

'I am leaving home for some time, and I beg of you not to give both of us more pain by trying to follow me. Oh, my dear, I cannot say how grieved I am.

'Your sincere friend,
'MADELEINE COBURN.'

Merriman was overwhelmed utterly by the blow. Mechanically he regained the taxi, where he lay limply back, gripping the note and unconscious of his position, while his bloodless lips repeated over and over again the phrase, 'I'll find her. I'll find her. If it takes me all my life I'll find her and I'll marry her.'

Like a man in a state of coma he returned to his hotel in Bordeaux, and there, for the first time in his life, he drank himself into forgetfulness.

CHAPTER XI

AN UNEXPECTED ALLY

FOR several days Merriman, sick at heart and shaken in body, remained on at Bordeaux, too numbed by the blow which had fallen on him to take any decisive action. He now understood that Madeleine Coburn had refused him because she loved him, and he vowed he would rest neither day nor night till he had seen her and obtained a reversal of her decision. But for the moment his energy had departed, and he spent his time smoking in the Jardin and brooding over his troubles.

It was true that on three separate occasions he had called at the manager's house, only to be told that Mr and Miss Coburn were still from home, and neither there nor from the foreman at the works could he learn their addresses or the date of their return. He had also written a couple of scrappy notes to Hilliard, merely saying he was on a fresh scent, and to make no move in the matter until he heard further. Of the Pit-Prop Syndicate as apart from Madeleine he was now profoundly wearied, and he wished for nothing more than never again to hear its name mentioned.

But after a week of depression and self-pity his natural good sense reasserted itself, and he began seriously to consider his position. He honestly believed that Madeleine's happiness could best be brought about by the fulfilment of his own, in other words by their marriage. He appreciated the motives which had caused her to refuse him, but he hoped that by his continued persuasion he might be able, as he put it to himself, to talk her round. Her very flight from him, for such he believed her absence to be, seemed to indicate that she herself was doubtful of her power to hold out against him, and to this extent he drew comfort from his immediate difficulty.

He concluded before trying any new plan to call once again at the clearing, in the hope that Mr Coburn at least might have returned. The next afternoon, therefore, saw him driving out along the now familiar road. It was still hot, with the heavy enervating heat of air held stagnant by the trees. The freshness of early summer had gone, and there was a hint of approaching autumn in the darker greenery of the firs, and the over maturity of such shrubs and wild flowers as could find along the edge of the road a precarious roothold on the patches of ground not covered by pine needles. Merriman gazed unceasingly ahead at the straight white ribbon of the road, as he pondered the problem of what he should do if once again he should be disappointed in his quest. Madeleine could not, he thought, remain indefinitely away. Mr Coburn at all events would have to return to his work, and it would be a strange thing if he could not obtain from the father some indication of his daughter's whereabouts.

But his call at the manager's house was as fruitless on this occasion as on those preceding. The woman from whom he had received the note opened the door and repeated her former statement. Mr and Miss Coburn were still from home.

Merriman turned away disconsolately, and walked slowly back across the clearing and down the lane. Though he told himself he had expected nothing from the visit, he was nevertheless bitterly disappointed with its result. And worse than his disappointment was his inability to see his next step, or even to think of any scheme which might lead him to the object of his hopes.

He trudged on down the lane, his head sunk and his brows knitted, only half conscious of his surroundings. Looking up listlessly as he rounded a bend, he stopped suddenly as if turned to stone, while his heart first stood still, then began thumping wildly as if to choke him. A few yards away and coming to meet him was Madeleine!

She caught sight of him at the same instant and stopped with a low cry, while an expression of dread came over her face. So for an appreciable time they stood looking at one another, then Merriman, regaining the power of motion, sprang forward and seized her hands.

'Madeleine! Madeleine!' he cried brokenly. 'My own one! My beloved!' He almost sobbed as he attempted to strain her to his heart.

But she wrenched herself from him.

'No, no!' she gasped. 'You must not! I told you. It cannot be.'

He pled with her, fiercely, passionately, and at last despairingly. But he could not move her. Always she repeated that it could not be.

'At least tell me this,' he begged at last. 'Would you marry me if this syndicate did not exist; I mean if Mr Coburn was not mixed up with it?'

At first she would not answer, but presently overcome by his persistence, she burst once again into tears and admitted that her fear of disgrace arising through discovery of the syndicate's activities was her only reason for refusal.

'Then,' said Merriman resolutely, 'I will go back with you now and see Mr Coburn, and we will talk over what is to be done.'

At this her eyes dilated with terror.

'No, no!' she cried again. 'He would be in danger. He would try something that might offend the others, and his life might not be safe. I tell you I don't trust Captain Beamish and Mr Bulla. I don't think they would stop at anything to keep their secret. He is trying to get out of it, and he must not be hurried. He will do what he can.'

'But, my dearest,' Merriman remonstrated, 'it could do no harm to talk the matter over with him. That would commit him to nothing.'

But she would not hear of it.

'If he thought my happiness depended on it,' she declared, 'he would break with them at all costs. I could not risk it. You must go away. Oh, my dear, you must go. Go, go!' she entreated almost hysterically, 'it will be best for us both.'

Merriman, though beside himself with suffering, felt he could no longer disregard her.

'I shall go,' he answered sadly, 'since you require it, but I will never give you up. Not until one of us is dead, or you marry some one else—I will never give you up. Oh, Madeleine, have pity and give me some hope; something to keep me alive till this trouble is over.'

She was beginning to reply when she stopped suddenly and stood listening.

'The lorry!' she cried, 'Go! Go!' Then pointing wildly in the direction of the road, she turned and fled rapidly back towards the clearing.

Merriman gazed after her until she passed round a corner of the lane and was lost to sight among the trees. Then, with a weight of hopeless despair on his heart, he began to walk towards the road. The lorry, driven by Henri, passed him at the next bend, and Henri, though he saluted with a show of respect, smiled sardonically as he noted the other's woebegone appearance.

But Merriman neither knew nor cared what the driver thought. Almost physically sick with misery and disappointment he regained his taxi and was driven back to Bordeaux.

The next few days seemed to him like a nightmare of hideous reality and permanence. He moved as a man in a dream, living under a shadow of almost tangible weight, as a criminal must do who has been sentenced to early execution. The longing to see Madeleine again, to hear the sound of her voice, to feel her presence, was so intense as to be almost unendurable. Again and again he said to himself that had she cared for another, had she even told him that she could not care for him, he would have taken his dismissal as irrevocable and gone to try and drag out the remainder of his life elsewhere as best he could. But he was maddened to think that the major difficulty—the overwhelming, insuperable difficulty—of his suit had been overcome. She loved him! Miraculous and incredible though it might seem—though it was—it was the amazing truth. And that being so, it was beyond bearing that a mere truckling to convention should be allowed to step in and snatch away the ecstasy of happiness that was within his grasp. And worse still, this truckling to convention was to save—*him*! What, he asked himself savagely, did it matter about *him*? Even if the worst happened and she suffered shame through her father, wasn't all he wanted to be allowed to share it with her? And if narrow, stupid fools did talk, what matter? They could do without their companionship.

Fits of wild rage alternated with periods of cold and numbing despair, but as day succeeded day the desire to be near her grew until it could no longer be denied. He dared not again attempt to force himself into her presence, lest she should be angry and shatter irrevocably the hope to which he still clung with desperation. But he might without fear of disaster be nearer to her for a time. He hired a bicycle, and after dark had fallen that evening he rode out to the lane, and leaving his machine on the road, walked to the edge of the clearing. It was a perfect night, calm and silent, though with a slight touch of chill in the air. A crescent moon shone soft and silvery, lighting up pallidly the open space, gleaming on the white wood of the freshly cut stumps, and throwing black shadows from the ghostly looking buildings. It was close on midnight, and Merriman looked eagerly across the clearing to the manager's house. He was not disappointed. There, in the window that he knew belonged to her room, shone a light.

He slowly approached, keeping on the fringe of the clearing and beneath the shadow of the trees. Some shrubs had taken root on the open ground, and behind a clump of these, not far from the door, he lay down, filled his pipe, and gave himself up to dreams. The light still showed in the window, but even as he looked it went out, leaving the front of the house dark and, as it seemed to him, unfriendly and forbidding. 'Perhaps she'll look out before going to bed,' he thought, as he gazed disconsolately at the blank, unsympathetic opening. But he could see no movement therein.

He lost count of time as he lay dreaming of the girl whose existence had become more to him than his very life, and it was not until he suddenly realised that he had become stiff and cramped from the cold that he looked at his watch. Nearly two! Once more he glanced sorrowfully at the window, realising that no comfort was to be obtained therefrom, and decided he might as well make his way back, for all the ease of mind he was getting.

He turned slowly to get up, but just as he did so he noticed a slight movement at the side of the house before him, and he remained motionless, gazing intently forward. Then, spellbound, he watched Mr Coburn leave by the side door, walk quickly to the shed, unlock a door, and disappear within.

There was something so secretive in the way the manager looked around before venturing into the open, and so stealthy about his whole walk and bearing, that Merriman's heart beat more quickly as he wondered if he was now on the threshold of some revelation of the mystery of that outwardly innocent place. Obeying a sudden instinct, he rose from his hiding-place in the bushes and crept silently across the sward to the door by which the other had entered.

It was locked, and the whole place was dark and silent. Were it not for what he had just seen, Merriman would have believed it deserted. But it was evident that some secret and perhaps sinister activity was in progress within, and for the moment he forgot even Madeleine in his anxiety to learn its nature.

He crept silently round the shed, trying each door and peering into each window, but without result. All remained fast and in darkness, and though he listened with the utmost intentness of which he was capable, he could not catch any sound.

His round of the building completed, he paused in doubt. Should he retire while there was time, and watch for Mr

Coburn's reappearance with perhaps some of his accomplices, or should he wait at the door and tackle him on the matter when he came out? His first preference was for the latter course, but as he thought over it he felt it would be better to reserve his knowledge, and he turned to make for cover.

But even as he did so he heard the manager say in low, harsh tones: 'Hands up now, or I fire!' and swinging round, he found himself gazing into the bore of a small, deadly looking repeating pistol.

Automatically he raised his arms, and for a few moments both men stood motionless, staring perplexedly at one another. Then Mr Coburn lowered the pistol and attempted a laugh, a laugh nervous, shaky, and without merriment. His lips smiled, but his eyes remained cold and venomous.

'Good heavens, Merriman, but you did give me a start,' he cried, making an evident effort to be jocular. 'What in all the world are you doing here at this hour? Sorry for my greeting, but one has to be careful here. You know the district is notorious for brigands.'

Merriman was not usually very prompt to meet emergencies. He generally realised when it was too late what he ought to have said or done in any given circumstances. But on this occasion a flash of veritable inspiration revealed a way by which he might at one and the same time account for his presence, disarm the manager's suspicions, and perhaps even gain his point with regard to Madeleine. He smiled back at the other.

'Sorry for startling you, Mr Coburn. I have been looking for you for some days to discuss a very delicate matter, and I came out late this evening in the hope of attracting your attention after Miss Coburn had retired, so that our chat could be quite confidential. But in the darkness I fell and hurt my knee, and I spent so much time waiting for it to get better that I was ashamed to go to the house. Imagine my delight when, just as I was turning to leave, I saw you coming down to the shed, and I followed with the object of trying to attract your attention.'

He hardly expected that Mr Coburn would have accepted his statement, but whatever the manager believed privately, he gave no sign of suspicion.

'I'm glad your journey was not fruitless,' he answered courteously. 'As a matter of fact, my neuralgia kept me from sleeping, and I found I had forgotten my bottle of aspirin down here, where I had brought it for the same purpose this morning. It seemed worth the trouble of coming for it, and I came.'

As he spoke Mr Coburn took from his pocket and held up for Merriman's inspection a tiny phial half full of white tablets.

It was now Merriman's turn to be sceptical, but he murmured polite regrets in as convincing a way as he was able.

'Let us go back into my office,' the manager continued. 'If you want a private chat we can have it there.'

He unlocked the door, and passing in first, lit a reading-lamp on his desk. Then relocking the door behind his visitor and unostentatiously slipping the key into his pocket, he sat down at the desk, waved Merriman to a chair, and producing a box of cigars, passed it across.

The windows, Merriman noticed, were covered by heavy blinds, and it was evident that no one could see into the room, nor could the light be observed from without. The door behind him was locked, and in Mr Coburn's pocket was the key as well as a revolver, while Merriman was unarmed. Moreover, Mr Coburn was the larger and heavier, if not the stronger man of the two. It was true his words and manner were those of a friend, but the cold hatred in his eyes revealed his purpose. Merriman instantly realised he was in very real personal danger, and it was borne in on him that if he was to get out of that room alive, it was to his own wits he must trust.

But he was no coward, and he did not forget to limp as he crossed the room, nor did his hand shake as he stretched it out to take a cigar. When he came within the radius of the lamp he noticed with satisfaction that his coat was covered with fragments of moss and leaves, and he rather ostentatiously brushed these away, partly to prove to the other his calmness, and partly to draw attention to them in the hope that they would be accepted as evidence of his fall.

Fearing lest if they began a desultory conversation he might be tricked by his astute opponent into giving himself away, he left the latter no opportunity to make a remark, but plunged at once into his subject.

'I feel myself, Mr Coburn,' he began, 'not a little in your debt for granting me this interview. But the matter on which I wish to speak to you is so delicate and confidential, that I think you will agree that any precautions against eavesdroppers are justifiable.'

He spoke at first somewhat formally, but as interest in his subject quickened, he gradually became more conversational.

'The first thing I have to tell you,' he went on, 'may not be very pleasing hearing to you, but it is a matter of almost life and death importance to me. I have come, Mr Coburn, very deeply and sincerely to love your daughter.'

Mr Coburn frowned slightly, but he did not seem surprised, nor did he reply except by a slight bow. Merriman continued:

'That in itself need not necessarily be of interest to you, but there is more to tell, and it is in this second point that the real importance of my statement lies, and on it hinges everything that I have to say to you. Madeleine, sir, has given me a definite assurance that my love for her is returned.'

Still Mr Coburn made no answer, save than by another slight inclination of his head, but his eyes had grown anxious and troubled.

'Not unnaturally,' Merriman resumed, 'I begged her to marry me, but she saw fit to decline. In view of the admission she had just made, I was somewhat surprised that her refusal was so vehement. I pressed her for the reason, but she utterly declined to give it. Then an idea struck me, and I asked her if it was because she feared that your connection with this syndicate might lead to unhappiness. At first she would not reply nor give me any satisfaction, but at last by persistent questioning, and only when she saw I knew a great deal more about the business than she did herself, she admitted that that was indeed the barrier. Not to put too fine a point on it—it is better, is it not, sir, to be perfectly candid—she is living in terror and dread of your arrest, and she won't marry me for fear that if it were to happen she might bring disgrace on me.'

Mr Coburn had not moved during this speech, except that his face had become paler and the look of cold menace in his eyes seemed charged with a still more vindictive hatred. Then he answered slowly:

'I can only assume, Mr Merriman, that your mind has become temporarily unhinged, but even with such an excuse, you cannot really believe that I am going to wait here and listen to you making such statements.'

Merriman bent forward.

'Sir,' he said earnestly, 'I state on my honour as a gentleman, and I ask you to believe, that I am approaching you as a friend. I am myself an interested party. I have sought this interview for Madeleine's sake. For her sake, and for her sake only, I have come to ask you to discuss with me the best way out of the difficulty.'

Mr Coburn rose abruptly.

'The best way out of the difficulty,' he declared, no longer attempting to disguise the hatred he felt, 'is for you to take yourself off and never to show your face here again. I am amazed at you.' He took his automatic pistol out of his pocket. 'Don't you know that you are completely in my power? If I chose I could shoot you like a dog and sink your body in the river, and no one would ever know what had become of you.'

Merriman's heart was beating rapidly. He had the uncomfortable suspicion that he had only to turn his back to get a bullet into it. He assumed a confidence he was far from feeling.

'On the contrary, Mr Coburn,' he said quietly, 'it is you who are in our power. I'm afraid you don't quite appreciate the situation. It is true you could shoot me now, but if you did, nothing could save you. It would be the rope for you and prison for your confederates, and what about your daughter then? I tell you, sir, I'm not such a fool as you take me for. Knowing what I do, do you think it likely I should put myself into your power unless I knew I was safe?'

His assurance was not without its effect. The other's face grew paler and he sat heavily down in his chair.

'I'll hear what you have to say,' he said harshly, though without letting go his weapon.

'Then let me begin at the beginning. You remember that first evening I was here, when you so kindly supplied me with petrol? Sir, you were correct when you told Captain Beamish and Mr Bulla that I had noticed the changing of the lorry number plate. I had.'

Mr Coburn started slightly, but he did not speak, and Merriman went on:

'I was interested, though the thing conveyed nothing to me. But some time later I mentioned it casually, and Hilliard, who has a mania for puzzles, overheard. He suggested my joining him on his trip, and calling to see if we could solve it. You, Mr Coburn, said another thing to your friends—that though I might have noticed about the lorry, you were certain neither Hilliard nor I had seen anything suspicious at the clearing. There, sir, you were wrong. Though at that time we could not tell what was going on, we knew it was something illegal.'

Coburn was impressed at last. He sat motionless staring at the speaker. As Merriman remained silent, he moved.

'Go on,' he said hoarsely, licking his dry lips.

'I would ask you please to visualise the situation when we left. Hilliard believed he was on the track of a criminal organisation, carrying on illicit operations on a large scale. He believed that by lodging with the police the information he had gained, the break-up of the organisation and the capture of its members would be assured, and that he would stand to gain much kudos. But he did not know what the operations were, and he hesitated to come forward, lest by not waiting and investigating further he should destroy his chance of handing over to the authorities a complete case. He was therefore exceedingly keen that we should carry on inquiries at what I may call the English end of the business. Such was Hilliard's attitude. I trust I make myself clear.'

Again Coburn nodded without speaking.

'My position was different. I had by that time come to care for Madeleine, and I saw the effect any disclosure must have on her. I therefore wished things kept secret, and I urged Hilliard to carry out his second idea and investigate further so as to make his case complete. He made my assistance a condition of agreement, and I therefore consented to help him.'

Mr Coburn was now ghastly, and was listening with breathless earnestness to his visitor. Merriman realised what he had always suspected, that the man was weak and a bit of a coward, and he began to believe his bluff would carry him through.

'I need not trouble you,' he went on, 'with all the details of our search. It is enough to say that we found out what we wanted. We went to Hull, discovered the wharf at Ferriby, made the acquaintance of Benson, and witnessed what went on there. We know all about Archer and how he plants your stuff, and Morton, who had us under observation and whom we properly tricked. I don't claim any credit for it; all that belongs to Hilliard. And I admit we did not learn certain small details of your scheme. But the main points are clear—clear enough to get convictions anyway.'

After a pause to let his words create their full effect, Merriman continued:

'Then arose the problem that had bothered us before. Hilliard was wild to go to the authorities with his story; on Madeleine's account I still wanted it kept quiet. I needn't recount our argument. Suffice it to say that at last we compromised. Hilliard agreed to wait for a month. For the sake of our friendship and the help I had given him, he undertook to give me a month to settle something about Madeleine. Mr Coburn, nearly half that month is gone and I am not one step farther on.'

The manager wiped the drops of sweat from his pallid brow. Merriman's quiet, confident manner, with its apparent absence of bluff or threat had had its effect on him. He was evidently thoroughly frightened, and seemed to think it no longer worth while to plead ignorance. As Merriman had hoped and intended, he appeared to conclude that conciliation would be his best chance.

'Then no one but you two know so far?' he asked, a shifty, sly look passing over his face.

Merriman read his thoughts and bluffed again.

'Yes and no,' he answered. 'No one but we two knows at present. On the other hand, we have naturally taken all reasonable precautions. Hilliard prepared a full statement of the matter which we both signed, and this he sent to his banker with the request that unless he claimed it in person before the given date, the banker was to convey it to Scotland Yard. If anything happens to me here, Hilliard will go at once to the Yard, and if anything happens to him our document will be sent there. And in it we have suggested that if either of us disappear, it will be equivalent to adding murder to the other charges made.'

It was enough. Mr Coburn sat, broken and completely cowed. To Merriman he seemed suddenly to have become an old man. For several minutes silence reigned and then at last the other spoke.

'What do you want me to do?' he asked, in a tremulous voice, hardly louder than a whisper.

Merriman's heart leaped.

'To consider your daughter, Mr Coburn,' he answered promptly. 'All I want is to marry Madeleine, and for her sake I want you to get out of this thing before the crash comes.'

Mr Coburn once more wiped the drops of sweat from his forehead.

'My God!' he cried hoarsely. 'Ever since it started I have been trying to get out of it. I was forced into it against my will and I would give my soul if I could do as you say and get free. But I can't—I can't.'

He buried his head in his hands and sat motionless, leaning on his desk.

'But your daughter, Mr Coburn,' Merriman persisted. 'For her sake something must be done.'

Mr Coburn shook his clenched fists in the air.

'Damnation take you!' he cried, with a sudden access of rage, 'do you think I care about myself? Do you think I'd sit here and listen to you talking as you've done if it wasn't for her? By God! I'd shoot you as you sit, if I didn't know from my own observation that she is fond of you. I swear it's the only thing that has saved you.' He rose to his feet and began pacing jerkily to and fro. 'See here,' he continued wildly, 'Go away from here before I do it. I can't stand any more of you at present. Go now and come back on Friday night at the same time, and I'll tell you my decision. Here's the key,' he threw it down on the desk. 'Get out quick before I do for you!'

Merriman was for a moment inclined to stand his ground, but, realising that not only had he carried his point as far as he could have expected, but also that his companion was in so excited a condition as hardly to be accountable for his actions, he decided discretion was the better part, and merely saying: 'Very well, Friday night,' he unlocked the door and took his leave.

On the whole he was well pleased with his interview. In the first place, he had by his readiness escaped an imminent personal danger. What was almost as important, he had broken the ice with Mr Coburn about Madeleine, and the former had not only declared that he was aware of the state of his daughter's feelings, but he had expressed no objection to the proposed match. Further, an understanding as to Mr Coburn's own position had been come to. He had practically admitted that the syndicate was a felonious conspiracy, and had stated that he would do almost anything to get out of it. Finally he had promised a decision on the whole question in three days' time. Quite a triumph, Merriman thought.

On the other hand, he had given the manager a warning of danger which the latter might communicate to his fellow-conspirators, with the result that all of them might escape from the net in which Hilliard, at any rate, wished to enmesh them. And just to this extent he had become a co-partner in their crime. And though it was true that he had escaped from his immediate peril, he had undoubtedly placed himself and Hilliard in very real danger. It was by no means impossible that the gang would decide to murder both of the men whose knowledge threatened them, in the hope of bluffing the bank manager out of the letter which they would believe he held. Merriman had invented this letter on the spur of the moment, and he would have felt a good deal happier if he knew that it really existed. He decided he would write to Hilliard immediately and get him to make it a reality.

A great deal, he thought, depended on the character of Coburn. If he was weak and cowardly he would try to save his own skin and let the others walk into the net. Particularly might he do this if he had suffered at their hands in the way he suggested. On the other hand, a strong man would undoubtedly consult his fellow-conspirators and see that a pretty determined fight was made for their liberty and their source of gain.

He had thought of all this when it suddenly flashed into his mind that Mr Coburn's presence in the shed at two in the morning in itself required a lot of explanation. He did not for a moment believe the aspirin story. The man had looked so shifty while he was speaking, that even at the time Merriman had decided he was lying. What then could he have been doing?

He puzzled over the question, but without result. Then it occured to him that as he was doing nothing that evening he might as well ride out again to the clearing and see if any nocturnal activities were undertaken.

Midnight therefore found him once more ensconced behind a group of shrubs in full view of both the house and the shed. It was again a perfect night, and again he lay dreaming of the girl who was so near in body and in spirit, and yet so infinitely far beyond his reach.

Time passed slowly, but the hours wore gradually round until his watch showed two o'clock. Then, just as he was thinking that he need hardly wait much longer, he was considerably thrilled to see Mr Coburn once more appear at the side door of the house, and in the same stealthy, secretive way as on the previous night, walk hurriedly to the shed and let himself in by the office door.

At first Merriman thought of following him again in the hope of learning the nature of these strange proceedings, but a moment's thought showed him he must run no risk of discovery. If Coburn learned that he was being spied on he would at once doubt Merriman's statement that he knew the syndicate's secret. It would be better, therefore, to lie low and await events.

But the only other interesting event that happened was that some fifteen minutes later the manager left the shed, and with the same show of secrecy returned to his house, disappearing into the side door.

So intrigued was Merriman by the whole business that he determined to repeat his visit the following night also. He did so, and once again witnessed Mr Coburn's stealthy walk to the shed at two a.m., and his equally stealthy return at two-fifteen.

Rack his brains as he would over the problem of these nocturnal visits, Merriman could think of no explanation. What for three consecutive nights could bring the manager down to the sawmill? He could not imagine, but he was clear it was not the pit-prop industry.

If the *Girondin* had been in he would have once more suspected smuggling, but she was then at Ferriby. No, it certainly did not work in with smuggling. Still less did it suggest false note printing, unless—Merriman's heart beat more quickly as a new idea entered his mind. Suppose the notes were printed there, at the mill! Suppose there was a cellar under the engine house, and suppose the work was done at night? It was true they had not seen signs of a cellar, but if this surmise was correct it was not likely they should.

At first sight this theory seemed a real advance, but a little further thought showed it had serious objections. Firstly, it did not explain Coburn's nightly visits. If the manager had spent some hours in the works it might have indicated the working of a press, but what in that way could be done in fifteen minutes? Further, and this seemed to put the idea quite out of court, if the notes were being produced at the clearing, why the changing of the lorry numbers? That would then be a part of the business quite unconnected with the illicit traffic. After much thought, Merriman had to admit to himself that here was one more of the series of insoluble puzzles with which they found themselves faced.

The next night was Friday, and in accordance with the arrangement made with Mr Coburn, Merriman once again went out to the clearing, presenting himself at the works door at two in the morning. Mr Coburn at once opened to his knock, and after locking the door, led the way to his office. There he wasted no time in preliminaries.

'I've thought this over, Merriman,' he said, and his manner was very different from that of the previous interview, 'and I'm bound to say that I've realised that, though interested, your action towards me has been very decent, not to say generous. Now I've made up my mind what I'll do, and I trust you will see your way to fall in with my ideas. There is a meeting of the syndicate on Thursday week. I should have been present in any case, and I have decided that, whatever may be the result, I will tell them I am going to break with them. I will give ill-health as my reason for this step, and fortunately or unfortunately I can do this with truth, as my heart is seriously diseased. I can easily provide the necessary doctor's certificates. If they accept my resignation, well and good—I will emigrate to my brother in South America and you and Madeleine can be married. If they decline, well'—Mr Coburn shrugged his shoulders—'your embarrassment will be otherwise removed.'

He paused. Merriman would have spoken, but Mr Coburn held up his hand for silence and went on:

'I confess I have been terribly upset for the last three days to discover my wisest course, and even now I am far from certain that my decision is best. I do not want to go back on my former friends, and on account of Madeleine I cannot go back on you. Therefore I cannot warn the others of their danger, but on the other hand I won't give your life into their hands. For if they knew what I know now, you and Hilliard would be dead men inside twenty-four hours.'

Mr Coburn spoke simply and with a certain dignity, and Merriman found himself disposed not only to believe what he had heard, but even to understand and sympathise with the man in the embarrassing circumstances in which he found himself. That his difficulties were of his own making there could be but little doubt, but how far he had put himself in the power of his associates through deliberate evil doing, and how far through mistakes or weakness, there was of course no way of learning.

At the end of an hour's discussion, Mr Coburn had agreed at all costs to sever his connection with the syndicate, to emigrate to his brother in Chile, and to do his utmost to induce his daughter to remain in England and to marry Merriman. On his side, Merriman undertook to hold back the lodging of information at Scotland Yard for one more week, to enable the other's arrangements to be carried out.

There being nothing to keep him in Bordeaux, Merriman left for London that day, and the next evening he was closeted with Hilliard in the latter's rooms, discussing the affair. Hilliard at first was most unwilling to postpone their visit to the Yard, but he agreed on Merriman's explaining that he had pledged himself to the delay.

So the days, for Merriman heavily weighted with anxiety and suspense, began slowly to drag by. His fate and the fate of the girl he loved hung in the balance, and not the least irksome feature of his position was his own utter impotence. There was nothing that he could do—no action which would take him out of himself and ease the tension of his thoughts. As day succeeded day and the silence remained unbroken, he became more and more upset. At the end of a week he was almost beside himself with worry and chagrin, so much so that he gave up attending his office altogether, and was only restrained from rushing back to Bordeaux by the knowledge that to force himself once more on Madeleine might be to destroy, once and for ever, any hopes he might otherwise have had.

It was now four days since the Thursday on which Mr Coburn had stated that the meeting of the syndicate was to have been held, and only three days to the date on which the friends had agreed to tell their story at Scotland Yard. What if he received no news during those three days? Would Hilliard agree to a further postponement? He feared not, and he was racked with anxiety as to whether he should cross that day to France and seek another interview with Mr Coburn.

But, even as he sat with the morning paper in his hand, news was nearer than he imagined. Listlessly he turned over the sheets, glancing with but scant attention to the headlines, automatically running his eyes over the paragraphs. And when he came to one headed 'Mystery of a Taxi-cab', he absent-mindedly began to read it also.

But he had not gone very far when his manner changed. Starting to his feet, he stared at the column with horror-stricken eyes, while his face grew pallid and his pipe dropped to the floor from his open mouth. With the newspaper still tightly grasped in his hand, he ran three steps at a time down the stairs of his flat, and calling a taxi, was driven to Scotland Yard.

PART II

THE PROFESSIONALS

CHAPTER XII

MURDER!

ALMOST exactly fifteen hours before Merriman's call at Scotland Yard, to wit, about eight o'clock on the previous evening, Inspector Willis of the Criminal Investigation Department was smoking in the sitting-room of his tiny house in Brixton. George Willis was a tall, somewhat burly man of five-and-forty, with heavy, clean shaven, expressionless features which would have made his face almost stupid, had it not been redeemed by a pair of the keenest of blue eyes. He was what is commonly known as a safe man, not exactly brilliant, but plodding and tenacious to an extraordinary degree. His forte was slight clues, and he possessed that infinite capacity for taking pains which made his following up of them approximate to genius. In short, though a trifle slow, he was already looked on as one of the most efficient and reliable inspectors of the Yard.

He had had a heavy day, and it was with a sigh of relief that he picked up the evening paper and stretched himself luxuriously in his easy-chair. But he was not destined to enjoy a long rest. Hardly had he settled himself to his satisfaction when the telephone bell rang. He was wanted back at the Yard immediately.

He swore under his breath, then, calling the news to his wife, he slipped on his waterproof and left the house. The long spell of fine weather had at last broken and the evening was unpleasant, indeed unusually inclement for mid-September. All day the wind had been gusty and boisterous, and now a fine drizzle of rain had set in, which was driven in sheets against the grimy buildings and whirled in eddies round the street corners. Willis walked quickly along the shining pavements, and in a few minutes reached his destination. His chief was waiting for him.

'Ah, Willis,' the great man greeted him, 'I'm glad you weren't out. A case has been reported which I want you to take over; a suspected murder; man found dead in a taxi at King's Cross.'

'Yes, sir,' Willis answered unemotionally. 'Any details forward?'

'None, except that the man is dead and that they're holding the taxi at the station. I have asked Dr Horton to come round, and you had both better get over there as quickly as possible.'

'Yes, sir,' Willis replied again, and quietly left the room.

His preparations were simple. He had only to arrange for a couple of plain clothes men and a photographer with a flashlight apparatus to accompany him, and to bring from his room a handbag containing his notebook and a few other necessary articles. He met the police doctor in the corridor and, the others being already in waiting, the five men immediately left the great building and took a taxi to the station.

'What's the case, inspector, do you know?' Dr Horton inquired as they slipped deftly through the traffic.

'The Chief said suspected murder; man found dead in a taxi at King's Cross. He had no details.'

'How was it done?'

'Don't know, sir. Chief didn't say.'

After a few brief observations on the inclemency of the weather, conversation waned between the two men, and they followed the example of their companions, and sat watching with a depressed air the rain-swept streets and the hurrying foot passengers on the wet pavements. All five were annoyed at being called out, as all were tired and had been looking forward to an evening of relaxation at their homes.

They made a quick run, reaching the station in a very few minutes. There a constable identified the inspector.

'They've taken the taxi round to the carriers' yard at the west side of the station, sir,' he said to Willis. 'If you'll follow me, I'll show the way.'

The officer led them to an enclosed and partially roofed area at the back of the parcels office, where the vans from the shops unloaded their traffic. In a corner under the roof and surrounded by a little knot of men stood a taxi-cab. As Willis and his companions approached, a sergeant of police separated himself from the others and came forward.

'We have touched nothing, sir,' he announced. 'When we found the man was dead we didn't even move the body.'

Willis nodded.

'Quite right, sergeant. It's murder, I suppose?'

'Looks like it, sir. The man was shot.'

'Shot? Anything known of the murderer?'

'Not much, I'm afraid, sir. He got clear away in Tottenham Court Road, as far as I can understand it. But you'll hear what the driver has to say.'

Again the inspector nodded, as he stepped up to the vehicle.

'Here's Dr Newman,' the sergeant continued, indicating an exceedingly dapper and well groomed little man with medico written all over him. 'He was the nearest medical man we could get.'

Willis turned courteously to the other.

'An unpleasant evening to be called out, doctor,' he remarked. 'The man's dead, I understand? Was he dead when you arrived?'

'Yes, but only a very little time. The body was quite warm.'

'And the cause of death?'

'Seeing that I could do nothing, I did not move the body until you Scotland Yard gentlemen had seen it, and therefore I cannot say professionally. But there is a small hole in the side of the coat over the heart.' The doctor spoke with a slightly consequential air.

'A bullet wound?'

'A bullet wound unquestionably.'

Inspector Willis picked up an acetylene bicycle lamp which one of the men had procured and directed its beam into the cab.

The corpse lay in the back corner seat on the driver's side, the head lolling back sideways against the cushions and crushing into a shapeless mass the gray Homburg hat. The mouth and eyes were open and the features twisted as if from sudden pain. The face was long and oval, the hair and eyes dark, and there was a tiny black moustache with waxed ends. A khaki coloured waterproof, open in front, revealed a gray tweed suit, across the waistcoat of which shone a gold watch chain. Tan shoes covered the feet. On the left side of the body just over the heart was a little round hole in the waterproof coat. Willis stooped and smelt the cloth.

'No blackening and no smell of burnt powder,' he thought. 'He must have been shot from outside the cab.' But he found it hard to understand how such a shot could have been fired from the populous streets of London. The hole also seemed too far round towards the back of the body to suggest that the bullet had come in through the open window. The point was puzzling, but Willis pulled himself up sharply with the reminder that he must not begin theorising until he had learnt all the facts.

Having gazed at the gruesome sight until he had impressed its every detail on his memory, he turned to his assistant. 'Get ahead with your flashlight, Kirby,' he ordered. 'Take views from all the angles you can. The constable will give you a hand. Meantime, sergeant, give me an idea of the case. What does the driver say?'

'He's here, sir,' the officer returned, pointing to a small, slight individual in a leather coat and cap, with a sallow, frightened face and pathetic, dog-like eyes which fixed themselves questioningly on Willis's face as the sergeant led their owner forward.

'You might tell me what you know, driver.'

The man shifted nervously from one foot to the other.

'It was this way, sir,' he began. He spoke earnestly, and to Willis, who was accustomed to sizing up rapidly those with whom he dealt, he seemed a sincere and honest man. 'I was driving down Piccadilly from Hyde Park Corner looking out for a fare, and when I gets just by the end of Bond Street two men hails me. One was this here man what's dead, the other was a big, tall gent. I pulls in to the kerb, and they gets in, and the tall gent he says "King's Cross". I starts off by Piccadilly Circus and Shaftesbury Avenue, but when I gets into Tottenham Court Road about the corner of Great Russell Street, one of them says through the tube, "Let me down here at the corner of Great Russell Street," he sez. I pulls over to the kerb, and the tall gent he gets out and stands on the kerb and speaks in to the other one. "Then I shall follow by the three o'clock tomorrow," he sez, and he shuts the door and gives me a bob and sez, "That's for yourself," he sez, "and my friend will square up at the station," he sez. I came on here, and when this here man opens the door,' he indicated a porter standing by, 'why, the man's dead. And that's all I knows about it.'

The statement was made directly and convincingly, and Willis frowned as he thought that such apparently simple cases proved frequently to be the most baffling in the end. In his slow, careful way he went over in his mind what he had heard, and then began to try for further details.

'At what time did you pick up the men?' he inquired.

'About half-past seven or maybe twenty to eight.'

'Did you see where they were coming from?'

'No, sir. They were standing on the kerb, and the tall one he holds up his hand for me to pull over.'

'Would you know the tall man again?'

The driver shook his head.

'I don't know as I should, sir. You see, it was raining, and he had his collar up round his neck and his hat pulled down over his eyes, so as I couldn't right see his face.'

'Describe him as best you can.'

'He was a tall man, longer than what you are, and broad too. A big man, I should call him.'

'How was he dressed?'

'He had a waterproof, khaki colour—about the colour of your own—with the collar up round his neck.'

'His hat?'

'His hat was a soft felt, dark, either brown or green, I couldn't right say, with the brim turned down in front.'

'And his face? Man alive, you must have seen his face when he gave you the shilling.'

The driver stared helplessly. Then he answered:

'I couldn't be sure about his face, not with the way he had his collar up and his hat pulled down. It was raining and blowing something crool.'

'Did the other man reply when the tall one spoke into the cab?'

'Didn't hear no reply at all, sir.'

Inspector Willis thought for a moment and then started on another tack.

'Did you hear a shot?' he asked sharply.

'I heard it, sir, right enough, but I didn't think it was a shot at the time, and I didn't think it was in my cab. It was just when we were passing the Apollo Theatre, and there was a big block of cars setting people down, and I thought it was a burst tyre. "There's somebody's tyre gone to glory," I sez to myself, but I give it no more thought, for it takes you to be awake to drive up Shaftesbury Avenue when the theatres are starting.'

'You said you didn't think the shot was in your cab; why do you think so now?'

'It was the only sound like a shot, sir, and if the man has been shot, it would have been then.'

Willis nodded shortly. There was something puzzling here. If the shot had been fired by the other occupant of the cab, as the man's evidence seemed to indicate, there would certainly have been powder blackening on the coat. If not, and if the bullet had entered from without, the other passenger would surely have stopped the car and called a policeman. Presently he saw that some corroborative evidence might exist. If the bullet came from without the left-hand window must have been down, as there was no hole in the glass. In this case the wind, which was blowing from the north-west, would infallibly have driven in the rain, and drops would still show on the cushions. He must look for them without delay.

He paused to ask the driver one more question, whether he could identify the voice which told him through the speaking tube to stop with that of the man who had given him the shilling. The man answering affirmatively, Willis turned to one of the plain clothes men.

'You have heard this driver's statement, Jones,' he said. 'You might get away at once and see the men who were on point duty both at the corner of Great Russell Street where the tall man got out, and in Piccadilly where both got in. Try the hotels thereabouts, the Albemarle and any others you can think of. If you can get any information follow it up and keep me advised at the Yard of your movements.'

The man hurried away and Willis moved over once more to the taxi. The assistant had by this time finished his flashlight photographs, and the inspector, picking up the bicycle lamp, looked again into the interior. A moment's examination showed him there were no raindrops on the cushions, but his search nevertheless was not unproductive. Looking more carefully this time than previously, he noticed on the floor of the cab a dark object almost hidden beneath the seat. He drew it out. It was a piece of thick black cloth about a yard square.

Considerably mystified he held it up by two corners, and then his puzzle became solved. In the cloth were two small holes, and round one of them the fabric was charred and bore the characteristic smell of burnt powder. It was clear what had been done. With the object doubtless of hiding the flash as well as of muffling the report, the murderer had covered his weapon with a double thickness of heavy cloth. No doubt it had admirably achieved its purpose, and Willis seized it eagerly in the hope that it might furnish him with a clue as to its owner.

He folded it and set it aside for further examination, turning back to the body. Under his direction it was lifted out, placed on an ambulance stretcher provided by the railwaymen, and taken to a disused office close by. There the clothes were removed and, while the doctors busied themselves with the remains, Willis went through the pockets and arranged their contents on one of the desks.

The clothes themselves revealed but little information. The waterproof and shoes, it is true, bore the makers' labels, but both these articles were the ready-made products of large firms, and inquiry at their premises would be unlikely to lead to any result. None of the garments bore any name or identifiable mark.

Willis then occupied himself with the contents of the pockets. Besides the gold watch and chain, bunch of keys, knife, cigarette case, loose coins and other small objects which a man such as the deceased might reasonably be expected to carry, there were two to which the inspector turned with some hope of help.

The first was a folded sheet of paper which proved to be a receipted hotel bill. It showed that a Mr Coburn and another had stayed in the Peveril Hotel in Russell Square during the previous four days. When Willis saw it he gave a grunt of satisfaction. It would doubtless offer a ready means to learn the identity of the deceased, as well possibly as of that other, in whom Willis was already even more interested. Moreover, so good a clue must be worked without delay. He called over the second plain clothes man.

'Take this bill to the Peveril, Matthews,' he ordered. 'Find out if the dead man is this Coburn, and if possible get on the track of his companion. If I don't get anything better here I shall follow you round, but keep the Yard advised of your movements in any case.'

Before the man left, Willis examined the second object. It was a pocket-book, but it proved rather disappointing. It contained two five pound Bank of England notes, nine one pound and three ten shilling Treasury notes, the return half of a third-class railway ticket from Hull to King's Cross, a Great Northern cloakroom ticket, a few visiting cards inscribed 'Mr Francis Coburn', and lastly, the photograph by Cramer of Regent Street of a pretty girl of about twenty.

Willis mentally noted the three possible clues these articles seemed to suggest; inquiries in Hull, the discovery of the girl through Messrs Cramer, and third and most important, luggage or a parcel in some Great Northern cloakroom, which on recovery might afford him help. The presence of the money also seemed important, as this showed that the motive for the murder had not been robbery.

Having made a parcel of the clothes for transport to the Yard, reduced to writing the statements of the driver and of the porter who had made the discovery, and arranged with the doctors as to the disposal of the body, Willis closed and locked the taxi, and sent it in charge of a constable to Scotland Yard. Then with the cloakroom ticket he went round to see if he could find the office which had issued it.

The rooms were all shut for the night, but an official from the stationmaster's office went round with him, and after a brief search they found the article for which the ticket was a voucher. It was a small suitcase, locked, and Willis brought it away with him, intending to open it at his leisure.

His work at the station being by this time complete, he returned to the Yard, carrying the suitcase. There, though it was growing late, he forced the lock, and sat down to examine the contents. But from them he received no help. The bag contained just the articles which a man in middle-class circum-stances would naturally carry on a week or a fortnight's trip—a suit of clothes, clean linen, toilet appliances, and such like. Nowhere could Willis find anything of interest.

Telephone messages, meanwhile, had come in from the two plain clothes men. Jones reported that he had interviewed all the constables who had been on point duty at the places in question, but without result. Nor could any of the staffs of the neighbouring hotels or restaurants assist him.

The call from the Peveril conveyed slightly more information. The manageress, so Matthews said, had been most courteous and had sent for several members of her staff in the hope that some of them might be able to answer his questions. But the sum total of the knowledge he had gained was not great. In the first place, it was evident that the deceased was Mr Coburn himself. It appeared that he was accompanied by a Miss Coburn, whom the manageress believed to be his daughter. He had been heard addressing her as Madeleine. The two had arrived in time for dinner five days previously, registering 'F. Coburn and Miss Coburn', and had left about eleven on the morning of the murder. On each of the four days of their stay they had been out a good deal, but they had left and returned at different hours, and therefore appeared not to have spent their time together. They seemed, however, on very affectionate terms. No address had been left to which letters might be forwarded, and it was not known where the two visitors had intended to go when they left. Neither the manageress nor any of the staff had seen any one resembling the tall man.

Inspector Willis was considerably disappointed by the news. He had hoped that Mr Coburn's fellow-guest would have been the murderer, and that he would have left some trace from which his identity could have been ascertained. However, the daughter's information would no doubt be valuable, and his next care must be to find her and learn her story.

She might of course save him the trouble by herself coming forward. She would be almost certain to see an account of the

murder in the papers, and even if not, her father's disappear-
ance would inevitably lead her to communicate with the police.

But Willis could not depend on this. She might, for example,
have left the previous day on a voyage, and a considerable time
might elapse before she learned of the tragedy. No; he would
have to trace her as if she herself were the assassin.

He looked at his watch and was surprised to learn that it
was after one o'clock. Nothing more could be done that night,
and with a sigh of relief he turned his steps homewards.

Next morning he was back at the Yard by eight o'clock. His
first care was to re-examine the taxi by daylight for some mark
or article left by its recent occupants. He was extraordinarily
thorough and painstaking, scrutinising every inch of the floor
and cushions, and trying the door handles and window straps
for finger marks, but without success. He then went over once
again the clothes the dead man was wearing as well as those in
the suitcase, took prints from the dead man's fingers, and began
to get things in order for the inquest. Next he saw Dr Horton,
and learned that Mr Coburn had been killed by a bullet from
an exceedingly small automatic pistol, one evidently selected
to make the minimum of noise and flash, and from which a
long carry was not required.

When the details were complete he thought it would not be
too early to call at the Peveril and begin the search for Miss
Coburn. He therefore sent for a taxi, and a few minutes later
was seated in the office of the manageress. She repeated what
Matthews had already told him, and he personally interviewed
the various servants with whom the Coburns had come in
contact. He also searched the rooms they had occupied, examined with a mirror the blotting paper on a table at which the
young lady had been seen to write, and interrogated an elderly
lady visitor with whom she had made acquaintance.

But he learnt nothing. The girl had vanished completely, and
he could see no way in which he might be able to trace her.

He sat down in the lounge and gave himself up to thought.

And then suddenly an idea flashed into his mind. He started, sat for a moment rigid, then gave a little gasp.

'Lord!' he muttered. 'But I'm a blamed idiot. How in Hades did I miss that?'

He sprang to his feet and hurried out of the lounge.

CHAPTER XIII

A PROMISING CLUE

THE consideration which had thus suddenly occurred to Inspector Willis was the extraordinary importance of the fact that the tall traveller had spoken through the tube to the driver. He marvelled how he could have overlooked its significance. To speak through a taxi tube one must hold up the mouthpiece, and that mouthpiece is usually made of vulcanite or some similar substance. What better surface, Willis thought delightedly but anxiously, could be found for recording finger-prints? If only the tall man had made the blunder of omitting to wear gloves, he would have left evidence which might hang him! And he, Willis, like the cursed imbecile that he was, had missed the point! Goodness only knew if he was not already too late. If so, he thought grimly, it was all u.p. with his career at the Yard.

He ran to the telephone. A call to the Yard advised him that the taxi driver, on being informed he was no longer required, had left with his vehicle. He rapidly rang up the man's employers, asking them to stop the cab directly they came in touch with it, then hurrying out of the hotel, he hailed a taxi and drove to the rank on which the man was stationed.

His luck was in. There were seven vehicles on the stand, and his man, having but recently arrived, had only worked up to the middle of the queue. The sweat was standing in large drops on Inspector Willis's brow as he eagerly asked had the tube been touched since leaving Scotland Yard, and his relief when he found he was still in time was overwhelming. Rather unsteadily he entered the vehicle and ordered the driver to return to the Yard.

On arrival he was not long in making his test. Sending for

his finger-print apparatus, he carefully powdered the vulcanite mouthpiece, and he could scarcely suppress a cry of satisfaction when he saw shaping themselves before his eyes three of the clearest prints he had ever had the good fortune to come across. On one side of the mouthpiece was the mark of a right thumb, and on the other those of a first and second finger.

'Lord!' he muttered to himself, 'that was a near thing. If I had missed it, I could have left the Yard for good and all. It's the first thing the Chief would have asked about.'

His delight was unbounded. Here was as perfect and definite evidence as he could have wished for. If he could find the man whose fingers fitted the marks, that would be the end of his case.

He left the courtyard intending to return to the Peveril and resume the tracing of Miss Coburn, but before he reached the door of the great building he was stopped. A gentleman had called to see him on urgent business connected with the case.

It was Merriman—Merriman almost incoherent with excitement and distress. He still carried the newspaper in his hand, and with trembling finger pointed to the paragraph which had so much upset him. Willis pulled forward a chair, invited the other to be seated, and took the paper. The paragraph was quite short, and read:

'MYSTERY OF A TAXI-CAB

'A tragedy which recalls the well-known detective novel *The Mystery of a Hansom Cab* occurred last evening in one of the most populous thoroughfares in London. It appears that about eight o'clock two men engaged a taxi in Piccadilly to take them to King's Cross. Near the Oxford Street end of Tottenham Court Road the driver was ordered to stop. One of the men alighted, bid good-night to his companion, and told the driver to proceed to King's Cross, where his friend would settle up. On reaching the station there was no sign of the friend, and a search revealed him lying dead in the taxi with a bullet wound in his heart. From papers found on the body the deceased is believed to be a Mr Francis Coburn, but his residence has not yet been ascertained.'

Inspector Willis laid down the paper and turned to his visitor.

'You are interested in the case, sir?' he inquired.

'I knew him, I think,' Merriman stammered. 'At least I know some one of the name. I—'

Willis glanced keenly at the newcomer. Here was a man who must, judging by his agitation, have been pretty closely connected with Francis Coburn. Suspicious of every one, the detective recognised that there might be more here than met the eye. He drew out his notebook.

'I am glad you called, sir,' he said pleasantly. 'We shall be very pleased to get any information you can give us. What was your friend like?'

His quiet, conversational manner calmed the other.

'Rather tall,' he answered anxiously, 'with a long, pale face, and small, black, pointed moustache.'

'I'm afraid, sir, that's the man. I think if you don't mind you had better see if you can identify him.'

'I want to,' Merriman cried, leaping to his feet. 'I must know at once.'

Willis rose also.

'Then come this way.'

They drove quickly across town. A glance was sufficient to tell Merriman that the body was indeed that of his former acquaintance. His agitation became painful.

'My God!' he cried. 'It is he! And it's my fault! Oh, if I had only done what she said! If I had only kept out of it!'

He wrung his hands in his anguish.

Willis was much interested. Though this man could not be personally guilty—he was not tall enough, for one thing—he must surely know enough about the affair to put the inspector on the right track. The latter began eagerly to await his story.

Merriman, for his part, was anxious for nothing so much as to tell it. He was sick to death of plots and investigations and machinations, and while driving to the Yard he had made up his mind that if the dead man were indeed Madeleine's father, he would tell the whole story of his and Hilliard's investigations into the doings of the syndicate. When therefore they were back in the inspector's room, he made a determined effort to pull himself together and speak calmly.

'Yes,' he said, 'I know him. He lived near Bordeaux with his daughter. She will be absolutely alone. You will understand that I must go out to her by the first train, but until then I am at your service.'

'You are a relation perhaps?'

'No, only an acquaintance, but—I'm going to tell you the whole story, and I may as well say, once for all, that it is my earnest hope some day to marry Miss Coburn.'

Willis bowed and inquired, 'Is Miss Coburn's name Madeleine?'

'Yes,' Merriman answered, surprise and eagerness growing in his face.

'Then,' Willis went on, 'you will be pleased to learn that she is not in France—at least, I think not. She left the Peveril Hotel in Russell Square about eleven o'clock yesterday morning.'

Merriman sprang to his feet.

'In London?' he queried excitedly. 'Where? What address?'

'We don't know yet, but we shall soon find her. Now, sir, you can't do anything for the moment, and I am anxious to hear your story. Take your own time, and the more details you can give me the better.'

Merriman controlled himself with an effort.

'Well,' he said slowly, sitting down again, 'I *have* something to tell you, inspector. My friend Hilliard—Claud Hilliard of the Customs Department—and I have made a discovery. We have accidentally come on what we believe is a criminal conspiracy, we don't know for what purpose, except that it is something big and fraudulent. We were coming to the Yard in any case to tell what we had learnt, but this murder has precipitated things. We can no longer delay giving our information. The only thing is that I should have liked Hilliard to be here to tell it instead of me, for our discovery is really due to him.'

'I can see Mr Hilliard afterwards. Meantime tell me the story yourself.'

Merriman thereupon related his and Hilliard's adventures and experiences from his own first accidental visit to the clearing when he noticed the changing of the lorry number, right up to his last meeting with Mr Coburn, when the latter expressed his intention of breaking away from the gang. He hid nothing, explaining without hesitation his reasons for urging the delay in informing the authorities, even though he quite realised his action made him to some extent an accomplice in the conspiracy.

Willis was much more impressed by the story than he would have admitted. Though it sounded wild and unlikely, there was a ring of truth in Merriman's manner which went far to convince the other of its accuracy. He did not believe, either, that any one could have invented such a story. Its very improbability was an argument for its truth.

And if it were true, what a vista it opened up to himself! The solution of the murder problem would be gratifying enough, but it was a mere nothing compared to the other. If he could search out and bring to naught such a conspiracy as Merriman's story indicated, he would be a made man. It would be the crowning point of his career, and would bring him measurably nearer to that cottage and garden in the country to which for years past he had been looking forward. Therefore no care and no trouble would be too great to spend on the matter.

Putting away thoughts of self, therefore, and deliberately concentrating on the matter in hand, he set himself to consider in detail what his visitor had told him and get the story clear in his mind. Then slowly and painstakingly he began to ask questions.

'I take it, Mr Merriman, that your idea is that Mr Coburn was murdered by a member of the syndicate?'

'Yes, and I think he foresaw his fate. I think when he told them he was going to break with them they feared he might betray them, and wanted to be on the safe side.'

'Any of them a tall, stoutly built man?'

'Captain Beamish is tall and strongly built, but I should not say he was stout.'

'Describe him.'

'He stooped and was a little round shouldered, and even then he was tall. If he had held himself up he would have been a big man. He had a heavy face with a big jaw, thin lips, and a vindictive expression.'

Willis, though not given to jumping to conclusions, felt suddenly a little thrilled, and he made up his mind that an early development in the case would be the taking of the impressions of Captain Beamish's right thumb and forefinger.

He asked several more questions and, going over the story again, took copious notes. Then for some time he sat in silence considering what he had heard.

At first sight he was inclined to agree with Merriman, that the deceased had met his death at the hands of a member of the syndicate, and if so, it was not unlikely that all or most of the members were party to it. From the mere possibility of this it followed that the most urgent thing for the moment was to prevent the syndicate suspecting his knowledge. He turned again to his visitor.

'I suppose you realise, Mr Merriman, that if all these details you have given me are correct, you yourself are in a position of some danger?'

'I know it, but I am not afraid. It is the possible danger to Miss Coburn that has upset me so much.'

'I understand, sir,' the inspector returned sympathetically, 'but it follows that for both your sakes you must act very cautiously, so as to disarm any suspicions these people may have of you.'

'I am quite in your hands, inspector.'

'Good. Then let us consider your course of action. Now, first of all about the inquest. It will be held this evening at five o'clock. You will have to give evidence, and we shall have to settle very carefully what that evidence will be. No breath of suspicion against the syndicate must leak out.'

Merriman nodded.

'You must identify the deceased, and, if asked, you must tell the story of your two visits to the clearing. You must speak without the slightest hesitation. But you must of course make no mention of the changing of the lorry numbers nor of your suspicions, nor will you mention your visit to Hull. You will explain that you went back to the clearing on the second occasion because it was so little out of your way and because you were anxious to meet the Coburns again, while your friend wanted to see the forests of Les Landes.'

Merriman again nodded.

'Then both you and your friend must avoid Scotland Yard. It was quite natural that you should rush off here as you did, but it would not be natural for you to return. And there is no reason why Mr Hilliard should come at all. If I want to see either of you I shall ring up and arrange a place of meeting. And just two other things. The first is that I need hardly warn you to be as circumspect in your conversation as in your evidence. Keep in mind that each stranger that you may meet may be Morton or some other member of the gang. The second is that I should like to keep in touch with you for the remainder of the day in case any question might crop up before the inquest. Where will you be?'

'I shall stay in my club, the Rover's, in Cranbourne Street. You can ring me up.'

'Good,' Willis answered, rising to his feet. 'Then let me say again how pleased I am to have met you and heard your story. Five o'clock, then, if you don't hear to the contrary.'

When Merriman had taken his leave the inspector sat on at his desk, lost in thought. This case bade fair to be the biggest he had ever handled, and he was anxious to lay his plans so as to employ his time to the best advantage. Two clearly defined lines of inquiry had already opened out, and he was not clear which to follow. In the first place, there was the obvious routine investigation suggested directly by the murder. That comprised the finding of Miss Coburn, the learning of Mr Coburn's life history, the tracing of his movements during the last four or five days, the finding of the purchaser of the black cloth, and the following up of clues discovered during these inquiries. The second line was that connected with the activities of the syndicate, and Willis was inclined to believe that a complete understanding of these would automatically solve the problem of the murder. He was wondering whether he should not start an assistant on the routine business of the tragedy, whilst himself concentrating on the pit-prop business, when his cogitations were brought to an end by a messenger. A lady had called in connection with the case.

'Miss Madeleine Coburn,' thought Willis, as he gave orders for her to be shown to his room, and when she entered he instantly recognised the original of the photograph.

Madeleine's face was dead white and there was a strained look of horror in her eyes, but she was perfectly calm and self-possessed.

'Miss Coburn?' Willis said, as he rose and bowed. 'I am afraid I can guess why you have called. You saw the account in the paper?'

'Yes.' She hesitated. 'Is it—my father?'

Willis told her as gently as he could. She sat quite still for a few moments, while he busied himself with some papers, then she asked to see the body. When they had returned to Willis's room he invited her to sit down again.

'I very deeply regret, Miss Coburn,' he said, 'to have to trouble you at this time with questions, but I fear you will have to give evidence at the inquest this afternoon, and it will be easier for yourself to make a statement now, so that only what is absolutely necessary need be asked you then.'

Madeleine seemed stunned by the tragedy, and she spoke as if in a dream.

'I am ready to do what is necessary.'

He thanked her, and began by inquiring about her father's history. Mr Coburn, it appeared, had had a public school and college training, but, his father dying when he was just twenty, and leaving the family in somewhat poor circumstances, he had gone into business as a clerk in the Hopwood Manufacturing Company, a large engineering works in the Midlands. In this he had risen until he held the important position of cashier, and he and his wife and daughter had lived in happiness and comfort during the latter's girlhood. But some six years previous to the tragedy which had just taken place a change had come over the household. In the first place, Mrs Coburn had developed a painful illness and had dragged out a miserable existence for the three years before her death. At the same time, whether from the expense of the illness or from other causes Miss Coburn did not know, financial embarrassment seemed to descend on her father. One by one their small luxuries were cut off, then their house had to be given up, and they had moved to rooms in a rather poor locality of the town. Their crowning misfortune followed rapidly. Mr Coburn gave up his position at the works, and for a time actual want stared them in the face. Then this Pit-Prop Syndicate had been formed, and Mr Coburn had gone into it as the manager of the loading station. Miss Coburn did not know the reason of his leaving the engineering works, but she suspected there had been friction, as his disposition for a time had changed, and he had lost his bright manner and vivacity. He had, however, to a large extent recovered while in France. She was not aware, either, of the terms on which he had entered the syndicate, but she imagined he shared in the profits instead of receiving a salary.

These facts, which Willis obtained by astute questioning, seemed to him not a little suggestive. From what Mr Coburn had himself told Merriman, it looked as if there had been some secret in his life which had placed him in the power of the syndicate, and the inspector wondered whether this might not be connected with his leaving the engineering works. At all events inquiries there seemed to suggest a new line of attack, should such become necessary.

Willis then turned to the events of the past few days. It appeared that about a fortnight earlier, Mr Coburn announced that he was crossing to London for the annual meeting of the syndicate, and, as he did not wish his daughter to be alone at the clearing, it was arranged that she should accompany him. They travelled by the *Girondin* to Hull, and coming on to London, put up at the Peveril. Mr Coburn had been occupied off and on during the four days they had remained there, but the evenings they had spent together in amusements. On the night of the murder, Mr Coburn was to have left for Hull to return to France by the *Girondin*, his daughter going by an earlier train to Eastbourne, where she was to have spent ten days with an aunt. Except for what Mr Coburn had said about the meeting of the syndicate, Madeleine did not know anything of his business in town, nor had she seen any member of the syndicate after leaving the ship.

Having taken notes of her statements, Willis spoke of the inquest and repeated the instructions he had given Merriman as to the evidence. Then he told her of the young man's visit, and referring to his anxiety on her behalf, asked if he might acquaint him of her whereabouts. She thankfully acquiesced, and Willis, who was anxious that her mind should be kept occupied until the inquest, pushed his good offices to the extent of arranging a meeting between the two.

The inquest elicited no further information. Formal evidence of identification was given, the doctors deposed that death was due to a bullet from an exceedingly small bore automatic pistol, the cab driver and porter told their stories, and the jury returned the obvious verdict of murder against some person or persons unknown. The inspector's precautions were observed, and not a word was uttered which could have given a hint to any member of the Pit-Prop Syndicate that the *bona fides* of his organisation was suspected.

Two days later, when the funeral was over, Merriman took Miss Coburn back to her aunt's at Eastbourne. No word of love passed his lips, but the young girl seemed pleased to have his company, and before parting from her he obtained permission to call on her again. He met the aunt for a few moments, and was somewhat comforted to find her a kind, motherly woman, who was evidently sincerely attached to the now fatherless girl. He had told Madeleine of his interview with her father, and she had not blamed him for his part in the matter, saying that she had believed for some time that a development of the kind was inevitable.

So, for them, the days began to creep wearily past. Merriman paid as frequent visits to Eastbourne as he dared, and little by little he began to hope that he was making progress in his suit. But try as he would, he could not bring the matter to a head. The girl had evidently had a more severe shock than they had realised at first, and she became listless and difficult to interest in passing events. He saw there was nothing for it but to wait, and he set himself to bide his time with the best patience he could muster.

CHAPTER XIV

A MYSTIFYING DISCOVERY

INSPECTOR WILLIS was more than interested in his new case. The more he thought over it, the more he realised its dramatic possibilities and the almost worldwide public interest it was likely to arouse, as well as the importance which his superiors would certainly attach to it; in other words, the influence a successful handling of it would have on his career.

He had not been idle since the day of the inquest, now a week past. To begin with he had seen Hilliard secretly, and learned at first hand all that that young man could tell him. Next he had made sure that the finger-prints found on the speaking tube were not those of Mr Coburn, and he remained keenly anxious to obtain impressions from Captain Beamish's fingers to compare with the former. But inquiries from the port officials at Hull, made by wire on the evening of the inquest, showed that the *Girondin* would not be back at Ferriby for eight days. There had been no object, therefore, in his leaving London immediately, and instead he had busied himself by trying to follow up the deceased's movements in the metropolis, and learn with whom he had associated during his stay. In his search for clues he had even taken the hint from Merriman's newspaper and bought a copy of *The Mystery of a Hansom Cab*, but though he saw that this clever story might easily have inspired the crime, he could find from it no help towards its solution.

He had also paid a flying visit to the manager of the Hopwood Manufacturing Company in Sheffield, where Coburn had been employed. From him he had learnt that Madeleine's surmise was correct, and that there had been 'friction' before her father left. In point of fact a surprise audit had revealed discrepancies in the accounts. Some money was missing, and what was suspiciously like an attempt to falsify the books had taken place. But the thing could not be proved. Mr Coburn had paid up, but though his plea that he had made a genuine clerical error had been accepted, his place had been filled. The manager expressed the private opinion that there was no doubt of his subordinate's guilt, saying also that it was well known that during the previous months Coburn had been losing money heavily through gambling. Where he had obtained the money to meet the deficit the manager did not know, but he believed some one must have come forward to assist him.

This information interested Willis keenly, supporting, as it seemed to do, his idea that Coburn was in the power of the syndicate or one of its members. If, for example, one of these men, on the lookout for helpers in his conspiracy, had learned of the cashier's predicament, it was conceivable that he might have obtained his hold by advancing the money needed to square the matter in return for a signed confession of guilt. This was of course the merest guesswork, but it at least indicated to Willis a fresh line of inquiry in case his present investigation failed.

And with the latter he was becoming exceedingly disappointed. With the exception of the facts just mentioned, he had learned absolutely nothing to help him. Mr Coburn might as well have vanished into thin air when he left the Peveril Hotel, for all the trace he had left. Willis could learn neither where he went nor whom he met on any one of the four days he had spent in London. He congratulated himself, therefore, that on the following day the *Girondin* would be back at Ferriby, and he would then be able to start work on the finger-print clue.

That evening he settled himself with his pipe to think over once more the facts he had already learnt. As time passed he found himself approaching more and more to the conclusion reached by Hilliard and Merriman several weeks before—that the secret of the syndicate was the essential feature of the case. What were these people doing? That was the question which at all costs he must answer.

His mind reverted to the two theories already in the field. At first sight that of brandy smuggling seemed tenable enough, and he turned his attention to the steps by which the two young men had tried to test it. At the loading end their observations were admittedly worthless, but at Ferriby they seemed to have made a satisfactory investigation. Unless they had unknowingly fallen asleep in the barrel, it was hard to see how they could have failed to observe contraband being set ashore, had such been unloaded. But he did not believe they had fallen asleep. People were usually conscious of awakening. Besides there was the testimony of Menzies, the pilot. It was hardly conceivable that this man also should have been deceived. At the same time Willis decided he must interview him, so as to form his own opinion of the man's reliability.

Another possibility occurred to him which none of the amateur investigators appeared to have thought of. North Sea trawlers were frequently used for getting contraband ashore. Was the *Girondin* transferring illicit cargo to such vessels while at sea?

This was a question Inspector Willis felt he could not solve. It would be a matter for the Customs Department. But he knew enough about it to understand that immense difficulties would have to be overcome before such a scheme could be worked. Firstly, there was the size of the fraud. Six months ago, according to what Miss Coburn overheard, the syndicate were making £6800 per trip, and probably, from the remarks then made, they were doing more today. And £6800 meant—the inspector buried himself in calculations—at least one thousand gallons of brandy. Was it conceivable that trawlers could get rid of one thousand gallons every ten days—one hundred gallons a day? Frankly he thought it impossible. In fact, in the face of the Customs officers activities, he doubted if such a thing could be done by any kind of machinery that could be devised. Indeed, the more Willis pondered the smuggling theory, the less likely it seemed to him, and he turned to consider the possibilities of Miss Coburn's suggestion of false note printing.

Here at once he was met by a fact which he had not mentioned to Merriman. As it happened, the circulation of spurious Treasury notes was one of *the* subjects of interest to Scotland Yard at the moment. Notes *were* being forged and circulated, and in large numbers. Furthermore, the source of supply was believed to be some of the large towns of the Midlands, Leeds being particularly suspected. But Leeds was on the direct line through Ferriby, and comparatively not far away. Willis felt that it was up to him to explore to the uttermost limit all the possibilities which these facts opened up.

He began by looking at the matter from the conspirators' point of view. Supposing they had overcome the difficulty of producing the notes, how would they dispose of them?

Willis could appreciate the idea of locating the illicit press in France. Firstly, it would be obvious to the gang that the early discovery of a fraud of the kind was inevitable. Its existence, indeed, would soon become common property. But this would but slightly affect its success. It was the finding of the source of supply that mattered, and the difficulty of this was at once the embarrassment of the authorities and the opportunity of the conspirators.

Secondly, English notes were to be forged and circulated in England, therefore it was from the English police that the source of supply must be hidden. And how better could this be done than by taking it out of England altogether? The English police would look in England for what they wanted. The attention of the French police, having no false French notes to deal with, would not be aroused. It seemed to Willis that so far he was on firm ground.

The third point was that, granting the first two, some agency would be required to convey the forged notes from France to

England. But here a difficulty arose. The pit-prop plan seemed altogether too elaborate and cumbrous for all that was required. Willis, as Merriman had done earlier, pictured the passenger with the padded overcoat and the double-bottomed handbag. This traveller, it seemed, would meet the case.

But did he? Would there not, with him, be a certain risk? There would be continuous passing through Customs houses, frequent searchings of the faked suitcase. Accidents happened. Suppose the traveller held on to his suitcase too carefully? Some sharp-eyed Customs officer might become suspicious. Suppose he didn't hold on carefully enough and it were lost? Yes, there would be risks. Small, doubtless, but still risks. And the gang couldn't afford them.

As Willis turned the matter over in his mind, he came gradually to the conclusion that the elaboration of the pit-prop business was no real argument against its having been designed merely to carry forged notes. As a business, moreover, it would pay or almost pay. It would furnish a secret method of getting the notes across at little or no cost. And as a blind, Willis felt that nothing better could be devised.

The scheme visualised itself to him as follows: Somewhere in France, probably in some cellar in Bordeaux, was installed the illicit printing-press. There the notes were produced. By some secret method they were conveyed to Henri when his lorry driving took him into the city, and he in turn brought them to the clearing and handed them over to Coburn. Captain Beamish and Bulla would then take charge of them, probably hiding them on the *Girondin* in some place which would defy a surprise Customs examination. Numbers of such places, Willis felt sure, could be arranged, especially in the engine room. The cylinders of a duplicate set of pumps, disused on that particular trip, occurred to him as an example. After arrival at Ferriby there would be ample opportunity for the notes to be taken ashore and handed over to Archer, and Archer 'could plant stuff on Old Nick himself.'

The more he pondered over it, the more tenable this theory seemed to Inspector Willis. He rose and began pacing the room, frowning heavily. More than tenable, it seemed a sound scheme cleverly devised and carefully worked out. Indeed he could think of no means so likely to mislead and delude suspicious authorities in their search for the criminals as this very plan.

Two points, however, think as he might, he could not reconcile. One was that exasperating puzzle of the changing of the lorry number plates, the other how the running of a second boat to Swansea would increase the profits of the syndicate.

But everything comes to him who waits, and at last he got an idea. What if the number of the lorry was an indication to the printers of the notes as to whether Henri was or was not in a position to take over a consignment? Would some such sign not be necessary? If Henri suspected he was under observation, or if he had to make calls in unsuitable places, he would require a secret method of passing on the information to his accomplices. And if so, could a better scheme be devised than that of showing a prearranged number on his lorry? Willis did not think so, and he accepted the theory for what it was worth.

Encouraged by his progress, he next tackled his second difficulty—how the running of a second boat would dispose of more notes. But try as he would he could arrive at no conclusion which would explain the point. It depended obviously on the method of distribution adopted, and of this part of the affair he was entirely ignorant. Failure to account for this did not therefore necessarily invalidate the theory as a whole.

And with the theory as a whole he was immensely pleased. As far as he could see it fitted all the known facts, and bore the stamp of probability to an even greater degree than that of brandy smuggling.

But theories were not enough. He must get ahead with his investigation.

Accordingly next morning he began his new inquiry by sending a telegram.

'To BEAMISH, Landes Pit-Prop Syndicate, Ferriby, Hull.
'Could you meet me off London train at Paragon Station
at 3.09 tomorrow re death of Coburn. I should like to get
back by 4.00. If not would stay and go out to Ferriby.

'WILLIS,
'Scotland Yard.'

He travelled that same day to Hull, having arranged for the
reply to be sent after him. Going to the first-class refreshment
room at Paragon, he had a conversation with the barmaid in
which he disclosed his official position and passed over a ten
shilling note in account for services about to be rendered. Then,
leaving by the evening train, he returned to Doncaster, where
he spent the night.

On the next day he boarded the London train which reaches
Hull at 3.09. At Paragon Station he soon singled out Beamish
from Merriman's description.

'Sorry for asking you to come in, Captain Beamish,' he apologised, 'but I was anxious if possible to get back to London
tonight. I heard of you from Miss Coburn and Mr Merriman,
both of whom read of the tragedy in the papers, and severally
came to make inquiries at the Yard. Lloyd's Register told me
your ship came in here, so I came along to see you in the hope
that you might be able to give me some information about the
dead man which might suggest a line of inquiry as to his
murderer.'

Beamish replied politely and with a show of readiness and
candour.

'No trouble to meet you, inspector. I had to come up to Hull
in any case, and I shall be glad to tell you anything I can about
poor Coburn. Unfortunately I am afraid it won't be much. When
our syndicate was starting we wanted a manager for the export
end. Coburn applied, there was a personal interview, he seemed
suitable and he was appointed on trial. I know nothing whatever
about him otherwise, except that he made good, and I may say

that in the two years of our acquaintance I always found him not only pleasant and agreeable to deal with, but also exceedingly efficient in his work.'

Willis asked a number of other questions—harmless questions, easily answered—about the syndicate and Coburn's work, ending up with an expression of thanks for the other's trouble and an invitation to adjourn for a drink.

Beamish accepting, the inspector led the way to the first-class refreshment room and approached the counter opposite the barmaid whose acquaintance he had made the previous day.

'Two small whiskies, please,' he ordered, having asked his companion's choice.

The girl placed the two small tumblers of yellow liquid before her customers and Willis added a little water to each.

'Well, here's yours,' he said, and raising his glass to his lips, drained the contents at a draught. Captain Beamish did the same.

The inspector's offer of a second drink having been declined, the two men left the refreshment room, still chatting about the murdered man. Ten minutes later Captain Beamish saw the inspector off in the London train. But he did not know that in the van of that train there was a parcel, labelled to 'Inspector Willis, passenger to Doncaster by 4.00 p.m.', which contained a small tumbler, smelling of whisky, and carefully packed so as to prevent the sides from being rubbed.

The inspector was the next thing to excited when, some time later, he locked the door of his bedroom in the Stag's Head Hotel at Doncaster and, carefully unpacking the tumbler, he took out his powdering apparatus and examined it for prints. With satisfaction he found his little ruse had succeeded. The glass bore clearly defined marks of a right thumb and two fingers.

Eagerly he compared the prints with those he had found on the taxi call-tube. And then he suffered disappointment keen and deep. The two sets were dissimilar.

So his theory had been wrong, and Captain Beamish was not the murderer after all! He realised now that he had been much more convinced of its truth than he had had any right to be, and his chagrin was correspondingly greater. He had indeed been so sure that Beamish was his man that he had failed sufficiently to consider other possibilities, and now he found himself without any alternate theory to fall back on.

But he remained none the less certain that Coburn's death was due to his effort to break with the syndicate, and that it was to the syndicate that he must look for light on the matter. There were other members of it—he knew of two, Archer and Morton, and there might be more—one of whom might be the man he sought. It seemed to him that his next business must be to find those other members, ascertain if any of them were tall men and, if so, obtain a copy of their finger-prints.

But how was this to be done? Obviously from the shadowing of the members whom he knew, that was, Captain Beamish, Bulla, and Benson, the Ferriby manager. Of these, Beamish and Bulla were for the most part at sea; therefore, he thought, his efforts should be concentrated on Benson.

It was with a view to some such contingency that he had alighted at Doncaster instead of returning to London, and he now made up his mind to return on the following day to Hull and, the *Girondin* having by that time left, to see what he could learn at the Ferriby depot.

He spent three days shadowing Benson, without coming on anything in the slightest degree suspicious. The manager spent each of the days at the wharf until about six o'clock. Then he walked to Ferriby Station and took the train to Hull, where he dined, spent the evening at some place of amusement, and returned to the depot by a late train.

On the fourth day, as the same programme seemed to be in progress, Willis came to the conclusion that he was losing time and must take some more energetic step. He determined that if Benson left the depot in the evening as before, he would try to effect an entrance to his office and have a look through his papers.

Shortly after six, from the hedge behind which he had concealed himself, he saw Benson appear at the door in the corrugated iron fence, and depart in the direction of Ferriby. The five employees had left about an hour earlier, and the inspector believed the works were entirely deserted.

After giving Benson time to get clear away, he crept from his hiding place, and approaching the depot, tried the gate in the fence. It was locked, but few locks were proof against the inspector's prowess, and with the help of a bent wire he was soon within the enclosure. He closed the gate behind him, and glancing carefully round, approached the shed.

The door to the office was also locked, but the bent wire conquered it too, and in a couple of minutes he pushed it open, passed through, and closed it behind him.

The room was small, finished with yellow match-boarded walls and ceiling, and containing a closed roll top desk, a table littered with papers, a vertical file, two cupboards, a telephone, and other simple office requisites. Two doors led out of it, one to the manager's bedroom, the other to the shed. Thinking that these could wait, Willis settled down to make an examination of the office.

He ran rapidly though methodically through the papers on the table without finding anything of interest. All referred to the pit-prop industry, and seemed to indicate that the business was carried on efficiently. Next he tackled the desk, picking the lock with his usual skill. Here also, though he examined everything with meticulous care, his search was fruitless.

He moved to the cupboards. One was unfastened and contained old ledgers, account books and the like, none being of any interest. The other cupboard was locked, and Willis's quick eyes saw that the woodwork round the keyhole was much scratched, showing that the lock was frequently used. Again the wire was brought into requisition, and in a moment the door swung open, revealing to the inspector's astonished gaze—a telephone.

Considerably puzzled, he looked round to the wall next the door. Yes, he had not been mistaken; there also was affixed a telephone. He crossed over to it, and following with his eye the run of the wires, saw that it was connected to those which approached the shed from across the railway.

With what, then, did this second instrument communicate? There were no other wires approaching the shed, nor could he find any connection to which it could be attached.

He examined the instrument more closely, and then he saw that it was not of the standard government pattern. It was marked 'The A.M. Curtiss Co., Philadelphia, Pa.' It was therefore part of a private installation and, as such, illegal, as the British Government hold the monopoly for all telephones in the country. At least it would be illegal if it were connected up.

But was it? The wires passed through the back of the cupboard into the wall, and, looking down, Willis saw that one of the wall sheeting boards, reaching from the cupboard to the floor, had at some time been taken out and replaced with screws.

To satisfy his curiosity he took out his combination pocket knife, and deftly removing the screws, pulled the board forward. His surprise was not lessened when he saw that the wires ran down inside the wall and, heavily insulated, disappeared into the ground beneath the shed.

'Is it possible that they have a cable?' thought the puzzled man, as he replaced the loose board and screwed it fast.

The problem had to stand over, as he wished to complete his investigation of the remainder of the building. But though he searched the entire premises with the same meticulous thoroughness that he had displayed in dealing with the papers, he came on nothing else which in any way excited his interest.

He let himself out and, relocking the various doors behind him, walked to Hessle and from there returned to his hotel in Hull.

He was a good deal intrigued by his discovery of the secret

telephone. That it was connected up and frequently used he was certain, both from the elaboration of its construction and from the marking round the cupboard keyhole. He wondered if he could without discovery tap the wires and overhear the business discussed. Had the wires been carried on poles the matter would have been simple, but as things were he would have to make his connection under the loose board, and carry his cable out through the wall and along the shore to some point at which the receiver would be hidden—by no means an easy matter.

But in default of something better he would have tried it, had not a second discovery he made later on the same evening turned his thoughts into an entirely new channel.

It was in thinking over the probable purpose of the telephone that he got his idea. It seemed obvious that it was used for the secret side of the enterprise, and if so, would it not most probably connect the import depot of the secret commodity with that of its distribution? Ferriby wharf was the place of import, but the distribution, as the conversations overheard indicated, lay not in the hands of Benson but of Archer. What if the telephone led to Archer?

There was another point. The difficulty of laying a secret land wire would be so enormous that in the nature of things the line must be short. It must either lead, Willis imagined, to the southern bank of the estuary or to somewhere quite near.

But if both these conclusions were sound, it followed that Archer himself must be found in the immediate neighbourhood. Could he learn anything from following up this idea?

He borrowed a directory of Hull and began looking up all the Archers given in the alphabetical index. There were fifteen, and of these one immediately attracted his attention. It read:

'Archer, Archibald Charles, The Elms, Ferriby.'

He glanced at his watch. It was still but slightly after ten. Taking his hat he walked to the police station and saw the sergeant on duty.

'Yes, sir,' said the man in answer to his inquiry. 'I know the gentleman. He is the managing director of Ackroyd and Holt's distillery, about half-way between Ferriby and Hessle.'

'And what is he like in appearance?' Willis continued, concealing the interest this statement had aroused.

'A big man, sir,' the sergeant answered. 'Tall, and broad too. Clean shaven, with heavy features, very determined looking.'

Willis had food for thought as he returned to his hotel. Merriman had been thrilled when he learnt of the proximity of the distillery to the syndicate's depot, seeing therein an argument in favour of the brandy smuggling theory. This new discovery led Willis at first to take the same view, but the considerations which Hilliard had pointed out occurred to him also, and though he felt a little puzzled, he was inclined to dismiss the matter as a coincidence.

Though after his recent experience he was even more averse to jumping to conclusions than formerly, Willis could not but believe that he was at last on a hopeful scent. At all events his first duty was clear. He must find this Archibald Charles Archer, and obtain prints of his fingers.

Next morning found him again at Ferriby, once more looking southwards from the concealment of a cluster of bushes. But this time the object of his attention was no longer the syndicate's depot. Instead he focussed his powerful glasses on the office door of the distillery.

About nine-thirty a tall, stoutly built man strode up to the building and entered. His dress indicated that he was of the employer class, and from the way in which a couple of workmen touched their caps as he passed, Willis had no doubt he was the managing director.

For some three hours the inspector lay hidden, then he suddenly observed the tall man emerge from the building and walk rapidly in the direction of Ferriby. Immediately the inspector crept down the hedge nearer to the road, so as to see his quarry pass at closer quarters.

It happened that as the man came abreast of Willis, a small two seater motor-car coming from the direction of Ferriby also reached the same spot. But instead of passing, it slowed down and its occupant hailed the tall man.

'Hallo, Archer,' he shouted. 'Can I give you a lift?'

'Thanks,' the big man answered. 'It would be a kindness. I have unexpectedly to go into Hull, and my own car is out of order.'

'Run you in in a quarter of an hour.'

'No hurry. If I am in by half-past one it will do. I am lunching with Frazer at the Criterion at that time.'

The two seater stopped, the big man entered, and the vehicle moved rapidly away.

As soon as it was out of sight, Willis emerged from his hiding-place, and hurrying to the station, caught the 1.17 train to Hull. Twenty minutes later he passed through the swing doors of the Criterion.

The hotel, as is well known, is one of the most fashionable in Hull, and at the luncheon hour the restaurant was well filled. Glancing casually round, Willis could see his new acquaintance seated at a table in the window, in close conversation with a florid, red-haired individual of the successful business man type.

All the tables in the immediate vicinity were occupied, and Willis could not get close by in the hope of overhearing some of the conversation, as he had intended. He therefore watched the others from a distance, and when they moved to the lounge he followed them.

He heard them order coffee and liqueurs, and then a sudden idea came into his head. Rising he followed the waiter through the service door.

'I want a small job done,' he said, while a ten shilling note changed hands. 'I am from Scotland Yard, and I want the finger-prints of the men who have just ordered coffee. Polish the outsides of the liqueur glasses thoroughly, and only lift them by the stems. Then when the men have gone let me have the glasses.'

He returned to the lounge, and presently had the satisfaction of seeing Archer lift his glass by the bowl between the fingers and thumb of his right hand, to empty the liqueur into his coffee. Half an hour later he was back in his hotel with the carefully packed glass.

A very few minutes sufficed for the test. The impressions showed up well, and this time the inspector gave a sigh of relief as he compared them with those of the taxi speaking-tube. They were the same. His quest was finished. Archer was the murderer of Francis Coburn.

For a minute or two, in his satisfaction, the inspector believed his work was done. He had only to arrest Archer, take official prints of his fingers, and he had all the necessary proof for a conviction. But a moment's consideration showed him that his labours were very far indeed from being over. What he had accomplished was only a part of the task he had set himself. It was a good deal more than likely that the other members of the syndicate were confederates in the murder as well as in the illicit trade. He must get his hands on them too.

But if he arrested Archer he would thereby destroy all chance of accomplishing the greater feat. The very essence of success lay in lulling to rest any doubts that their operations were suspect which might have entered into the minds of the members of the syndicate. No, he would do nothing at present, and he once more felt himself up against the question which had baffled Hilliard and Merriman—What was the syndicate doing? Until he had answered this, therefore, he could not rest.

And how was it to be done? After some thought he came to the conclusion that his most promising clue was the secret telephone, and he made up his mind that next day he would try to find its other end, and if necessary tap the wires and listen in to any conversation which might take place.

CHAPTER XV

INSPECTOR WILLIS LISTENS IN

INSPECTOR WILLIS was a good deal exercised by the question of whether or not he should have Archer shadowed. If the managing director conceived the slightest suspicion of his danger he would undoubtedly disappear, and a man of his ability would not be likely to leave many traces. On the other hand Willis wondered whether even Scotland Yard men could shadow him sufficiently continuously to be a real safeguard, without giving themselves away. And if that happened he might indeed arrest Archer, but it would be good-bye to any chance of getting his confederates.

After anxious thought he decided to take the lesser risk. He would not bring assistants into the matter, but would trust to his own skill to carry on the investigation unnoticed by the distiller.

Though the discovery of Archer's identity seemed greatly to strengthen the probability that the secret telephone led to him, Willis could not state this positively, and he felt it was the next point to be ascertained. The same argument that he had used before seemed to apply—that owing to the difficulty of the wiring, the point of connection must be close to the depot. Archer's office was not more than three hundred yards away, while his house, The Elms, was over a mile. The chances were therefore in favour of the former.

It followed that he must begin by searching Archer's office for the other receiver, and he turned his attention to the problem of how this could best be done.

And first, as to the lie of the offices. He called at the Electric Generating Station, and having introduced himself confidentially to the manager in his official capacity, asked to see the man whose business it was to inspect the lights at the distillery. From him he had no difficulty in obtaining a rough plan of the place.

It appeared that the offices were on the first floor, fronting along the lane, Archer's private office occupying the end of the suite and the corner of the building nearest to the syndicate's wharf, and therefore to Ferriby. The supervisor believed that it had two windows looking to the front and side respectively, but was not sure.

That afternoon Inspector Willis returned to the distillery, and secreting himself in the same hiding-place as before, watched until the staff had left the building. Then strolling casually along the lane, he observed that the two telephone wires which approached across the fields led to the third window from the Ferriby end of the first floor row.

'That'll be the main office,' he said to himself, 'but there will probably be an extension to Archer's own room. Now I wonder—'

He looked about him. The hedge bounding the river side of the lane ran up to the corner of the building. After another hasty glance round Willis squeezed through and from immediately below scrutinised the side window of the managing director's room. And then he saw something which made him chuckle with pleasure.

Within a few inches of the architrave of the window there was a downspout, and from the top of the window to the spout he saw stretching what looked like a double cord. It was painted the same colour as the walls, and had he not been looking out specially he would not have seen it. A moment's glance at the foot of the spout showed him his surmise was correct. Pushed in behind it and normally concealed by it were two insulated wires, which ran down the wall from the window and disappeared into the ground with the spout.

'Got it first shot,' thought the inspector delightedly, as he moved away so as not to attract the attention of any chance onlooker.

Another idea suddenly occurred to him and, after estimating the height and position of the window, he turned and ran his eye once more over his surroundings. About fifty yards from the distillery, and behind the hedge fronting the lane, stood the cottage which Hilliard and Merriman had noticed. It was in a bad state of repair, having evidently been unoccupied for a long time. In the gable directly opposite the managing director's office was a broken window. Willis moved round behind the house, and once again producing his bent wire, in a few moments had the back door open. Slipping inside, he passed through the damp smelling rooms and up the decaying staircase until he reached the broken window. From it, as he had hoped, he found he had a good view into the office.

He glanced at his watch. It was ten minutes past seven.

'I'll do it tonight,' he murmured, and quietly leaving the house, he hurried to Ferriby Station and so to Hull.

Some five hours later he left the city again, this time by motor. He stopped at the end of the lane which ran past the distillery, dismissed the vehicle, and passed down the lane. He was carrying a light, folding ladder, a spade, a field telephone, a coil of insulated wire and some small tools.

The night was very dark. The crescent moon would not rise for another couple of hours, and a thick pall of cloud cut off all light from the stars. A faint wind stirred the branches of the few trees in the neighbourhood and sighed gently across the wide spaces of open country. The inspector walked slowly, being barely able to see against the sky the tops of the hedges which bounded the lane. Except for himself no living creature seemed to be abroad.

Arrived at his destination, Willis felt his way to the gap in the hedge which he had used before, passed through, and with infinite care raised his ladder to the window of Archer's office. He could not see the window, but he checked the position of the ladder by measurements from the hedge. Then he slowly ascended.

He found he had gauged his situation correctly, and he was soon on the sill of the window, trying with his knife to push back the hasp. This he presently accomplished, and then, after an effort so great that he thought he would be beaten, he succeeded in raising the sash. A minute later he was in the room.

His first care was to pull down the thick blinds of blue holland with which the windows were fitted. Then tiptoeing to the door, he noiselessly shot the bolt in the lock.

Having thus provided against surprise, he began his investigation. There in the top corner of the side window were the wires. They followed the mitre of the window architrave—white enamelled to match—and then, passing down for a few inches at the outside of the mouldings, ran along the picture rail round the room, concealed in the groove behind it. Following in the same way the mitre of the architrave, they disappeared through a door in the back wall of the office.

Willis softly opened the door, which was not locked, and peered into a small store, evidently used for filing. The wires were carried down the back of the architrave moulding and along the top of the wainscoting, until finally they disappeared into the side of one of a series of cupboards which lined the wall opposite the door. The cupboard was locked, but with the help of the bent wire it soon stood open and Willis, flashing in a beam from his electric torch, saw with satisfaction that he had attained at least one of his objects. A telephone receiver similar to that at the syndicate's depot was within.

He examined the remaining contents of the room, but found nothing of interest until he came to the door. This was solidly made and edged with rubber, and he felt sure that it would be almost completely sound proof. It was, moreover, furnished with a well-oiled lock.

'Pretty complete arrangement,' Willis thought as he turned back to the outer office. Here he conducted another of his meticulous examinations, but unfortunately with a negative result.

Having silently unlocked the door and pulled up the blinds, he climbed out on the window sill and closed the window. He was unable to refasten the hasp, and had therefore to leave this evidence of his visit, though he hoped and believed it would not be noticed.

Lifting down the ladder, he carried it to the cottage and hid it therein. Part of his task was done, and he must wait for daylight to complete the remainder.

When some three hours later the coming dawn had made objects visible, he again emerged armed with his tools and coil of insulated wire. Digging a hole at the bottom of the down pipe, he connected his wires just below ground level to those of the telephone. Then inserting his spade along the face of the wall from the pipe to the hedge, he pushed back the adjoining soil, placed the wires in the narrow trench thus made, and trod the earth back into place. When the hole at the downspout had been filled, practically no trace remained of the disturbance.

The ground along the inside of the hedge being thickly grown over with weeds and grass, he did not think it necessary to dig a trench for the wire, simply bedding it beneath the foliage. But he made a spade cut across the sward from the hedge to the cottage door, sank in the wire, and trod out the cut. Once he had passed the tiny cable beneath the front door he no longer troubled to hide it, but laid it across the floors and up the stairs to the broken window. There he attached the field receiver, affixing it to his ear so as to be ready for eventualities.

It was by this time half-past six and broad daylight, but Willis had seen no sign of life and he believed his actions had been unobserved. He ate a few sandwiches, then lighting his pipe, he lay down on the floor and smoked contentedly.

His case at last was beginning to prosper. The finding of Coburn's murderer was of course an event of outstanding importance, and now this discovery of the telephone was not only valuable for its own sake, but was likely to bring in a rich harvest of information from the messages he hoped to intercept. Indeed he believed he could hardly fail to obtain from this source a definite indication of the nature and scope of the conspiracy.

About eight o'clock he could see from his window a number of workmen arrive at the distillery, followed an hour later by the clerical staff. After them came Archer, passing from his car to the building with his purposeful stride. Almost immediately he appeared in his office, sat down at his desk, and began to work.

Until nearly midday Willis watched him going through papers, dictating letters, and receiving subordinates. Then about two minutes to the hour he saw him look at his watch, rise, and approach the door from the other office, which was in Willis's line of vision behind the desk. He stooped over the lock as if turning the key, and then the watcher's excitement rose as the other disappeared out of sight in the direction of the filing room.

Willis was not disappointed. Almost immediately he heard the faint call of the tiny buzzer, and then a voice—Archer's voice, he believed, from what he had heard in the hotel lounge—called softly, 'Are you there?'

There was an immediate answer. Willis had never heard Benson speak, but he presumed that the reply must be from him.

'Anything to report?' Archer queried.

'No. Everything going on as usual.'

'No strangers poking round and asking questions?'

'No.'

'And no traces of a visitor while you were away?'

'None.'

'Good. It's probably a false alarm. Beamish may have been mistaken.'

'I hope so, but he seemed very suspicious of that Scotland Yard man—said he was sure he was out for more than he pretended. He thought he was too easily satisfied with the information he got, and that some of his questions were too foolish to be genuine.'

Inspector Willis sat up sharply. This was a blow to his dignity, and he felt not a little scandalised. But he had no time to consider his feelings. Archer was speaking again.

'I think we had better be on the safe side. If you have the slightest suspicion don't wait to report to me. Wire at once to Henri at the clearing this message—take it down so that there'll be no mistake—"Six hundred four-foot props wanted. If possible send next cargo." Got that? He will understand. It is our code for "Suspect danger. Send blank cargoes until further notice." Then if a search is made nothing will be found, because there won't be anything there to find.'

'Very good. It's a pity to lose the money, but I expect you're right.'

'We can't take avoidable risks. Now about yourself. I see you brought no stuff up last night?'

'Couldn't. I had a rotten bilious attack. I started, but had to go back to bed again. Couldn't stand.'

'Better?'

'Yes, alright now, thanks.'

'Then you'll bring the usual up tonight?'

'Certainly.'

'Very well. Now, what about ten forty-five for tomorrow?'

'Right.'

The switch snapped, and in a few seconds the watcher saw Archer return to his office, bend for a moment over the lock of the door, then reseat himself at his desk.

Inspector Willis was as much excited as his professional calm would allow.

'I've got them now,' he thought triumphantly. 'I've got them at last. Tonight I'll take them red-handed in whatever they're doing.' He smiled in anticipation. 'By Jove,' he went on, 'it was lucky they sent nothing up last night, or they would have taken *me* red-handed, and that might have been the end of me!'

He was greatly impressed by the excellence of the telephone scheme. There was nothing anywhere about it to excite suspicion, and it kept Archer in touch with the illicit undertaking, while enabling him to hold himself absolutely aloof from all its members. If the rest of the organisation was as good, it was not surprising that Hilliard and Merriman had been baffled.

But the puzzle was now solved, the mystery at an end. That night, so Willis assured himself, the truth would be known.

He remained in his hiding-place all day, until, indeed, he had watched the workers at the distillery leave and the gray shadows of evening had begun to descend. Then he hid the telephone and wire in a cupboard, stealthily left the house, and after a rapid glance round hurried along the lane towards Ferriby.

He caught the 6.57 train to Hull, and in a few minutes was at the police station. There he saw the superintendent, and after a little trouble got him to fall in with the plan which he had devised.

As a result of their conference a large car left the city shortly before nine, in which were seated Inspector Willis and eight picked constables in plain clothes. They drove to the end of the Ferriby Lane, where the men dismounted and took cover behind some shrubs, while the car returned towards Hull.

It was almost, but not quite dark. There was no moon, but the sky was clear and the stars were showing brightly. A faint air, in which there was already a touch of chill, sighed gently through the leaves, rising at intervals almost to a breeze, then falling away again to nothing. Lights were showing here and there—yellow gleams from unshaded windows, signal lamps from the railway, navigation lights from the river. Except for the sound of the retreating car and the dull roar of a distant train, the night was very still, a night, in fact, pre-eminently suitable for the inspector's purpose.

The nine men moved silently down the lane at intervals of a few minutes, their rubber shod feet making no sound on the hard surface. Willis went first, and as the others reached him he posted them in the positions on which he had previously decided. One man took cover behind the hedge of the lane a short distance on the distillery side of the wharf, another behind a pile of old material on the railway at the same place, a third hid himself among some bushes on the open ground between the railway and the river, while a fourth crept as near to the end of the wharf as the tide would allow, so as to watch approaches from the water. When they were in position, Willis felt convinced no one could leave the syndicate's depot for the distillery without being seen.

The other four men he led on to the distillery, placing them in a similar manner on its Ferriby side. If by some extraordinary chance the messenger with the 'stuff' should pass the first cordon, the second, he was satisfied, would take him. He left himself free to move about as might appear desirable.

The country was extraordinarily deserted. Not one of the nine men had seen a living soul since they left their motor, and Willis felt certain that his dispositions had been carried out in absolute secrecy.

He crossed the fence on to the railway. By climbing half-way up the ladder of a signal he was able to see the windows of the shed over the galvanised fence. All were in darkness, and he wondered if Benson had gone on his customary expedition into Hull.

To satisfy himself on this point he hid beneath a wagon which was standing on the siding close to the gate in the fence. If the manager were returning by his usual train he would be due in a few minutes, and Willis intended to wait and see.

It was not long before a sharp footfall told that some one was coming along the lane. The unknown paused at the stile, climbed over, and, walking more carefully across the rails, approached the door. Willis, whose eyes were accustomed to the gloom, could make out the dim form of a man, showing like a smudge of intensified blackness against the obscurity beyond. He unlocked the door, passed through, slammed it behind him, and his retreating steps sounded from within. Finally another door closed in the distance and silence again reigned.

Willis crawled out from beneath his truck and once more climbed the signal ladder. The windows of Benson's office were now lighted up, but the blinds being drawn, the inspector could see nothing within.

After about half an hour he observed the same phenomenon as Hilliard and Merriman had witnessed—the light was carried from the office to the bedroom, and a few minutes later disappeared altogether.

The ladder on which he was standing appearing to Willis to offer as good an observation post as he could hope to get, he climbed to the little platform at the top, and seating himself, leaned back against the timber upright and continued his watch.

Though he was keenly interested by his adventure, time soon began to drag. It was cramped on the little seat, and he could not move freely for fear of falling off. Then to his dismay he began to grow sleepy. He had of course been up all the previous night, and though he had dozed a little during his vigil in the deserted house, he had not really rested. He yawned, stretched himself carefully, and made a determined effort to overcome his drowsiness.

He was suddenly and unexpectedly successful. He got the start of his life, and for a moment he thought an earthquake had come. The signal post trembled and swayed, while with a heavy metallic clang objects moved through the darkness near his head. He gripped the rail, and then he laughed as he remembered that railway signals were movable. This one had just been lowered for a train.

Presently it roared past beneath him, enveloping him in a cloud of steam, which for an instant was lit bright as day by the almost white beam that poured out of the open door of the engine firebox. Then, the steam clearing, there appeared a strip of faintly lit ground on either side of the flying carriage roofs; it promptly vanished; red tail lamps appeared, leaping away; there was the rattle of wheels over siding connections, and with a rapidly decreasing roar the visitation was past. For a moment there remained the quickly moving spot of lighted steam, then it too vanished. Once again the signal post swayed as the heavy mechanism of the arm dropped back into the 'on' position, and then all was once more still.

The train had effectually wakened Willis, and he set himself with a renewed vigour to his task. Sharply he watched the dark mass of the shed with its surrounding enclosure, keenly he listened for some sound of movement within. But all remained dark and silent.

Towards one in the morning he descended from his perch and went the round of his men. All were alert, and all were unanimous that no one had passed.

The time dragged slowly on. The wind had risen somewhat and clouds were banking towards the north-west. It grew colder, and Willis fancied there must be a touch of frost.

About four o'clock he went round his pickets for the second time. He was becoming more and more surprised that the attempt had been delayed so long, and when some two hours later the coming dawn began to brighten the eastern sky and still no sign had been observed, his chagrin waxed keen. As the light increased he withdrew his men to cover, and about seven o'clock, when it was no longer possible that anything would be attempted, he sent them by ones and twos to await their car at the agreed rendezvous.

He was more disappointed at the failure of his trap than he would have believed possible. What, he wondered, could have happened? Why had the conspirators so unexpectedly abandoned their purpose? Had he given himself away? He went over in his mind every step he had taken, and he did not see how any one of them could have become known to his enemies, or how any of his actions could have aroused their suspicions.

No; it was not, he felt sure, that they had realised their danger. Some other quite accidental circumstance had intervened to cause them to postpone the transfer of the 'stuff' for that night.

But what extraordinarily hard luck for him! He had obtained his helpers from the superintendent only after considerable trouble, and the difficulty of getting them again would be much greater. And not the least annoying thing was that he, a London man, one, indeed, of the best men at the Yard, had been made to look ridiculous in the eyes of these provincial police!

Dog-tired and hungry though he was, he set his teeth and determined that he would return to the cottage in the hope of learning the reason of his failure from the conversation which he expected would take place between Archer and Benson at a quarter to eleven that day.

Repeating, therefore, his proceedings of the previous morning, he regained his point of vantage at the broken window. Again he watched the staff arrive, and again observed Archer enter and take his place at his desk. He was desperately sleepy, and it required all the power of his strong will to keep himself awake. But at last his perseverance was rewarded, and at 10.45 exactly he saw Archer bolt his door and disappear towards the filing room. A moment later the buzzer sounded.

'Are you there?' once again came in Archer's voice, followed by the astounding phrase, 'I see you brought up that stuff last night.'

'Yes, I brought up two hundred and fifty,' was Benson's equally amazing reply.

Inspector Willis gasped. He could scarcely believe his ears. So he had been tricked after all! In spite of his carefully placed pickets, in spite of his own ceaseless watchfulness, he had been tricked. Two hundred and fifty of the illicit somethings had been conveyed, right under his and his men's noses, from the depot to the distillery. Almost choking with rage and amazement he heard Archer continue:

'I had a lucky deal after our conversation yesterday, got

seven hundred unexpectedly planted. You may send up a couple of hundred extra tonight if you like.'

'Right. I shall,' Benson answered, and the conversation ceased.

Inspector Willis swore bitterly as he lay back on the dusty floor and pillowed his head on his hands. And then while he still fumed and fretted, outraged nature asserted herself and he fell asleep.

He woke, ravenously hungry, as it was getting dusk, and he did not delay long in letting himself out of the house, regaining the lane, and walking to Ferriby Station. An hour later he was dining at his hotel in Hull.

CHAPTER XVI

THE SECRET OF THE SYNDICATE

A NIGHT'S rest made Willis once more his own man, and next morning he found that his choking rage had evaporated, and that he was able to think calmly and collectedly over the failure of his plans.

As he reconsidered in detail the nature of the watch he had kept, he felt more than ever certain that his cordons had not been broken through. No one, he felt satisfied, could have passed unobserved between the depot and the distillery.

And in spite of this the stuff had been delivered. Archer and Benson were not bluffing to put him off the scent. They had no idea that they were overheard, and therefore had no reason to say anything except the truth.

How then was the communication being made? Surely, he thought, if these people could devise a scheme, he should be able to guess it. He was not willing to admit his brain inferior to any man's.

He lit his pipe and drew at it slowly as he turned the question over in his mind. And then a possible solution occurred to him. What about a subterranean connection? Had these men driven a tunnel?

Here undoubtedly was a possibility. To drive three hundred yards of a heading large enough for a stooping man to pass through, would be a simple matter to men who had shown the skill of these conspirators. The soil was light and sandy, and they could use without suspicion as much timber as they required to shore up their work. It was true they would have to pass under the railway, but that again was a matter of timbering.

Their greatest difficulty, he imagined, would be in the

214

disposal of the surplus earth. He began to figure out what it would mean. The passage way could hardly be less than four feet by five, to allow for lining, and this would amount to about two yards of material to the yard run, or say six hundred or seven hundred cubic yards altogether. Could this have been absorbed in the filling of the wharf? He thought so. The wharf was a large structure, thirty yards by thirty at least and eight or nine feet high; more than two thousand cubic yards of filling would have been required for it. The disposal of the earth, therefore, would have presented no difficulty. All that came out of a tunnel could have gone into the wharf three times over.

A tunnel seemingly being a practical proposition, he turned his attention to his second problem. How could he find out whether or not it had been made?

Obviously only from examination at one or other end. If it existed it must connect with cellars at the depot and the distillery. And of these there could be no question of which he ought to search. The depot was not only smaller and more compact, but it was deserted at intervals. If he could not succeed at the syndicate's enclosure he would have no chance at the larger building.

It was true he had already searched it without result, but he was not then specially looking for a cellar, and with a more definite objective he might have better luck. He decided that if Benson went up to Hull that night he would have another try.

He took an afternoon train to Ferriby, and walking back towards the depot, took cover in the same place that he had previously used. There, sheltered by a hedge, he watched for the manager's appearance.

The weather had, from the inspector's point of view, changed for the worse. The sunny days had gone, and the sky was overladen with clouds. A cold wind blew in gustily from the south-east, bringing a damp fog which threatened every minute to turn to rain, and flecking the lead coloured waters of the estuary with spots of white. Willis shivered and drew up his collar higher round his ears as he crouched behind the wet bushes.

'Confound it,' he thought, 'when I get into that shed I shall be dripping water all over the floor.'

But he remained at his post, and in due course he was rewarded by seeing Benson appear at the door in the fence, and after locking it behind him, start off down the railway towards Ferriby.

As before, Willis waited until the manager had got clear away, then slipping across the line, he produced his bent wire, opened the door, and five minutes later stood once more in the office.

From the nature of the case it seemed clear that the entrance to the cellar, if such existed, would be hidden. It was therefore for secret doors or moving panels that he must look.

He began by ascertaining the thickness of all the walls, noting the size of the rooms so as to calculate those he could not measure directly. He soon found that no wall was more than six inches thick, and none could therefore contain a concealed opening.

This narrowed his search. The exit from the building could only be through a trap-door in the floor.

Accordingly he set to work in the office, crawling torch in hand along the boards, scrutinising the joints between them for any that were not closed with dust, feeling for any that might be loose. But all to no purpose. The boards ran in one length across the floor and were obviously firmly nailed down on fixed joists.

He went to the bedroom, rolling aside the mats which covered the floor and moving the furniture back and forwards. But here he had no better result.

The remainder of the shed was floored with concrete, and a less meticulous examination was sufficient to show that the surface was unbroken. Nor was there anything either on the wharf itself or in the enclosure behind the shed which could form a cover to a flight of steps.

Sorely disappointed, Willis returned once more to the office and, sitting down, went over once again in his mind what he had done, trying to think if there was a point on the whole area of the depot which he had overlooked. He could recall none except the space beneath a large wardrobe in the next room which, owing to its obvious weight, he had not moved.

'I suppose I had better make sure,' he said to himself, though he did not believe so massive a piece of furniture could have been pulled backwards and forwards without leaving scratches on the floor.

He returned to the bedroom. The wardrobe was divided into two portions, a single deep drawer along the bottom, and above it a kind of large cupboard with a central door. He seized its end. It was certainly very heavy; in fact, he found himself unable to move it.

He picked up his torch and examined the wooden base. And then his interest grew, for he found it was strongly stitchnailed to the floor.

Considerably mystified he tried to open the door. It was locked, and though with his wire he eventually shot back the bolt, the trouble he had proved that the lock was one of first quality. Indeed, it was not a cupboard lock screwed to the inside of the door, as might have been expected, but a small-sized mortice lock hidden in the thickness of the wood, and the keyhole came through to the inside; just the same arrangement as is usual in internal house doors.

The inside of the wardrobe revealed nothing of interest. Two coats and waistcoats, a sweater, and some other clothes were hanging from hooks at the back. Otherwise the space was empty.

'Why,' he wondered as he stood staring in, 'should it be necessary to lock up clothes like these?'

His eyes turned to the drawer below, and he seized the handles and gave a sharp pull. The drawer was evidently locked. Once again he produced his wire, but for the first time it failed him. He flashed a beam from his lamp into the hole, and then he saw the reason.

The hole was a dummy. It entered the wood but did not go through it. It was not connected to a lock.

He passed the light round the edges of the drawer. If there was no lock to fasten it why had he been unable to open it? He took out his penknife and tried to push the blade into the surrounding space. It would not penetrate, and he saw that there was no space, but merely a cut half an inch deep in the wood. There was no drawer. What seemed a drawer was merely a blind panel.

Inspector Willis grew more and more interested. He could not see why all that space should be wasted, as it was clear from the way in which the wardrobe was finished that economy in construction had not been the motive.

Once again he opened the door of the upper portion, and putting his head inside passed the beam of the lamp over the floor. This time he gave a little snort of triumph. The floor did not fit tight to the sides. All round was a space of some eighth of an inch.

'The trap-door at last,' he muttered, as he began to feel about for some hidden spring. At last, pressing down on one end of the floor, he found that it sank and the other end rose in the air, revealing a square of inky blackness out of which poured a stream of cold, damp air, and through which he could hear, with the echoing sound peculiar to vaults, the splashing and churning of the sea.

His torch revealed a flight of steps leading down into the darkness. Having examined the pivoted floor to make sure there was no secret catch which could fasten and imprison him below, he stepped on to the ladder and began to descend. Then the significance of the mortice lock in the wardrobe door occurred to him, and he stopped, drew the door to behind him, and with his wire locked it. Descending farther he allowed the floor to drop gently into place above his head, thus leaving no trace of his passage.

He had by this time reached the ground, and he stood flashing his torch about on his surroundings. He was in a cellar, so low in the roof that except immediately beneath the stairs he could not stand upright. It was square, some twelve feet either way, and from it issued two passages, one apparently running down under the wharf, the other at right angles and some two feet lower in level, leading as if towards the distillery. Down the centre of this latter ran a tiny tramway of about a foot gauge, on which stood three kegs on four-wheeled frames. In the upper side of each keg was fixed a tundish, to the under side a stop-cock. Two insulated wires came down through the ceiling below the cupboard in which the telephone was installed, and ran down the tunnel towards the distillery.

The walls and ceiling of both cellar and passages were supported by pit-props, discoloured by the damp and marked by stains of earthy water which had oozed from the spaces between. They glistened with moisture, but the air, though cold and damp, was fresh. That and the noise of the waves which reverberated along the passage under the wharf seemed to show that there was an open connection to the river.

The cellar was empty except for a large wooden tun or cask which reached almost to the ceiling, and a gun-metal hand pump. Pipes led from the latter, one to the tun, the other along the passage under the wharf. On the side of the tun and connected to it at top and bottom was a vertical glass tube protected by a wooden casing, evidently a gauge, as beside it was a scale headed 'gallons', and reading from oo at the bottom to 2000 at the top. A dark coloured liquid filled the tube up to the figure 1250. There was a wooden spigot tap in the side of the tun at floor level, and the tramline ran beneath this so that the wheeled kegs could be pushed below it and filled.

The inspector gazed with an expression almost of awe on his face.

'Lord!' he muttered. 'Is it brandy after all?'

He stooped and smelled the wooden tap, and the last doubt was removed from his mind.

He gave vent to a comprehensive oath. Right enough it was hard luck! Here he had been hoping to bring off a forged note coup which would have made his name, and the affair was a job for the Customs Department after all! Of course a pretty substantial reward would be due to him for his discovery, and there was his murder case all quite satisfactory, but forged notes were more in his line, and he felt cheated out of his due.

But now that he was so far he might as well learn all he could. The more complete the case he gave in, the larger the reward. Moreover, his own curiosity was keenly aroused.

The cellar being empty save for the tun, the pump and the small tramway and trucks, he turned, and flashing his light before him, walked slowly along the passage down which ran the pipe. He was, he felt sure, passing under the wharf and heading towards the river.

Some sixty feet past the pump the floor of the passage came to an abrupt end, falling vertically as by an enormous step to the churning waters of the river some six feet below. At first in the semi-darkness Willis thought he had reached the front of the wharf, but he soon saw he was still in the cellar. The roof ran on at the same level for some twenty feet farther, and the side walls, here about five feet apart, went straight down from it into the water. Across the end was a wall, sloping outwards at the bottom and made of horizontal pit-props separated by spaces of two or three inches. Willis immediately realised that these props must be those placed behind the inner or raking row of piles which supported the front of the wharf.

Along one side wall for its whole length was nailed a series of horizontal laths twelve inches apart. What their purpose was he did not know, but he saw that they made a ladder twenty feet wide, by which a man could work his way from the passage to the end wall and reach the water at any height of the tide.

Above this ladder was an object which at first puzzled the

inspector, then as he realised its object, it became highly illu-
minating. On a couple of brackets secured to the wall lay a pipe
of thin steel covered with thick black baize, and some sixteen
feet long by an inch in diameter. Through it ran the light copper
pipe which was connected at its other end to the pump. At the
end of the passage this pipe had several joints like those of a
gas bracket, and was folded on itself concertina-wise.

The inspector stepped on to the ladder and worked his way
across it to the other end of the steel pipe, close by the end wall.
The copper pipe protruded and ended in a fitting like the half
of a union. As Willis gazed he suddenly grasped its significance.

The side of the *Girondin*, he thought, would lie not more
than ten feet from where he was standing. If at night some one
from within the cellar were to push the end of the steel tube
out through one of the spaces between the horizontal timbers
of the end wall, it could be inserted into a port-hole, supposing
one were just opposite. The concertina joints would make it
flexible and allow it to extend, and the baize covering would
prevent its being heard should it inadvertently strike the side
of the ship. The union on the copper tube could then be fixed
to some receptacle on board, the brandy being pumped from
the ship to the tun.

And no outsider could possibly be any the wiser! Given a
dark night and careful operators, the whole thing would be
carried out invisibly and in absolute silence.

Now Willis saw the object of the peculiar construction of
the front of the wharf. It was necessary to have two lines of
piles, so that the deck between might overshadow and screen
from view the openings between the horizontal beams at the
front of the cellar. He stood marvelling at the ingenuity of the
plan. No wonder Hilliard and Merriman had been baffled.

But if he were to finish his investigations, he must no longer
delay. He worked back across the side of the cellar, regained the
passage, and returned to the pump room. Then turning into the
other passage, he began to walk as quickly as possible along it.

The tunnel was barely four feet high by three wide, and he found progress very tiring. After a slight curve at the mouth it ran straight and almost dead level. Its construction was the same as that of the cellar, longitudinal timber lining supported behind verticals and lintels spaced about six feet apart. When he had gone about two hundred yards it curved sharply to the left, ran heavily timbered for some thirty yards in the new direction, and then swung round to the right again.

'I suppose the railway crosses here,' Willis thought, as he passed painfully round the bends.

The sweat stood in drops on his forehead when he reached the end, and he breathed a sigh of relief as he realised he could once more stand upright and stretch his cramped back. He found himself in another cellar, this time about six feet by twelve. The tramway ran along it, stopping at the end wall. The place was otherwise empty, save for a wooden grating or tundish with a hinged lid, which was fixed between the rails near the entrance. The telephone wires, which had followed the tunnel all the way, here vanished into the roof.

Willis concluded he must be standing beneath some part of the distillery, and a very little thought was required to make clear to him the *raison d'être* of what he saw. He pictured the kegs being pushed under the tap of the large tun in the pump-room and filled with brandy pumped in from the *Girondin*, In imagination he saw Benson pushing his loaded trucks through the tunnel—a much easier thing to do than to walk without something to stoop over—stopping them one by one over the grating and emptying the contents therein. No doubt that grating was connected to some vat or tun buried still deeper beneath the distillery, in which the brandy mingled with the other brandy brought there by more legitimate means, and which was sold without documentary evidence of its surprising increase in bulk.

It was probable, thought Willis, that some secret door must connect the chamber in which he stood with the distillery, but a careful search revealed no trace of any opening, and he was forced to the conclusion that none existed. Accordingly, he turned and began to retrace his steps through the tunnel.

The walk back seemed even longer and more irksome than his first transit, and he stopped here and there and knelt down in order to straighten his aching back. As he advanced, the booming sound of the waves, which had died down to a faint murmur at the distillery, grew louder and louder. At last he reached the pump-cellar, and was just about to step out of the tunnel when his eye caught the flicker of a light at the top of the stepladder. Some one was coming down!

Willis instantly snapped off his own light, and for the fraction of a second he stood transfixed, while his heart thumped and his hand slid round to his revolver pocket. Breathlessly he watched a pair of legs step on to the ladder and begin to descend the steps.

Like a flash he realised what he must do. If this was Benson coming to 'take up stuff', to remain in the tunnel meant certain discovery. But if only he could reach the passage under the wharf, he might be safe. There was nothing to bring Benson into it.

But to cross the cellar he must pass within two feet of the ladder, and the man was half-way down. For a moment it looked quite hopeless, then unexpectedly he got his chance. The man stopped to lock the wardrobe door. When he had finished, Willis was already across the cellar and hurrying down the other passage. Fortunately the noise of the waves drowned all other sounds.

By the time the unknown had reached the bottom of the ladder, Willis had stepped on to the cross laths and was descending by them. In a moment he was below the passage level. He intended, should the other approach, to hide beneath the water in the hope that in the darkness his head would not be seen.

But the light remained in the cellar, and Willis raised himself and cautiously peeped down the passage. Then he began to congratulate himself on what he had just been considering his misfortune. For, watching there in the darkness, he saw Benson carry out the very operations he had imagined were performed. The manager wheeled the kegs one by one beneath the great barrel, filled them from the tap, and then, setting his lamp on the last of the three, pushed them before him down the tunnel towards the distillery.

Inspector Willis waited until he judged the other would be out of sight, then left his hiding-place and cautiously returned to the pump-room. The gauge now showed 1125 gallons, and he noted that 125 gallons was put up per trip. He rapidly ascended the steps, passed out through the wardrobe, and regained the bedroom. A few minutes later he was once more out on the railway.

He had glanced at his watch in the building and found that it was but little after ten. Benson must therefore have returned by an earlier train than usual. Again the inspector congratulated himself that events had turned out as they had, for though he would have had no fear for his personal safety had he been seen, premature discovery might have allowed the other members of the gang to escape.

The last train for Hull having left, he started to walk the six miles to the city. The weather had still further changed for the worse, and now half a gale of wind whirled round him in a pandemonium of sound and blew blinding squalls of rain into his eyes. In a few moments he was soaked to the skin, and the buffeting of the wind made his progress slow. But he struggled on, too well pleased by the success of his evening's work to mind the discomfort.

And as he considered the affair on the following morning he felt even more satisfied. He had indeed done well! Not only had he completed what he set out to do—to discover the murderer of Coburn—but he had accomplished vastly more. He had brought to light one of the greatest smuggling conspiracies o modern times. It was true he had not followed up and completed the case against the syndicate, but this was not his business. Smuggling was not dealt with by Scotland Yard. It was a matter for the Customs Department. But if only it had been forged notes! He heaved a sigh as he thought of the kudos which might have been his.

But when he had gone so far, he thought he might as well make certain that the brandy was discharged as he imagined. He calculated that the *Girondin* would reach Ferriby on the following day, and he determined to see the operation carried out.

He followed the plan of Hilliard and Merriman to the extent of hiring a boat in Hull and sculling gently down towards the wharf as dusk fell. He had kept a watch on the river all day without seeing the motor ship go up, but now she passed him a couple of miles above the city. He turned inshore when he saw her coming, lest Captain Beamish's binoculars might reveal to him a familiar countenance.

He pulled easily, timing himself to arrive at the wharf as soon as possible after dark. The evening was dry, but the south-easterly wind still blew cold and raw, though not nearly so strongly as on the night of his walk.

There were a couple of lights on the *Girondin*, and he steered by these till the dark mass of her counter, looming up out of the night, cut them off. Slipping round her stern, as Hilliard had done in the River Lesque, he unshipped his oars and guided the boat by his hands into the V-shaped space between the two rows of piles fronting the wharf. As he floated gently forward he felt between the horizontal props which held back the filling until he came to a vacant space, then knowing he was opposite the cellar, he slid the boat back a few feet, tied her up, and settled down to wait.

Though sheltered from the wind by the hull, it was cold and damp under the wharf. The waves were lapping among the timbers, and the boat moved uneasily at the end of her short painter. The darkness was absolute—an inky blackness unrelieved by any point of light. Willis realised that waiting would soon become irksome.

But it was not so very long before the work began. He had been there, he estimated, a couple of hours when he saw, not ten feet away, a dim circle of light suddenly appear on the *Girondin's* side. Some one had turned on a faint light in a cabin whose open porthole was immediately opposite the cellar. Presently Willis, watching breathlessly, saw what he believed was the steel pipe impinge on and enter the illuminated ring. It remained projecting into the porthole for some forty minutes, was as silently withdrawn, the porthole was closed, a curtain drawn across it, and the light turned up within. The brandy had been discharged.

The thing had been done inaudibly, and invisibly to any one on either wharf or ship. Marvelling once more at the excellence and secrecy of the plan, Willis gently pushed his boat out from among the piles and rowed back down the river to Hull. There he tied the boat up, and returning to his hotel, was soon fast asleep.

In spite of his delight at the discovery, he could not but realise that much still remained to be done. Though he had learned how the syndicate was making its money, he had not obtained any evidence of the complicity of its members in the murder of Coburn.

Who, in addition to Archer, could be involved? There were, of course, Beamish, Bulla, Benson and Henri. There was also a man, Morton, whose place in the scheme of things had not yet been ascertained. He, Willis realised, must be found and identified. But were these all? He doubted it. It seemed to him that the smuggling system required more helpers than these. He now understood how the brandy was got from the ship to the distillery, and he presumed it was loaded at the clearing in the same manner, being brought there in some unknown way by the motor lorries. But there were two parts of the plan of which nothing was yet known. Firstly, where was the brandy obtained from originally, and, secondly, how was it distributed from the distillery? It seemed to Willis that each of these operations would require additional accomplices. And if so, these persons might also have been implicated in Coburn's death.

He thought over the thing for three solid hours before coming to a decision. At the end of that time he determined to return to London and, if his chief approved, lay the whole facts before the Customs Departments of both England and France, asking them to investigate the matter in their respective countries. In the meantime he would concentrate on the question of complicity in the murder.

He left Hull by an afternoon train, and that night was in London.

CHAPTER XVII

'ARCHER PLANTS STUFF'

WILLIS'S chief at the Yard was not a little impressed by his subordinate's story. He congratulated the inspector on his discovery, commended him for his restraint in withholding action against Archer until he had identified his accomplices, and approved his proposals for the further conduct of the case. Fortified by this somewhat unexpected approbation, Willis betook himself forthwith to the headquarters of the Customs Department and asked to see Hilliard.

The two men were already acquainted. As has been stated, the inspector had early called at Hilliard's rooms and learned all that the other could tell him of the case. But for prudential reasons they had not met since.

Hilliard was tremendously excited by the inspector's news, and eagerly arranged the interview with his chief which Willis sought. The great man was not engaged, and in a few minutes the others were shown into his presence.

'We are here, sir,' Willis began, when the necessary introductions had been made, 'to tell you jointly a very remarkable story. Mr Hilliard would doubtless have told you his part long before this, had I not specially asked him not to. Now, sir, the time has come to put the facts before you. Perhaps as Mr Hilliard's story comes before mine in point of time, he should begin.'

Hilliard thereupon began. He told of Merriman's story in the Rovers' Club, his own idea of smuggling based on the absence of return cargoes, his proposition to Merriman, their trip to France and what they learned at the clearing. Then he described their visit to Hull, their observations at the Ferriby wharf, the experiment carried out with the help of Leatham, and, finally, what Merriman had told him of his second visit Bordeaux.

Willis next took up the tale and described the murder of Coburn, his inquiries thereinto and identification of the assassin, and his subsequent discoveries at Ferriby, ending up by stating the problem which still confronted him, and expressing the hope that the chief in dealing with the smuggling conspiracy would co-operate with him in connection with the murder.

The latter had listened with an expression of amazement, which towards the end of the inspector's statement changed to one of the liveliest satisfaction. He gracefully congratulated both men on their achievements, and expressed his gratification at what had been discovered and his desire to co-operate to the full with the inspector in the settling up of the case.

The three men then turned to details. To Hilliard's bitter disappointment it was ruled that, owing to his being known to at least three members of the gang, he could take no part in the final scenes, and he had to be content with the honour of, as it were, a seat on the council of war. For nearly an hour they deliberated, at the end of which time it had been decided that Stopford Hunt, one of the Customs Department's most skilful investigators, should proceed to Hull and tackle the question of the distribution of the brandy. Willis was to go to Paris, interest the French authorities in the Bordeaux end of the affair, and then join Hunt in Hull.

Stopford Hunt was an insignificant looking man of about forty. All his characteristics might be described as being of medium quality. He was five feet nine in height, his brown hair was neither fair nor dark, his dress suggested neither poverty nor opulence, and his features were of the type known as ordinary. In a word, he was not one whose appearance would provoke a second glance, or who would be credited with taking an important part in anything that might be in progress.

But for his job these very peculiarities were among his chief assets. When he hung about in an aimless, loafing way, as he very often did, he was overlooked by those whose actions he was so discreetly watching, and where mere loafing would look suspicious, he had the inestimable gift of being able to waste time in an *affairé* and preoccupied manner.

That night Willis crossed to Paris, and next day he told his story to the polite chief of the French Excise. M. Max was almost as interested as his English *confrère*, and readily promised to have the French end of the affair investigated. That same evening the inspector left for London, going on in the morning to Hull.

He found Hunt a shrewd and capable man of the world, as well as a pleasant and interesting companion.

They had engaged a private sitting-room at their hotel, and after dinner they retired thither to discuss their plan of campaign.

'I wish,' said Willis, when they had talked for some moments, 'that you would tell me something about how this liquor distribution business is worked. It's outside my job, and I'm not clear on the details. If I understood I could perhaps help you better.'

Hunt nodded and drew slowly at his pipe.

'The principle of the thing,' he answered, 'is simple enough, though in detail it becomes a bit complicated. The first thing we have to remember is that in this case we're dealing, not with distillers, but with rectifiers. Though in loose popular phraseology both businesses are classed under the term "distilling", in reality there is a considerable difference between them. Distillers actually produce the spirit in their buildings, rectifiers do not. Rectifiers import the spirit produced by distillers, and refine or prepare it for various specified purposes. The check required by the Excise authorities is therefore different in each case. With rectifiers it is only necessary to measure the stuff that goes into and comes out of the works. Making due allowance for variation during treatment, these two figures will balance if all is right.'

Willis nodded, and Hunt resumed.

'Now, the essence of all fraud is that more stuff goes out of the works than is shown on the returns. That is, of course, another way of saying that stuff is sold upon which duty has not been paid. In the case of a rectifying house, where there is no illicit still, more also comes in than is shown. In the present instance you yourself have shown how the extra brandy enters. Our job is to find out how it leaves.'

'That part of it is clear enough anyway,' Willis said, with a smile. 'But brandy smuggling is not new. There must surely be recognised ways of evading the law?'

'Quite. There are. But to follow them you must understand how the output is measured. For every consignment of stuff that leaves the works a permit or certificate is issued and handed to the carrier who removes it. This is a kind of waybill, and of course a block is kept for the inspection of the surveying officer. It contains a note of the quantity of stuff, date and hour of starting, consignee's name and other information, and it is the authority for the carrier to have the liquor in his possession. An Excise officer may stop and examine any dray or lorry carrying liquor, or railway wagon, and the driver or other official must produce his certificate so that his load may be checked by it. All such, what I may call surprise examinations, together with the signature of the officer making them, are recorded on the back of the certificate. When the stuff is delivered, the certificate is handed over with it to the consignee. He signs it on receipt. It then becomes his authority for having the stuff on his premises, and he must keep it for the Excise officer's inspection. Do you follow me so far?'

'Perfectly.'

'The fraud, then, consists in getting more liquor away from the works than is shown on the certificates, and I must confess it is not easy. The commonest method, I should think, is to fill the kegs or receptacles slightly fuller than the certificate shows. This is sometimes done simply by putting extra stuff in the ordinary kegs. It is argued that an Excise officer cannot by his eye tell a difference of five or six per cent.; that, for example, twenty-six gallons might be supplied on a twenty-five gallon certificate without any one being much the wiser. Variants of this method are to use slightly larger kegs, or, more subtly, to use normal sized kegs of which the wood at the ends has been thinned down, and which therefore when filled to the same level hold more, while showing the same measure with a dipping rod. But all these methods are risky. On the slightest suspicion the contents of the kegs are measured and the fraud becomes revealed.'

Willis, much interested, bent forward eagerly as the other, after a pause to relight his pipe, continued:

'Another common method is to send out liquor secretly, without a permit at all. This may be done at night, or the stuff may go through an underground pipe, or be hidden in innocent looking articles such as suitcases or petrol tins. The pipe is the best scheme from the operator's point of view, and one may remain undiscovered for months, but the difficulty usually is to lay it in the first instance.

'A third method can be used only in the case of rectifiers, and it illustrates one of the differences between rectifiers and distillers. Every permit for the removal of liquor from a distillery must be issued by the Excise surveyor of the district, whereas rectifiers can issue their own certificates. Therefore in the case of rectifiers there is the possibility of the issuing of forged or fraudulent certificates. Of course this is not so easy as it sounds. The certificates are supplied in books of two hundred by the Excise authorities, and the blocks must be kept available for the supervisor's scrutiny. Any certificates can be obtained from the receivers of the spirit, and compared with the blocks. Forged permits are very risky things to work with, as all genuine ones bear the government watermark, which is not easy to reproduce. In fact, I may say about this whole question of liquor distribution generally, that fraud has been made so difficult that the only hope of those committing it is to avoid arousing suspicion. Once suspicion is aroused, discovery follows almost as a matter of course.'

'That's hopeful for us,' Willis smiled.

'Yes,' the other answered, 'though I fancy this case will be more difficult than most. There is another point to be taken into consideration which I have not mentioned, and that is, how the perpetrators of the fraud are going to get their money. In the last resort it can only come in from the public over the counters of the licensed premises which sell the smuggled spirits. But just as the smuggled liquor cannot be put through the books of the house selling it, so the money received for it cannot be entered either. This means that some one in authority in each licensed house must be involved. It also carries with it a suggestion, though only a suggestion, that the houses in question are tied houses. The director of a distillery company would have more hold on the manager of one of their own tied houses than over an outsider.'

Again Willis nodded without replying, and Hunt went on:

'Now it happens that these Ackroyd & Holt people own some very large licensed houses in Hull, and it is to them, I imagine, that we should first direct our attention.'

'How do you propose to begin?'

'I think we must first find out how the Ferriby liquor is sent to these houses. By the way, you probably know that already. You watched the distillery during working hours, didn't you?'

The inspector admitted it.

'Did you see any lorries?'

'Any number; large blue machines. I noticed them going and coming in the Hull direction loaded up with barrels.'

Hunt seemed pleased.

'Good,' he commended. 'That's a beginning anyway. Our next step must be to make sure that all these lorries carry certificates. We had better begin tomorrow.'

Willis did not quite see how the business was to be done,

but he forbore to ask questions, agreeing to fall in with his companion's arrangements.

These arrangements involved the departure from their hotel by taxi at six o'clock the next morning. It was not fully light as they whirled out along the Ferriby road, but the sky was clear and all the indications pointed to a fine day.

They dismounted at the end of the lane leading to the works, and struck off across the fields, finally taking up their position behind the same thick hedge from which Willis had previously kept watch.

They spent the whole of that day, as well as of the next two, in their hiding-place, and at the end of that time they had a complete list of all lorries that entered or left the establishment during the period. No vehicles other than blue lorries appeared, and Hunt expressed himself as satisfied that if the smuggled brandy was not carried by them it must go either by rail or at night.

'We can go into those other contingencies later if necessary,' he said, 'but on the face of it I am inclined to back the lorries. They supply the tied houses in Hull, which would seem the obvious places for the brandy to go, and, besides, railway transit is too well looked after to attract the gang. I think we'll follow this lorry business through first on spec.'

'I suppose you'll compare the certificate blocks with the list we have just made?' Willis asked.

'Of course. That will show if all carry certificates. But I don't want to do that yet. Before alarming them I want to examine the contents of a few of the lorries. I think we might do that tomorrow.'

The next morning, therefore, the two detectives again engaged a taxi and ran out along the Ferriby road until they met a large blue lorry loaded with barrels and bearing on its side the legend 'Ackroyd & Holt, Ltd., Licensed Rectifiers'. When it had lumbered past on its way to the city, Hunt called to the driver and ordered him to follow it.

The chase led to the heart of the town, ending in a street which ran parallel to the Humber Dock. There the big machine turned into an entry.

'The Anchor Bar,' Hunt said, in satisfied tones. 'We're in luck. It's one of the largest licensed houses in Hull.'

He jumped out and disappeared after the lorry, Willis following. The vehicle had stopped in a yard at the back of the great public house, where were more barrels than the inspector ever remembered having seen together, while the smell of various liquors hung heavy in the air. Hunt, having shown his credentials, demanded the certificate for the consignment. This was immediately produced by the driver, scrutinised, and found in order. Hunt then proceeded to examine the consignment itself, and Willis was lost in admiration at the rapidity as well as the thoroughness of his inspection. He tested the nature of the various liquids, measured their receptacles, took dippings in each cask, and otherwise satisfied himself as to quality and quantity. Finally he had a look over the lorry, then expressing himself satisfied, he indorsed the certificate, and with a few civil words to the men in charge, the two detectives took their leave.

'That's all square anyway,' Hunt remarked, as they re-entered their taxi. 'I suppose we may go and do the same thing again.'

They did. Three times more on that day, and four times on the next they followed Messrs Ackroyd & Holt's lorries, in every instance with the same result. All eight consignments were examined with the utmost care, and all were found to be accurately described on the accompanying certificate. The certificates themselves were obviously genuine, and everything about them, so far as Hunt could see, was in order.

'Doesn't look as if we were going to get it that way,' he commented, as late that second evening they sat once more discussing matters in their private sitting-room.

'Don't you think we have frightened them into honesty by our persistence?' Willis queried.

'No doubt,' the other returned. 'But that couldn't apply to

the first few trips. They couldn't possibly have foretold that we should examine those consignments yesterday, and today I expect they thought their visitation was over. But we have worked it as far as it will go. We shall have to change our methods.'

The inspector looked his question and Hunt continued:

'I think tomorrow I had better go out to the works and have a look over those certificate blocks. But I wonder if it would be well for you to come? Archer has seen you in that hotel lounge, and at all events he has your description.'

'I shall not go,' Willis decided. 'See you when you get back.'

Hunt, after showing his credentials, was received with civility at Messrs Ackroyd & Holt's. When he had completed the usual examination of the stills and apparatus he asked for certain books. He took them to a desk, and sitting down, began to study the certificate blocks.

His first care was to compare the list of outward lorries which he and Willis had made with the blocks for the same period. A short investigation convinced him that here also everything was in order. There was a certificate for every lorry which had passed out, and not only so, but the number of the lorry, the day and hour at which it left and the load were all correct so far as his observations had enabled him to check them. It was clear that here also he had drawn blank, and for the fiftieth time he wondered with a sort of rueful admiration how the fraud was being worked.

He was idly turning over the leaves of the blocks, gazing vacantly at the lines of writing while he pondered his problem, when his attention was attracted to a slight difference of colour in the ink of an entry on one of the blocks. The consignment was a mixed one, containing different kinds of spirituous liquors. The lowest entry was for three twenty-five gallon kegs of French brandy. This entry was slightly paler than the remainder.

At first Hunt did not give the matter serious thought. The

page had evidently been blotted while the ink was wet, and the lower items should therefore naturally be the fainter. But as he looked more closely he saw that this explanation would not quite meet the case. It was true that the lower two or three items above that of the brandy grew gradually paler in proportion to their position down the sheet, and to this rule Archer's signature at the bottom was no exception. In these Hunt could trace the gradual fading of colour due to the use of blotting paper. But he now saw that this did not apply to the brandy entry. It was the palest of all—paler even than Archer's name, which was below it.

He sat staring at the sheet, whistling softly through his teeth and with his brow puckered into a frown, as he wondered whether the obvious suggestion that the brandy item had been added after the sheet had been completed, was a sound deduction. He could think of no other explanation, but he was loath to form a definite opinion on such slight evidence.

He turned back through the blocks to see if they contained other similar instances, and as he did so his interest grew. Quite a number of the pages referring to mixed consignments had for their last item kegs of French brandy. He scrutinised these entries with the utmost care. A few seemed normal enough, but others showed indications which strengthened his suspicions. In three more the ink was undoubtedly paler than on the remainder of the sheet, in five it was darker, while in several others the handwriting appeared slightly different—more upright, more sloping, more heavily or more lightly leant on. When Hunt had examined all the instances he could find stretching over a period of three months, he was convinced that his deduction was correct. The brandy items had been written at a different time from the remainder, and this could only mean that they had been added after the certificate was complete.

His interest at last keenly aroused, he began to make an analysis of the blocks in question in the hope of finding some other peculiarity common to them which might indicate the direction in which the solution might lie.

And first as to the consignees. Ackroyd & Holt evidently supplied a very large number of licensed houses, but of these the names of only five appeared on the doubtful blocks. But these five were confined to houses in Hull, and each was a large and important concern.

'So far, so good,' thought Hunt, with satisfaction. 'If they're not planting their stuff in those five houses, I'm a Dutchman!'

He turned back to the blocks and once again went through them. This time he made an even more suggestive discovery. Only one lorry-man was concerned in the transport of the doubtful consignments. All the lorries in question had been in charge of a driver called Charles Fox.

Hunt remembered the man. He had driven three of the eight lorries Hunt had himself examined, and he had been most civil when stopped, giving the investigator all possible assistance in making his inspection. Nor had he at any time betrayed embarrassment. And now it seemed not improbable that this same man was one of those concerned in the fraud.

Hunt applied himself once again to a study of the blocks, and then he made a third discovery, which, though he could not at first see its drift, struck him nevertheless as being of importance. He found that the faked block was always one of a pair. Within a few pages either in front of or behind it was another block containing particulars of a similar consignment, identical, in fact, except that the brandy item was missing.

Hunt was puzzled. That he was on the track of the fraud he could not but believe, but he could form no idea as to how it was worked. If he were right so far, the blocks had been made out in facsimile in the first instance, and later the brandy item had been added to one of each pair. Why? He could not guess.

He continued his examination, and soon another interesting fact became apparent. Though consignments left the works at all hours of the day, those referred to by the first one of each pair of blocks had all been sent out between the hours of one and two in the afternoon, and those referred to by the second between the hours of four and five. Further, the number of minutes past one and past four were always identical on each pair. That showing the brandy item was nearly always the later of the two, but occasionally the stuff had gone with the one o'clock trip.

Hunt sat in the small office, of which he had been given undisturbed possession, pondering over his problem and trying to marshal the facts he had learnt in such a way as to extract their inner meaning. As far as he could follow them they seemed to show that three times each day driver Charles Fox took a lorry of various liquors into Hull. The first trip was irregular, that is, he left at anything between seven-thirty and ten-thirty a.m., and his objective extended over the entire city. The remaining two trips were regular. Of these the first always left between one and two and the second the same number of minutes past four; both were invariably to the same one of the five large tied houses already mentioned; the load of each was always identical except that one—generally the second—had some kegs of brandy additional, and, lastly, the note of this extra brandy appeared always to have been added to the certificate after the latter had been made out.

Hunt could make nothing of it. In the evening he described his discoveries to Willis, and the two men discussed the affair exhaustively, though still without result.

That night Hunt could not sleep. He lay tossing from side to side and racking his brains to find a solution. He felt subconsciously that it was within his reach, and yet he could not grasp it.

It was not far from dawn when a sudden idea flashed into his mind, and he lay thrilled with excitement as he wondered if at last he held the clue to the mystery. He went over the details in his mind, and the more he thought over his theory the more likely it seemed to grow.

But how was he to test it? Daylight had come before he saw his way; but at last he was satisfied, and at breakfast he told Willis his idea and asked his help to carry out his plan.

'You're not a photographer, by any chance?' he asked.

'I'm not A1, but I dabble a bit at it.'

'Good. That will save some trouble.'

They called at a photographic outfitters, and there, after making a deposit, succeeded in hiring two large-size Kodaks for the day. With these and a set of climbing irons they drove out along the Ferriby road, arriving at the end of the lane to the works shortly after midday. There they dismissed their taxi.

As soon as they were alone their actions became somewhat bewildering to the uninitiated. Along one side of the road ran a seven-foot wall bounding the plantation of a large villa. Over this Willis, with the help of his friend, clambered. With some loose stones he built himself a footing at the back, so that he could just look over the top. Then, having focussed his camera for the middle of the road, he retired into obscurity behind his defences.

His friend settled to his satisfaction, Hunt buckled on the climbing irons, and crossing the road, proceeded to climb a telegraph pole which stood opposite the lane. He fixed his camera to the lower wires—carefully avoiding possible short-circuitings—and having focussed it for the centre of the road, pulled a pair of pliers from his pocket and endeavoured to simulate the actions of a lineman at work. By the time these preparations were complete it was close on one o'clock.

Some half-hour later a large blue lorry came in sight bearing down along the lane. Presently Hunt was able to see that the driver was Fox. He made a prearranged sign to his accomplice behind the wall, and the latter, camera in hand, stood up and peeped over. As the big vehicle swung slowly round into the main road both men from their respective positions photographed it. Hunt indeed, rapidly changing the film, took a second view as the machine retreated down the road towards Hull.

When it was out of sight, Hunt descended and with some difficulty climbed the wall to his colleague. There in the shade of the thick belt of trees both men lay down and smoked peacefully until nearly four o'clock. Then once more they took up their respective positions, watched until about half an hour later the lorry again passed out, and photographed it precisely as before. That done, they walked to Hessle station, and took the first train to Hull.

By dint of backsheesh they persuaded the photographer to develop the films there and then, and that same evening they had the six prints.

As it happened they turned out exceedingly good photographs. The definition was excellent, and each view included the whole of the lorry. The friends found, as Hunt had hoped and intended, that owing to the height from which the views had been taken, each several keg of the load showed out distinctly. They counted them. Each picture showed seventeen.

'You see?' cried Hunt triumphantly. 'The same amount of stuff went out on each load! We shall have them now, Willis!'

Next day Hunt returned to the Ferriby works ostensibly to continue his routine inspection. But in three minutes he had seen what he wanted. Taking the certificate book, he looked up the blocks of the two consignments they had photographed, and he could have laughed aloud in his exultation as he saw that what he had suspected was indeed the fact. The two certificates were identical except that to the second an item of four kegs of French brandy had been added! Hunt counted the barrels. The first certificate showed thirteen and the last seventeen.

'Four kegs of brandy smuggled out under our noses yesterday,' he thought delightedly. 'By Jove! but it's a clever trick. Now to test the next point.'

He made an excuse for leaving the works, and returning to Hull, called at the licensed house to which the previous afternoon's consignment had been despatched. There he asked to see the certificates of the two trips. On seeing his credentials these were handed up without demur, and he withdrew with them to his hotel.

'Come,' he cried to Willis, who was reading in the lounge, 'and see the final act in the drama.'

They retired to their private room, and there Hunt spread the two certificates on the table. Both men stared at them, and Hunt gave vent to a grunt of satisfaction.

'I was right,' he cried delightedly. 'Look there! Why, I can see it with the naked eye!'

The two certificates were an accurate copy of their blocks. They were dated correctly, both bore Fox's name as driver, and both showed consignments of liquor, identical except for the additional four kegs of brandy on the second. There was, furthermore, no sign that this had been added after the remainder. The slight lightening in the colour towards the bottom of the sheet, due to the use of blotting paper, was so progressive as almost to prove the whole had been written at the same time.

The first certificate was timed 1.15 p.m., the second 4.15 p.m., and it was to the 4 of this second hour that Hunt's eager finger pointed. As Willis examined it he saw that the lower two strokes were fainter than the remainder. Further, the beginning of the horizontal stroke did not quite join the first vertical stroke.

'You see?' Hunt cried excitedly. 'That figure is a forgery. It was originally a 1, and the two lower strokes have been added to make it a 4. The case is finished!'

Willis was less enthusiastic.

'I'm not so sure of that,' he returned cautiously. 'I don't see light all the way through. Just go over it again, will you?'

'Why to me it's as clear as daylight,' the other asserted impa- tiently. 'See here. Archer decides, let us suppose, that he will send out four kegs, or one hundred gallons, of the smuggled brandy to the Anchor Bar. What does he do? He fills out certificates for two consignments each of which contain an identical assortment of various liquors. The brandy he shows on one certificate only. The blocks are true copies of the certificates except that the brandy is not entered on either. The two blocks he times for a quarter past one and past four respectively, but both certificates he times for a quarter past one. He hands the two certificates to Fox. Then he sends out on the one o'clock lorry the amount of brandy shown on one of the certificates.'

Hunt paused and looked interrogatively at his friend, then, the latter not replying, he resumed:

'You follow now the position of affairs? In the office is Archer with his blocks, correctly filled out as to time, but neither showing the brandy. On the one o'clock lorry is Fox, with one hundred gallons of brandy among his load. In his pocket are the two certificates, both timed for one o'clock, one showing the brandy and the other not.'

The inspector nodded as Hunt again looked at him.

'Now suppose,' the latter went on, 'that the one o'clock lorry gets through to its destination unchallenged, and the stuff is unloaded. The manager arranges that the four kegs of brandy will disappear. He takes over the certificate which does not show brandy, signs it, and the transaction is complete. Everything is in order, and he has got his four kegs smuggled in.'

'Good,' Willis interjected.

'On the other hand, suppose the one o'clock trip is held up by an exciseman. This time Fox produces the other certificate, the one which shows the brandy. Once again everything is in order, and the Excise officer is satisfied. It is true that on this occasion Fox has been unable to smuggle out his brandy, and on that which he carries duty must be paid, but this rare contingency will not matter to him as long as his method of fraud remains concealed.'

'Seems very sound so far.'

'I think so. Let us now consider the four o'clock trip. Fox arrives back at the works with one of the two certificates still in his pocket, and the make up of his four o'clock load depends on which that is. He attempts no more smuggling that day. If his remaining certificate shows brandy he carries brandy, if not, he leaves it behind. In either case his certificate is in order if an Excise officer holds him up. That is, when he has attended to one little point. He has to add two strokes to the i of the hour to make it into a 4. The ease of doing this explains why these two hours were chosen. Is that all clear?'

'Clear, indeed, except for the one point of how the brandy item is added to the correct block.'

'Obviously Archer does that as soon as he learns how the first trip has got on. If the brandy was smuggled out on the first trip, it means that Fox is holding the brandy bearing certificate for the second, and Archer enters brandy on his second block. If, on the contrary, Fox has had his first load examined, Archer will make his entry on the first block.'

'The scheme,' Willis declared, 'really means this. If Archer wants to smuggle out one hundred gallons of brandy, he has to send out another hundred legitimately on the same day? If he can manage to send out two hundred altogether then one hundred will be duty clear, but in any case he must pay on one hundred?'

'That's right. It works out like that.'

'It's a great scheme. The only weak point that I can see is that an Excise officer who has held up one of the trips might visit the works and look at the certificate block before Archer gets it altered.'

Hunt nodded.

'I thought of that,' he said, 'and it can be met quite easily. I bet the manager telephones Archer on receipt of the stuff. I am going into that now. I shall have a note kept at the Central of conversations to Ferriby. If Archer doesn't get a message by a certain time, I bet he assumes the plan has miscarried for that day and fills in the brandy on the first block.'

During the next two days Hunt was able to establish the truth of his surmise. At the same time Willis decided that his co-operation in the work at Hull was no longer needed. For Hunt there was still plenty to be done. He had to get direct evidence against each severally of the managers of the five tied houses in question, as well as to ascertain how and to whom they were passing on the 'stuff', for that they were receiving more brandy than could be sold over their own counters was unquestionable. But he agreed with Willis that these five men were more than likely in ignorance of the main conspiracy, each having only a private understanding with Archer. But whether or not this was so, Willis did not believe he could get any evidence that they were implicated in the murder of Coburn.

The French end of the affair, he thought, the supply of the brandy in the first instance, was more promising from this point of view, and next morning he took an early train to London as a preliminary to starting work in France.

CHAPTER XVIII

THE BORDEAUX LORRIES

Two days later Inspector Willis sat once again in the office of M. Max, the head of the French Excise Department in Paris. The Frenchman greeted him politely, but without enthusiasm.

'Ah, monsieur,' he said. 'You have not received my letter? No? I wrote to your department yesterday.'

'It hadn't come, sir, when I left,' Willis returned. 'But perhaps if it is something I should know, you could tell me the contents?'

'But certainly, monsieur. It is easily done. A thousand regrets, but I fear my department will not be of much service to you.'

'No, sir?' Willis looked his question.

'I fear not. But I shall explain.' M. Max gesticulated as he talked. 'After your last visit here I send two of my men to Bordeaux. They make examination, but at first they see nothing suspicious. When the *Girondin* comes in they determine to test your idea of the brandy loading. They go in a boat to the wharf at night. They pull in between the rows of piles. They find the spaces between the tree trunks which you have described. They know there must be a cellar behind. They hide close by; they see the porthole lighted up; they watch the pipe go in, all exactly as you have said. There can be no doubt brandy is secretly loaded at the Lesque.'

'It seemed the likely thing, sir,' Willis commented.

'Ah, but it was good to think of. I wish to congratulate you on finding it out.' M. Max made a little bow. 'But to continue. My men wonder how the brandy reaches the saw-mill. Soon they think that the lorries must bring it. They think so for two reasons. First, they can find no other way. The lorries are the only vehicles which approach; nothing goes by water; there

246

cannot be a tunnel, because there is no place for the other end. There remains only the lorries. Second, they think it is the lorries because the drivers change the numbers. It is suspicious, is it not? Yes? You understand me?'

'Perfectly, sir.'

'Good. My men then watch the lorries. They get help from the police at Bordeaux. They find the firewood trade is a nothing.' M. Max shrugged his shoulders. 'There are five firms to which the lorries go, and of the five, four—' His gesture indicated a despair too deep for words. 'To serve them, it is but a blind; so my men think. But the fifth firm, it is that of Raymond Fils, one of the biggest distilleries of Bordeaux. That Raymond Fils are sending out the brandy suggests itself to my men. At last the affair marches.'

M. Max paused, and Willis bowed to signify his appreciation of the point.

'My men visit Raymond Fils. They search—into everything. They find the law is not broken. All is in order. They are satisfied.'

'But, sir, if these people are smuggling brandy into England—' Willis was beginning when the other interrupted him.

'But yes, monsieur, I grasp your point. I speak of French law; it is different from yours. Here duty is not charged on just so much spirit as is distilled. We grant the distiller a licence, and it allows him to distil any quantity up to the figure the licence bears. But, monsieur, Raymond Fils are—how do you say it?—well within their limit; is it not? Yes? They do not break the French law.'

'Therefore, sir, you mean that you cannot help further?'

M. Max spread out his hands deprecatingly.

'My dear monsieur, what would you? I have done my best for you. I make inquiries. The matter is not for me. With the most excellent wish to assist, what more can I?'

Willis, realising he could get no more, rose.

'Nothing, sir, except to accept on my own part and that of

my department our hearty thanks for what you have done. I can assure you, sir, I quite understand your position, and I greatly appreciate your kindness.'

M. Max also had risen. He politely repeated his regrets, and with mutual compliments the two men parted.

Willis had once spent a holiday in Paris, and he was slightly acquainted with the city. He strolled on through the busy streets, brilliant in the pale autumn sunlight, until he reached the Grands Boulevards. There entering a café, he sat down, called for a bock, and settled himself to consider his next step.

The position created by M. Max's action was disconcerting. Willis felt himself stranded, literally a stranger in a strange land, sent to carry out an investigation among a people whose language he could not even speak! He saw at once that his task was impossible. He must have local help or he could proceed no further.

He thought of his own department. The Excise had failed him. What about the Sûreté?

But a very little thought convinced him that he was even less likely to obtain help from this quarter. He could only base an appeal on the possibility of a future charge of conspiracy to murder, and he realised that the evidence for such was too slight to put forward seriously.

What was to be done? So far as he could see, but one thing. He must employ a private detective. This plan would meet the language difficulty by which he was so completely hung up.

He went to a call office and got his chief at the Yard on the long distance wire. The latter approved his suggestion, and recommended M. Jules Laroche of the Rue du Sommerard near the Sorbonne. Half an hour later Willis reached the house.

M. Laroche proved to be a tall, unobtrusive looking man of some five-and-forty, who had lived in London for some years and spoke as good English as Willis himself. He listened quietly and without much apparent interest to what his visitor had to tell him, then said he would be glad to take on the job.

'We had better go to Bordeaux this evening, so as to start fresh tomorrow,' Willis suggested.

'Two o'clock at the d'Orsay station,' the other returned. 'We have just time. We can settle our plans in the train.'

They reached the St Jean station at Bordeaux at 10.35 that night, and drove to the Hotel d'Espagne. They had decided that they could do nothing until the following evening, when they would go out to the clearing and see what a search of the mill premises might reveal.

Next morning Laroche vanished, saying he had friends in the town whom he wished to look up, and it was close on dinner-time before he put in an appearance.

'I have got some information that may help,' he said, as Willis greeted him. 'Though I'm not connected with the official force, we are very good friends and have often worked into each other's hands. I happen to know one of the officers of the local police, and he got me the information. It seems that a M. Pierre Raymond is practically the owner of Raymond Fils, the distillers you mentioned. He is a man of about thirty, and the son of one of the original brothers. He was at one time comfortably off, and lived in a pleasant villa in the suburbs. But latterly he has been going the pace, and within the last two years he let his villa and bought a tiny house next door to the distillery, where he is now living. It is believed his money went at Monte Carlo, indeed it seems he is a wrong 'un all round. At all events he is known to be hard up now.'

'And you think he moved in so that he could load up that brandy at night?'

'That's what I think,' Laroche admitted. 'You see, there is the motive for it as well. He wouldn't join the syndicate unless he was in difficulties. I fancy M. Pierre Raymond will be an interesting study.'

Willis nodded. The suggestion was worth investigation, and he congratulated himself on getting hold of so excellent a colleague as this Laroche seemed to be.

The Frenchman during the day had hired a motor bicycle and sidecar, and as dusk began to fall the two men left their hotel and ran out along the Bayonne road until they reached the Lesque. There they hid their vehicle behind some shrubs, and reaching the end of the lane, turned down it.

It was pitch dark among the trees, and they had some difficulty in keeping the track until they reached the clearing. There a quarter moon rendered objects dimly visible, and Willis at once recognised his surroundings from the description he had received from Hilliard and Merriman.

'You see, somebody is in the manager's house,' he whispered, pointing to a light which gleamed in the window. 'If Henri has taken over Coburn's job he may go down to the mill in the night as Coburn did. Hadn't we better wait and see?'

The Frenchman agreeing, they moved round the fringe of trees at the edge of the clearing, just as Merriman had done on a similar occasion some seven weeks earlier, and as they crouched in the shelter of a clump of bushes in front of the house, they might have been interested to know that it was from these same shrubs that that disconsolate sentimentalist had lain dreaming of his lady love, and from which he had witnessed her father's stealthy journey to the mill.

It was a good deal colder tonight than on that earlier occasion when watch was kept on the lonely house. The two men shivered as they drew their collars higher round their necks, and crouched down to get shelter from the bitter wind. They had resigned themselves to a weary vigil, during which they dared not even smoke.

But they had not to wait so long after all. About ten the light went out in the window, and not five minutes later they saw a man appear at the side door and walk towards the mill. They could not see his features, though Willis assumed he was Henri. Twenty minutes later they watched him return, and then all once more was still.

'We had better give him an hour to get to bed,' Willis whispered.

'If he were to look out it wouldn't do for him to see two detectives roaming about his beloved clearing.'

'We might go at eleven,' Laroche proposed, and so they did.

Keeping as much as possible in the shelter of the bushes, they approached the mill. Willis had got a sketch-plan of the building from Merriman, and he moved round to the office door. His bent wire proved as efficacious with French locks as with English, and in a few moments they stood within, with the door shut behind them.

'Now,' said Willis, carefully shading the beam of his electric torch, 'let's see those lorries first of all.'

As has already been stated, the garage was next to the office, and passing through the communicating door, the two men found five of the ponderous vehicles therein. A moment's examination of the number plates showed that on all the machines the figures were separate from the remainder of the lettering, being carried on small brass plates which dropped vertically into place through slots in the main castings. But the joint at each side of the number was not conspicuous because similar vertical lines were cut into the brass between each letter of the whole legend.

'That's good,' Laroche observed. 'Make a thing unnoticeable by multiplying it!'

Of the five lorries, two were loaded with firewood and three empty. The men moved round examining them with their torches.

'Hallo,' Laroche called suddenly in a low voice, 'what have we here, Willis?'

The inspector crossed over to the other, who was pointing to the granolithic floor in front of him. One of the empty lorries was close up to the office wall, and the Frenchman stood between the two. On the floor were three drops of some liquid.

'Can you smell them?' he inquired.

Willis knelt down and sniffed, then slowly got up again.

'Good man,' he said, with a trace of excitement in his manner. 'It's brandy right enough.'

'Yes,' returned the other. 'Security has made our nocturnal friend careless. The stuff must have come from this lorry, I fancy.'

They turned to the vehicle and examined it eagerly. For some time they could see nothing remarkable, but presently it gave up its secret. The deck was double! Beneath it was a hollow space some six feet wide by nine long, and not less than three inches deep. And not only so. This hollow space was continued up under the unusually large and wide driver's seat, save for a tiny receptacle for petrol. In a word, the whole top of the machine was a vast secret tank.

The men began measuring and calculating, and they soon found that no less than one hundred and fifty gallons of liquid could be carried therein.

'One hundred and fifty gallons of brandy per trip!' Willis ejaculated. 'Lord! It's no wonder they make it pay.'

They next tackled the problem of how the tank was filled and emptied, and at last their perseverance was rewarded. Behind the left trailing wheel, under the framing, was a small hinged door about six inches square, and fastened by a spring operated by a mock rivet head. This being opened, revealed a cavity containing a pipe connected to the tank and fitted with a stop-cock and the half of a union coupling.

'The pipe which connects with that can't be far away,' Laroche suggested. 'We might have a look round for it.'

The obvious place was the wall of the office, which ran not more than three feet from the vehicle. It was finished with vertical tongued and V-jointed sheeting, and a comparatively short search revealed the loose board the detectives were by this time expecting. Behind it was concealed a pipe, jointed concertina-wise, and ending in the other half of the union coupling. It was evident the joints would allow the half coupling to be pulled out and connected up with that on the lorry. The pipe ran down through the floor, showing that the lorry could be emptied by gravity.

'A good, safe scheme,' Laroche commented. 'If I had seen that lorry a hundred times I never should have suspected a tank. It's well designed.'

They turned to examine the other vehicles. All four were identical in appearance with the first, but all were strictly what they seemed, containing no secret receptacle.

'Merriman said they had six lorries,' Willis remarked. 'I wonder where the sixth is.'

'At the distillery, don't you think?' the Frenchman returned. 'Those drops prove that manager fellow has just been unloading this one. I expect he does it every night. But if so, Raymond must load a vehicle every night too.'

'That's true. We may assume the job is done every night, because Merriman watched Coburn come down here three nights running. It was certainly to unload the lorry.'

'Doubtless; and he probably came at two in the morning on account of his daughter.'

'That means there are two tank lorries,' Willis went on, continuing his own line of thought. 'I say, Laroche, let's mark this one so that we may know it again.'

They made tiny scratches on the paint at each corner of the big vehicle, then Willis turned back to the office.

'I'd like to find that cellar when we're here,' he remarked. 'We know there is a cellar, for those Customs men saw the *Girondin* loaded from it. We might have a look round for the entrance.'

Then ensued a search similar to that which Willis had carried out in the depot at Ferriby, except that in this case they found what they were looking for in a much shorter time. In the office was a flat roll-topped desk, with the usual set of drawers at each side of a central knee well, and when Willis found it was clamped to the floor he felt he need go no farther. On the ground in the knee well, and projecting out towards the revolving chair in front, was a mat. Willis raised it, and at once observed a joint across the boards where in ordinary circumstances no joint should be. He fumbled and pressed and pulled, and in a couple of minutes he had the satisfaction of seeing the floor under the well rise and reveal the head of a ladder leading down into the darkness below.

'Here we are,' he called softly to Laroche, who was searching at the other side of the room.

The cellar into which the two detectives descended was lined with timber like that at Ferriby. Indeed the two were identical, except that only one passage—that under the wharf—led out of this one. It contained a similar large tun with a pipe leading down the passage under the wharf, on which was a pump. The only difference was in the connection of the pipes. At Ferriby the pump conveyed from the wharf to the tun, here it was from the tun to the wharf. The pipe from the garage came down through the ceiling and ran direct into the tun.

The two men walked down the passage towards the river. Here also the arrangement was the same as at Ferriby, and they remained only long enough for Willis to point out to the Frenchman how the loading apparatus was worked.

'Well,' said the former, as they returned to the office, 'that's not so bad for one day. I suppose it's all we can do here. If we can learn as much at that distillery we shall soon have all we want.'

Laroche pointed to a chair.

'Sit down a moment,' he invited. 'I have been thinking over that plan we discussed in the train, of searching the distillery at night, and I don't like it. There are too many people about, and we are nearly certain to be seen. It's quite different from working a place like this.'

'Quite,' Willis answered rather testily. 'I don't like it either, but what can we do?'

'I'll tell you what I should do.' Laroche leaned forward and checked his points on his fingers. 'That lorry has just been unloaded. It's empty now, and if our theory is correct it will be taken to the distillery tomorrow and left there over night to be filled up again. Isn't that so?'

Willis nodded impatiently and the other went on:

'Now, it is clear that no one can fill up that tank without leaving finger-prints on the pipe connections in that secret box. Suppose we clean those surfaces now, and suppose we come back here the night after tomorrow, *before* the man here unloads, we could get the prints of the person who filled up in the distillery.'

'Well,' Willis asked sharply, 'and how would that help us?'

'This way. Tomorrow you will be an English distiller with a forest you could get cheap near your works. You have an idea of running your stills on wood fires. You naturally call to see how M. Raymond does it, and you get shown over his works. You have prepared a plan of your proposals. You hand it to him when he can't put it down on a desk. He holds it between his fingers and thumb, and eventually returns it to you. You go home and use powder. You have his finger-prints. You compare the two sets.'

Willis was impressed. The plan was simple, and it promised to gain for them all the information they required without recourse to a hazardous nocturnal visit to the distillery. But he wished he had thought of it himself.

'We might try it,' he admitted, without enthusiasm. 'It couldn't do much harm anyway.'

They returned to the garage, opened the secret lid beneath the lorry, and with a cloth moistened with petrol cleaned the fittings. Then after a look round to make sure that nothing had been disturbed, they let themselves out of the shed, regained the lane and their machine, and some forty minutes later were in Bordeaux.

On reconsideration they decided that as Raymond might have obtained Willis's description from Captain Beamish, it would be wiser for Laroche to visit the distillery. Next morning, therefore, the latter bought a small writing block, and taking an inside leaf, which he carefully avoided touching with his hands, he drew a cross-section of a wood-burning fire-box copied from an illustration in a book of reference in the city library, at the same time reading up the subject so as to be able to talk on it without giving himself away. Then he set out on his mission.

In a couple of hours he returned.

'Got that all right,' he exclaimed, as he rejoined the inspector. 'I went and saw the fellow; said I was going to start a distillery in the Ardennes where there was plenty of wood, and wanted to see his plant. He was very civil, and took me round and showed me everything. There is a shed there above the still furnaces with hoppers for the firewood to go down, and in it was standing the lorry—*the* lorry, I saw our marks on the corner. It was loaded with firewood, and he explained that it would be emptied last thing before the day-shift left, so as to do the stills during the night. Well, I got a general look round the concern, and I found that the large tuns which contain the finished brandy were just at the back of the wall of the shed where the lorry was standing. So it is easy to see what happens. Evidently there is a pipe through the wall, and Raymond comes down at night and fills up the lorry.'

'And did you get his finger-prints?'

'Have 'em here.'

Locking the door of their private room, Laroche took from his pocket the sketch he had made.

'He held this up quite satisfactorily,' he went on, 'and there should be good prints.'

Willis had meanwhile spread a newspaper on the table and taken from his suitcase a small bottle of powdered lamp-black and a camel's-hair brush. Laying the sketch on the newspaper he gently brushed some of the black powder over it, blowing off the surplus. To the satisfaction of both men, there showed up near the left bottom corner the distinct mark of a left thumb.

'Now the other side.'

Willis turned the paper and repeated the operation on the back. There he got prints of a left fore and second finger.

'Excellent, clear prints, those,' Willis commented, continuing: 'And now I have something to tell you. While you were away I have been thinking over this thing, and I believe I've got an idea.'

Laroche looked interested, and the other went on slowly:

'There are two brandy carrying lorries. Every night one of these lies at the distillery and the other at the clearing; one is being loaded and the other unloaded; and every day the two change places. Now we may take it that neither of those lorries are sent to any other place in the town, lest the brandy tanks might be discovered. For the same reason, they probably only make the one run mentioned per day. Is that right so far?'

'I should think so,' Laroche replied cautiously.

'Very well. Let us suppose these two lorries are Nos. 1 and 2. No. 1 goes to the distillery, say, every Monday, Wednesday and Friday, and returns on the other three days, while No. 2 does vice versa, one trip each day, remember. And this goes on day after day, week after week, month after month. Now is it too much to assume that sooner or later some one is bound to notice this—some worker at the clearing or the distillery, some policeman on his beat, some clerk at a window overlooking the route? And if any one notices it will he not wonder why it *always* happens that these two lorries go to this one place and to no other, while the syndicate has six lorries altogether trading into the town? And if this observer should mention his discovery to some one who could put two and two together, suspicion might be aroused, investigation undertaken, and presently the syndicate is up a tree. Now do you see what I'm getting at?'

Laroche had been listening eagerly, and now he made a sudden gesture.

'But of course!' he cried delightedly. 'The changing of the numbers!'

'The changing of the numbers,' Willis repeated. 'At least, it looks like that to me. No. 1 does the Monday run to the distillery. They change the number plate, and No. 4 does it on Wednesday, while No. 1 runs to some other establishment, where it can be freely examined by any one who is interested. How does it strike you?'

'You have got it. You have certainly got it.' Laroche was more enthusiastic than the inspector had before seen him. 'It's what you call a cute scheme, quite on a par with the rest of the business. They didn't leave much to chance, these! And yet it was this very precaution that gave them away.'

'No doubt, but that was an accident.'

'You can't,' said the Frenchman sententiously, 'make *anything* completely watertight.'

The next night they went out to the clearing, and as soon as it was dark once more entered the shed. There with more powder—white this time—they tested the tank lorry for finger-marks. As they had hoped, there were several on the secret fittings, among others a clear print of a left thumb on the rivet head of the spring.

A moment's examination only was necessary. The prints were those of M. Pierre Raymond.

Once again Inspector Willis felt that he ought to have completed his case, and once again second thoughts showed him that he was as far away from that desired end as ever. He had been trying to find accomplices in the murder of Coburn, and by a curious perversity, instead of finding them he had bit by bit solved the mystery of the Pit-Prop Syndicate. He had shown, firstly, that they were smuggling brandy, and, secondly, how they were doing it. For that he would no doubt get a reward, but such was not his aim. What he wanted was to complete his own case and get the approval of his own superiors and bring promotion nearer. And in this he had failed.

For hours he pondered over the problem, then suddenly an idea which seemed promising flashed into his mind. He thought it over with the utmost care, and finally decided that in the absence of something better he must try it.

In the morning the two men travelled to Paris, and Willis, there taking leave of his colleague, crossed to London, and an hour later was with his chief at the Yard.

CHAPTER XIX

WILLIS SPREADS HIS NET

THOUGH Inspector Willis had spent so much time out of London in his following up of the case, he had by no means lost sight of Madeleine Coburn and Merriman. The girl, he knew, was still staying with her aunt at Eastbourne, and the local police authorities, from whom he got his information, believed that her youth and health were reasserting themselves, and that she was rapidly recovering from the shock of her father's tragic death. Merriman haunted the town. He practically lived at the George, going up and down daily to his office, and spending as many of his evenings and his Sundays at Mrs Luttrell's as he dared.

But though the young man had worn himself almost to a shadow by his efforts, he felt that the realisation of his hopes was as far off as ever. Madeleine had told him that she would not marry him until the mystery of her father's murder was cleared up and the guilty parties brought to justice, and he was becoming more and more afraid that she would keep her word. In vain he implored her to consider the living rather than the dead, and not to wreck his life and her own for what, after all, was but a sentiment. But though she listened to his entreaties and was always kind and gentle, she remained inflexible in her resolve. Merriman felt that his only plan, failing the discovery of Mr Coburn's assassin, was unobtrusively to keep as much as possible in her company, in the hope that she would grow accustomed to his presence, and perhaps in time come to need it.

Under these circumstances his anxiety as to the progress of the case was very great, and on several occasions he had written to Willis asking him how his inquiry was going on. But the inspector had not been communicative, and Merriman had no idea how matters actually stood.

It was therefore with feelings of pleasurable anticipation that he received a telephone call from Willis at Scotland Yard.

'I have just returned from Bordeaux,' the inspector said, 'and I am anxious to have a chat with Miss Coburn on some points that have arisen. I should be glad of your presence also, if possible. Can you arrange an interview?'

'Do you want her to come to town?'

'Not necessarily; I will go to Eastbourne if more convenient. But our meeting must be kept strictly secret. The syndicate must not get to know.'

Merriman felt excitement and hope rising within him.

'Better go to Eastbourne then,' he advised. 'Come down with me tonight by the 5.20 from Victoria.'

'No,' Willis answered, 'we mustn't be seen together. I shall meet you at the corner of the Grand Parade and Carlisle Road at nine o'clock.'

This being agreed on, both men began to make their arrangements. In Merriman's case these consisted in throwing up his work at the office and taking the first train to Eastbourne. At five o'clock he was asking for Miss Coburn at Mrs Luttrell's door.

'Dear Madeleine,' he said, when he had told her his news, 'you must not begin to expect things. It may mean nothing at all. Don't build on it.'

But soon he had made her as much excited as he was himself. He stayed for dinner, leaving shortly before nine to keep his appointment with Willis. Both men were then to return to the house, when Madeleine would see them alone.

Inspector Willis did not travel by Merriman's train. Instead he caught the 5.35 to Brighton, dined there, and then slipping out of the hotel, motored over to Eastbourne. Dismissing his vehicle at the Grand Hotel, he walked down the Parade and found Merriman at the rendezvous. In ten minutes they were in Mrs Luttrell's drawing-room.

'I am sorry, Miss Coburn,' Willis began politely, 'to intrude on you in this way, but the fact is, I want your help and indirectly the help of Mr Merriman. But it is only fair, I think, to tell you first what has transpired since we last met. I must warn you, however, that I can only do so in the strictest confidence. No whisper of what I am going to say must pass the lips of either of you.'

'I promise,' said Merriman instantly.

'And I,' echoed Madeleine.

'I didn't require that assurance,' Willis went on. 'It is sufficient that you understand the gravity of the situation. Well, after the inquest I set to work,' and he briefly related the story of his investigations in London and in Hull, his discoveries at Ferriby, his proof that Archer was the actual murderer, the details of the smuggling organisation and, finally, his suspicion that the other members of the syndicate were privy to Mr Coburn's death, together with his failure to prove it.

His two listeners heard him with eager attention, in which interest in his story was mingled with admiration of his achievement.

'So Hilliard was right about the brandy after all!' Merriman exclaimed. 'He deserves some credit for that. I think he believed in it all the time, in spite of our conclusion that we had proved it impossible. *By* Jove! *How* you can be had!'

Willis turned to him.

'Don't be disappointed about your part in it, sir,' he advised. 'I consider that you and Mr Hilliard did uncommonly well. I may tell you that I thought so much of your work that I checked nothing of what you had done.'

Merriman coloured with pleasure.

'Jolly good of you to say so, I'm sure, inspector,' he said; 'but I'm afraid most of the credit for that goes to Hilliard.'

'It was your joint work I was speaking of,' Willis insisted.

'But now to get on to business. As I said, my difficulty is that I suspect the members of the syndicate of complicity in Mr Coburn's death, but I can't prove it. I have thought out a plan which may or may not produce this proof. It is in this that I want your help.'

'Mr Inspector,' cried Madeleine reproachfully, 'need you ask for it?'

Willis laughed.

'I don't think so. But I can't very well come in and command it, you know.'

'Of course you can,' Madeleine returned. 'You know very well that in such a cause Mr Merriman and I would do *anything*.'

'I believe it, and I am going to put you to the test. I'll tell you my idea. It has occurred to me that these people might be made to give themselves away. Suppose they had one of their private meetings to discuss the affairs of the syndicate, and that, unknown to them, witnesses could be present to overhear what was said. Would there not at least be a sporting chance that they would incriminate themselves?'

'Yes!' said Merriman, much interested. 'Likely enough. But I don't see how you could arrange that.'

Willis smiled slightly.

'I think it might be managed,' he answered. 'If a meeting were to take place we could easily learn where it was to be held and hear what went on. But the first point is the difficulty—the question of the holding of the meeting. In the ordinary course there might be none for months. Therefore we must take steps to have one summoned. And that,' he turned to Madeleine, 'is where I want your help.'

His hearers stared, mystified, and Willis resumed.

'Something must happen of such importance to the welfare of the syndicate that the leaders will decide that a full conference of the members is necessary. So far as I can see, you alone can cause that something to happen. I will tell you how. But I must warn you that I fear it will rake up painful memories.'

Madeleine, her lips parted, was hanging on his words.

'Go on,' she said quickly, 'we have settled all that.'

'Thank you,' said Willis, taking a sheet of paper from his pocket. 'I have here the draft of a letter which I want you to write to Captain Beamish. You can phrase it as you like; in fact, I want it in your own words. Read it over and you will understand.'

The draft ran as follows:

> 'SILVERDALE ROAD,
> 'EASTBOURNE.

> 'DEAR CAPTAIN BEAMISH,—In going over some papers belonging to my late father, I learn to my surprise that he was not a salaried official of your syndicate, but a partner. It seems to me, therefore, that as his heir I am entitled to his share of the capital of the concern, or at all events to the interest on it. I have to express my astonishment that no recognition of this fact has as yet been made by the syndicate.

> 'I may say that I have also come on some notes relative to the business of the syndicate, which have filled me with anxiety and dismay, but which I do not care to refer to in detail in writing.

> 'I think I should like an interview with you to hear your explanation of these two matters, and to discuss what action is to be taken with regard to them. You could perhaps find it convenient to call on me here, or I could meet you in London if you preferred it.

> 'Yours faithfully,
> 'MADELEINE COBURN.'

Madeleine made a grimace as she read this letter. 'Oh,' she cried, 'but how could I do that? I didn't find any notes, you know, and besides—it would be so dreadful—acting as a decoy—'

'There's something more important than that,' Merriman burst in indignantly. 'Do you realise, Mr Inspector, that if Miss Coburn were to send that letter she would put herself in very real danger?'

'Not at all,' Willis answered quietly. 'You have not heard my whole scheme. My idea is that when Beamish gets that letter he will lay it before Archer, and they will decide that they must find out what Miss Coburn knows, and get her quieted about the money. They will say: "We didn't think she was that kind, but it's evident she is out for what she can get. Let's pay her a thousand or two a year as interest on her father's alleged share—it will be a drop in the bucket to us, but it will seem a big thing to her—and that will give us a hold on her keeping silence, if she really does know anything." Then Beamish will ask Miss Coburn to meet him, probably in London. She will do so, not alone, but with some near friend, perhaps yourself, Mr Merriman, seeing you were at the clearing and know something of the circumstances. You will be armed, and in addition I shall have a couple of men from the Yard within call—say, disguised as waiters, if a restaurant is chosen for the meeting. You, Miss Coburn, will come out in a new light at that meeting. You will put up a bluff. You will tell Captain Beamish you know he is smuggling brandy, and that the money he offers won't meet the case at all. You must have £25,000 down, paid as the value of your father's share in the concern, and in such a way as will raise no suspicion that you knew what was in progress. The interview we can go into in detail later, but it must be so arranged that Beamish will see Mr Merriman's hand in the whole thing. On the £25,000 being paid the incriminating notes will be handed over. You will explain that as a precautionary measure you have sent them in a sealed envelope to your solicitor, together with a statement of the whole case, with instructions to open the same that afternoon if not reclaimed before that by yourself in person. Now with regard to your objection, Miss Coburn. I quite realise what an exceedingly nasty job this will be for you. In ordinary circumstances I should not suggest it. But the people against whom I ask you to act did not hesitate to lure your father into the cab in which they intended to shoot him. They did this by a show of friendliness, and by playing on the trust he reposed in them, and they did it deliberately and in cold blood. You need not hesitate from nice feeling to act as I suggest in order to get justice for your father's memory.'

Madeleine braced herself.

'I know you are right, and if there is no other way I shall not hesitate,' she said, but there was a piteous look in her eyes. 'And you will help me, Seymour?' She looked appealingly at her companion.

Merriman demurred on the ground that, even after taking all Willis's precautions, the girl would still be in danger, but she would not consider that aspect of the question at all, and at last he was overborne. Madeleine with her companion's help then rewrote the letter in her own phraseology, and addressed it to Captain Beamish, c/o Messrs The Landes Pit-Prop Syndicate, Ferriby, Hull. Having arranged that he would receive immediate telephonic information of a reply, Willis left the house and was driven back to Brighton. Next morning he returned to London.

The *Girondin*, he reckoned, would reach Ferriby on the following Friday, and on Thursday he returned to Hull. He did not want to be seen with Hunt, as he expected the latter's business would by this time be too well known. He therefore went to a different hotel, ringing up the Excise man and arranging a meeting for that evening.

Hunt turned up about nine, and the two men retired to Willis's bedroom, where the inspector described his doings at Bordeaux. Then Hunt told of his discoveries since the other had left.

'I've got all I want at last,' he said. 'You remember we both realised that those five houses were getting in vastly more brandy than they could possibly sell? Well, I've found out how they are getting rid of the surplus.'

Willis looked his question.

'They are selling it round to other houses. They have three men doing nothing else. They go in and buy anything from a bottle up to three or four kegs, and there is always a good reason for the purchase. Usually it is that they represent a publican whose stock is just out, and who wants a quantity to keep him going. But the point is that all the purchases are perfectly in order. They are openly made and the full price is paid. But, following it up, I discovered that there is afterwards a secret rebate. A small percentage of the price is refunded. This pays every one concerned and ensures secrecy.'

Willis nodded.

'It's well managed all through,' he commented. 'They deserved to succeed.'

'Yes, but they're not going to. All the same my discoveries won't help you. I'm satisfied that none of these people know anything of the main conspiracy.'

Early on the following morning Willis was once more at work. Dawn had not completely come when he motored from the city to the end of the Ferriby lane. Ten minutes after leaving his car he was in the ruined cottage. There he unearthed his telephone from the box in which he had hidden it, and took up his old position at the window, prepared to listen in to whatever messages might pass.

He had a longer vigil than on previous occasions, and it was not until nearly four that he saw Archer lock the door of his office and move towards the filing-room. Almost immediately came Benson's voice calling: 'Are you there?'

They conversed as before for a few moments. The *Girondin*, it appeared, had arrived some two hours previously with a cargo of '1375'. It was clear that the members of the syndicate had agreed never to mention the word 'gallons.' It was, Willis presumed, a likely enough precaution against eavesdroppers, and he thought how much sooner both Hilliard and himself would have guessed the real nature of the conspiracy, had it not been observed.

Presently they came to the subject about which Willis was expecting to hear. Beamish, the manager explained, was there and wished to speak to Archer.

'That you, Archer?' came in what Willis believed he recognised as the captain's voice. 'I've had rather a nasty jar, a letter from Madeleine Coburn. Wants Coburn's share in the affair, and hints at knowledge of what we're really up to. Reads as if she was put up to it by some one, probably that—Merriman. Hold on a minute and I'll read it to you.' Then followed Madeleine's letter.

Archer's reply was short, but lurid, and Willis, notwithstanding the seriousness of the matter, could not help smiling.

There was a pause, and then Archer asked:

'When did you get that?'

'Now, when we got in; but Benson tells me the letter has been waiting for me for three days.'

'You might read it again.'

Beamish did so, and presently Archer went on:

'In my opinion, we needn't be unduly alarmed. Of course she may know something, but I fancy it's what you say; that Merriman is getting her to put up a bluff. But it'll take thinking over. I have an appointment presently, and in any case we couldn't discuss it adequately over the telephone. We must meet. Could you come up to my house tonight?'

'Yes, if you think it wise.'

'It's not wise, but I think we must risk it. You're not known here. But come alone; Benson shouldn't attempt it.'

'Right. What time?'

'What about nine? I often work in the evenings, and I'm never disturbed. Come round to my study window and I shall be there. Tap lightly. The window is on the right-hand side of the house as you come up the drive, the fourth from the corner.

You can slip round to it in the shadow of the bushes, and keep on the grass the whole time.'

'Right. Nine o'clock, then.'

The switch of the telephone clicked, and presently Willis saw Archer reappear in his office.

The inspector was disappointed. He had hoped that the conspirators would have completed their plans over the telephone, and that he would have had nothing to do but listen to what they arranged. Now he saw that if he were to gain the information he required, it would mean a vast deal more trouble, and perhaps danger as well.

He felt that at all costs he must be present at the interview in Archer's study, but the more he thought about it, the more difficult the accomplishment of this seemed. He was ignorant of the plan of the house, or what hiding-places, if any, there might be in the study, nor could he think of any scheme by which he could gain admittance. Further, there was but little time in which to make inquiries or arrangements, as he could not leave his present retreat until dark, or say six o'clock. He saw the problem would be one of the most difficult he had ever faced.

But the need for solving it was paramount, and when darkness had set in he let himself out of the cottage and walked the mile or more to Archer's residence. It was a big square block of a house, approached by a short winding drive, on each side of which was a border of rhododendrons. The porch was in front, and the group of windows to the left of it were lighted up—the dining-room, Willis imagined. He followed the directions given to Beamish and moved round to the right, keeping well in the shadow of the shrubs. The third and fourth windows from the corner on the right side were also lighted up, and the inspector crept silently up and peeped over the sill. The blinds were drawn down, but that on the third window was not quite pulled to the bottom, and through the narrow slit remaining he could see into the room.

It was empty, but evidently only for the time being, as a cheerful fire burned in the grate. Furnished as a study, everything bore the impress of wealth and culture. By looking from each end of the slot in turn, nearly all the floor area and more than half that of the walls became visible, and a glance showed the inspector that nowhere in his purview was there anything behind which he might conceal himself, supposing he could obtain admission.

But could he obtain admission? He examined the sashes. They were of steel, hinged and opening inwards in the French manner, and were fastened by a handle which could not be turned from without. Had they been the ordinary English sashes fastened with snibs he would have had the window open in a few seconds, but with these he could do nothing.

He moved round the house examining the other windows. All were fitted with the same type of sash, and all were fastened. The front door also was shut, and though he might have been able to open it with his bent wire, he felt that to adventure himself into the hall without any idea of the interior would be too dangerous. Here, as always, he was hampered by the fact that discovery would mean the ruin of his case.

Having completed the circuit of the building, he looked once more through the study window. At once he saw that his opportunity was gone. At the large desk sat Archer, busily writing.

Various expedients to obtain admission to the house passed through his brain, all to be rejected as impracticable. Unless some unexpected incident occurred of which he could take advantage, he began to fear he would be unable to accomplish his plan.

As by this time it was half-past eight, he withdrew from the window and took up his position behind a neighbouring shrub. He did not wish to be seen by Beamish, should the latter come early to the rendezvous.

He had, however, to wait for more than half an hour before

a dark form became vaguely visible in the faint light which shone through the study blinds. It approached the window, and a tap sounded on the glass. In a moment the blind went up, the sash opened, the figure passed through, the sash closed softly, and the blind was once more drawn down. In three seconds Willis was back at the sill.

The slot under the blind still remained, the other window having been opened. Willis first examined the fastening of the latter in the hope of opening the sash enough to hear what was said, but to his disappointment he found it tightly closed. He had therefore to be content with observation through the slot.

He watched the two men sit down at either side of the fire, and light cigars. Then Beamish handed the other a paper, presumably Madeleine's letter. Archer having read it twice, a discussion began. At first Archer seemed to be making some statement, to judge by the other's rapt attention and the gestures of excitement or concern which he made. But no word of the conversation reached the inspector's ears.

He watched for nearly two hours, getting gradually more and more cramped from his stooping position, and chilled by the sharp autumn air. During all that time the men talked earnestly, then, shortly after eleven, they got up and approached the window. Willis retreated quickly behind his bush.

The window opened softly and Beamish stepped out to the grass, the light shining on his strong, rather lowering face. Archer leant out of the window after him, and Willis heard him say in low tones, 'Then you'll speak up at eleven?' to which the other nodded and silently withdrew. The window closed, the blind was lowered, and all remained silent.

Willis waited for some minutes to let the captain get clear away, then leaving his hiding-place and again keeping on the grass, he passed down the drive and out on to the road. He was profoundly disappointed. He had failed in his purpose, and the only ray of light in the immediate horizon was that last remark of Archer's. If it meant, as he presumed it did, that the men were to communicate by the secret telephone at eleven in the morning, all might not yet be lost. He might learn then what he had missed tonight.

It seemed hardly worth while returning to Hull. He therefore went to the Raven Bar in Ferriby, knocked up the landlord, and by paying four or five times the proper amount, managed to get a meal and some food for the next day. Then returning to the deserted cottage, he let himself in, closed the door behind him, and lying down on the floor with his head on his arm, fell asleep.

Next morning found him back at his post at the broken window, with the telephone receiver at his ear. His surmise of the meaning of Archer's remark at the study window proved to be correct, for precisely at eleven he heard the familiar: 'Are you there?' which heralded a conversation. Then Beamish's voice went on:

'I have talked this business over with Benson, and he makes a suggestion which I think is an improvement on our plan. He thinks we should have our general meeting in London immediately after I have interviewed Madeleine Coburn. The advantage of this scheme would be that if we found she possessed really serious knowledge, we could immediately consider our next move, and I could, if necessary, see her again that night. Benson thinks I should fix up a meeting with her at say 10.30 or 11, that I could then join you at lunch at 1.30, after which we could discuss my report, and I could see the girl again at 4 or 5 o'clock. It seems to me a sound scheme. What do you say?'

'It has advantages,' Archer answered slowly. 'If you both think it best, I'm quite agreeable. Where then should the meetings be held?'

'In the case of Miss Coburn there would be no change in our last night's arrangement; a private sitting-room at the Gresham would still do excellently. If you're going to town you could fix up some place for our own meeting—preferably fairly close by.'

'Very well, I'm going up on Tuesday in any case, and I'll arrange something. I shall let Benson know, and he can tell you and the others. I think we should all go up by separate trains. I shall probably go by the 5.03 from Hull on the evening before. Let's see, when will you be in again?'

'Monday week about midday, I expect. Benson could go up that morning, Bulla and I separately by the 4, and Fox, Henri and Raymond, if he comes, by the first train next morning. How would that do?'

'All right, I think. The meetings then will be on Tuesday at 11 and 1.30, Benson to give you the address of the second. We can arrange at the meeting about returning to Hull.'

'Righto,' Beamish answered shortly, and the conversation ended.

Willis for once was greatly cheered by what he had overheard. His failure on the previous evening was evidently not going to be so serious as he had feared. He had in spite of it gained a knowledge of the conspirators' plans, and he chuckled with delight as he thought how excellently his ruse was working, and how completely the gang were walking into the trap which he had prepared. As far as he could see, he held all the trump cards of the situation, and if he played his hand carefully he should undoubtedly get not only the men, but the evidence to convict them.

To learn the rendezvous for the meeting of the syndicate he would have to follow Archer to town, and shadow him as he did his business. This was Saturday, and the managing director had said he was going on the following Tuesday. From that there would be a week until the meeting, which would give more than time to make the necessary arrangements.

Willis remained in the cottage until dark that evening, then making his way to Ferriby station, returned to Hull. His first action on reaching the city was to send a letter to Madeleine, asking her to forward Beamish's reply to him at the Yard.

On Monday he began his shadowing of Archer, lest the latter should go to town that day. But the distiller made no move until the Tuesday, travelling up that morning by the 6.15. from Hull.

At 12. 25 they reached King's Cross. Archer leisurely left the train, and crossing the platform, stepped into a taxi and was driven away. Willis, in a second taxi, followed about fifty yards behind. The chase led westwards along the Euston Road until, turning to the left down Gower Street, the leading vehicle pulled up at the door of the Gresham Hotel in Bedford Square. Willis's taxi ran on past the other, and through the backlight the inspector saw Archer alight and pass into the hotel.

Stopping at a door in Bloomsbury Street, Willis sat watching. In about five minutes Archer reappeared, and again entering his taxi, was driven off southwards. Willis's car slid in once more behind the other, and the chase recommenced. They crossed Oxford Street, and passing down Charing Cross Road stopped at a small foreign restaurant in a narrow lane off Cranbourne Street.

Willis's taxi repeated its previous manœuvre, and halted opposite a shop from where the inspector could see the other vehicle through the backlight. He thought he had all the information he needed, but there was the risk that Archer might not find the room he required at the little restaurant, and have to try elsewhere.

This second call lasted longer than the first, and a quarter of an hour had passed before the distiller emerged and re-entered his taxi. This time the chase was short. At the Trocadero Archer got out, dismissed his taxi, and passed into the building. Willis, following discreetly, was in time to see the other seat himself at a table and leisurely take up the bill of fare. Believing the quarry would remain where he was for another half-hour at least, the inspector slipped unobserved out of the room, and jumping once more into his taxi, was driven back to the little restaurant off Cranbourne Street.

He sent for the manager and drew him aside.

'I'm Inspector Willis from Scotland Yard,' he said, with a sharpness strangely at variance with his usual easy-going mode of address. 'See here.' He showed his credentials, at which the manager bowed obsequiously. 'I am following that gentleman who was in here inquiring about a room a few minutes ago. I want to know what passed between you.'

The manager, who was a sly, evil-looking person seemingly of Semitic blood, began to hedge, but Willis cut him short with scant ceremony.

'Now look here, my friend,' he said brusquely, 'I haven't time to waste with you. That man that you were talking to is wanted for murder, and what you have to decide is whether you're going to act with the police or against them. If you give us any trouble you may find yourself in the dock as an accomplice after the fact. In any case it's not healthy for a man in your position to run up against the police.'

His bluff had more effect than it might have had with an Englishman in similar circumstances, and the manager became polite and anxious to assist. Yes, the gentleman had come about a room. He had ordered lunch in a private room for a party of seven for 1.30 on the following Tuesday. He had been very particular about the room, had insisted on seeing it, and had approved of it. It appeared the party had some business to discuss after lunch, and the gentleman had required a guarantee that they would not be interrupted. The gentleman had given his name as Mr Hodgson. The price had been agreed on.

Willis in his turn demanded to see the room, and he was led upstairs to a small and rather dark chamber, containing a fair-sized oval table surrounded by red plush chairs, a red plush sofa along one side, and a narrow sideboard along another. The walls supported tawdry and dilapidated decorations, in which bevelled mirrors and faded gilding bore a prominent part. Two large but quite worthless oil paintings hung above the fireplace and the sideboard respectively, and the window was covered with gelatine paper simulating stained glass.

Inspector Willis stood surveying the scene with a frown on his brow. How on earth was he to secrete himself in this barely furnished apartment? There was not room under the sofa, still less beneath the sideboard. Nor was there any adjoining room or cupboard in which he could hide, his keen ear pressed to the keyhole. It seemed to him that in this case he was doing nothing but coming up against one insoluble problem after another. Ruefully he recalled the conversation in Archer's study, and he decided that, whatever the cost in time and trouble, there must be no repetition of that fiasco.

He stood silently pondering over the problem, the manager obsequiously bowing and rubbing his hands. And then the idea for which he was hoping flashed into his mind. He walked to the wall behind the sideboard and struck it sharply. It rang hollow.

'A partition?' he asked. 'What is behind it?'

'Anozzer room, sair. A private room, same as dees.'

'Show it to me.'

The 'ozzer room' was smaller, but otherwise similar to that they had just left. The doors of the two rooms were beside each other, leading on to the same passage.

'This will do,' Willis declared. 'Now look here, Mr Manager, I wish to overhear the conversation of your customers, and I may or may not wish to arrest them. You will show them up and give them lunch exactly as you have arranged. Some officers from the Yard and myself will previously have hidden ourselves in here. See?'

The manager nodded.

'In the meantime I shall send a carpenter and have a hole made in that partition between the two rooms, a hole about two feet by one, behind the upper part of that picture that hangs above the sideboard. Do you understand?'

The manager wrung his hands.

'Ach!' he cried. 'But *meine Zimmern!* Mine rooms, zey veel pe deestroyed!'

'Your rooms will be none the worse,' Willis declared. 'I will have the damage made good, and I shall pay you reasonably well for everything. You'll not lose if you act on the square, but if not—' he stared aggressively in the other's face—'if the slightest hint of my plan reaches any of the men—well, it will be ten years at least.'

'It shall pe done! All shall happen as you say!'

'It had better,' Willis rejoined, and with a menacing look strode out of the restaurant.

'The Gresham Hotel,' he called to his driver, as he re-entered his taxi.

His manner to the manageress of the Bedford Square hotel was very different from that displayed to the German Jew. Introducing himself as an inspector from the Yard, he inquired the purpose of Archer's call. Without hesitation he was informed. The distiller had engaged a private sitting-room for a business interview which was to take place at eleven o'clock on the following Tuesday between a Miss Coburn, a Mr Merriman and a Captain Beamish.

'So far so good,' thought Willis exultingly, as he drove off. 'They're walking into the trap! I shall have them all. I shall have them in a week.'

At the Yard he dismissed his taxi, and on reaching his room he found the letter he was expecting from Madeleine. It contained that from Beamish, and the latter read:

'FERRIBY, YORKS,
'*Saturday*.

'DEAR MISS COBURN,—I have just received your letter of 25th inst., and I hasten to reply.

'I am deeply grieved to learn that you consider yourself badly treated by the members of the syndicate, and I may say at once that I feel positive that any obligations which they may have contracted will be immediately and honourably discharged.

'It is, however, news to me that your late father was a partner, as I always imagined he held his position as I do my own, namely, as a salaried official who also receives a bonus based on the profits of the concern.

'With regard to the notes you have found on the operations of the syndicate, it is obvious that these must be capable of a simple explanation, as there was nothing in the operations complicated or difficult to understand.

'I shall be very pleased to fall in with your suggestion that we should meet and discuss the points at issue, and I would suggest 11 a.m. on Tuesday, 10th prox., at the Gresham Hotel in Bedford Square, if this would suit you.

'With kind regards,
'Yours sincerely,
'WALTER BEAMISH.'

Willis smiled as he read this effusion. It was really quite well worded, and left the door open for any action which the syndicate might decide on. 'Ah, well, my friend,' he thought grimly, 'you'll get a little surprise on Tuesday. You'll find Miss Coburn is not to be caught as easily as you think. Just you wait and see.'

For the next three or four days Willis busied himself in preparing for his great coup. First he went down again to Eastbourne via Brighton, and coached Madeleine and Merriman in the part they were to play in the coming interview. Next he superintended the making of the hole through the wall dividing the two private rooms at the Cranbourne Street restaurant, and drilled the party of men who were to occupy the annexe. To his unbounded satisfaction, he found that every word uttered at the table in the larger room was audible next door to any one standing at the aperture. Then he detailed two picked men to wait within call of the private room at the Gresham during the interview between Madeleine and Beamish. Finally, all his preparations in London complete, he returned to Hull, and set himself, by means of the secret telephone, to keep in touch with the affairs of the syndicate.

CHAPTER XX

THE DOUBLE CROSS

INSPECTOR WILLIS spent the Saturday before the fateful Tuesday at the telephone in the empty cottage. Nothing of interest passed over the wire, except that Benson informed his chief that he had had a telegram from Beamish saying that, in order to reach Ferriby at the prearranged hour, he was having to sail without a full cargo of props, and that the two men went over again the various trains by which they and their confederates would travel to London. Both items pleased Willis, as it showed him that the plans originally made were being adhered to.

On Monday morning, as the critical hours of his coup approached, he became restless and even nervous—so far, that is, as an inspector of the Yard on duty can be nervous. So much depended on the results of the next day and a half! His own fate hung in the balance as well as that of the men against whom he had pitted himself, Miss Coburn and Merriman too would be profoundly affected however the affair ended, while to his department, and even to the nation at large, his success would not be without importance.

He determined he would, if possible, see the various members of the gang start, travelling himself in the train with Archer, as the leader and the man most urgently 'wanted'. Benson, he remembered, was to go first. Willis therefore haunted the Paragon station, watching the trains leave, and he was well satisfied when he saw Benson get on board the 9.10 a.m. By means of a word of explanation and the passing of a couple of shillings, he induced an official to examine the traveller's ticket, which proved to be a third return to King's Cross.

Beamish and Bulla were to travel by the 4 p.m., and Willis,

carefully disguised as a deep-sea fisherman, watched them arrive separately, take their tickets, and enter the train. Beamish travelled first, and Bulla third, and again the inspector had their tickets examined, and found they were for London.

Archer was to leave at 5.03, and Willis intended as a precautionary measure to travel up with him and keep him under observation. Still in his fisherman's disguise, he took his own ticket, got into the rear of the train, and kept his eye on the platform until he saw Archer pass, suitcase and rug in hand. Then cautiously looking out, he watched the other get into the through coach for King's Cross.

As the train ran past the depot at Ferriby, Willis observed that the *Girondin* was not discharging pit-props, but instead was loading casks of some kind. He had noted on the previous Friday, when he had been in the neighbourhood, that some wagons of these casks had been shunted inside the enclosure, and were being unloaded by the syndicate's men. The casks looked like those in which the crude oil for the ship's Diesel engines arrived, and the fact that she was loading them unemptied—he presumed unemptied—seemed to indicate that the pumping plant on the wharf was out of order.

The 5.03 p.m. ran, with a stop at Goole, to Doncaster, where the through carriage was shunted on to one of the great expresses from the north. More from force of habit than otherwise, Willis put his head out of the window at Goole to watch if any one should leave Archer's carriage. But no one did.

At Doncaster Willis received something of a shock. As his train drew into the station another was just coming out, and he idly ran his eye along the line of coaches. A figure in the corner of a third-class compartment attracted his attention. It seemed vaguely familiar, but it was already out of sight before the inspector realised that it was a likeness to Benson that had struck him. He had not seen the man's face, and he at once dismissed the matter from his mind with the careless thought that every one has his double. A moment later they pulled up at the platform.

Here again he put out his head, and it was not long before he saw Archer alight and, evidently leaving his suitcase and rug to keep his seat, move slowly down the platform. There was nothing remarkable in this, as no less than seventeen minutes elapsed between the arrival of the train from Hull and the departure of that for London, and through passengers frequently left their carriage while it was being shunted. At the same time Willis unostentatiously followed, and presently saw Archer vanish into the first-class refreshment-room. He took up a position where he had a good view of the door, and waited for the other's reappearance.

But the distiller was in no hurry. Ten minutes elapsed, and still he made no sign. The express from the north thundered in, the engine hooked off, and shunting began. The train was due out at 6.22, and now the hands of the great clock pointed to 6.19. Willis began to be perturbed. Had he missed his quarry?

At 6.20 he could stand it no longer, and at risk of meeting Archer, should the latter at that moment decide to leave the refreshment-room, he pushed open the door and glanced in. And then he breathed freely again. Archer was seated at a table sipping what looked like a whisky and soda. As Willis looked he saw him glance up at the clock—now pointing to 6.21—and calmly settle himself more comfortably in his chair!

Why, the man would miss the train! Willis, with a sudden feeling of disappointment, had an impulse to run over and remind him of the hour at which it left. But he controlled himself in time, slipped back to his post of observation, and took up his watch. In a few seconds the train whistled, and pulled majestically out of the station.

For fifteen minutes Willis waited, and then he saw the distiller leave the refreshment-room and walk slowly down the platform. As Willis followed, it was clear to him that the other had deliberately allowed his train to start without him, though what his motive had been the inspector could not imagine. He now approached the booking-office and apparently bought a ticket, afterwards turning back down the platform.

Willis slipped into a doorway until he had passed, then hurrying to the booking-window, explained who he was and asked to what station the last comer had booked. He was told 'Selby,' and he retreated, exasperated and puzzled beyond words. What *could* Archer be up to?

He bought a time-table and began to study the possibilities. First he made himself clear as to the lie of the land. The main line of the great East Coast route from London to Scotland ran almost due north and south through Doncaster. Eighteen miles to the north was Selby, the next important station. At Selby a line running east and west crossed the other, leading in one direction to Leeds and the west, and in the other to Hull.

About half-way between Selby and Hull, at a place called Staddlethorpe, a line branched off and ran south-westerly through Goole to Doncaster. Selby, Staddlethorpe, and Doncaster therefore formed a railway triangle, one of the sides of which, produced, led to Hull. From this it followed, as indeed the inspector had known, that passengers to and from Hull had two points of connection with the main line, either direct to Selby, or through Goole to Doncaster.

He began to study the trains. The first northwards was the 4 p.m. dining-car express from King's Cross to Newcastle. It left Doncaster at 7.56 and reached Selby at 8.21. Would Archer travel by it? And if he did, what would be his next move?

For nearly an hour Willis sat huddled up in the corner of a seat, his eye on Archer in the distance, and his mind wrestling with the problem. For nearly an hour he racked his brains without result, then suddenly a devastating idea flashed before his consciousness, leaving him rigid with dismay. For a moment his mind refused to accept so disastrous a possibility, but as he continued to think over it he found that one puzzling and unrelated fact after another took on a different complexion from that it had formerly borne; that, moreover, it dropped into place and became part of a connected whole.

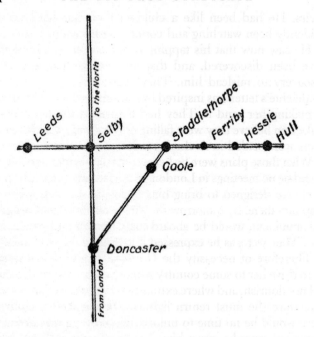

He saw now why Archer could not discuss Madeleine's letter over the telephone, but was able to arrange in that way for the interview with Beamish. He understood why Archer, standing at his study window had mentioned the call at eleven next morning. He realised that Benson's amendment was probably arranged by Archer on the previous evening. He saw why the *Girondin* had left the Lesque without her full cargo, and why she was loading barrels at Ferriby. He knew who it was he had seen passing in the other train as his own reached Doncaster, and he grasped the reason for Archer's visit to Selby.

In a word, he saw he had been hoaxed—fooled—carefully, systematically and at every point. While he had been congratulating himself on the completeness with which the conspirators had been walking into his net, he had in reality been caught in theirs. He had been like a child in their hands. They had evidently been watching and countering his every step.

He saw now that his tapping of the secret telephone must have been discovered, and that his enemies had used their discovery to mislead him. They must have recognised that Madeleine's letter was inspired by himself, and read his motives in making her send it. They had then used the telephone to make him believe they were falling into his trap, while their real plans were settled in Archer's study.

What those plans were he believed he now understood. There would be no meetings in London on the following day. The meetings were designed to bring him, Willis, to the metropolis and keep him there. By tomorrow the gang, convinced that discovery was imminent, would be aboard the *Girondin* and on the high seas. They were, as he expressed it to himself, 'doing a bunk'.

Therefore of necessity the *Girondin* would load barrelled oil to drive her to some country where Scotland Yard detectives did not flourish, and where extradition laws were of no account. Therefore she must return light, or, he suspected, empty, as there would be no time to unload. Moreover, a reason for this 'lightness' must be given him, lest he should notice the ship sitting high out of the water, and suspect. And he now knew that it was really Benson that he had seen returning to Ferriby via Goole, and that Archer was doing the same via Selby.

He looked up the trains from Selby to Ferriby. There was only one. It left Selby at 9.19, fifty-eight minutes after the Doncaster train arrived there, and reached Ferriby at 10.07. It was now getting on towards eight. He had nearly two and a half hours to make his plans.

Though Willis was a little slow in thought, he was prompt in action. Feeling sure that Archer would indeed travel by the 7.56 to Selby, he relaxed his watch and went to the telephone call office. There he rang up the police station at Selby, asking for a plain clothes man and two constables to meet him at the train to make an arrest. Also he asked for a fast car to be engaged to take him immediately to Ferriby. He then called up the police in Hull, and had a long talk with the superintendent. Finally it was arranged that a sergeant and twelve men were to meet him on the shore at the back of the signal cabin near the Ferriby depot, with a boat and a grappling ladder for getting aboard the *Girondin*. This done, Willis hurried back to the platform, reaching it just as the 7.56 came in. He watched Archer get on board, and then himself entered another compartment.

At Selby the quarry alighted, and passed along the platform towards the booking-office. Willis's police training instantly revealed to him the plain clothes man, and him he instructed to follow Archer and learn to what station he booked. In a few moments the man returned to say it was Ferriby. Then calling up the two constables, the four officers followed the distiller into the first-class waiting-room, where he had taken cover. Willis walked up to him.

'Archibald Charles Archer,' he said impressively, 'I am Inspector Willis of Scotland Yard. I have a warrant for your arrest on a charge of murdering Francis Coburn in a cab in London on 12th September last. I have to warn you that anything you say may be used in evidence against you.'

For a moment the distiller seemed so overwhelmed with surprise as to be incapable of movement, and before he could pull himself together there was a click, and handcuffs gleamed on his wrists. Then his eyes blazed, and with the inarticulate roar of a wild beast he flung himself wildly on Willis, and, manacled as he was, attempted to seize his throat. But the struggle was brief. In a moment the three other men had torn him off, and he stood glaring at his adversary, and uttering savage curses.

'You look after him, sergeant,' Willis directed a little breathlessly, as he tried to straighten the remnants of his tie. 'I must go on to Ferriby.'

A powerful car was waiting outside the station, and Willis, jumping in, offered the driver an extra pound if he was at Ferriby within fifty minutes. He reckoned the distance was about twenty-five miles, and he thought he should maintain an average of thirty miles an hour.

The night was intensely dark as the big vehicle swung out of Selby, eastward bound. A slight wind blew in from the east, bearing a damp, searching cold, more trying than frost. Willis, who had left his coat in the London train, shivered as he drew the one rug the vehicle contained up round his shoulders.

The road to Howden was broad and smooth, and the car made fine going. But at Howden the main road turned north, and speed on the comparatively inferior cross roads to Ferriby had to be reduced. But Willis was not dissatisfied with their progress when at 9.38, fifty-four minutes after leaving Selby, they pulled up in the Ferriby lane, not far from the distillery and opposite the railway signal cabin.

Having arranged with the driver to run up to the main road, wait there until he heard four blasts on the *Girondin's* horn, and then make for the syndicate's depot, the inspector dismounted, and forcing his way through the railway fence, crossed the rails and descended the low embankment on the river side. A moment later, just as he reached the shore, the form of a man loomed up dimly through the darkness.

'Who is there?' asked Willis softly.

'Constable Jones, sir,' the figure answered. 'Is that Inspector Willis? Sergeant Hobbs is here with the boats.'

Willis followed the other for fifty yards along the beach, until they came on two boats, each containing half a dozen policemen. It was still very dark, and the wind blew cold and raw. The silence was broken only by the lapping of the waves on the shingle. Willis felt that the night was ideal for his purpose. There was enough noise from wind and water to muffle any sounds that the men might make in getting aboard the *Girondin*, but not enough to prevent him overhearing any conversation which might be in progress.

'We have just got here this minute, sir,' the sergeant said. 'I hope we haven't kept you waiting.'

'Just arrived myself,' Willis returned. 'You have twelve picked men?'

'Yes, sir.'

'Armed?'

'Yes, sir.'

'Good. I need not remind you all not to fire except as a last resort. What arrangements have you made for boarding?'

'We have a ladder with hooks at the top for catching on the taffrail.'

'Your oars muffled?'

'Yes, sir.'

'Very well. Now listen, and see that you are clear about what you are to do. When we reach the ship get your ladder in position, and I'll go up. You and the men follow. Keep beside me, sergeant. We'll overhear what we can. When I give the signal, rush in and arrest the whole gang. Do you follow?'

'Yes, sir.'

'Then let us get under way.'

They pushed off, passing like phantoms over the dark water. The ship carried a riding light, to which they steered. She was lying, Willis knew, bow up-stream. The tide was flowing, and when they were close by they ceased rowing and drifted down on to her stern. There the leading boat dropped in beneath her counter, and the bowman made the painter fast to her rudder post. The second boat's painter was attached to the stern of the first, and the current swung both alongside. The men, fending off, allowed their craft to come into place without sound. The ladder was raised and hooked on, and Willis, climbing up, steathily raised his head above the taffrail.

The port side of the ship was, as on previous occasions, in complete darkness, and Willis jerked the ladder as a signal to the others to follow him. In a few seconds the fourteen men stood like shadows on the lower deck. Then Willis, tiptoeing forward, began to climb the ladder to the bridge deck, just as Hilliard had done some four months earlier. As on that occasion, the starboard side of the ship, next the wharf, was dimly lighted up. A light also showed in the window of the captain's cabin, from which issued the sound of voices.

Willis posted his men in two groups at either end of the cabin, so that at a given signal they could rush round in opposite directions and reach the door. Then he and the sergeant crept forward and put their ears to the window.

This time, though the glass was hooked back as before, the curtain was pulled fully across the opening, so that the men could see nothing and only partially hear what was said. Willis therefore reached in and very gradually pulled it a little aside. Fortunately no one noticed the movement, and the talk continued uninterruptedly.

The inspector could now see in. Five men were squeezed round the tiny table. Beamish and Bulla sat along one side, directly facing him. At the end was Fox. The remaining two had their backs to the window, and were, the inspector believed, Raymond and Henri. Before each man was a long tumbler of whisky and soda, and a box of cigars lay on the table. All seemed nervous and excited, indeed as if under an intolerable strain, and kept fidgeting and looking at their watches. Conversation was evidently maintained with an effort, as a thing necessary to keep them from a complete breakdown. Raymond was speaking.

'And you saw him come out?' he was asking.

'Yes,' Fox answered. 'He came out sort of stealthy and looked around. I didn't know who it was then, but I knew no one had any business in the cottage at that hour, so I followed him to Ferriby Station. I saw his face by the lamps there.'

'And you knew him?'

'No, but I recognised him as having been around with that Excise inspector, and I guessed he was on to something.'

'*Oui, oui.* Yes?' The Frenchman interrogated.

'Well, naturally I told the chief. He knew who it was.'

'*Bien!* There is not—how do you say—flies on Archer, *n'est-ce pas?* And then?'

'The chief guessed who it was from the captain's description.' Fox nodded his head at Beamish. 'You met him, eh, captain?'

'He stood me a drink,' the big man answered, 'but what he did it for I don't know.'

'But how did he get wise to the telephone?' Bulla rumbled.

'Can't find out,' Fox replied, 'but it showed he was wise to the whole affair. Then there was that letter from Miss Coburn. That gave the show away, because there could have been no papers like she said, and she couldn't have discovered anything then that she hadn't known at the clearing. Archer put Morton on to it, and he found that this Willis went down to Eastbourne one night about two days before the letter came. So that was that. Then he had me watch the boy going to the telephone, and he has fooled him about proper. I guess he's in London now, arranging to arrest us all tomorrow.'

Bulla chuckled fatly.

'As you say,' he nodded at Raymond, 'there ain't no flies on Archer, what?'

'I've always thought a lot of Archer,' Beamish remarked, 'but I never thought so much of him as that night we drew lots for who should put Coburn out of the way. When he drew the long taper he never as much as turned a hair. That's the last time we had a full meeting, and we never reckoned that this would be the next.'

At this moment a train passed going towards Hull.

'There's his train,' Fox cried. 'He should be here soon.'

'How long does it take to get from the station?' Raymond inquired.

'About fifteen minutes,' Captain Beamish answered. 'We're time enough making a move.'

The men showed more and more nervousness, but the talk dragged on for some quarter of an hour. Suddenly from the wharf sounded the approaching footsteps of a running man. He crossed the gangway and raced up the ladder to the captain's cabin. The others sprang to their feet as the door opened and Benson appeared.

'He hasn't come!' he cried excitedly. 'I watched at the station and he didn't get out!'

Consternation showed on every face, and Beamish swore bitterly. There was a variety of comments and conjectures.

'There's no other train?'

'Only the express. It doesn't stop here, but it stops at Hessle on notice to the guard.'

'He may have missed the connection at Selby,' Fox suggested. 'In that case he would motor.'

Beamish spoke authoritatively.

'I wish, Benson, you would go and ring up the Central and see if there has been any message.'

Willis whispered to the sergeant, who, beckoning to two of his men, crept hurriedly down the port ladder to the lower deck. In a moment Benson followed down the starboard or lighted side. Willis, listening breathlessly above, heard what he was expecting—a sudden scuffle, a muffled cry, a faint click, and then silence. He peeped through the porthole. Fox was expounding his theory about the railway connections, and none of those within had heard the sounds. Presently the sergeant returned with his men.

'Trussed him up to the davit pole,' he breathed in the inspector's ear. '*He* won't give no trouble.'

Willis nodded contentedly. That was one out of the way out of six, and he had fourteen on his side.

Meanwhile the men in the cabin continued anxiously discussing their leader's absence, until after a few minutes Beamish swore irritably.

'Curse that fool Benson,' he growled. 'What the blazes is keeping him all this time? I had better go and hurry him up. If they've got hold of Archer, it's time we were out of this.'

Willis's hand closed on the sergeant's arm.

'Same thing again, but with three men,' he whispered.

The four had hardly disappeared down the port ladder, when Beamish left his cabin and began to descend the starboard.

Willis felt that the crisis was upon him. He whispered to the remaining constables, who closed in round the cabin door, then grasped his revolver, and stood tense.

Suddenly a wild commotion arose on the lower deck. There was a warning shout from Beamish, instantly muffled, the tramp of feet, a pistol shot, and sounds of a violent struggle.

For a moment there was silence in the cabin, the men gazing at each other with consternation on their faces. Then Bulla yelled: 'Copped, by God!' and with an agility hardly credible in a man of his years, whipped out a revolver, and sprang out of the cabin. Instantly he was seized by three constables, and the four went swinging and lurching across the deck, Bulla fighting desperately to turn his weapon on his assailants. At the same moment Willis leaped to the door, and with his automatic levelled, shouted, 'Hands up, all of you! You are covered from every quarter!'

Henri and Fox, who were next the door, obeyed as if in a stupor, but Raymond's hand flew out, and a bullet whistled past the inspector's head. Instantly Willis fired, and with a scream the Frenchman staggered back.

It was the work of a few seconds for the remaining constables to dash in under the inspector's pistol and handcuff the two men in the cabin, and Willis then turned to see how the contests on deck were faring. But these also were over. Both Beamish and Bulla, borne down by the weight of numbers, had been secured.

The inspector next turned to examine Raymond. His shot had been well aimed. The bullet had entered the base of the man's right thumb, and passed out through his wrist. His life was not in danger, but it would be many a long day before he would again fire a revolver.

Four blasts on the *Girondin's* horn recalled Willis's car, and when, some three hours later, the last batch of prisoners was safely lodged in the Hull police station, Willis began to feel that the end of his labours was at last coming in sight.

*

The arrests supplied the inspector with fresh material on which to work. As a result of his careful investigation of the movements of the prisoners during the previous three years, the entire history of the Pit-Prop Syndicate was unravelled, as well as the details of Coburn's murder.

It seemed that the original idea of the fraud was Raymond's. He looked round for a likely English partner, selected Archer, broached the subject to him, and found him willing to go in. Soon, from his dominating personality, Archer became the leader. Details were worked out, and the necessary confederates carefully chosen. Beamish and Bulla went in as partners, the four being bound together by their joint liability. The other three members were tools over whom the quartet had obtained some hold. In Coburn's case, Archer learned of the defalcations in time to make the erring cashier his victim. He met the deficit in return for a signed confession of guilt and an IOU for a sum which would have enabled the distiller to sell the other up, and ruin his home and his future.

An incompletely erased address in a pocket diary belonging to Beamish led Willis to a small shop on the south side of London, where he discovered an assistant who had sold a square of black serge to two men, about the time of Coburn's murder. The salesman remembered the transaction because his customers had been unable to describe what they wanted otherwise than by the word 'cloth', which was not the technical name for any of his commodities. The fabric found in the cab was identical with that on the roll this man stated he had used; moreover, he identified Beamish and Bulla as the purchasers.

Willis had a routine search made of the restaurants of Soho, and at last found that in which the conspirators had held their meetings previous to the murder. There had been two. At the first, so Willis learned from the descriptions given by the proprietor, Coburn had been present, but not at the second.

In spite of all his efforts he was unable to find the shop at which the pistol had been bought, but he suspected the transaction had been carried out by one of the other members of the gang, in order as far as possible to share the responsibility for the crime.

On the *Girondin* was found the false bulkhead in Bulla's cabin, behind which was placed the hidden brandy tank. The connection for the shore pipe was concealed behind the back of the engineer's wash-hand basin, which moved forward by means of a secret spring.

On the *Girondin* was also found something over £700,000, mostly in Brazilian notes, and Benson admitted later that the plan had been to scuttle the *Girondin* off the coast of Bahia, take to the boats and row ashore at night, remaining in Brazil at least till the hue and cry had died down. But instead all seven men received heavy sentences. Archer paid for his crimes with his life, the others got terms of from ten to fifteen years each. The managers of the licensed houses in Hull were believed to have been in ignorance of the larger fraud, and to have dealt privately and individually with Archer, and they and their accomplices escaped with lighter penalties.

The mysterious Morton proved to be a private detective, employed by Archer. He swore positively that he had no knowledge of the real nature of the syndicate's operations, and though the judge's strictures on his conduct were severe, no evidence could be found against him, and he was not brought to trial.

Inspector Willis got his desired promotion out of the case, and there was some one else who got more. About a month after the trial, in Holy Trinity Church, Eastbourne, a wedding was solemnised—Seymour Merriman and Madeleine Coburn were united in the bonds of holy matrimony. And Hilliard, assisting as best man, could not refrain from whispering in his friend's ear as they turned to leave the vestry, 'Three cheers for the Pit-Prop Syndicate!'

THE END

DANGER IN SHROUDE VALLEY

Although best remembered as a detective novelist, Crofts was also a prolific writer of short stories and his three published collections contain just over fifty stories, many of them very short. There are also a few uncollected stories, one of which is 'Danger in Shroude Valley', first published in a 1952 anthology for children, The Golden Book of the Year.

It has many Crofts motifs: a meticulous map of Shroude Valley, lots of railway detail and a young detective, Robin Brand, and his partner in crime detection, Jack Carr, both of whom had featured previously in their own novel, Young Robin Brand: Detective *(1947). Interestingly, that novel features not only Inspector French but also his nephew, Cyril.*

*

IT was the third evening of an unexpected and very delightful holiday. To the intense satisfaction of Robin Brand and his friend Jack Carr, several of their schoolfellows had gone down with measles, and now in early June the school had been closed. As on two previous occasions, Robin had been asked to spend the time with the Carrs. Jack's father was an engineer, and was now engaged in a large railway alteration near Swinleigh, in which town he had taken a house.

The boys had been seeing a friend off at the station, and as they left, Jack glanced at the clock.

'Nine-thirty-three,' he observed. 'We're not due home yet. What shall we do?'

Jack's passion was for railways, and he invariably spoke as if he and his friends were trains or bales of goods or perishable merchandise. Robin wouldn't have given two hoots for all the railways in creation, had these been offered to him at the price.

His hobby was detection. He was always discovering vital clues, though what these clues indicated he did not always seem to know.

'Too dark to do much in the town,' he pointed out. 'Let's go back and get on with the jigsaw.'

'Okay.'

It was unusual for Jack to agree so readily to a suggestion, and Robin listened with scepticism. He was soon justified. Jack stopped outside a paling.

'I say, here's a gap. Let's slip in and have a look round.'

The fence encircled the works of a new bus station. Jack despised buses as being mere poor relations of genuine coaching stock, but he was interested in any kind of engineering, and here work was in hand, even if for an inferior purpose.

Unseen from the not-too-well-lit street, they squeezed through the gap. The bus platforms had been laid down with their white kerbs, but their tarmac surfaces were still unfinished. Jack decided that each platform would contain six 'bays', and dilated on just how the buses would shunt to occupy them. Then they moved on to where a block of buildings was going up, the brick walls having reached a height of some eight feet.

'Offices, waiting-rooms, lavatories,' Jack declared. 'Let's poke through them.'

They moved silently over the soft clay to the first room, and were passing on to the next when they heard a man's voice. Under normal circumstances they would have backed quietly away, but the words caused them to stand rigid, scarcely daring to breathe.

'Aye,' rumbled the voice, ''e said as 'ow 'e'd knock 'em out an' tie 'em up. But 'e wouldn't do 'em no 'arm. 'E weren't goin' to stand for no chance of the rope, not for no money, 'e weren't.'

A higher-pitched voice murmured protestingly, but the words were inaudible.

''E ain't goin' to take no chances, nor me neither,' came again the deep growl. 'We're not standin' for no murder.'

The high-pitched voice sounded once more, but Robin was no longer listening. He put his lips to Jack's ear.

'Oh, Jack, they're plotting a crime! We should listen!'

Jack glanced round, then pointed to the bricklayers' scaffold. 'Give me a leg up on that and I'll look over. Steady,' as Robin began to move, 'wait till a bus is passing.'

In spite of the late hour, buses were continually starting up from the halts in the street. Their gears shattered the silence, completely covering the slight shuffling made by the boys. Robin helped Jack on to the scaffold and was then pulled up himself. While the next bus was passing, both crawled to the top of the wall and peeped over.

Two men were standing just below, and a third was approaching from the back of the area.

'Seen the boss?' The deep voice came from a gigantic man in dungarees.

'He's coming,' answered the newcomer, who was short and thickset, with fiery red hair. 'Here in a minute.'

A few more remarks passed and then a fourth individual walked quickly up from the rear. He was better dressed than the others and had an air of authority. He nodded briefly.

'Well, you're all here. Let's get down to it. But first, all right so far?'

The red-haired man replied: 'Goliath here's got the wind up about the chance of croaking the men. And so have I. We're not standing for any risk like that.'

'Tha's right,' the giant agreed succinctly.

'If I've told you once, I've told you a dozen times I don't want the men hurt.' The well-dressed man sounded testy. 'I only want them out of action till you get the thing started: a matter of three minutes. Has that sunk in?'

There were murmurs of satisfaction.

'Now see,' went on the boss, 'here's the scheme and don't you forget it.' He looked round aggressively. 'I'll take you first, Birkett. You ride out on your bicycle, hide it in the bushes, and go to the home signal. It'll be pulled off three or four minutes before the train comes, but don't do anything till you hear the train. We don't want to give the station people time to interfere. She'll be beating hard coming up the bank and you'll hear her a couple of miles away.'

'Okay, boss.'

'When you hear her, cut the distant and home signal wires. Then sprint down the line to Goliath and Ginger and help them through.'

'Suppose there's a down train and I can't hear ours?'

'Then cut two minutes after the signals go off.'

'I got you.'

The boss nodded and turned to Ginger. 'You, Ginger, get the car from me tomorrow night with the extra number plates. You put it in your shed.'

Ginger said he understood.

'On the night of the affair you change your plates and pick up Goliath where we agreed. You drive to near the station: I've explained where you should park, so that you can get away quick when you've finished. Both of you get on the line where the van will stop. Do you know the length of the train?'

'Yes,' answered Ginger, 'that's been measured different nights and it's always the same. And we've measured on the ground too. The place is marked.'

'Good. Then when the train stops tell the guard there's an obstruction ahead and to come down to arrange the shunting. When he does so, get a cloth over his head and gag and bind him. You can manage?'

'Sure, boss. Easy as wink.'

'I needn't go over the rest, we've been through it so often. You get the other fellows down, start the box, and then hook it. Now, any questions?'

'All clear to me,' declared Ginger.

'And to me,' added Birkett.

'Clear enough,' Goliath agreed, 'but wot abaht the dough?'

'What we settled; there's no change. I give each of you twenty-five now, and another twenty-five when the job's done. That'll be fifty pounds apiece.'

'Okay.'

Three lots of twenty-five notes were counted out and handed over. Then having recommended discretion to his accomplices, the boss disappeared.

When the next bus started up, Jack stabbed with his finger towards the ground, and quietly the boys lowered themselves from the scaffold.

'We'll shadow the last man,' whispered Jack as they crouched at a corner from which they could see the rear exit. First Goliath lumbered away, Ginger presently followed, and then it was Birkett's turn. As soon as his figure had become a dark smudge in the gloom, the boys crept silently after him.

At the back of the new station ran the River Swinn, here canalised and with a towpath along the bank. Birkett strolled along the path, and so naturally did the boys.

Some hundred yards away a side street crossed the river, and here steps led up to the bridge from the path. Birkett climbed the steps. Instantly the boys sprinted forward, but unhappily when they reached the street he had disappeared. They dashed to the big thoroughfare at the nearest corner. There was no sign of him, and a glance at the moving crowds showed the hopelessness of a search. Jack plumped for an immediate return home. 'Let's tell dad,' he suggested. 'He'll know what to do.'

'What's the idea of cutting the signal wires?' Robin panted as they hurried along.

'Puts the signals to danger. Those fellows are going to stop a non-stop train. They know what they're doing, too.'

'Why do you say that?'

'They're delaying cutting till the last minute. There are back-lights or electric repeaters on the signals which tell the signalman if they go up. It's not likely he'd notice, but he might.'

'You mean, the later the thing's done, the less chance of that?'

'Yes, and also if he did notice, there'd be less time to do anything about it.'

Mr Carr listened gravely to the story. 'The first part of it's clear enough, but what on earth does getting the other fellows down and starting the box mean? Sounds as if they were going to blow something up.'

'That's it, dad: the box is a magneto!' cried Jack.

'Could it mean that something valuable is going by that train, and they hope to get it after the explosion?' Robin suggested.

'Might. In any case I think the police should know of it. Suppose we walk round?'

Inspector Greer, to whom they reported, seemed really interested. He complimented the boys on their wise action, got from them as good descriptions of the four men as they could give, and said he would look into the matter and let them hear further. But if he had any idea of what was projected, he did not mention it. Nor did he ring up. The days went by and gradually the affair began to fade from the boys' minds.

Robin thought he had never known nicer people than the Carrs, especially Mrs Carr's younger sister, Joan. She was, so Jack explained, engaged to a young man named Redfern, who had just taken over a nearby training stables. He had a wonderful horse, Golden Crown, which he had entered for the chief race at a famous meeting near London during the following week.

Towards dusk on the Monday evening of that week of the races, the boys were cycling home when Robin noticed a cyclist who had just turned in from a side street and was pedalling on in front of them. His heart gave a leap. Could it be? Yes, he believed it was!

'Jack!' he cried. 'See that chap ahead there on the bike? I think it's Birkett!'

'Golly!' Jack declared. 'You're right! Let's drop back a bit and shadow him. If it's Birkett, we've got him!'

The unconscious quarry rode on at a leisurely pace, the boys following. Then the chase turned eastwards, out of the town.

'This road runs alongside the London railway,' grunted Jack suggestively.

Robin felt thrilled. 'Oh, Jack! Could he be going to do whatever it is? It was to be at a station. What stations are there?'

'Shroude's the first, four miles out, then Plumpton another four.'

'If there's a chance of anything, shouldn't we tell the police?'

Jack seemed doubtful. 'How could we? If we stop we'll lose Birkett. Besides, we're not sure. We daren't bring out the police on spec.'

Robin had a profound admiration for Jack's common sense, but now he disagreed with him. They could surely tell the police what they had seen, and leave the rest to them. The more he thought of it, the more uneasy he became. A move now might prevent a crime: if they waited it might be too late.

He rode on, thinking deeply, yet not too deeply to keep his eyes open. Presently they came to a suburban crossroads at which stood a telephone kiosk.

'Look, Jack,' he pointed to it. 'There's our chance! I'll report what we're doing and follow on. What about it?'

Jack nodded. 'I think you'd better. But don't tell them more than you know.'

Robin's emergency dialling and the word 'Police!' brought him an immediate reply. He quickly explained the circumstances and was cheered by the 'Good lads! I'll tell the inspector,' which resulted.

He put on speed after Jack. For a couple of miles out of the town the ground fell, till he crossed a river at the bottom of a wide valley. Then it began to rise again into a wilder district he and Jack had often explored, an area of hills and heather, of rocky outcrops and little mountain streams.

A mile beyond the river he overtook Jack. Here they entered the Shroude Valley, a wild and gloomy defile just wide enough for road, rail and a tumbling stream. At the entrance was a level-crossing, where the road passed from right to left of the line. Protecting the crossing were signals, operated from a gate-man's hut. A mile further up was the small roadside station of Shroude, where crossroads went up into the hills on either side.

A few score yards short of the station Birkett dismounted and wheeled his bicycle into a lane striking off to the left. The boys also dismounted.

'That just leads up on to the moor,' Jack said excitedly. 'He's hiding his bike in the bushes! It looks like a true bill!'

Robin made a gesture. 'We should get off the road in case he comes back and sees us.'

Jack swung his bicycle round. 'That's right. Let's go up to the ruined tower. From there we can see the whole valley, and if they try any tricks we can be at the station in a couple of minutes.'

This seemed sense, and they pushed their bicycles up a lane to the top of a little cliff on which the ruin stood. It was a place they had often visited. In the daytime, as Jack had said, the view was extensive. Directly below ran railway, road and stream, with, some quarter of a mile to the left, the station of Shroude. Nearly a mile in the opposite direction was the level-crossing, out of sight behind a bluff. Now in the growing dusk the lights of the station and signals had become the most prominent features of the landscape, but the outlines of the opposite hills were still clear and details below remained dimly visible.

'Look! There's Birkett!' Robin whispered suddenly, though they were far out of the man's earshot.

They could dimly see a black smudge on the road. It seemed to flit across it and become merged in the darker ground towards the railway.

'He's gone towards the signal, Jack! I'm glad we rang up the police!'

Jack agreed. There was silence for a moment, then he went

on tensely: 'Lucky we know the line here. A double line with a rising gradient of 1 in 100 all the way through the valley. That red spot to the left is what Birkett's heading for: the Shroude home signal. The crossing's away out of sight to the right. To protect the crossing there are catch-points on the up line, but of course you can't see them from here.'

'You did mention those,' Robin answered, 'but I didn't understand exactly what they were.'

In spite of their preoccupation, Jack could not resist the temptation to expound. 'Where you've a long gradient like this, there's always the danger of vehicles running away. For instance, a goods might break in two. Then the rear portion might run back down the hill, for the van brake mightn't hold it. It might go into a bus or something on the crossing and kill a lot of people. So catch-points are put into the track above the crossing to derail a runaway. The runaway would of course be smashed, but the public road or a following train would be safe.'

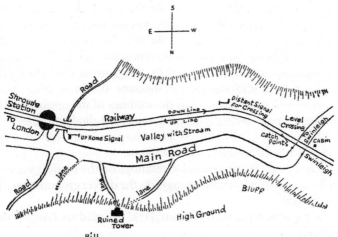

Sketch map of Shroude Valley, made by Robin for his case book

'Good notion,' Robin approved. 'But how do trains pass over it safely?'

'Trains on the up grade are naturally going in the opposite direction to a runaway, so they come on the points from behind instead of in front. The points are held open by a spring, and the wheel flanges of vehicles going up the grade simply force them shut. They spring open again automatically as soon as the wheels release them. If it's necessary to run trains downhill on the up line, as for example in emergency single-line working, the points can be closed by a lever which is kept beside them. It fits into a hole in a casting at the side of the track, and when you push it over the points close.'

Robin was about to comment further when Jack's hand closed like a vice on his wrist.

'There are the signals going off.' He glanced at his luminous-dialled watch. 'That'll be for the express: the 9.20 p.m. Swinleigh to London.'

The red light near the station had suddenly gone green. Robin stiffened. If anything was going to happen, they'd soon know about it now.

A couple of minutes passed, and then Jack shouted, 'Listen! She's coming!'

Far away the beat of an engine could be heard, faint at first, but quickly growing stronger and sharper. Soon was added the dull roar of an oncoming train. The engine was working hard up the hill, and the sound increased till the whole valley seemed full of it. Then traces of steam floated up over the bluff to the right.

Suddenly Jack gave a low cry. The green light had gone red! In a moment the headlights of the train appeared round the bluff. The engine gave a whistle, the beat ceased, and a spurt of steam roared from the safety-valve.

Robin gazed down breathlessly. He felt they ought to take some action, perhaps ring up the police again. But he seemed turned to stone, unable to do anything but watch what was happening. Jack also stood motionless, staring down with bulging eyes and open mouth.

With steadily falling speed the engine passed beneath them, followed by the long line of lighted coaches with two dark vehicles in the rear. The movement grew slower, till just before reaching the signal's red eye it ceased. There the train stood, a line of lights and jet against the grey darkness of the ground.

Now a narrow vertical rectangle of dim light appeared in the side of the first of the two dark rear vehicles. It dulled for a moment and then shone clear.

'That's the guard,' Jack breathed. 'He's got out.'

'Then,' Robin gasped, 'this *is* it!' Again he felt they ought to act, and again he seemed rooted to the ground.

Suddenly the same thing took place in the rear vehicle, a shorter one than the van. A vertical rectangle of light appeared in its side. This kept getting darker and lighter for a few seconds, and then disappeared.

'Golly!' Jack muttered. 'Someone's got out of that van too.'

'The other man!' Robin's voice was awestruck.

'Looks like it. What on earth can be going on?'

As transfixed they stared down, a narrow greyish gap appeared in the black line of the two last vehicles. Slowly it grew wider.

Jack stared as if his eyes would come out of their sockets, then he gave a scream. 'They've uncoupled the last vehicle! It's a horsebox! It'll run back down the hill and derail at the catch-points! Come on!'

He leaped for his bicycle, followed by Robin. They tore at breakneck speed down the rough lane from the tower, bumping and bouncing over the stones. Then Robin got the thrill of his life. Just before they reached the road, a police car whizzed past, going towards Shroude. So they had acted on his warning!

He thought Jack would have stopped, but Jack instead roared—'Never mind! Come on!'

By a miracle they reached the road without disaster, and

pedalled with all their strength down the hill towards the level-crossing. As he tried desperately to keep up with Jack, the probable explanation of the affair flashed into Robin's mind. A horse! The races! Something about betting! He recalled Sherlock Holmes' thrilling story of Silver Blaze, the favourite for the Wessex Cup, and how he was stolen just before the race. What if this horse was the favourite for some other important event? If the box was derailed it would be killed.

The wind whistled past their ears as they rushed along. Here was the bluff. They swung round it, cutting the corner to keep on the road. Fortunately nothing was coming in the opposite direction. There at last in front was the level-crossing. As they approached it they heard the telephone bell and saw the gate-keeper step to the instrument. He suddenly flung down the receiver and rushed out of the hut.

'Horsebox is running away,' roared Jack. 'Shall we close the catch-points?'

The man stared at them. 'Aye!' he shouted. 'Close them while I shut the gates!'

Jack tore up the line in the direction of the station, Robin panting behind him. Some fifty yards away were the catch-points, dimly visible. Jack stooped, seized a heavy lever which was lying on the ground, and felt feverishly with his hand.

'Can't find the hole in the dark!' he cried in desperation. 'A light! Quick!'

Robin turned to dash for a torch he had on his bicycle, then froze where he stood. Up the line a black, menacing shape with flaming red eyes was moving towards them through the grey dusk. Remorselessly it grew bigger. Now he heard the rolling of the wheels and the soft click of rail joints.

'The horsebox!' he yelled. 'It's coming!'

Jack was sobbing aloud in his extremity. Then he gave a shout. 'Got it!' He pushed the end of the lever into some socket, in which it stood nearly upright. Then he swung on its end. It did not move.

'Too heavy! Lend a hand!' he screamed.

The horsebox was close by, rolling forward inexorably. It seemed to grow monstrously. Robin hurled himself on the handle. The connections were stiff, and for a moment nothing happened. Then slowly the handle moved over. As the horsebox seemed right on top of them the points went home. Robin gave a choking gasp. Then the box had passed them and was moving on safely down the line.

When presently the boys learned that the horse they had saved was none other than Golden Crown, they could scarcely contain their delight. The engaged couple's gratitude knew no bounds.

Next evening there was a further meeting with Inspector Greer at police headquarters.

'A fine piece of work,' the Inspector declared. 'You boys saved a horse worth five thousand guineas and prevented an ugly bit of fraud. You rang us in the nick of time. A station in the direction you were going could only be Shroude or Plumpton, and when we saw the train stopped we knew it was Shroude. We took the three chaps redhanded as they were running from the station. And it'll not be long till we have the principal too.'

Robin's ears burned, and he was sure Jack's did also.

'The whole idea's pretty clear?' Mr Carr suggested.

'Perfectly,' Greer returned. 'North Star was the favourite for the principal race of the meeting and he had been heavily backed. Then news leaked out that this horse, Golden Crown, had done some extraordinary running. If he won, the North Star backers would be in the soup. What were three sums of fifty pounds to men who stood to lose thousands?'

'What exactly happened at the station?'

'They got the guard out and gagged and bound him. Then Goliath, as they called him, shouted up to the men in the horsebox—there were two. While they were speaking out of the window, Ginger and Birkett crept in by the other door and took them in the rear. They were quickly knocked out. The others uncoupled the horsebox, letting off its brake, and gave it a shove. The gradient did the rest.'

'The station people must have twigged what was happening?'

'We had warned all stations to be on the lookout, but they didn't jump to it till they went down and found the men tied up. Then they phoned the gatekeeper to close the gates and catch-points, for the section was clear of following trains and the horsebox would stop safely in the hollow at the bottom of the grade. But the man had only time to close the gates. And that'—the Inspector paused and turned to the boys—'is where you came in. As we police have learnt, it's teamwork that does it. Observation from Robin and initiative from Jack started the affair, and prompt help from both to the gateman completed it.'

Robin winked at Jack, but secretly his heart glowed.

THE END